MATAMOROS

MATAMOROS

James Kahn

Dedicated to Gene Ringgold

In 1848 the Mexican-American War resulted in Mexico losing almost 1/3 of its territory to the United States—including New Mexico, Arizona, California, Nevada, Utah, and the annexation of Texas. It was a bitter loss for Mexico; yet the U.S. celebration was brief.

In 1861—just 13 years later—the American Civil War began with a string of Southern victories. But by 1862 the Northern Navy had successfully blockaded all Southern ports. This was of critical importance to the Confederacy, since the Southern states had no industrial base of their own. All they had was cotton, and the slaves to pick it. So supporting their war effort depended on exporting cotton to Europe, and in return, importing guns, ammunition, and other essentials.

Matamoros, Mexico, was key in this. A sleepy village of 300 souls before the wars, it lay just across the mouth of the Rio Grande river from Brownsville, where the boot tip of Texas kicked into the Gulf of Mexico. Since Union gunships could not, by law, blockade foreign ports, Matamoros became the "back door of the Confederacy"—the port where Southern cotton was exported to the world, and war materiel smuggled into the South.

But 1862 was also the year that Napoleon III of France invaded Mexico with visions of conquest. Assisted by Mexican nobility who wanted a return to monarchy, French forces had the Mexican Army of President Benito Juarez on the run. In October of 1863 Napoleon named Archduke Maximilian of Austria as the Crowned Emperor of Mexico.

By July, 1863, the population of Matamoros had exploded to 40,000, and was host to 150 tall ships offshore daily, warships and commercial craft alike. It had become a hive of Northern and Southern spies, runaway slaves, Confederate deserters, escaped Yankee POW's, corrupt cotton brokers, profiteering weapons dealers, Mexican revolutionaries who wanted to take Texas back from the U.S., Texas Rangers determined to stop them, French Foreign Legionnaires, British merchant marines, Mexican resistance fighters, US naval blockade runners, Kiowa slave traders, bar girls, diplomats, bandits, matrons, lawyers and rogues of every stripe.

This is where our story begins.

ROSTER OF CHARACTERS

Clayton Wilkes: Confederate ex-patriate, owner of Brave River Gambling Emporium

Isaac: Clayton's partner/friend at Brave River

Tinbury: Aide to US Ambassador Leonard Pierce

Legionnaire Scully: Irish-born soldier of the French Foreign Legion

Teddy Beale: Union Corporal of the Guard

Aurelia: General Bee's housekeeper at his Matamoros *hacienda*

Major Charles Russell: Confederate Quartermaster of Fort Brown

General Hamilton Bee: Confederate Commandant of Fort Brown

Mildred Bee: Wife of General Hamilton Bee

Allie Stoneman: Recent cotton plantation owner

Jersey: Allie's teen house slave, married to Moon

Moon: Allie's house slave

Lieutenant Jessup: Texas Ranger

Captain Odeel: Confederate officer in the Cotton Bureau

Catherine Delacroix: French manager of the Opera House

Jose Agustin Quintero: Confederate States Special Consul to Mexico

Simon Wachtel: German editor of *The Daily Ranchero*

Leonard Pierce: United States Ambassador to Mexico

Ryburn Solomon: Scottish blockade runner

Claire: French understudy to the diva

Ned: Alcoholic Limey ship's deserter

INDIAN TERRITORY
FT. SMITH
ARKANSAS
RED RIVER
MISSISSIPPI R.
TEXARKANA
FT. WORTH
SHREVEPORT
TEXAS
LOUISIANA
SABINE R.
NATCHITOCHES
ALEXANDRIA
HOUSTON
BEAUMONT
LAFAYETTE
SAN ANTONIO
SABINE PASS
GALVESTON
MERMENTAU RIVER
NEW ORLEANS
RIO GRANDE R.
FT. RINGGOLD
PADRE IS.
LAREDO
KING RANCH
Brownsville
GULF
of
MEXICO
MATAMOROS
CLARKSVILLE
BRAZOS IS.
BAGDAD
MEXICO
N
W E
S

TEXAS
GULF of MEXICO
San Antonio
WILD HORSE DESERT
FORT RINGGOLD
Padre Island
RIO GRANDE RIVER
KING RANCH
BROWNSVILLE
CLARKSVILLE
PT. ISABEL
BRAZOS IS.
MATAMOROS
BAGDAD
MEXICO
N
W
E
S

CHAPTER 1

"WE WERE NORTH OF Denver," Clayton remembered, "winter of '58, packin' up the mountainside in a blizzard with a headwind, three of us spread out. I tripped and damned if it wasn't over the body of that very same lawman, frozen in ice, must've been two months dead—that's when he'd set out lookin' for us." Clayton laid his country accent on when he told tales to his bar crew.

"What'd you do then?" said Jim, the bartender.

"Well, I thought, I'm gonna have myself some fun with these boys. I brushed over my bootprints, backtracked a little, then walked around and twenty yards higher. Shot my pistol and the others come a-runnin'. They say, 'What's the matter?' I say I'm damned if I don't smell a dead body somewhere. O' course they snorted at that. 'Can't nobody smell a corpse in a blizzard,' Pete told me. I said I don't know about that, but I smell one, and it's comin' from down there somewhere. They give me even more shit then. 'The wind is blowin' *down* that way!' Oily yells at me. 'Can't smell *nothin'* if you're upwind from it.' I said I couldn't fault his logic, but I knew what I smelled."

The barkeep could hardly contain his glee at what was coming next. "Go on, what'd they say then?"

"They were all for movin' on. But I said it wasn't proper to leave a man dead where critters could pick his bones, and I was gonna go look for the body. They didn't like it, but they said okay, they'd help search for ten minutes, to humor me, but we had to make the miner's cabin by sunfall. I said Oily should look in the trees and Pete better check out that bare patch below us. I knew Pete had the best eyes, so if I put him in the right neighborhood he'd see the fellow. Sure enough, five minutes later a shot goes off and Pete's pointin' at that body froze in ice...."

Jim was laughing like he'd never stop now. "Go on, go on..."

"'How'd you smell that?' Pete says to me.

'I told you I was the best tracker in the county,' I told him. 'Nose like a bloodhound. So *now* will you pay me to find your miserable partner who run off with your stake?' He reaches into his pocket on the spot, pulls out his poke full of gold dust...."

At that moment Isaac walked up, looking serious. "Teamster at table four appears to be cheating," he said. "The fellow we discussed." Isaac was a muscular black man in red vest and cravatte. Dressed like a house slave, though there were, of course, no slaves here on the Mexican side of the river. There weren't even that many slaves across the border, in Texas—partly because escape into Mexico was so easy, partly because it was generally cheaper to hire Mexican labor and let them wade home at the end of the day than it was to keep and feed black American chattel.

Isaac spoke with an educated, vaguely New England accent. What he was doing south of the border was a matter of debate, and sometimes actual wagering, though neither Isaac nor Clayton offered any explanation. Their relationship alternated between fraternal and hierarchical, although it must have been a hierarchy of their own invention. In fact they acted a little like brothers; though obviously they were not.

Clayton, at 38, had straw-colored hair, clean-shaven face, a Louisiana lilt and a bent nose from a long-ago drubbing. His first offer was generally a smile. His second, less genial. As owner of the Brave River Gambling Emporium he dressed in the finest suits of London silk or linen. And though the summer temperature was still above 90 past midnight, Clayton gave the impression of never sweating. Some attributed this to pricey medicaments he purchased from a Kiowa medicine man he did business with from time to time; some to the good fortune of a cool-blooded ancestry. Clayton answered few questions of a personal nature, though. That would have been a tell, and Clayton was nothing if not a good gambler. Good gamblers hid their cards in plain sight, the way chameleons hid their skins. But the chameleon's gift was also its failure; for it could be said to have no true color of its own.

As Clayton stood, Isaac stopped him with a gentle hand. "You all right?"

Clayton had been having his dreams again lately, so he was looking a bit haggard. "I'm right as rain," he smiled, "but thank you for askin'." Then he turned back to Jim behind the bar. "I'll finish the story later," he said. Jim shook his head, still laughing, and walked over to try to tell his boss's tale to Rheumy, the other bartender, though he knew Rheumy wouldn't get it, and Jim would just end up aggravated with him.

Clayton followed Isaac slowly through the crowd, where he picked up the smell of gambler sweat mingled with a dozen other aromas: tobacco smoke, *chorizos* grilled in the kitchen by Milagra, his ancient Mexican cook; the sweet perfumed women at the bar, warm beer, burning kerosene and oiled boot-leather. Clayton took it all in, the scents and sights, the clatter and clamor. His domain.

Two faro setups, one monte, a dozen six-tops for poker. Three bagatelles and two billiard tables along the far wall, a cluster of Rebs playing Rattle-and-Snap in one corner. The long bar was filled with drinkers from several nations, hugging up to fancy girls and a few not so fancy. Laughing, telling whoppers, getting rowdy on whiskey and ale until occasionally some fell away to a row of small private cabins behind the casino.

Two main bartenders, Jim and Rheumy, were both on duty tonight. Jim was a big, cheerful bear of a man who rarely spoke, but big enough to stop fights just by walking up. The other barkeep, Rheumy, was a tough old, dark-skinned fellow, some Mestizo mix who kept a beehive out back, where he went to get swarmed once a week. Swore the beestings did wonders for his rheumatism. Clayton trusted them both to manage the room.

Draping the walls were flags from sixteen countries—mementos from the sailors who'd gambled away their shore leave. From above the bar a stuffed giraffe's head, neck included, stayed forever vigilant since being left on the doorstep by who-knows-who. Tattered crepe streamers still hung around the windows from some long-ago celebration, when mayors from three towns had come to a party *The Daily Ranchero* reported kept both sides of the Rio Grande awake all night. Only one celebrant died of alcohol poisoning and one from accidental gunfire, which Clayton called a good night and the sheriff called good riddance after seeing who the victims were. In any case the revelry went on for two days. Clayton was toasted many times, met many a lass in the stockroom for a few minutes of slap-and-tickle; and one in his office, for a bit longer.

He passed a roped-off corner where a Reb and a Yankee boxed—bare-chested, bare-knuckled, bloody-faced—a dozen bettors cheering or booing. A 9-year-old pickpocket lifted the money pouch of one of the spectators, but Clayton grabbed the kid, made him slip the purse back to its rightful owner, and gave the boy a scowl meant to look dangerous. The youngster just stuck out his tongue. Reminded Clayton of himself at that age, stabbing him with a keen momentary flash of longing for that innocent time. He took a licorice stick from a jar on the bar, gave it to the kid and pointed his thumb at the door. The little would-be thief grinned and ran off.

Clayton made his way across the floor, exchanging the occasional nod of hello or wide eyes of innuendo. Not that he ran all his flirtations to ground, but he liked having the reputation for excessive womanizing. It diminished him in the eyes of some men, which made them less on their guard in his presence, so more likely to speak of things they ought to have held close. Those casual divulgences were grist for Clayton's mill.

Tonight's crowd was relatively sedate: a couple deserters, both North and South; some British Royal Navy on shore leave; a few *Juaristas*—soldiers of the Mexican resistance army—currently surveilling the French invasion force, which tonight consisted of two besotted Frogs at the end of the bar having a drinking contest. And then there was Clayton's most reliable customer, Scully, the Irish-born French Foreign Legionnaire who always wore a leather glove on his left hand. But more of Scully later.

Clayton paused at one of the casualties of one of the wars—Hermano—a 40-year-old Mexican with a 3-year-old mind ever since an unrifled musket ball had creased his skull. Clayton let him live here, in a cabin out back, in return for work—though his only job was to crank a hand pump, moving water from a ground basin up to a cistern on the roof that provided indoor plumbing for the second floor. It was an occupation Hermano loved.

Clayton put a hand on his shoulder. "*Como estas, Hermano?*" Hermano smiled broadly, nodding his head like a nutating cow. "*Bien hecho,*" Clayton told him, patting his back with genuine affection. Good job. Clayton wished someone could tell him the same some day. Hermano patted his own back, feeling Clayton's pride in him.

Isaac and Clayton moved on. A longhaired gambler in elbow garters backed up his chair from a faro table, knocking into Isaac. "Whyn't you watch where the hell you walkin', boy?"

"Next time I'll try to step livelier, suh," Isaac replied, keeping his eyes downcast. He spoke Slave when he wanted to avoid trouble, or sometimes just to be a joker.

The gambler sensed insult. "Don't you backsass me." He spat on Isaac's chest.

As Isaac's fist clenched, Clayton whacked the dandy's head against the doorjamb. Stunned but not out, the man slid to the floor. Clayton grabbed a spittoon and emptied it over the fellow.

"I wouldn't want you to leave shy of spit," said Clayton. "Just don't come back for more, now, hear?" He rolled the soggy gambler out the door, waving off bartender Jim, who'd come up with a truncheon in case help was needed. Then he returned to Isaac. "You all right?" he asked, wiping the spittle off Isaac's vest with his handkerchief.

"You mean after you tried to show everyone you were faster than me?"

"Didn't have to try too hard, did I?"

They shared a quarter smile and walked side by side until they reached the table in question, where they paused to watch four men play out a hand of stud poker.

One wore the dented badge of a Texas Ranger, peevish but too drunk to focus.

Beside him was a young fellow named Tinbury, dressed in diplomat blue, for the past months trying desperately to grow a mustache. He was the Union *charge d'affaires* from Leonard Pierce's office, Pierce being the United States Ambassador in Matamoros, appointed by Lincoln himself. Tinbury, on the other hand, was a career bureaucrat, posted here through random assignment—bad luck, he'd say. Clayton nodded to this junior diplomat, whom he knew slightly, and disliked slightly more.

The third man at the table was a young, smooth-faced corporal in a Yankee blue uniform, with some kind of Grand Army of the Republic campaign medal pinned to his chest. Looked too young to be a soldier, really, but every year the recruits got younger, as the early enlistees got killed off. Clayton had seen this boy quite a bit lately, here and around town, though they'd never spoken. Tinbury made introductions.

"Wilkes, this is Beale, the new Corporal of the Guard at the embassy compound. Beale, Wilkes."

They nodded at each other, then Clayton's gaze moved on, while the corporal kept studying Clayton's face.

The last poker player was clearly the teamster Isaac had referred to, the man he'd said was cheating. Bewhiskered and weathered, his clothes were filthy, the way teamsters seemed to like them. He had the look of someone arrived in town that day, with a sizable stake by the looks of the mound in front of him. Clayton watched the man rake in another pot. Tinbury was watching as well, with more than a squint of suspicion.

Clayton began telling a story. "You boys know how a rattlesnake'll kill itself if it don't know when to slither away?"

"How's that, Mr. Wilkes?" smiled Isaac, who had long experience being the shill in Clayton's tales.

"Man just needs to bring up his pistol and wave it real slow, back and forth, in front of the rattler. Snake'll take a bead on the muzzle, follow its moves inch for inch, gettin' ready to strike. Thinks the gun muzzle is the eye of a hawk. That's when the man pulls the trigger. Blows the rattler's head off. Snake did all the aimin' for him—blind man coulda done it. O' course, if the snake had any sense it woulda just eased on out."

There was a confused silence. "What the hell's that mean?" said the Texas Ranger.

"Means there's a snake at this table who needs to ease on out," said Clayton. He walked behind the teamster, put a hand on the man's shoulder. "I'll have to ask you to divvy up your winnin's to the other men and vacate the premises, sir," Clayton addressed him with courteous regret.

"Ask away, friend. I'm here to gamble."

"You have done so, sir, and lost. Out you go."

"Who the hell are you?"

"I'm Clayton Wilkes, and this is my establishment."

"You got special house rules I don't know about?"

"The rules of the house are no cheatin'." Clayton grabbed him by the scruff of the shirt and pulled him upright. The man spun, drawing a Colt single-action from his belt. But Clayton brought up a derringer right quick, put the barrel to the teamster's chest and pulled the trigger. The blast from the small firearm was barely loud enough to rise above the din of the room—but strong enough to knock the man backwards onto his ass on the table. A bullet to the heart will do that. He lay still, on his back, as a bloody stain spread across his shirtfront and his poker mates got up, stunned.

"Oh, my Lord," said Tinbury.

"The teamster drew first, I saw it." This from the Texas Ranger, laconically indicating the recently deceased.

"That was…amazing," said Corporal Beale in awe, evidently new to gunplay.

Clayton reached under the dead man's sleeves and around his collar. Nothing there. But Isaac came forward to pop open the corpse's big belt buckle. An ace fell out. Isaac smiled. "Some men like to keep their secret treasures close to their family jewels."

"Sorry about this, gentlemen," said Clayton. "Y'all just split up his money."

The Ranger dug into the pile of cash between the cadaver's thighs and dispersed roughly equal portions to himself, the dumbfounded Yankee corporal, and Tinbury, who was methodically going through the dead man's pockets.

"Wish you hadn't done that, Wilkes," said Tinbury. "We had good reason to believe he was an agent for the Confederacy. I was all set to have Beale arrest him."

"Found out he was a spy you'd have hung him anyway."

"Yes, but if I'd been able to learn who his contact was, it might've shortened the war by a year."

"War's good for business, I got no use to shorten it. And folks hear I let cheats play at my place, it's bad for business. That's my only politics." He shrugged and turned to Isaac. "The water is wide, Isaac, you best send this boy home to Jesus."

"Yassuh, Mmmistah Wilkes, sssuh," Isaac stammered; then laughed as if it were the funniest thing he'd ever said. Clayton just shook his head patiently. Isaac picked up the body, flung it over his shoulder like an old coat and exited the back door. The Texas Ranger moved to a new poker table. Consular aide Tinbury drilled Clayton with a stare.

"That was a helluva thing. How'd you know he was a cheat?"

"Isaac told me."

"What if your boy'd been wrong?"

"He's not my boy. And the day he's wrong I'll wire you the news."

Though Tinbury had a Union posting, he'd grown up in southern Indiana and didn't much care for Negroes, though he knew it would be impolitic to say so if he expected advancement in the diplomatic corps of the North. But his childhood feelings crept out when he was under stress. And he was stressed now that the man he'd been following was dead. U.S. Ambassador Leonard Pierce would be irked, notwithstanding there was nothing Tinbury could have done about it. And nothing to be done about it now, Pierce be damned. So Tinbury just cursed his ill fortune and walked away.

"Damn!" said a voice cracked by excitement and youthful hormones. Clayton turned to see the young Yankee corporal looking at him with incredulous eyes. He'd forgotten the kid was still here. "That was so audacious," said the young soldier. "I mean, what guts it took, not to mention quick thinking. You are one cool customer."

"You run a place like this, you learn to anticipate behavior," Clayton demurred.

"Anticipate is one thing. Ricochet the hell out of it's another."

"We all have our own particular skills. I've no doubt you're a jim dandy sentry."

With that Clayton nodded politely and headed back upstairs to his office. The corporal watched him all the way.

Isaac felt someone watching him as he walked out the back door with the deadweight burden draping his shoulder, but he didn't look around to see who it was. Looking would have been a sign of weakness, or fear.

A light fog dampened his face as he made his way over the sandy earth, ground-covered with blue sage and sea grass, an easy walk to the river. The Rio Grande was shallow, twisting, muddy and wide. From here it rolled 25 miles east to the port of Bagdad, where it dumped into the Gulf of Mexico. Bagdad was the poor cousin to Matamoros, a hasty city of brothels and bars and tar-wood bonfires on the beach, where bales of cotton were piled high awaiting transfer to the ships offshore that would take them to the English mills. Isaac always expected to see Charon poised there on his ferry, readying to carry all those smokey souls across the river.

When he reached the water's edge he lowered the teamster to the sand and spoke softly. "Go with God, my friend." He rolled the body into the river, where it tumbled slowly in the current, reflecting the gibbous moonlight until it floated around a bend, lost to the world of concerns, out to the sea.

Isaac rose, turned, and just stood there for a moment to watch the city of Matamoros play its night games. Laughter and arguments in the *zocalo* were punctuated by an occasional gunshot, either celebratory or acrimonious. A chorus of opera from the magnificent *Teatro* crossed melodies with drunken sea shanties and *mariachis* rising from the bars. All brightly lit with lanterns, candle flame and intrigue. Isaac surely loved the clockworks of a city night, where everyone was a free agent.

A puff of wind flared up embers in a nearby, smoldering pile of charred dresses and satin bustiers, tin skirt hoops glowing orange. As sparks twisted up into the starry night, it seemed to Isaac as if the spirit of the South itself were turning to smoke and blowing away. If only it were that simple.

A man of the spirit, Isaac felt connected to all living things and made it his practice to experience that connection daily. Not that he wouldn't kill if he had to—but as he knew from Sun Tzu's *The Art of War*, great military conflicts are best won without doing battle. He'd studied the Sun Tzu text, along with other histories and philosophies, by reading them secretly at night, lifted from the shelves of his last owner—a Florida doctor who'd taught him medical arts as well, designating Isaac the caretaker of sick slaves on the doctor's plantation, so the doctor himself wouldn't have to dirty his hands.

But it was Shalako, the Zuni shaman, who'd taught Isaac that when he did have to kill an enemy—like he did that scrofulous doctor who'd owned him—he should always take a moment to thank the body for sharing that sacred moment of death. Same way you thanked the deer you killed for providing you with food. Because in being connected to all, Isaac touched his own mortality with every life he took.

Isaac walked back to the casino. He saw Tinbury watching from the shadows but gave no hint that he saw. Tinbury was a fool and would believe what he wanted to.

"Waterboy done tol' me," said Harley. "They found a beava dead in the wings."

"A beaver," said Clayton, holding a smile. "Son, where'd you hear that?"

"Waterboy said Miss Catherine tol' him. Was that singer what she called the beava."

"Diva, not beaver. The diva's dead? How'd that happen? Some patron of the opera not overly fond of Verdi?" Clayton had heard from the captain of the *Sea Queen* that *La Traviata* closed its run after just one week in Paris; but here in Matamoros audiences were generally more forgiving.

"Yellow fever took her, more like. Whole mess o' black flux out back."

"Have to burn her costumes, then, that'll cost the house a pretty penny. You give Catherine my regrets."

"Yessir, Cap'n." Harley called every man Cap'n. He was a

Confederate Army deserter, Alabama infantry, poorest of poor whites before the war, hardly better off now; so he felt deference to all was probably the safest way to stay out of hot water.

"Any talk of the invasion?"

"Everyone talks, Cap'n. Ain't nothin' to credit."

The impending invasion of Texas by the Yankee army was second only to the weather as a subject of speculation in Matamoros—and summer weather in the Rio Grande basin was a trial, going from heat so bad it was hard to breathe to tropical storms by September. They'd had torrential rain for just a single day the week before. Ever since then Yellow Fever cases had started hitting town; nothing like the epidemic of '58, but still enough to make a man wary, and would continue to do so until the weather turned cooler in the fall. As if there weren't enough cause to die in this season.

Times of drought the streets were arid with a fine dust swirling in on the desert wind, like the war rumors that blew through town. Some rumors were true, of course, whispered by officers through the cigar smoke between acts at the Opera House—the *Teatro de la Independencia*— where Harley worked as a janitor. He picked up details there as he swept out the *loggias*, keeping Clayton abreast of it all. For nickels mostly, but a half dollar for solid military rumors. Once, a Golden Eagle.

Though Clayton bought and sold information of all sorts, he didn't much care to trade with Yankees, reputedly due to their having burned down his family's plantation back in Louisiana. And because his sentiments were known around town, Union agents seldom approached him. If they did—even with cash on hand for intelligence about Southern troop movements—he usually declined their business. If accused of being a Reb sympathizer, he'd only say that he was a Mexican resident now, and took no sides in the American War Between the States. He was on his own side; in his own war.

Harley lingered another moment while Clayton found some coins in his pocket to give the man. "Thank you, Cap'n."

When Harley left, Clayton sipped his coffee—the real stuff, from Jamaica, strong and sober, a premium drink few in the Confederacy enjoyed—and walked to the French doors where Chinese silk curtains hung still in the windless night. He stepped out onto the *senorita* balcony. The view had a dreamlike hush to it, the fragmented reflection of the moon gliding on the slow current of the Rio Grande. Shards of moonlight, all broke to pieces. Made him glance over at the William Morris stained glass window he'd had shipped over from the 1862 London Exposition, shattered in a storm off Cuba, now lying in fragments on his workbench. Clayton had been piecing it together for weeks; like a puzzle. Maybe when he was done he'd have a go at fixing the river-splintered moon.

Clayton was, among other things, a fixer. People were in trouble, or in need, or in deep, Clayton was the man to fix you up. For a price, and with a sparkle in his eye. He bought and sold guns, cotton, documents, Confederate money and above all, information. Commonly to the highest bidder; but always as it pleased him.

Clayton inhaled deeply—another way to get information. He had a keen nose—not as good as he'd made out to his companions the day of that Colorado blizzard—but still, he'd been known to pick up clues on the air. It was clean now, though. No whiff of gunpowder, nor panic sweat, nor arson smoke; nor mercy, for that matter. Just the air, with a hint of moisture in it tonight, pure in its own way, devoid of artifice. He took a moment of peace before he stepped back inside. To his world of artifice.

Every curio in his office came with its own story. The Chinese curtains he'd bought from a whorehouse in San Francisco, the English rolltop rescued at the auction of a bankrupt Georgia peach plantation; the threadbare Persian carpet in which a fleeing pasha had been rolled to escape his enemies. He surrounded himself with objects of wonder; for life was short, was it not? And in that brief window, the senses might be soothed, even when the soul felt devoid of beauty.

Clayton walked to the workbench where the William Morris glass splinters lay. Picked up a red fragment and held it to the kerosene lamp on the desk. The color of blood, informed by fire. As if the war had seeped into everything.

He walked to his office door overlooking the gaming room and peered down through the stagnant layer of smoke that had found its level ten feet above the floor. It was four in the morning; quiet downstairs. Just French Foreign Legionnaire Scully out cold at a table, his leather-gloved hand gripping an empty shot glass; Little Andy, the dead-hours barkeep dozed against the backbar; and some lone banjo player picking a sad-wise tune for no one but himself. The place never closed, but business dropped off between three and ten a.m. Clayton knew he should go to sleep, but he rarely slept more than a few hours anyway. His dreams saw to that; bad dreams, bitter memories.

Clayton grew up on a cane plantation, the sole child of a doting mother and a strict father. His only friends were his father's slave children; and every summer, his Mother's siblings in France. But his mother was dead now, his father too, the plantation burned to ashes, Clayton vowing never to return. Sitting at his desk, he sipped a Tennessee whiskey until his head grew heavy, lulled by the banjo chords downstairs...

A banjoist plinked on the back step as two boys huddled nearby. Eight years old, one Negro, one white. The kitchen was abuzz with slaves preparing party food. The white boy nudged the black boy, who walked into the midst of the scurrying servants, took a handful of walnuts from a bowl and put them in his pockets. As he walked back to his co-conspirator he grabbed a dish of butter, and the boys ran out of the kitchen giggling.

The twilight party was a grand affair. Sixty ladies and gentlemen in fine gowns and elegant frock coats filled the drawing room, the gardens, the conservatory, drinking juleps and whatnot. Banjo and fiddle played, the moon was full, the magnolia sweet. The two boys crouched behind a wisteria in thrilled anticipation of the moment.

An old servant approached three ladies near the pond, bearing a silver tray of walnuts, figs and grapes. A young lady in a hoop dress reached for a walnut and nutcracker. The boys squeezed each other's hands tightly, stifling laughter. The lady cracked a nut. It split with ease into two perfect halves—each half filled with rancid butter. Without looking she reached into the shell for the nut-meat but only came back with a finger full of yellow goo. She looked at her finger, shrieked and slipped into the pond.

Next morning the Negro boy got tied to a post. All the slaves were made to watch, including his parents. Including the white boy. The overseer held a cat-o-nine-tails.

The white boy's father—the plantation owner—stood beside his son grimly. "This is your doin', Clay. You best not forget this." He nodded at the overseer.

The overseer whipped the black boy's back ten times. Every lash drew blood. The white boy twitched at each scourge. The eyes of the two boys met, until Clayton looked away.

When the whipping was done, Isaac's parents carried their unconscious son off to the slave quarters. Everyone dispersed quietly.

"That's what happens," the white boy's father told him, as Clay stood there, shaking…

Clayton startled awake, still sitting at his desk. He'd just heard a sound; or if not heard, at least sensed the vibration that living things sometimes make instead of sound.

A man stood silently behind him now, hidden in the Oriental curtains bracketing the open French doors. Motionless as granite and dripping wet. His shirt was stuck to his chest by the dark bloodstain the derringer ball had left. He stepped silently closer to Clayton. He wanted to be standing directly behind Wilkes before he made his presence known. Wanted to put his hand on Wilkes's shoulder, as Wilkes had done to him in the casino. He took one long stride toward the desk, then paused to set himself.

Clayton was able to estimate the size of his visitor by the almost soundless sag in the floorboard where the man stepped. He heard a few drops of water hit the floor with the man's step, too; river water, by the smell. That said it all. Clayton smiled. Without turning around, he lifted the whiskey bottle. "Will you join me?"

The man in the bloody shirt relaxed, his little surprise blown. It was the dead teamster. But not all that dead, apparently. His name was Dupree. "Make mine a double. This powder burn is killin' me."

CHAPTER 2

CLAYTON FILLED TWO SHOT glasses. "Sorry. I had to put an extra pinch of gunpowder in the wad to make certain that sack of pig's blood got tore."

"I didn't much like your buck puttin' hands on me to tape it there."

"Not my buck."

"What is he, then, a runaway?"

"Didn't you hear? Lincoln freed the slaves."

"Hell, he just did that so's England wouldn't recognize the sovereign Confederate States of America."

"Be that as it may. Isaac mostly does what I ask, if I ask polite, and it surely saved your skin."

"Well, I played it dead to the end. He said we was bein' watched. I didn't like that darkie puttin' hands on me, though." Dupree brought his own hand up to rub his sore, bloody chest. "Where'd y'all learn a trick like that blood pouch anyways?"

"I've a cousin who's an actor. It's a theater illusion. But that's no matter—I hear you've got somethin' to share. Go on now and share it."

Dupree pulled an upper set of false teeth from his mouth. Hidden in the bridge was a small oilcloth. "This is meant for Consul Jose Quintero. Can you get me to him?"

"No, he won't meet with anyone he don't know. I can get it to him though."

"It concerns the Union invasion of Texas. A lot depends on it."

"Then I'll be sure to get it to him." He took the oilcloth from

Dupree. "You best get back to New Orleans in a hush. You show your face around here, we're both for the gallows, after that little piece of theater. Tinbury thinks you're dead, remember."

Dupree raised his glass. "I regret I have but one life to give for my country."

"Or two."

They clinked and drank. Clayton wondered how many lives he had left himself.

As the sun rose over the Gulf, Clayton stood on his balcony to witness the huge Texican sky pushing the horizon out beyond its boundaries. Enormous clouds billowed in three distinct layers across the heavens, some appearing higher than last night's moon, some so low it seemed like you might hit one with a well-thrown rock. There was a balminess to the air this morning, a breeze coming in from the east. It meant the season was turning, from dry to wet. This change in weather always brought a characteristic aroma with it, the smells of Red Tide, dead fish and brine. All would wash away when the rains came in earnest a couple months from now.

Around ten he left the building and walked west to make his morning rounds. Small wooden houses with saggy planks, log columns and tin roofs lined the dirt streets. Crimson bougainvillea spilled around the *pueblos* in churning gushes of color. He admired the way bougainvillea thrived in the harshest terrain while sporting beautiful petals and dangerously spiky stems. It was a model Clayton tried to emulate.

This early in the day the outskirts of Matamoros were quiet. A pack of *zocalo* dogs ran a raccoon to ground in the bushes; then took off yowling when the feral scavenger rose on its hind legs to attack. A toothless old man slept off last night's mescal, snoring lightly. Somewhere a baby coughed in a high, wheezy bark. A *chachalaca* sat atop a low Texas palm, clutching a bullsnake in one talon and tearing out bits of meat with its beak. Flies buzzed over a dead skink.

Beyond the bushes, the raccoon mauled a three-legged mutt who'd gotten in over his head. Clayton kicked the raccoon soundly—the beast hissed at him but lumbered away. Squatting beside the wounded dog, Clayton could see it was done in this life but for the pain, staring at Clayton with huge pleading eyes. He twisted its neck in a quick act of mercy, though it felt like the end of everything trying to survive.

Nearing the *Plaza de Armas* he saw a few scattered debauchers going home; a *barrillero* rolling his keg of fresh water, calling out *"Agua puro!"* for two bits a jug, two bucks a barrel; merchants setting up their stalls with displays of *nopales*, jewelry, *maracas*, sandals, *tamales*; street musicians, tradesmen, scam artists and beggars. Storefront cotton traders were opening their shutters. Everywhere, cotton traders.

Matamoros was ground zero of *Los Algodones*, the "Cotton Times". Cotton was what kept the South alive in its struggle for independence— millions of bales ferried across the Rio Grande from Brownsville to Matamoros, then downriver to Bagdad, where lighters carried them to waiting foreign ships laden with guns to trade. People all over town were getting rich. Some within the law, some without it.

He passed the offices of *The Daily Ranchero*, the English speaking newspaper of record; and beyond that, at the edge of the plaza, the *Catedral de Notre Senora del Refugio*. The Cathedral of Our Lady of Refuge. The enormous ochre-brick church faced the *zocalo*, its three-story spires dominating the landscape. Clayton passed it without paying much attention. His faith resided in Lady Luck, his patron saints all sinners.

In the shadow of the central gazebo two *Cortinistas* beat a Texas Ranger unconscious. It was an old grudge, the Mexicans outraged that their land had been stolen by Texans. And the *Cortinistas*—followers of the *bandito*-turned-revolutionary Juan Cortina—wanted their land back. Failing that, they were happy to beat any old Texas Ranger into coma. Not Clayton's business.

Next came the Town Hall, whose bell rang for emergencies like fire, hurricane, or conquest. As Clayton walked past, an apparition— like the ghosts of all those catastrophes—emerged from behind the building, wafting across the courtyard: a single-file, black-and-white line of the French Order of Nuns of the Incarnate Word and Blessed Sacrament, floating across the landscape like stray, ungraspable thoughts.

Clayton never knew where they came from or where they went; they just appeared, like memories, or cautions.

At the far edge of the plaza he turned up Calle Abasolo, where the three-story *Teatro* at the corner filled the block. Modeled on the Paris Opera House, it boasted tall arches over the entryway and an exterior wrought-iron grillwork balcony overlooking the street. Most nights it was filled with gallant gents and fine ladies, smoking, drinking, talking of war and art, whispering about people they knew well, or slightly, or not at all. Clayton passed under the arches to enter the foyer.

A huge, marble hall lay in shadow at this hour, the massive chandeliers all extinguished, the ornate gilt lattice-work obscure in the half-light. The building was constructed with New York doors, Guatemalan lumber, Mexican bricks, Versailles candelabrae. The performance floor was raised or lowered on pulleys, for dances or orchestra pits. There was a *loggia* outside the balcony level for lounging between acts, and this grand lounge communicated with the outside balconies overlooking the street. A central staircase led up to the second floor, but Clayton walked behind it to a wall of cherub-encrusted portals. He knocked on the last door and entered.

The Confederate States of America Special Envoy to Mexico Jose Agustin Quintero reclined on a chaise, wearing a floorlength, violet brocade dressing gown, nursing a vindictive hangover with willow bark tea and the tender ministrations of the dead diva's understudy.

"Agustin, *mi viejo amigo.* I thought I might could find you here," said Clayton. Quintero's friends called him Agustin.

"Go away."

Many months ago at their first inebriated chess game, the goateed Quintero had told Clayton that he was a Cuban-born, Harvard-educated lawyer, poet and journalist who'd fled to America when the Spanish put a death sentence on his head for spreading revolutionary propaganda around Havana. His yen for rebellion brought him into contact with Jefferson Davis, who saw armed conflict as a last resort, a pragmatic means to an end. Quintero viewed revolution as more of a joyful, passionate obligation.

Once the Civil War began, Davis appointed Quintero chief diplomat to Mexico, where he established a working relationship with Mexican government officials who agreed—for a tariff—to provide security for the cotton trade, promising that Union troops would not be allowed to cross south of the border. So though Quintero was hardly a Son of the South, he'd become an indispensable Uncle to the Rebellion.

Clayton found different tactics useful in gaining the trust of different people. In Quintero's case it had been months of chess, philosophy, and Cuban rum. This morning, though, he could see a simple hangover might be all it took to help the man come to a decision Clayton wanted him to make.

Clayton poured a cup of tea and nodded to the young lady holding the damp cloth to Quintero's brow. "I'm afraid I'll have to ask you to leave us for the time bein', Miss. I'll keep up your good works with the Special Envoy, though."

"She speaks only French," said Quintero.

"*Alors, va-t'en, jolie mademoiselle*," said Clayton agreeably.

The young lady—wearing a white lace nightdress that exposed as much as it covered—smiled shyly and exited, brushing Clayton's arm with her breast on the way out, suggestively whispering, "*Bien, mon vieux.*" Made him think she might be a good source of Quintero's pillow talk if Clayton treated her right. "Pretty girl," he told Quintero.

"Go away," Quintero repeated.

"Say, did you hear the news from Charleston?" Clayton asked. "54th Massachusetts Colored troops have Fort Wagner surrounded."

"Of course, I heard. Now will you leave me alone?"

"Hell, Lincoln starts recruitin' all the ex-slaves into the Union army, the Confederacy's goose is cooked."

"It matters not what the *Yanquis* do. This may be a setback but revolution against tyranny is inevitable. The Rebels will triumph in the end."

"And to that end…" Clayton produced the small oilcloth given him by Dupree. "From our friends in New Orleans. Word of the Union advance, I'm given to believe."

Quintero walked unsteadily to the desk, opening the oilcloth as he spoke. "Their forces are amassing around Lafayette, I hear—a land invasion west into Texas. And now with momentum from Gettysburg, I fear it will launch before the new year." He'd lost most traces of his Spanish accent, but there remained a formality to his speech.

Inside the oilcloth was a small paper with a single line of writing, half the letters blurred by river water that had seeped in. Quintero held the paper to the light of the kerosene lamp. What was still legible read:

King   B   B   Si ster

"What is its meaning?" Quintero sounded annoyed.

Clayton shook his head. "Cipher, I expect. Don't you have a codebook or somethin' to unlock messages like this?"

"I do, but such scrawl looks like no code I have seen. '*King B B Sister*?' If this is to do with the Yankee invasion plans, it is lost on me."

"I can take it to someone I know," said Clayton. His tone conveyed helpfulness to a friend in need. He could see Quintero wanted nothing more than to go back to bed. "He's trustworthy, and he has the skills to bring out the smudged letters more clearly."

Quintero hesitated. He didn't like including strangers in his war games; but Wilkes had never let him down, and this was time-critical information. "Do what you can. We must learn if the Union troops in Louisiana are the main force or merely a diversion."

"I'll need some capital to pay my contact for his services."

"If a man is doing this for money, he may betray us for money just as easily."

"Even patriots need to eat. Besides, I'd rather a fellow be straightforward about his cash needs, means he's not tryin' to hide what he's after. I once had a man try to convince me I was the heir of a Dutch West Indies Company founder named Hendrik Wilkes who owned a big chunk of Manhattan—showed me the deeds, the marriage licenses, the genealogy comin' down to me—all he needed was a thousand dollars to bribe the New York City Clerk to open that record book."

"What did you do?"

"Took his documents to a slew of other Wilkeses I found in Boston, got them to give *me* a thousand each. Course, I only asked from those that could afford it—and only those with a little larceny in their hearts were tempted to give it to me."

Quintero nodded—point taken. "How much will your code breaker take?"

"He's a craftsman, it'd be foolish to insult him. Two hundred should cover it."

Quintero opened a large wall safe filled with paper.

"And no Confederate Treasury notes," Clayton advised.

Quintero moved one shelf of bills to the side, counted out ten gold pieces and gave them to Clayton. As Clayton put the specie in his pants pocket with the smudged code paper, Catherine Delacroix entered in high dudgeon, a low-cut gown, and a hint of French *cologne*. Catherine ran the place.

"Where is *mademoiselle*?" she inquired archly.

"I am certain I do not know to whom you refer." Quintero could be arch, too.

"I refer to Claire, whose slippers I see beside your bed, and who was due in my office ten minutes ago."

Clayton helped out. "I believe Catherine refers to the young lady who was soothin' your brow as I came in."

As general manager of the *Teatro*, Catherine had enough responsibilities to keep her miserable most of the time. These included playing hostess, booking performances and wrangling the talent. "*Tais-toi*," she said to Clayton without looking at him.

Her words gave him a fleeting memory of his French grandfather, but before he could savor it a young man appeared at the doorway. "These are the auditions?"

"No, the auditions are onstage! As the notice specified! Leave us!" Catherine shouted. Until she saw his face, and softened. "I will meet you there shortly, *mon petit. Ne se derange-toi pas*." She turned chilly eyes back on Quintero. "Where is the girl?"

Quintero closed his eyes, his headache expanding.

Clayton smiled sympathetically. "I'll let you two carry on your business in private, if I may." He bowed and left.

But as he rounded the curving staircase, Catherine caught up with him, pushing him flat against the bannister. "You are no gentleman," she said—and kissed him ripely on the mouth. He didn't protest, but he didn't give much back either. Catherine desisted. "Perhaps you are *trop fatigue?*" she queried, eyebrows up in arms.

"Never tired of a fine virtuoso like yourself."

She slapped him. "*Virtuoso* means you think I am old—so, as I said, no gentleman." But immediately rueful, she kissed the spot she'd stung.

"I'll keep that in mind," he said diplomatically and left. Though she was an excellent source of information, she excited little deep passion in him of late. Of course, not much did so any more.

Clayton returned to the *Plaza de Armas*, where he bought a *churro* from a rag-dressed *mestizo* boy on his payroll. "*Que pasa, amigo?*"

"*Nada de las guerras, mi capitan. Solo amor y beber.*" Nothing of the wars. Only love and drink.

Clayton paid the boy as a camel driver escorted his beast past them toward the river, one bale of cotton slung over either side of its hump. Camels were well suited for trekking cotton down the Wild Horse Desert but generally despised in town; smelly, mean, just badly behaved around civilized people, which Texans fancied themselves.

Clayton walked to *The Daily Ranchero*—a low, four room building housing two old Franklin presses, a half-dozen typesetters, and a cubicle where reporters came and went, writing their stories. The editor, Simon Wachtel, was a German Texas Unionist nearing seventy years old, with a cloud-colored beard that was at least fifty. He'd been run out of Ft. Worth by Secessionists for publishing abolitionist broadsides, but had found a happy home in Mexico. Printing was Simon's love, and here in this lawless town he could print what he wanted, in his own shop, where he hired mostly runaway slaves and Mexican orphans. He found them to be generally the most eager to learn a trade. Besides, it tickled him to be a burr in the saddle of the American racialists who'd kicked him out of Texas. Despite his Northern sympathies, he was a friend of Clayton's.

When Clayton entered the front office, he found Wachtel with a scrawny teenager named Jensen, whom Clayton knew to be a Union deserter from Ohio, instructing him in how to clean a press-bed with solvent. Simon—always dressed in suspendered tweed pants over ink-stained longjohns—looked more patient than usual. Clayton supposed the old coot couldn't afford to lose any more hired help with his short-fused temper. He walked past them without greeting, into Wachtel's back office.

The room appeared smaller than it was, cluttered as a newsman's stereotype. The desk was piled high with papers, books stuffed onto the shelves without order. Lying around were broken press parts, vats of ink, wooden job cases stacked on the floor to nearly tipping, lead letters pied in a corner. Today's front page lay on the desk, its headline proclaiming: NAPOLEON DECLARES MEXICO A CATHOLIC EMPIRE.

Clayton sat in the desk chair, picked up a well-thumbed catalogue from last year's London International Exposition and leafed through it, pausing at photographs of a new Analytical Engine that could make complex computations, invented by Charles Babbage; the creation of a new, strong, light material called "plastic;" a refrigeration machine; and the introduction of the hourglass to time-limit chess tournaments.

Wachtel came in and closed the door behind him. "*Es macht* rude, I say, to welcome a man into his own office."

Clayton shrugged, indicating the newspaper headline. "What's all this about a Catholic Empire?"

"The priests are in Napoleon's pocket. They think he is a *gut bollverk* against all your American Protestantism."

"Napoleon just wants his own country in this hemisphere. Catholics be damned, and the Monroe Doctrine too."

"This is all fascinating, but what do you want? I'm busy."

Clayton took the oilcloth from his vest, unfolded it and handed the paper to Wachtel, who read: "*King B B Sister.* You want I should print this for you?"

"No, I want you to translate it. It got dumped in the river and half the letters ran. I'd like to know what it really says."

Wachtel picked up a jeweler's loupe from the desk to examine the writing. "I cannot make out the *verschmiert* letters, the water blurred them too bad."

"So that's it? That's the best you can do?"

Wachtel wagged his finger. "I will not do this if it helps the Secessionists."

"Secession is just a political act, Simon, like any other."

"In the service of human slavery. This I will not support, you know that."

"Secession's about states' rights, that's all."

"*Ja*, the right to own slaves."

"Some slaves don't have it so bad, they do the master's work, but the owners feed them, house them, care for their physical and spiritual needs…"

"Enough! I will not support such an enterprise, *und* I will not…"

"All right, all right, I promise—translating this paper will not in any way promote that peculiar institution." Clayton took two of Quintero's ten $20 gold pieces out of his pocket and put them on Wachtel's desk. "Will that suffice to recompense your time?"

Wachtel sniffed. Clayton still hoped to keep the other eight gold pieces for himself, though. So he tried another tack. "You're afraid to try, aren't you. Afraid you can't restore the print, and you don't want me to see that."

"Insulting my skills now, *ja*?" he scowled. But Clayton pulled out his big guns.

"I'll spot you a bishop and two pawns in our next game."

Wachtel squinted at the offer, examining it for catches. "What stakes?"

"One pound of Jamaican coffee beans against that Spanish *porto* on your shelf."

Wachtel weighed the risk versus gain as he walked to a bank of flat files that he pulled out to reveal a dozen different weights of paper stock. He compared Clayton's small note to each of his own pieces until he found a match he liked.

"Here's what I can do. A technique I have heard called 'reverse engineering.'"

"Which is what?"

"*Ein freund* of mine in Leipzig built a *Koenig und Bauer* press by taking it apart *und* then building his own in back-to-front order with cheaper parts."

"And how does that tell us what this says, pray?"

"These blotches were letters before the water *verschmiert* them. I have similar paper stock here *und* I can make a good guess at the ink that was used. I will write a line of letters on this paper, wrap in an oilcloth, *und* stick in a bowl of water. Then if any of the smudges I get look like any of these smudges, I will know what letter made it."

"Sounds unlikely to me. When do you think you might know?"

"Come back tonight. Late."

"I will do that, sir. Until then, I'd brush up on the Benko Gambit, if I were you. It's what Steinitz used to win the Brilliancy Prize at the London Exposition, and it's how I plan to crush you." He poked his finger down on the Exposition catalogue page detailing the German chess master's unprecedented strategy, and left.

Time for lunch. Clayton headed for the ferry to Brownsville across the river. Along the way he passed an old man playing a warped guitar. He tossed the busker a few *pesos* for making the day sweeter. In the shallows of the river a white heron stood motionless, watching for fish to spear. Near the riverbank ox carts carried cotton from Matamoros to Bagdad. Clayton nodded to the ancient drivers as he made for the ferries—large flatboats operated with pullies and ropes going back and forth all day and night. Clayton always felt touched by these ferrymen, ox-cart haulers, herons and buskers—honest souls with small lives who plied their trades with pride. Clayton envied pride.

On reaching the dock he saw the young Yankee corporal who'd admired his feats at the poker table last night, standing behind a wagon 30 yards away. A horse crossed between them, though, and when it passed a moment later, the soldier was gone. Clayton was always on guard to being followed; but also to the tricks of his overactive imagination. Nothing to do now but just file the information away.

He boarded a flatboat as it pushed off, letting his gaze wander over the dirty water. Muddy rivers were like life, his mother used to say—you could float happily along, never seeing below the surface. But those depths were home to murky things; dreams lived there, too.

His mother'd told him he had that gift of dark sight, that his dreams could sometimes see portents, sometimes connections the angels might whisper in his ear—though he must never tell the Priest she'd said these things. He looked for connections now, peering into the murky flow all around him...

Clay and Isaac danced to the joyous spiritual an old black fiddler played in the backyard, when his father strode up and slapped him. "What do you think you're doin'?"

"Nothin', Daddy, I..."

"You playin' at music with a black boy? What're you thinkin'?" His father grabbed the fiddle from the old grandpa and hit Isaac in the face with it. Startled, Isaac sat down hard. Then Clay's daddy smashed the fiddle to the ground.

"Don't you ever dance to this Colored music again!" Slap...

"Senor!" The ferryman was jostling him. "We are here!"

Clayton looked around. Must have drifted off. Likely an unpleasant few minutes, too—his hands were clenched and the boatman was eyeing him with concern.

"I'm all right," he said, tipping the man a dollar. *"Todo esta bien."*

He stepped ashore and walked toward the fort. He'd be glad when these dreams left him.

CHAPTER 3

THE EMACIATED OX DROPPED to its knees and refused to get up, even after Jessup kicked it in the behind. A moment later it began bucking on the ground, some kind of fit.

Allie unholstered her pistol and head-shot the seizuring creature, though it took her three tries to actually kill it. "Best cut him from the yoke and replace him with an animal who can pull his own weight," she said; then hurried back to her tripod camera. Jessup watched her go, wondering not for the first time how he'd drawn this duty.

Allie Stoneman was the recent widow of Horace, whom she loved well; well, she loved him well enough, anyway. He was a sickly fellow, though, 40 years her senior, and required more care than she'd bargained for. But he'd given her the security she needed at a time she required, after all that bad business. Horace told her he cared not a whit about her past, though; he only wanted a loving wife to give him children, and nursing of his weak constitution. The nursing she had mastered, at least until the end.

When he finally passed, she ran Stoneman Plantation, just outside Shreveport, with a full measure of grit and then some. She'd taken control of pulling in this year's cotton crop, only to find that Horace's debts remained alive and well after he was put in the ground. There were two main creditors, with whom Allie negotiated a complicated deal. One took the cotton crop, the other took all 94 slaves, and Allie kept the plantation. But since she couldn't run the plantation without slaves, she sold it at a discount to creditor number two, and with the money, she bought back all the cotton, at a price far below what she knew she could get for it from the brokers in Matamoros. As a kindness the creditor let her retain her two personal slaves, Jersey and Moon, a young married couple who'd been with her ever since her own marriage to Horace.

She took her bales on the Cotton Road with all due speed—partly because she was done as done could be with Shreveport; partly because she believed that the Union troops rumored to be mustering down around Lafayette might send a contingent north to seize her goods before they martialed their forces west to invade Texas.

She made it to King Ranch with her 4600 bales without incident. Once there she took on a small escort of Texas Rangers for that last push down the Wild Horse Desert—a wasteland of dusty sand, Comanche and *banditos*. The trail was easy to follow, though—marked by the sun-parched bones of a thousand luckless men and beasts of burden. Once in Matamoros, her intention was to open her own import/export company and make a fortune off the war, like everyone one else there.

The convoy almost halfway down, Allie was feeling optimistic, having not yet lost a single bale. Unfortunately the animals had fared less well. One of the two water wagons had cracked, trickling half the supply into the hardpack before anyone noticed. Now a yoke of oxen, four horses and six head of cattle were fallen to a dry death. The dozen camels were doing fine, this godforsaken crucible like home to them; and Allie still had twenty-seven steers left to sell in Brownsville to the Confederate Army Quartermaster at Fort Brown, Major Russell. Then it was just a matter of paying the tariffs and bribes it took to ferry her load to Matamoros, and she'd be flush.

She stood behind her camera now, wearing a long cotton skirt, well-used riding boots, a man's shirt and a wide-brimmed church hat for sun shade. A fine-looking woman of 28 years, though not Southern-Belle pretty. Black hair, high cheeks and an aquiline nose had engendered some rumors about her ancestry when she'd settled in to Shreveport; but none dared speak of it to her face. Horace had cherished her, and she sat by him through his long ordeal with malaria—dosing him with quinine for the shaking chills and promising she'd not let the family farm fall to either Yankees or weevils. She didn't say anything about debt, and neither did he.

The tripod-mounted camera pointed the length of the caravan. Allie slipped her head under the canvas apron that shielded the viewfinder from light and waited until the muleskinner finished blowing his nose onto the ground. Then she raised her hand high, signaling everyone to be still—they all knew the drill by now—removed the dark slide that protected the glass negative from light and took the cap off the lens for one…two…three seconds. Then replaced the lens cap, inserted the dark slide back into the plate holder, and removed the holder assembly from the camera.

Quick-stepping the plate holder into the black tent behind her, Allie took out the collodion-and-silver-nitrate-coated glass negative from its frame and slipped it into the tray of pyrogallic acid. She watched as the image slowly developed, emerging like magic from the transparent glass. When the picture clarified, she removed the glass plate and lowered it into a tray of water, precious water. Next came the fixative, then a final water wash.

It dried quickly in this heat, and while it did, Allie took down her darkroom with the help of Moon and Jersey. "You two pack up fast, we can still make good time before this old Satan sun goes back down to hell."

"Yes, ma'am," said Jersey, a child bride of 14 or 15 who'd known her husband, Moon—a gangly, self-effacing 36 year old—most of her life, though she'd been born on a different plantation, so nobody really knew her birthday. They were an agreeable couple who loved to disagree. Allie felt they were more friends and confidantes to her than slaves. Though, of course, they weren't free to leave. And whether they considered *her* a friend wasn't exactly a subject of discussion.

"I don't reckon this the same sun we had in Lou'siana," said Moon. "If you want to send me back home, I'll be sure to grab the real one and tote it down to y'all in Texas." He grinned but Jersey poked him in the back, short-tempered in this furnace of a desert.

"You save your work for your arms, don't be exercisin' your jaw so much." Jersey was the sensible one.

While they stowed the photographic equipment onto a wagon, Allie varnished the dry glass plate and stored it in a special boxed rack with the other negatives. She'd print them up when she got to Brownsville. When all was finished, she mounted a haughty camel, which she was determined to teach some manners, and took a sip of hot water.

As this was going on, Jessup and a teamster yoked up a new ox. Jessup was a lieutenant in the Texas Rangers, leading the squad to guard Allie on this last leg of the journey. Not the command he preferred. He'd been taken off river patrol, where he'd been skirmishing with Cortina, the rebel leader who was still fighting the Mexican-American War, now 15 years past its conclusion; the old bandit just didn't know when to call it quits. Cortina hid on the *bancos* of the Rio Grande— islands in the middle of the wide river, formed when the river cut across its own loops. Considered neutral territory by international law, these islands provided havens for thieves who used them as base camps from which to raid Texas, terrorizing the settlers.

Jessup hated Cortina, whom he hadn't yet bested in a single fight; and whom he viewed as a common gangster. Cortina was a folk hero in Mexico, though; his own people wrote songs about him. *Cuando los Americanos duermen, Cortina visita sus suenos, y se despierta en Mexico.* When Americans sleep, Cortina visits their dreams, and they awake in Mexico. It was a catchy tune, which Jessup found himself singing sometimes, until he realized what it was and made himself stop. He'd crossed the border into Mexico once or twice in hot pursuit, though since the peace treaty of 1848 it was against the law to do so. In any case it was fruitless—every peasant in the country hid the old murdering *bandito.*

Still, Jessup loved chasing him, and had been doing so for almost four years under the command of Colonel John Salmon "Rip" Ford. Ford had been given the nickname "Rip" because he ended every letter to the family of a fallen comrade "Rest In Peace," which, when casualties began mounting, he abbreviated RIP. Jessup wanted to rejoin him, to take Cortina to ground once and for all—but here he was babysitting this woman's crop. Well, Brownsville was only three days away—if they didn't keep making these insane camera picture stops.

And though they only had two good days' worth of water left, they could make it last if they let another couple animals die of thirst.

Clenching his impatience, he paused before her, perched atop her camel. "You sure you don't want to rest a bit longer, Mrs. Stoneman? Maybe take a few more photographs?" He didn't try too hard to keep the sarcasm out of his voice.

"Quite sure, Lieutenant Jessup." She knew he was being high-handed with her, but it was of little moment as long as he did his job. She sat atop her desert mount and took in the horizon. A stand of prickly pear to the east, coarse sandstone and low hills to the west, a dust devil due south. When she nudged her animal forward it turned its head to nip her, luckily only getting her boot heel. Deeply annoyed, she slipped down off the saddle and berated the creature. "You're too damn smelly to ride anyway." She remounted, up on her horse, and moved off at a slow walk.

Jessup called back to the teamsters. "Move out!" He took the reins of his horse, walking him back down the line, inspecting the procession as it started moving again. Mule teams pulled the flat wagons loaded with cotton bales; a few cowboys lazily herded the cattle, whipping those that didn't want to move; four Texas Rangers rode as outliers, scanning the distance for hostiles.

Allie's house slaves monitored the loads, making sure they were roped down tight. "I hope this ain't all what Texas like," said Moon, "nothin' but sand."

"They got a big river called the Rio, I heard," said Jersey, trying to reassure him.

"Yeah, a river o' sand, most likely, so wide you cain't see the other side, so deep you could drown." His image put him to mind of a favorite church tune, so he sang. "*So high, you cain't get over it, so wide you cain't get 'crost it, so deep, you cain't get…*"

"You got too much 'magination for this family," she interrupted. "I don't like to think o' no sand river, and I don't like you puttin' it in my mind, fool."

She knew she ought to let him fantasize whatever he wanted to in order to get through this trek, but his stories just irritated her.

Stories were made up. Didn't have a single thing to do with real life, so what was the point in going on about them? Just made life harder in comparison as far as she could tell. Try to tell that to Moon, though.

All day the expeditioners walked, sipping from canteens, nodding off from time to time under the relentless sun dessicating their skin. And the desert so unending, the only thing to mark their progress were the mummified beasts littering the way.

Allie hated this climate. She'd grown up in the muggy sweet basin of Louisiana, redolent of magnolia and wisteria. Her father was a merchant. Her mother, Rachel, insane by local accounts, had killed herself when Allie was 12—an act that left its mark on Allie, some would later say. The family wasn't rich by a long shot—certainly not slave owners—but what money her father had he put into his children's education—three boys and two girls—leaving Allie with a foundation in the Classics and a healthy familiarity with a wide range of subjects, including literature, poetry, painting, mathematics and natural history; she especially had a head for math.

But it was the delayed aftereffects of her mother's suicide—or possibly a congenital inclination—that led her to run away at the age of sixteen, taking her on an odyssey from Memphis to the coast for five months before she was found by detectives and returned home. She refused to speak of it to anyone, including the family doctor her father insisted she see. And she only brought back one memento. The camera.

She took photos all the time once back home, and though her father thought it unseemly for a young lady, he didn't forbid it. For Allie the new science of photography had gripped her imagination. It more than made painting obsolete. Like some magical alchemy, it seemed to register not just the surface of what it recorded but seared right into its soul. Seared, and revealed—which, in the circuitous way these things sometimes go, determined the next path her life would take.

A wealthy plantation owner, Horace Stoneman, saw her working in her father's dry goods shop one day and fell in love with her. Her initial response was amusement—the man was nearing 70 years old. But he pressed his case, and though she resisted at first, two events came to pass. The first was her father's accident. His horse bolted at a snake in the road and threw him. He was laid up for two weeks with a head injury that most feared would lead to his demise. It was during this period he begged his daughter to marry Stoneman. She promised to give it her sincerest consideration. But it was her father's second request that bore fruit.

Knowing her passion for the camera, he asked Allie to take a formal photographic portrait of Stoneman and keep it at her bedside. This she did. And the soul she found there, revealed in the eyes of her subject, contained a deep, abiding kindness that somehow spoke to her. So to everyone's surprise, she agreed to marry him.

Life was sweet until the war came. In short order her brothers all joined up and got killed at the Battle of Manassas, what the Union called Bull Run. Not long after that Yankee raiders looted her father's store and raped her sister, who subsequently threw herself into Lake Ponchartrain. Her father, bereft, left home and never came back.

Allie spiraled into a black study for some months, but Stoneman remained kind, and she was determined not to follow her mother and sister down that rabbit hole. She emerged a hardened, capable woman, intent on making better the good life her husband had given her. Things began to look up a bit; the war usually seemed far off and unreal. Sadly, Horace took ill, and despite her nursing, died more or less peacefully.

So fate had once again turned her life upside down. Alone in the world now, in charge of tens of thousands of dollars' worth of goods, she journeyed through the desert toward new dangers and opportunities. Allie knew her constitution would serve her in this rough world; and her head for numbers would keep her trading business prosperous. But it was photography that would be her solace when life grew strained.

She was pulled out of the reverie she'd fallen into by a subtle, distant, moaning. "What is that?" she asked.

"What is what?" said Jessup.

"That wailing sound."

He smiled. "Maybe *la llorona*."

"I beg your pardon?"

"*La llorona*'s the ghost of a woman who lost her children, they say.

Been wandering the border hills ever since, lookin' for 'em and crying all along the way."

"Well, I don't believe in ghosts."

"Then I suppose it's just the wind."

It didn't sound like any wind she'd ever heard, though. It sounded twisted and heartbreaking. But the Wailing Woman was interrupted by one of the outrider Texas Rangers, coming in at a gallop and shouting, "Raiding party! Comanche!"

"Make side-by-sides! Double time!" Jessup bellowed.

The front ten wagons stopped in place. The back half of the caravan pulled around and drove forward until there were two lines of wagons side by side, a space between them. The lead wagon of one line pulled over to the front, closing the gap between the two rows; and a rear wagon did the same at the back end. Everyone collected inside the barriers, pulling out guns and opening boxes of ammunition.

The cowboys hobbled the steers, tying them to the wagons and to each other. The animals would serve as extra fortification, and they couldn't be driven off. Now it was only left to wait the few minutes until the attacking braves arrived.

"You ever fight Indians, Lieutenant?"

"I've fought just about whatever likes to fight, that being Yankees, *banditos*, Comanche, *Cortinistas*, mountain lion, bear and snake. *Cortinistas* my favorite."

"And how do you mean to deal with this bunch?"

"Depends how many there are. Once we pick a few off, if there's still too many we'll let some cows go. Likely that's all they want anyway. Just hungry."

Allie hoped that was all they wanted. She'd heard stories, of course—who hadn't? But she also knew people liked to scare themselves, and she wasn't a woman who scared easily. Even so she felt her pulse quicken. This was her first frontier trial by fire; she expected to get burned. She just didn't want to get charred to a cinder.

The raiding party came, ten strong. Not Comanche, though. Comancheros. A feral bunch of rogue Kiowa, Mexican cutthroats, alcoholic Indian traders and other murderous Whites painted up like devils; renegades from all societies who were just out to steal and kill. Some rode around the wagons, fierce and whooping, loosing arrows, firing long guns. Some lay back, unmoving, beyond accurate rifle range, carefully shooting arrows in a high arc, to come down inside the fortress of wagons. Three steers were hit, then two camels, whose height made them easier targets. One of the Rangers took an arrow in the belly and pulled it right out—but blood poured from the hole that was left, like wine from an open keg, and the poor fellow was dead in a minute.

Fortunately Mrs. Stoneman seemed to be holding her own, getting off a patient, occasional shot. Not only that, she often hit something. Once, she took down an Indian pony. The brave rolled away and hid behind a mummified ox carcass. A few minutes later she hit a Comanchero square in the chest.

Allie felt her fear rise, but it was controllable. She knew she could shoot as well as any man, better than most with a rifle—another part of her schooling. She brought down a second horse, its painted rider running away, his flesh the color of brass, long black hair streaming like pennants. Another attacker veered away before she could get off a shot when she froze at the sight of him—bald, lipless, and tattooed like a demon.

One foolhardy Ranger stood to get better aim and caught an arrow in the neck; a young cowboy, paralyzed with fear, hid against a dead camel. Seeing the encounter wasn't going well, Jessup cut loose three steers and shot his pistol beside them to make them run. One of the Comancheros collected the animals and rode them off. All at once the raiders stopped shooting, looked east, and rode west amidst yowls of glory. Jessup jumped up on a wagon to see what was what—and Lord bless the CSA, it was Confederate troops bearing down hard. Most of the horse soldiers stopped when they reached the wagon train, but a few kept on riding after the renegades.

The Rebel troopers dismounted to cheers from the cotton train. Allie nodded to Jessup. "You acquitted yourself well, Lieutenant." The man didn't wither under fire, and she appreciated that kind of mettle.

"I could say the same for you," he said, and meant it.

They approached the Reb commander. Jessup stuck out his hand.

"Lieutenant Jessup, Ford's Texas Rangers, now guard escort to the Stoneman cotton convoy."

Allie extended her hand before the officer could respond. "I am Mrs. Stoneman, and these are my goods which you have so kindly protected from those miscreants."

"Madam, sir. I am Captain Odeel, 21st Cavalry, 1st Arkansas Lancers, at your service." He bowed slightly, his gray uniform a patchwork of sweat, blood, and dust. "Miscreants they are. Two off-reservation Kiowa, a crazy White whiskey trader, and a Yankee who escaped the gallows in Alexandria and favors collecting Southern scalps."

"Lucky for us they weren't Comanche or we'd likely be dead by now," said Jessup. And to Allie: "Comanche's the fiercest warrior on a horse or with a rifle."

"The bunch that came at you were nasty enough," said Odeel, "and I hope to string 'em all up if I may do."

"You may as far as I am concerned, sir. Can we give you anything for your men from our provisions?"

"That is most appreciated, ma'am. You are bound for Brownsville, I expect?"

"We are that," said Allie. "Perhaps you'd care to join us for the duration? I know I'd feel safer with a larger escort." And with a gentle nod at Jessup, "Not that Lieutenant Jessup hasn't done us all proud."

Jessup nodded modestly. "I think I have the situation pretty well in hand."

The captain hesitated. "Madame, I regret I am obliged to seize your cotton."

Allie paused, to assimilate this new information. "I beg your pardon?"

"I'm under orders to impress all cotton stores for the war effort."

"You mean to steal my cotton."

"No, madam. You shall of course be paid full value in Confederate Graybacks, which you may redeem for gold at the end of the war."

"Unless the South loses. At which time that paper is worth nothin'. Until then it's worth puttin' in a tub of hot water and usin' to dye my old clothes."

"Madame, that talk sounds frightful close to treason."

Jessup stepped in. "Politics aside, this cotton belongs to the lady. If you'd care to purchase it for gold at a Matamoros price, I'm sure she'd do the patriotic thing."

"Let me speak plainly, Lieutenant. This isn't a negotiation. And I ain't about to let some tin-star Texican misuse Confederate property. I'm taking these goods to trade the British for arms that'll win the war."

"The hell." Jessup drew his gun, and so did Captain Odeel. Jessup punched him in the nose.

Odeel went sprawling, raising his gun to shoot—but Allie stepped on his wrist, pinning it to the ground. "Gentlemen, please. You're both sons of the South. I'm sure we don't want to give Mr. Lincoln's Army any more advantage than it has. Put up your weapons, I adjure you."

Jessup and Odeel gave each other the stink-eye, reluctantly holstering their guns. Allie went on. "As you can see, Captain, I'm vexed by your temerity. But I won't have violence between soldiers of the Confederacy. You go ahead, take possession of the wagons and have your man settle up the money with me. I'll ride on ahead—and perhaps Lieutenant Jessup would be so kind as to accompany me to guard my banknotes until we reach civilization."

It took all of Jessup's willpower not to just shoot the bastard. Captain Odeel stood up, giving them both a steely squint—"Admirable decision."—and walked off.

"You just gonna let him do that?" demanded Jessup. He hated to lose a fight.

"I'll get what's mine and make sure that peacock gets what's his. I don't mean to be labeled a traitor to the Cause, though—and whoever gets to Brownsville first gets to do the labeling, I judge. Without the wagons, you and I ought to make pretty fair time."

He agreed with her calculations and her conclusion. "I may be able to help you there. The fellow in charge at Fort Brown is General Hamilton Bee—he appreciates what the Texas Rangers do for law and order in the Rio Grande valley. Plus, Major Russell oversees the movement of cotton through town, and I'll talk to him for you."

She was liking Jessup's pluck but regarded him with a studied glance. "You and I haven't seen eye to eye much yet, Lieutenant. Why would you take my side in this dispute?"

"I'm a Ranger, Mrs. Stoneman. We got a workin' relationship with the CSA, and even been commissioned by them. But the Rebs' fight ain't always ours. Some Rangers hold that Texas oughta be its own country, and if workin' with the Confederate cause helps get us there in the long run, well, so be it. That don't mean I have to like every Rebel officer who thinks he can steal a lady's goods under color of authority."

"Odeel did save our necks from those desperados."

"He just didn't want what he saw as his cotton gettin' set afire. Ain't the same as savin' you. But for now I'd advise you leave your camel with the wagon train and find you a good strong pony to ride south."

With that the four of them provisioned and rode off—Jessup and Allie each ahorse, Moon and Jersey sitting in a loaded cart pulled by four swayback mules.

"Moon, sing us a song," Allie called to him. "You know how much your singin' pleases me when life gets aggravatin'."

And dry as he was, Moon sang for his mistress's pleasure. *"Was a fine lady, had a little baby, Jesus was the baby, glory hallelujah…"*

Allie didn't think she'd ever been so thirsty. Every breath stabbed her throat, and her skin was white with the dried salt of perspiration. She felt so light, it was as if she were dissolving in the air itself and floating off into the sun. Jessup had seen people give up in the desert when the water was gone. But sometimes their bodies could be persuaded to trudge on if they just had mundane tasks to perform. Like talking. "What's your plan once we get to Matamoros, Mrs. Stoneman?"

She looked at him like he was far away, like she couldn't make out his face. But his question registered, jogging a response. "Why, I intend to start a substantial import-export business. And of course, the photography."

"Photography? Is that a business?"

"A lucrative one in Matamoros, with all the grandiose personalities I've heard tell of there. No doubt they flatter themselves that posterity demands a portrait of their glory. Cortina, Juarez, Ford. I might even wrangle a sitting with Napoleon if he gets to town."

"And you think you can make a livin' takin' pictures?"

"Well…that and importin' goods to sell. I aim to find out what the locals lack and make it available to them."

"That sounds like a shrewd business sense, there. Was your daddy a businessman?"

"Yes, he was," she said more softly, "though the poor man was mad with grief, all his children but me lost to the war." She was speaking more to herself than to him now. "It was wrong of those Bluecoats to do to us like they did. Took our land, took our lives, I hate them. I hate their arrogance and their beastliness."

"There's brutes on both sides o' this war, what I been able to tell. That stickler Odeel was no Southern gentleman. Republic of Texas, that's the only true free place I ever seen. O' course the land itself can be a harsh thing, but there's a purity to it, not like the backstabbin' people you deal with in so-called civilization. Just lookit that sky, how big, and open as anything. You couldn't ask for a more honest piece of territory."

Jessup could see she was calmed by his words, so he just kept talking to keep them both on the move, with stories of his mining days near Santa Fe, his Apache fighting, his run-ins with Juan Cortina. Allie sat a little more firm in the saddle now, and Jessup felt she'd probably do all right. He mostly kept his eyes closed after that, to save them from the blinding brightness. He knew his horse would walk true toward the river, however far it was, and he had nothing better to add in the way of direction.

Behind them Jersey and Moon had gotten out of the cart miles ago, so the mules wouldn't have as much weight to pull. Moon had stopped singing hours before, too dry to make much sound. But he did carve little animals as they walked, carved them out of dead cactus roots and gave them to his traveling companions to talk to as they wandered in the desert. "Don't matter if they talk back or not," he'd say, "they good listeners."

The horizon was flat in every direction; effectively nonexistent, since the line between white sky and white sand was indistinguishable. Jessup kept his eyes closed, and hoped for the best.

CHAPTER 4

BROWNSVILLE, TEXAS, WAS A bustling community of mostly Mexican families, annexed by the United States at the end of the Mexican-American War and overseen by Fort Brown's 1200 Confederate soldiers. The garrison's other jobs included protecting the cotton trade, skirmishing with the Comanche, battling the private Mexican armies that spilled over the border from time to time; and by all means, preparing for the long rumored Union invasion of Texas by the damn Yankees. General Hamilton Bee was in overall charge of the operation. But the hands on, day-to-day business of management was handled by the fort's Quartermaster, Major Charles Russell.

And every bale of cotton that went through Brownsville into Matamoros left a bit of gold in Russell's palm; the Russell Tax some called it. If anyone complained to General Bee about the situation—some defrauded cotton trader, or foreign arms dealer, say—why, the General would huff and puff and swear to get to the bottom of it, and call Major Russell into his office. Russell would grease the commanding officer's palm with a kickback of his own, then General Bee would tell him not to let it happen again, and they'd have a drink. After which Bee would be too busy to see the complainant in chambers again. It was a fine war for those two.

The noontime after Clayton Wilkes had made his deciphering arrangement with newsman Simon Wachtel, he made his way to Fort Brown. Walking past the main gate he passed the gallows, where a man was hanging by the neck, a paper pinned to his chest scrawled with the word TRAITOR. Clayton didn't know the fellow but figured one way or another he hadn't played his cards right. It was a cruel world, he thought, if a man took things too seriously, or not seriously enough. Clayton knew he'd never fall into either of those traps.

He went direct to Major Russell's post. Russell had just seized a consignment of sugar cane trekked in from a Louisiana plantation, and was waiting for the foreman to show up to start negotiations for allowing its transit.

"How goes the war, Major Russell?" asked Clayton.

"I'd have said peachy until I heard the news from Gettysburg."

"Damn Yanks finally found a general who knew a thing or two."

"More like Lee got too cocky."

"Charleston's about lost to the 54th Massachusetts as well, I'm told."

"I hadn't heard that," said Russell.

"By God, you're the one supposed to be sellin' *me* inside tips."

"Who won a particular fight is hardly pricey news. Anyway, I might have a thing or two on the hush for you." Russell grinned, knowing he was about to do some business.

"All right, don't be shy. What have you come up with?"

"We're sending infantry units to Lafayette to face off the Union build-up there."

"That ain't exactly what I call privileged information. I surely hope you don't expect me to pay you for the same damn song every bar fly on the river's singin'."

"Well, I don't know why not. How else am I supposed to make an honest wage?" Russell was of a mind that he had no real skills, and if he couldn't get rich leveraging the unique position he found himself in here during a war, he sure as hell would never get rich once the war was over, which it one day certainly would be.

"I'll be sure to let the general staff know of your concerns about a soldier's pay," said Clayton. "What's the other scuttlebutt you have?" He came up with one of Quintero's twenty-dollar gold pieces and tossed it onto the desk.

Russell picked up the coin and rubbed its face with his thumb like the soft cheek of a beautiful woman. "There's a blockade runner,

The Buccaneer, skipper's a fellow name of Solomon. A Hebrew, from Scotland. He tried bringing rifles out of Havana to our troops in Galveston but Farragut's fleet chased him south. Word is a four-pound ball found its mark and he grounded somewhere on Padre Island."

Clayton didn't see the point of the story. "Why is that news worth my while?"

"You interested in secret Union troop movements out of New Orleans?"

"What would Solomon know about that?"

"His ship's cook was an omnibus boy at Antoine's, where the Yankee officers favor taking their grub. They caught the boy eavesdropping but he escaped to Solomon's boat. Signed on as cook. They sailed to Cuba and came right back with guns for Galveston 'til they got chased off. So what's that news worth to you?"

Clayton considered the problem. "Depends what this omnibus boy actually knows. Padre Island's a mighty long spit. You know where they went aground?"

"You want me to do all your work for you?"

"No, that wouldn't be gentlemanly." He stood up and laid two more gold pieces on the desk. "But I thank you for the dispatch. Now I have a request. There's a tall ship comin' in soon, the *Defiant*, out of Birmingham. It's carryin' a special load for me."

"And what would that be?"

"India tea is what the Customs declaration asserts. I'd consider it a favor if you notified me of its arrival and detailed a few men to guard its transport to my Emporium."

Russell smiled. "I believe I can help you out with your shipment, Wilkes. My usual compensation, and half again if there's any trouble."

Just then a ragtag PFC ran in, all atwitter. "Major! Three Yankee prisoners unaccounted for, and their cell doors is unlocked!"

"Close down the fort, Private. Mount a detail, search every room and closet. And have every damn soldier on guard duty report to me double time."

"Yes, sir!" The soldier saluted and ran out.

Russell raised his eyebrows at Clayton. "One of them Yanks was stationed at New Orleans. He's the one clued me in to the omnibus boy from Antoine's."

"And now he's escaped. Sounds like you might could have a Leonard Pierce collaborator lurkin' in your ranks." Rumor had it that Ambassador Pierce was organizing a private army of escaped Union POWs, runaway slaves, and *Cortinistas* who wanted to take Texas back.

"If there's a collaborator I'll string the man up, by God," said Russell with a smile.

He stormed out, Clayton following calmly. He knew the escaped Yanks were good as gone. Leonard Pierce had a large store of gold from the Union mint, more than enough to provision a small army, let alone bribe some hungry Mississippi jailer to leave a cell door open. But Clayton knew the bigger bribe had likely been to Russell himself—to order the guard to take a piss outside while the jailbreak was in progress. Then Russell would put a reprimand in the jailer's record and slip him an extra twenty dollars.

It was a well-oiled system for those who knew how to use it.

Clayton took the ferry back to Matamoros as he considered his options for finding the cook of that Hebrew sea captain, Solomon, to learn about Union troop movements. Best to head down to Bagdad tonight, hire a smuggler captain he knew and set sail in search of Solomon's crippled ship. As his plan came together he found himself at *Le Bon Marche*, a café with a dozen patio tables. Clayton took one, ordered his coffee thick and grabbed a copy of today's *Daily Ranchero* to peruse as he contemplated the day.

Stories ran the gamut from news of the cotton trade to news of war; news of the building boom, the opera, the racetrack; news of break-ins, murders, thefts; birth announcements, fever outbreaks, storm warnings; high and low tides, services offered, rooms for rent and all manner of social puffery. It was, in sum, a local newspaper.

Clayton's coffee arrived; he took a sip. It had a chicory aura that took him to Louisiana back in the day, and his mind drifted to the sounds in the Quarter, street corner music, his mother trading jokes in French with the rivermen, Clayton not understanding but laughing like he did. "Pretend you know everything and people will believe you," his French uncles used to tell him.

His mother's ritual was to take him back to Marseilles, to live with her family for one month every summer when he was a boy. Her own father was a fisherman, her mother a fishwife, her eight siblings a careless mix of urchins, thieves, lollygaggers, and one Jesuit priest. So Clayton's Augusts were an education in the backstreet world his mother had been rescued from, due to her singular charms. Clayton's father had met her while arranging a new shipping deal to bring his cane crop to France, and was arrested by her beauty. Over the course of his two weeks in Marseilles he fell in love with her and asked her to be his wife.

Clayton loved his mother's family. He loved the excitement running with his cousins stealing *du pain* from a street market. But if one of you is caught, his mother instructed him, you must always help your family. No matter what. Your family is part of you. His mother's birds were family, as well. Homing pigeons, tender by nature, mated for life, they flew long distances from a deep loyalty to geography. Though some said it was apocryphal, he'd once been told that carrier pigeons sent the results of the triumphant Battle of Waterloo to the Bank of Rothschild in London before anyone else in England got the news—so Rothschild quickly bought up millions in English government bonds, thereby cementing his fortune. Legend or not, *les pigeons de guerre* were now used by some to pass secret information at the speed of birdflight.

Clayton's mother was the keeper of the pigeon nest in her family, and his time tending them with her remained one of his fondest memories. He thought of his mother as every August approached; the memory filled him with a longing he couldn't articulate. Something to do with the perfume she wore to hide the smell of fish in her family home; the love in the midst of misdemeanor lives; the windborne vapors of the Mediterranean harbor; and the beating wings of birds at dusk, when flocks crossed the water to their nesting grounds. If he listened closely, these longings never left him.

A chair scraped back across the flagstone of the café patio. "I thought I might find you idling here." Catherine Delacroix took a seat, jostling him out of his fugue state—first with her voice, then with a hand on his thigh.

He smiled at her warmly. "Solve your problem with the new diva yet?"

"We had words. She will be *prete* by tonight's performance. Are you coming?"

"Sadly, no. I have to make a trip down to Bagdad."

She stuck out her lower lip, a cartoon of a pout. *"Je suis desole."*

He put his lips seductively to her ear and whispered. "Feel free to give my box to whomever you choose."

"I may do just that and join him there myself."

A nattily dressed gent in a manicured beard strolled by—but Catherine stuck out her hand to stop him. "Leonard! Please join us!"

"Catherine, what a pleasure. But I'm afraid I must…"

"No excuses, what you must do is sit for five minutes or I shall be quite insulted."

Leonard Pierce bowed stiffly and sat. An uncomfortable pause filled the space between the two men. Pierce was at the nexus of Union activity south of the border, while Clayton was a palpably Southern gentleman by stock.

"Mr. Pierce," Clayton said stiffly. "Good of you to join us."

"Mr. Wilkes. May I offer my condolences that your little stateside rebellion is faring less well these days?"

"Not my rebellion, sir. I'm a Mexican businessman now."

"No politics in my presence!" shouted Catherine. "Can a lady not pass a pleasant moment with two gentlemen without a duel in the offing?"

"Duels have been outlawed in the United States, Catherine," Pierce smiled. "Some of us still try to be civilized."

"I will not rise to your bait, sir," said Clayton. "Rather let me buy you some refreshment. We can toast the Union soldiers who escaped Fort Brown this morning."

"I was unaware of the news."

"The prison break was a great success. Give them my best when you see them."

Pierce turned to Catherine. "He's a bit arrogant, even for a slaveholder."

"If you're referin' to Isaac, he is a free man. To imply otherwise is an insult to…"

"*Arete!*" she commanded.

Silence descended. Pierce stood. "If you'll excuse me, I do have business." He left without waiting for a response.

Catherine gave Clayton a dour glance. "Was that *necessaire?*" She stood, out of patience. "I'm giving your box at the opera to him tonight." She strode off. Clayton finished his coffee and returned to the offices of *The Daily Ranchero.*

Clayton entered to find Jensen, the young printer's devil, unlocking the lead type of today's pages from the bed of the press, to distribute into the cubbies of the job case.

"Learnin' your way around all right?" asked Clayton.

"Not that hard."

"The old man can be a taskmaster, I expect."

"That don't get far with me. I left home for less than that."

"Left the field of battle, too, way I hear it."

Clayton was testing the kid, but Jensen didn't rattle. "Wasn't what I expected. You have a problem with that?"

"No, young man, I don't. And neither does the country of Mexico, so you're safe from both of us. Your only worry is if you set a 'b' instead of a 'd' on a front page story—then you'll have hell and Simon Wachtel to pay."

The office door opened and Simon stuck his head out, looking annoyed at Clayton. "I told you come back late in the day. I got a press to run."

Clayton walked past Simon and into his office. Wachtel followed, shutting the door behind him. "I did your job, *ja,*" he groused. "But you have no reason to expect it done so soon."

As the man rifled through the mountain of papers on his desk, Clayton paused over the chessboard now set up, with the white King's pawn two squares forward, and the black side missing the Queen's Bishop and two Knight's pawns.

"After the advantage I gave you in pieces you still went first?" Clayton demanded with mock incredulity.

"Take your turn without whining, please."

Clayton studied the board as Wachtel came up with a small scrap of paper. "I cannot promise you this is a perfect translation. But it probably is."

Clayton looked at the short line of script Wachtel had written below the smudges streaked across the porous paper. *Kingston Bar Bar Sinister.*

"I know the Kingston Bar, all right." Clayton nodded. "Homesick Limeys take their ale there. I can't credit what's sinister about it, but I'll take a look. I thank you for this, sir. You can be sure you're the first person I give any news of record to."

"Your news is all off the record. But I will call in the favor, you can bet on this, *ja.*"

Clayton jumped his knight over his pawn. "King's Knight to King's Rook 3," said Clayton. "You should have read up on Benko. Now I've got you on the run."

Clayton left, a jaunty spring to his stride, as Wachtel sat down and studied the board with a furrowed brow.

The Kingston Bar was a replica pub where sailors from Great Britain and other grog-shop loafers congregated to get insensate drunk. It sold imported ale and gin, as well as cheaper local brews. The interior was low-ceilinged pinewood lit by whale-oil lanterns, the walls covered with dartboards, coats-of-arms and etchings of great sea adventure. Booths lined one wall, rough wooden tables filled the floor. The place was always jammed with English drinkers and the *senoritas* they called wenches.

Clayton squeezed up to the bartop and ordered porter from Georgie, a Canadian bartender he trusted. "Anything sinister about this bar you know of?" Clayton asked.

"The foock does 'sinister' mean?" The barman glared at him.

"Evil, dark. Disturbin'."

"Only the Micks. Wouldn't say sinister, exactly, though. More likes just arses."

Clayton nodded, turned his back to the bar and looked around. A bunch from the *Sir William Peel* laughed it up at one long table—some Royal Navy in their bell-bottom blues, some merchant seamen less well attired. Two old salts in the corner were trading kisses with a salty Mexican *tia* amidst negotiations for a room upstairs. There was a friendly game of darts against the back wall. None of it looked very sinister to Clayton.

He saw a second mate he knew fairly well; the fellow spent a good deal of time at the Brave River bar, among myriad other watering holes. At the moment he was nursing a gin, looking darker in mood than Clayton's stout. Ned something. Clayton paid the bartender for a half bottle of gin and brought it over to Ned's table. "Mind if I join you?"

Ned waved a muddled hand at the bench opposite him. "It's a free country, they say. America, that is." He raised his glass, tossed it back like water.

"Free enough since the Emancipation Proclamation," Clayton smiled like a friend. "And Mexico has its peons, and England its Irish, so we're all our brothers' keepers, one way or another." Clayton refilled Ned's glass.

Ned squinted suspiciously. "I thank 'ee. But what is it you want?"

"I'm not altogether sure. Ever hear anyone call this a sinister bar?"

"Sinister, is it?" He began to sip the gin, but interrupted himself with a sudden suspicion. "They don't keep dogs in this pub, do they? Dogs is a sinister thing."

"No dogs. But sinister is what the gentleman was heard to say." Clayton knew Ned's ties ran wide in the seafaring world, so worth pushing to jog his tattered memory. "Come on, mate. Think about it. 'Sinister bar,' who do you know might have said that?"

"Sinister bar. Sinister bar..." He grabbed Clayton's gin bottle and finished it off in a series of gulps. Suddenly his eyes lit up, he jumped onto the table, danced a lively reel, and accompanied himself with Clayton's lyrics, to a melody of his own invention.

"Sinister bar! Sinister bar! Sinister bar sinister bar sinister bar sinister..." As he danced, other bar patrons laughed, clapped, or stomped in rhythm. Which only encouraged old Ned. "…bar sinister bar sinister bar sinister…"

A large man entered, crossed to them and swept a truncheon through the sailor's jigging legs. Ned tumbled to the floor, unconscious before he hit the ground. A shout of protest went up across the tavern, a few patrons even making a move. But the large man stood his ground, happy to take on all comers. "This swine jumped ship and if he ain't keelhauled by sunset he's luckier than the last one tried that."

The room went quiet. This was one of those unthinkable transgressions that every tar in the bar had thought of doing at one time or another. Not a soul challenged the burly fellow as he grabbed Ned at the beltline and dragged him out of the pub. Immediately the noise and drink level rushed in to fill the vacuum of silence. Over the din, Clayton was just close enough to the dartboard to hear one of the gamers crow loudly, "Bar sinister, is it? Bend sinister's what we used to call it."

Clayton watched the man toss his three darts, and ambled over to him. "Excuse me sir, I couldn't help overhearin'. What exactly did you mean by 'bar sinister'?"

He was a garrulous fellow, happy to share. "Just what I said. There's some as calls it 'bar sinister,' but 'bend' is the way I learned."

"Learned what?"

"The wood crafts, o' course. Ship's carpenter I be now, but I was apprenticed to a master what carved heralds for many a peer of the realm. Duke o' Richmond, Earl o' Derby, all them fine gents."

"What's carving heralds to do with a bar sinister?"

The carpenter slapped the coat-of-arms beside the dartboard. Red crown, blue shield, white stripe crossing down from left to right. "This crest is for the Earldom of Fortescue. See the stripe there? That's what some calls the bar. This one goes from left shoulder down to right hip. Sinister is when the bar goes the other way, from right to left. Means it's a cursed family betimes, more likely a bastard in the family."

"A bastard."

"Illegitimate, what you genteel folk say. Like Arthur Plantagenet of the House o' York. That's where I learned bar sinisters." He went back to his dart game, clearly pleased with himself for being able to school a gentleman.

Clayton glanced around the tavern—for the first time fully aware of all the coats-of-arms on the walls. "Thank you, sir," he said more to himself than his informant, and slowly walked the perimeter, checking each hung shield, and the cant of its bar.

Every coat on the wall showed stripes upper right down to left. Gold lions, rampant; white horses rearing before a crown; red stags, yellow flags, rippling pennants. And finally, the herald of a bastard in a dark corner near the unlit fireplace: gold shield, lions, *fleurs de lis*, and a blue bar sinister. Upper right, down to lower left. Here was the bar sinister at the Kingston Bar. Kingston Bar Bar Sinister.

Clayton ran his hands over the wood, testing for hidden compartments or loose pieces. He tipped it up from its hook on the wall and felt along the back. Tacked to the hindside was a square of paper attached by sealing wax. He tugged and it came free.

He exited by the rear door, peering at the paper in the waning light of day. It was a page of random letters: *erf ltllgmn soqec mtlell...* Code, obviously. He knew where to get it translated but he didn't have the time to make that connection right now. The last coach to Bagdad today left in an hour. He might ride his horse but a rider alone was always subject to highwaymen on the route to Bagdad, and he couldn't risk that now. There was just time to tell Isaac his plan and run to the coach station.

He slipped the cipher into his vest pocket; had a few more words with the ship's carpenter; reached an agreement, money changed hands; and he went to Brave River.

Darkness was setting in as he neared the building. The sun's last copper sparkles had disappeared from the surface of the river winding toward the Gulf. The overhead sky was a deep blue, with orange-pink underlighting the thunderheads hanging above the western horizon. Clayton neared the back of the casino, taking a wide detour around old Rheumy the barman, who was gleefully stirring up his therapeutic beehive in the crotch of a dead oak, angering enough bees to sting away his arthritis. As Clayton made his way around, he saw the young

Yankee corporal again, standing in the shadows of a pecan grove. Once might have been coincidence, but seeing the fellow twice today sealed it; he had to know what this was about. Did Ambassador Pierce's lackey Tinbury want a tail on Clayton? He strolled past the stalker as if unaware; but a little further on, cut into the grove and circled around behind the lad. As the boy made a move forward to see where Clayton had gone, Wilkes put a hand on his shoulder.

"You best tell me what you're up to or pay the price."

The kid nearly jumped out of his boots. "I...I didn't mean anything..."

"You meant somethin', doggin' my steps. Now tell me who's puttin' you up to it."

The Yankee was wearing civilian clothes, most likely to avoid detection. Clayton's assumption had been the boy was a military spy. But maybe he simply needed money and had been paid by one of the warring factions around town, to run down Clayton's sources. Or maybe just rob him after a sale of some kind. But now the kid looked so anxious, Clayton shifted his expectations, though he didn't let down his guard.

"Nobody's putting me up to anything, sir. This is just me, being some kind of fool. I meant no harm. I don't always know how to comport myself when I hit civilization."

Clayton also knew information sometimes showed up in odd ways. Maybe the Yank had some for him, but had been reluctant to share it, out of fear, or loyalty to country. And secrets of any ilk were not to be turned away.

"All right, then, spit it out. What are you up to? Come on, I won't bite."

"This is hard for me," said the young man. "It's just...the way you took charge with that cheat at poker last night, never a flutter, I mean there's a lot of men can subdue a drunk, or quiet a fool...what I mean to say is..."

He looked all tied up in knots. To put him at ease, Clayton laid a hand comfortingly on the boy's shoulder. "It's all right, son. You can tell me."

"I don't rightly know how to say it. Or when I could, if I don't now. Or how to lead up to it. Or..." He just shook his head, his cheeks a little flush. "Aw, hell." He wrapped his arms around Clayton and hugged him with an abundance of feeling.

Clayton was so surprised he just took it for a moment; until his discomfort made him push the boy gently back. "Here, now, what's this about?"

"I'm sorry, I couldn't think what else to do..."

"Well you can't go about huggin' another man without warnin'. It's just bad behavior."

"I judge I didn't think this out as clear as I ought. I shoulda seen what to expect."

"Well...what'd you expect?"

"I don't know, I surely don't. But I fear I must tell you one more thing, so's not to be completely misunderstood." He turned away.

Clayton knew about men who loved men; he even knew one or two firsthand, and wasn't much bothered in his business dealings with them. But there was an urgency in this corporal's hug he thought he ought to nip in the bud. "I believe I'd just as soon not know one more thing you had to tell me about misunderstandin's..."

But when the junior officer turned back to face him, Clayton saw he had his shirt open and was just about done unraveling a swath of binding around his chest. Was he wounded? Did he not have long to live? Clayton was so taken aback—for the second time in a minute—all he could do was say, "What the hell."

The boy's chest swaddling fell to the ground, revealing...breasts. A woman's breasts. Not overly large, but definitely female. To be so open was quite a bold move on her part. "I just never met a man like you," she said in a voice husky with wanting, wrapping her arms around his waist, her short, mussed-up hair tucking into his neck.

"By God, I never met a man like you, either," Clayton said, uncertain what to do with his hands. "But darlin'...why are you pretendin' like this?"

"Because they won't let a woman join the army to fight for what she believes in. I hate slavery with an abiding passion and I wanted to strike a blow for freedom in these terrible times. But I couldn't do that without I misrepresented my sex first."

Clayton was having a hard time with this. "You wanted to be a foot soldier?"

"I been a good one, too. Performed with valor at Second Bull Run and got a medal." He—she, that is—pursed her lips now. "Being a good soldier was my downfall, though, I guess. I got promoted and transferred here to guard Mr. Lincoln's ambassador. It's an honor, I suppose, and a good soldier does what he's told. Doesn't feel much like abolition work, though."

"How'd you ever get so good at soldierin' to begin with?"

"Grew up on my daddy's ranch, I learned how to sit a horse and I'm pretty fair with a rope. My mama was full Cheyenne, daddy'd won her in a card game from the preacher who owned her. We had some vigilante troubles after that, which is when I got good with a gun. Mama taught me the keeping of slaves was an abomination—but the army won't let a woman be a damn soldier. So I dressed up like a man and they gave me a uniform. Kept to myself in camp, so the boys just counted me as shy." She tipped her head up, kept her eyes firmly on his face. "That doesn't mean I can't be a woman off the battlefield, though. I have a woman's feelings, too." She regarded him with such longing he had to look away, it pinched his heart to see anyone that revealed.

Clayton was rarely without words, yet speech defied him now. But the corporal had enough womanly skills to see he was more open than some, which gave her the courage to elaborate. "I've enjoyed the company of men at war. Their comradely spirit in the face of fear has been an inspiration to me." She squeezed her arms around him even tighter. "But I have a woman's feelings in the quiet of a day."

He pushed her gingerly back, at arm's length. "What's your first name, girl?"

"My soldier name's Teddy Beale. But you can call me Theodora in private."

"Well, here's the lay of the land, Theodora. You've taken me unawares but I don't hold that against you. Fact is, I admire a person who can keep a secret good as you've done." He pulled her shirt closed, to cover the secret.

At that, she knew her play had failed. "I know you have your pick of women, everyone says so. But I can make you feel good."

"I've no doubt of it. But to be inelegantly blunt—I don't have sentiments for you in that regard." Clayton was well aware of the many disadvantages to being so widely known as an indiscriminate lover; he just never suspected this could be one of them.

She pulled her shirt tight, to take charge of her own dignity. "You won't tell on me?"

"No, of course not. You put yourself together and go be the best damn soldier out there, guardin' Ambassador Pierce. You want to come in my place to gamble, you do that, too. Just don't be pullin' your shirt open to me again and we'll do fine."

A small smile came to her mouth as she picked up the swaddling from the dirt and began binding her breasts. "I've never been this forward before. It's just, I didn't see another chance coming, and…you looked so bold in the casino last night."

"Button your shirt, girl," he scolded her softly.

She complied, but not without a final half-smiled rejoinder. "Don't know that I'm all done with you yet, Mr. Wilkes." She tucked in her shirt and left.

Clayton admired her pluck. Moreover, he had a certain respect for anyone who could put one over on him. He considered her potential utility as a spy but put the question aside until he had all his wits again. While he was used to being thought of as a lothario around town, this little interlude had unaccountably undone him. So he walked to Brave River as he contemplated his chagrin and the countless ways he was blind to the people around him. One day that would surely get him killed.

CHAPTER 5

Early evening Clayton entered his gambling hall with a nod at two *Juaristas* who were still celebrating the French defeat at the Battle of Puebla on May 5; a much-needed victory for Benito Juarez, leader of the collapsing Mexican government. *Juaristas* were nominally in control of Matamoros, since the French expedition hadn't yet reached this far; but in fact it was an open city, a free market zone where anyone could play. And everyone did at Clayton Wilkes's casino. As long as half the world was at war, right here on the river it was good for business.

At the bar two of the bandit Cortina's *Cortinistas* were harmonizing badly but warmly about their leader: "*Cuando los Americanos duermen, Cortina visita sus suenos, y se despierta en Mexico.*" Clayton wondered if someone would make up a song about him one day. Not likely. Maybe he'd make one up about himself; that way he might not forget who he was.

He stopped by the small kitchen to dip a spoon into the pot of beans Milagra was cooking up. She was a large woman with wonderful laugh lines at her eyes, and she made the best *mole poblano* Clayton had ever tasted. He considered it almost sacred.

"*Esto es damasiado Bueno para mi,*" he told her. This is too good for me.

She laughed gaily, saying, "*Se que se.*" I know, I know. They both laughed at that, and he left her to her holy work, heading toward the bar.

Redheaded Scully, the French Foreign Legionnaire, was drinking hard there. Scully was born Irish. But the French Foreign Legion was composed of French non-nationals, except for the officers—and these soldiers of fortune swore loyalty to no nation. Only to the Legion, which invented the concept of *esprit de corps*. They were men without a country—until wounded in battle, that is. At that point they became citizens of France. *Francais par le sang verse*, French by spilled blood.

Scully had been a hunted man in Ireland, sought by the British for treason, robbery and mayhem. Many joined the Legionnaires under similar circumstances, but Scully had reason to join beyond just wanting to escape the long arm of John Law. He volunteered because he hated the British, hated how they'd enslaved the Irish people. He hoped one day France would invade England, and the Legion would spearhead that assault. Instead Scully got sent to Mexico.

He'd been one of an infantry patrol of 62 Legionnaires who got cornered at a *hacienda* near Camaron, surrounded by 3000 Mexican Cavalry. When only six of the French corps were left alive, they launched a fierce bayonet attack on the Mexicans, in a heroic gesture of suicidal folly. Three of the six were killed, the last three captured. Scully was one of these. He and his comrades were escorted back to the French lines as a tribute to their bravery and an honor guard for their fallen commander—Scully's best friend—Captain Danjou. But Scully lost more than Danjou and 58 comrades; he lost his left arm below the elbow. What he had now was a wood prosthetic, girdled in leather and iron, always gloved to spare him pitying glances.

Scully sulked around the bars of Matamoros, now, released from service, dressed in Danjou's own black tunic with gold epaulets. His final order on mustering out of the Legion was to maintain reconnaissance and report his findings to French Headquarters; but he couldn't be bothered. His dream of liberating Ireland had been replaced with the nightmare of being part of a colonizing force at the back end of the world in a subtropical cesspool that could only be cleansed with drink. Clayton liked him.

"Legionnaire Scully, may I buy you another?"
"You may buy me several, and I'll race you to hell."
"You have the advantage on me there, sir, you've got a head start."

"You've got the endurance, though, Boyo, I can see it in your soul." He emptied his glass and held it out to the bartender for another. Clayton gestured to Jim, who refilled Scully's whiskey. Clayton enjoyed the man's honesty. A lot of people suspected Clayton was going to hell; not many told him so and demanded a free drink in return.

"You tell me what a man has to do to join the Confederation of Clayton Wilkes, and I'll become a citizen—if you take cripples." Scully raised his wooden arm in salute.

"I never mark a man good or bad by how many knuckles he has. Look at General Santa Anna. After his victory at the Alamo, he lost his leg in another campaign. Did he mourn it? He did not. He held a state funeral for the errant limb and buried the damn thing with honors. Had a jim dandy new one fitted and wore it into the very next battle."

"I'd have to go back to Camaron to look for me arm, and I'm afraid I'd find someone else's. Imagine havin' a wake for some stranger's lopped-off hand that never saw the inside of a church and wouldn't know how to cross itself. It don't seem right."

"You wouldn't like the Republic of Clayton Wilkes anyway. Too cold."

"Try me." Scully said this without humor, and Clayton knew the fellow was ready to sell his soul, or whatever still resembled such a thing.

"I'll keep it in mind," Clayton told him. They held eyes a moment, each taking the other's measure—then Clayton walked to the end of the bar, where Isaac was shaking hands with a sinewy Negro who left by the time Clayton arrived. "Haven't seen him around before."

"Man just got back from Liberia, looking for work. I told him he could start tomorrow, haul in the liquor from that Belgian schooner." Liberia was the newly proclaimed country in Africa populated by some 20,000 freed American slaves, sent back to their home continent by the abolitionist American Colonization Society.

"What's the word in Liberia?"

"Fever took half the immigrants. Then the Malinke tribes attacked them—African natives don't want anything to do with Americans setting up on their land, even if they're all the same color skin."

"Didn't you ever flirt with the idea of sailin' there?"

"My family's been here four generations—Africa's no home to me. I allow as how we of the black race are just God's lost children."

Clayton signaled the barman. "Rheumy, give my good friend, here, a strong enough drink to make his ears glow. It might help God find him again."

Rheumy brought over the bottle of hundred proof rye, his face all swollen red with bee stings, and poured Isaac a glass, which Isaac raised.

"The Roman God Jupiter gifted bees with stingers to protect their honey, but he told them they would die if they stung anyone. Noble Rheumy, here, allows them to make their sacrifice on the altar of his face." He swigged the rye.

Rheumy regarded Isaac in complete bafflement, then walked away. Clayton got down to business. "I'm off to Bagdad now, so you're the house until I get back. If I'm still gone in four days, come alookin'."

"Speaking of journeys, word came. The *Defiant* just left England with your cargo."

"It was supposed to leave well over a month ago. What happened?"

Isaac shrugged. While Clayton had been involved with contraband for almost two years, this shipment was a prize like no other, transcending war and politics. But there were more pressing matters now.

He left Isaac, walking past Claire, the seductive understudy-turned-diva, her pupils now big with belladonna—the tincture well known to make a lady's eyes alluring. Clayton looked away to avoid capture and walked upstairs. Past his office to the end of the hall, then another flight up to the roof. A wide deck was cut into the slope. Buttressed on one side was the large cistern that Hermano happily pumped water up to. The other side of the deck sported a wire cage containing six pigeons, cooing and darting their querulous heads from side to side. He removed a small piece of paper from his vest, wrote a terse instruction on it, extracted one of the birds from the cage and held it gently in his hands.

"Madeira," he whispered, "you're my favorite, but don't tell the others." He petted her gently from nape to tail with a tenderness he felt for no human. The homing pigeons always reminded him of his mother, and her family. Always protect your family, she'd told him; for better or worse, they are part of you. He just sat there, now, eyes closed, sensing the humid, briny air, trying to bring back the felt sounds of the beating wings of birds at dusk; trying to bring back that other time.

It seemed to him there was no time now, no expansiveness of time as there had once been in his life. There was only each moment's requirement, and an endless stream of them, every one demanding a response, an action, each action leading to the next, like the beads on his mother's perfumed rosary. The smells of Marseilles came back to him now—the nets of fish, the baking bread, the beery breath of his *grandpere* shouting at the head of the dinner table for everyone to shut up—*Tais-toi!*—so they could hear *grandmama* pray thanks for their home, their meal, their loving kinship. Then Emile would kick him under the table, and Lisette would steal Odilon's cheese, and his mother would wink at him, like a secret message between them no one else could see, a special bond. Maybe this was the birth of his love of secrets. Clayton smiled deeply at the unexpected, unexpectedly tender, memory.

Opening his watery eyes, he fastened his message to the cooing bird's leg. Then he stood looking out over the great river to the north, twisting off east and west. Dark clouds roiled high above as the rising wind tousled his hair, carrying the smell of rain. He raised his arms quickly, releasing the war pigeon. It swirled and banked until it found its direction; then flew eastward to Bagdad, propelled by the thrill of sensing home. Clayton had given up on ever again longing for that particular thrill.

Bagdad at night resembled a village in hell; a shanty town lit everywhere by torches and bonfires reflecting off torn tents, shacks built on pilings, beached boats, great mounds of stinking garbage, and the wandering shadows of misbegotten souls.

The rat-infested streets often held mud 12 inches deep, sometimes filling with filthy water that coalesced into mosquito-filled canals. Walkways consisted of planks up on two-foot pilings, so people could get around when the streets were flooded from river tide or storm surge. The beaches themselves looked like a refugee camp. Mountains of cotton bales were surrounded by armed guards, waiting for transport out to tall ships. Durable goods sat in locked sheds, ready for loading on paddle steamers up the twisting river to Matamoros, bound for points northeast, into the heart of Dixie. Guns, shoes, powder, copper, tin, tea, saltpeter. All for the armies of the South.

If Matamoros was the Back Door of the Confederacy, Bagdad was the fetid crawlspace. While the Spanish and French colonial architecture of Matamoros housed the military, diplomatic, cultural and mercantile classes, the hovels of Bagdad were dens of dock workers, whores, teamsters, thieves, con artists, sailors and pirates, the waywardest people of every nationality and ethnicity, sharing quarters with each other and the oxen that hauled their trappings.

Hundreds of filthy rooming houses populated the alleyways, interspersed with a few well-appointed hotels for the gentry. With 150 European ships in the harbor on any given day, there were always captains, owners and gentlemen who needed lodging—arriving at night and unable to get to Matamoros or Brownsville until the next afternoon. None stayed in Bagdad long, though. To do so risked theft, disease, or death by thug.

Clayton jumped off the coach and looked out on the harbor. Here at the ocean's edge the muscular wind swept in like a following sea. Sails on the nearest ships could be heard snapping wildly as crews made to take them down before they ripped. But the gale blew the mosquitos away too, which was a blessing. He made his way from the coach station across a sandy promenade, where he tripped over six inches of longbone sticking upright out of the ground. Somebody's forearm, it looked like, ending at the wrist with barely a stump of tendon-tied fingers. It gave him only momentary pause before walking on to the smugglers' bar where his pigeon had instructed Captain Brancado to meet him.

The air was thick with tobacco, opium and the black issue of camphine lamps. As soon as he stepped up to the bar he was accosted by a mangy wretch with a rolled-up scroll who was willing to sell him the map to Jean Laffite's treasure for a hundred dollars in gold coin. When

Clayton declined, the price dropped to fifty, a one-time offer. When Clayton let show the .41 caliber Philadelphia Derringer in his belt, the man backed off to seek more agreeable pickings.

Clayton walked through the warren of rooms, many of them filled tonight with Austrian troops—allies of Napoleon, scouting Rio Grande positions for a good French beachhead. Clayton didn't much like these soldiers of Archduke Maximilian, they were too in love with their uniforms, medals and feathered hats. They tended to keep to themselves, though—in their arrogance—so they were easy to avoid. Clayton soon located Captain Brancado in a dark corner, grinding his hips into the backside of a portly lass bent over the table, her dress pulled up around her head. As Clayton approached, Brancado barked one loud growl, spanked the woman's wide bottom and sat himself down as he buttoned himself up. The woman rearranged her dress, picked up the folding money on the table, winked at Clayton and left.

Brancado came up with a price to sail Wilkes and the ship's carpenter from the Kingston Bar—his name was Quail—up Padre Island, where Brancado knew all the coves the Scottish blockade runner had likely gone to ground. Details out of the way, they departed, to sleep on the ship and leave on the tide.

They set sail before dawn on Brancado's sternwheeler, the *Neer-do-well*, a low draft mudskimmer that could glide the coastal waters and shallow inlets. The ship was "whitewashed"—its name had been changed and its papers reregistered to Mexico, so it couldn't be seized by U.S. Navy blockade gunboats.

Two hours at full steam took them to the southern tip of Padre, a barrier island less than two miles wide and over a hundred miles long, stretching from Corpus Christi in the north all the way down to Point Isabel on the Brownsville side of the Rio Grande. Brancado guided his ship up Laguna Madre, the narrow waterway separating the island from the mainland, where Captain Solomon had likely beached his craft to make repairs in the marshes. That's where they'd look first.

Six hours into the day they saw it—the masthead of the *Bucanneer* peeking from behind a grassy dune. It appeared to be accessible up an inlet that feathered into marshes. But Clayton didn't want to scare Solomon or risk an ambush by his men. So Brancado dropped anchor just offshore and remained on board with the rest of his crew while Clayton and carpenter Quail rowed a skiff in to the beach.

As they followed the inlet around the dune, there it was: the 80-foot *Bucanneer*, listing in shallow water against the marshy sand. And there stood Solomon with three crewmen, pointing rifles at Clayton's landing party of two. Clayton's hands went up.

"Hold! We're unarmed friends of the Confederacy, here to give aid to brothers in distress, if you are Captain Solomon."

"Ye nae best move further, 'til I have some proof of what ye say."

"Of proof I've none. But my name is Clayton Wilkes, I run a gamblin' concession in Matamoros, where I heard of your troubles. I've brought a master ship's carpenter and materials to make your repairs. We're laid in offshore just beyond the dune, there."

Solomon was looking for a catch. "And what's yer stake, lad?"

"I'm a Son of the South, plain and simple. If you let us approach, my friend Mr. Quail can assess your damages. We can help you or not—you're the captain here."

Solomon kept his stern face, but lowered his gun. "Come ahead, then."

It was a ragged hole at the waterline, considerably bigger than the size of a four-pound ball. Mr. Quail wasn't much fazed by it, though. He set about repairing the damage with wood, bolts and tar, while the two crews shared a jug of grog Clayton had brought for the occasion. Finally, to cement the bond of trust he was trying to build with Solomon, Clayton pulled a dozing pigeon from his pack and released it into the wild.

Solomon looked baffled. "And what might that have been?"

"One of my homin' pigeons. I brought it to send for help in case you were inhospitable. But looks like I don't need it now, and it's wantin' to go home for food."

"And how do I know you didn't just send it out for reinforcements?"

Clayton pulled out a fifth of fine, aged scotch. "I didn't bring enough refreshment for that, sir." Whereupon he and Solomon traded stories, half of them true.

"At heart I'm a pirate," laughed Solomon, "so if nae for smuggling I wouldn't know what else to do. I come from Havana this run, with a heavy load. Had to dump it all when the Yankee gunboat gave chase, though. If they'd boarded us carrying that kind of contraband, there'd be nothin' for it but the stockade."

"A ship ought to be free to go anywhere it wants in international waters."

"Oh, they'd have to have let us go eventually. But if they decided to lose the paperwork, I could rot in Parish Prison for months. So tell me, how was it you appointed your wee self my savior?"

"Keepin' my ear to the ground. Back in '61 I got my gamblin' hall, which is a fine place to listen for careless talk and pick up useful tidbits."

"So I was someone's useful tidbit, is it?"

"Indeed. A friend of the Cause, is what they said about you, though you weren't ashamed to make yourself a little coin in the bargain. I've done as much myself."

"And tell me what that might've been, lad." Looking for Clayton's *bona fides*.

"Well...I once ran a herd of cattle to Dodge, to sell to the Union Army. But I stopped lettin' the beeves drink three days before we got there. Night before the sale we drove 'em to a river where they drank themselves silly. Sold 'em by weight to the Yankee captain the next day and left with a handy profit before the cows pissed themselves skinny again."

"The poor beasts!" Solomon roared.

"True, but they were to be slaughtered soon anyway, and I like to think of their profound pleasure at the riverside. Besides, the purse was too good to pass up, and I got to thumb my nose at those arrogant Bluecoats while I was at it."

Solomon chuckled, pulled on the bottle and squinted at Clayton. "What is it you're after now, man? You didnae come all this way just to help an old Scot get seaworthy."

One of Clayton's *fortes* was knowing when to drop subterfuge and play it straight. He thought Solomon could read him cold. "I'm after information I hope to sell, and I've been led to believe your cook has war news. If he'd care to pass it on to me, I'm in a position to make certain it gets into Rebel hands."

Solomon liked Clayton's plain talk. He took him into a plantain grove where the cook—an octagenarian Cuban named Raoulito—was roasting a four-foot turtle in an open pit of coals under a canopy of wide leaves. Raoulito was brown as rum, with laugh lines spoking from the corners of his eyes and an Adam's Apple big as a plum pit.

"*Buenas dias, Senor,*" Clayton shook the old man's hand. "I'm told you were the omnibus boy at Antoine's in New Orleans. Is that a fact?"

"*Si, mi amigo.* But I learn to cook fancy from the *jefe* in the kitchen there, and I a good cook now, by God."

"I can see you're doin' wonders with that tortoise. I've had the turtle soup at *Antoine's* and there's none finer. But you can keep your cookin' secrets to yourself. I'm only interested in what you heard at the Yankee officers' table."

Raoulito looked at Solomon for direction; Solomon gave him a nod. Raoulito went on. "*Si,* they talk yap yap yap 'cause they think I only espeak espanish. Later I gotta run pretty damn quick when they hear me take English orders from that ginger Mick waiter."

"Tell me about the invasion."

"All those Union troops at Lafayette? Is a trick. To make the Rebels send their soldiers there. The real attack is from the sea, by God. At Galveston."

"You sure about this?"

"*Es verdad.*"

"They have a date set for the attack?"

"Not that they espoke to me."

Clayton shook his hand. "Thank you, *Senor.* I'll put this information to good use, I assure you." And to Solomon: "I best be goin'."

"Will you nae stay for a fine dinner?"

"I thank you, but no. Your ship looks seaworthy enough now to make it to Bagdad for a boatyard repair—so I'll bid you farewell, and hope we meet again."

As Clayton walked back to the mudskimmer, Solomon stood on a dune with an *Ybor Royale* cigar-box fiddle made of fine Havana cedar, and played an air taken from an old Scottish tune, with words he made up on the spot. "*There once was a gambler, a high rovin' rambler, kept his cattle from water, 'til ready to sell…*"

Wilkes made it back to Bagdad on the *Ne'er-do-well* after dark and paid extra for an upriver trip back to Matamoros. Because the Rio Grande had so many coiling twists, it was twice as many miles as the land route, taking hours more for the journey. But Clayton was exhausted, and lay on the deck in a liminal state staring up at the black, star-turning sky until his eyes merged with the darkness and he rose into its embrace…

They ran through the Spanish Moss to the edge of Bayou Nezpique and crouched in a clump of Mangroves, panting from the run. Going on sixteen, bold as brass. Clay pulled out a tortoise shell comb, the one he'd just stolen from the windowsill of the mayor's daughter. "Bet her hair smells nice," he said, bringing it to his nose.

"Your daddy gonna whup you sure," said Isaac.

There was a noise down by the river bank. They lay flat on their bellies, peering through the foliage. A young gent was helping his lady out of a scull he'd pulled half up onto shore. They walked up the bank hand in hand and he spread a blanket for a picnic.

"We could get home quicker in that little boat," whispered Clay.

"Man see us in his boat he shoot us right off."

They watched the man give the lady a kiss. She resisted, but not much.

"He won't even know we doin' it," said Clay. "Come on."

The man and woman rolled in each other's arms as Clay and Isaac slithered like marbled salamanders down to the water, where they eased the little vessel into the river and floated downstream, hanging on until they were out of sight. Then they climbed in.

"They in for a surprise when it's goin' home time," said Isaac with a chuckle.

At the bow of the skiff was a basket of apples, tarts and a bottle of wine. "Why those fine folks left the picnic for us!"

They broke out the feast over a wide-ranging conversation about love, bravery, and how the Nezpique River was like a Tattooed Nose. As the stars came out, Clay looked up at the storied constellations, wondering if life could possibly ever again feel so right...

Until the star clusters high above him on the Rio Grande took Clayton finally into the resting sleep he sought, undisturbed by dreams, memories, or regrets.

When the *Ne'er-do-well* reached Matamoros the next morning, Clayton walked back to Brave River, trotted upstairs past his suite and knocked on Isaac's door.

"Come."

Clayton entered the monkish quarters. Whitewashed walls, a mat on the floor. A tiny juniper tree grew in a pot on the windowsill; Isaac called it *bonsai*. Isaac himself sat at the only piece of furniture in the room, a writing desk beside the window, with a view of the river. He was shirtless, his back crisscrossed with dozens of old whip scars, enlarged by cheloid to look like thick, twisted ropes in a dense mesh. He practiced calligraphy on a large sheet of rice paper, line after line of italic *O*'s.

"Am I interruptin'?"

"I'm just doing my practice. Quiet night here. Was your trip fruitful?"

"Most likely. I need you to go down to *The Daily Ranchero* and place an ad in the classified section."

"Saying what?"

"'*Bar Sinister: Reply at Brave River.*'"

"Anything else?"

"Yes, sir, there is. I want you to make a wooden plaque, about one by two feet, and paint this design on it." He drew a rough coat-of-arms with a bar sinister crossing from upper right to lower left. "Make the crown red, the pennants gray...and see if you can't make these animals look like polecats."

"Skunks?"

"I believe that should give the flavor of Southern royalty. Let's write a motto in the pennants, too—something in your beautiful calligraphy."

"What kind of motto? Like 'Never Kick a Polecat'?"

"Perfect. But write it in Latin."

"*Non Calcitrare Polecatus.* I will enjoy that."

"I thought you might. Hang it on the wall across from the bar. I want to know who shows an interest in it. Tell the barkeeps too."

Clayton went downstairs as Isaac nodded, putting on his shirt. He'd learned Latin and calligraphy both while slave to his last owner, a Florida doctor named Ellengill. The man had fancied himself quite enlightened, educating Isaac in philosophies most slave-owners thought the black race incapable of grasping. They discussed literature, science, art, history, mythology, Isaac consumed it all—which became a problem for Dr. Ellengill as Isaac began to surpass him, and even challenge some of his dearly held notions. Things went downhill after that.

When Clayton got downstairs he noticed Legionnaire Scully introducing himself to the new diva, Claire, who seemed to like the cut of Scully's jib. It was a bartop romance Clayton would enjoy watching unfold. But that would have to wait until later. For now he had to make his rounds of the city.

And so he did.

CHAPTER 6

"MAJOR RUSSELL, I'D LIKE to introduce you to Mrs. Allison Stoneman."

"How do you do, Mrs. Stoneman? It's an honor to meet you." Russell had an open face that invited conversation.

"The honor is mine, Major. And I beg your forgiveness, I must look a fright."

"I wish Lieutenant Jessup always presented me with such frights."

"We made it down the Sands with spit and a prayer," said Jessup, "and I haven't had spit for the last forty miles."

"Comanche steal your goods?"

"Confederate Major named Odeel," said Jessup. "Impressed all of her cotton."

"I'm sorry to hear that, Mrs. Stoneman. Some of these so-called officers have little respect for private property rights."

The way he said it, the way he looked at her, gave Allie to hope there was some wiggle room with this Rebel officer. "I don't suppose there's any way you can get my bales back when the wagon train pulls in, can you, Major?"

"That's a tricky thing, to make something like that happen. It's for the war effort, you know, and I've got little to say against that. Little I can do. Usually." He watched her latch onto his last word. Might be something to pursue. "Is your husband joining you?"

There was a commotion down the hall, then a herd of footsteps and several people pushed in through the door. Jessup and Russell straightened and saluted, as a 50-year-old paunchy officer wearing double button dress grays entered, followed by a pretty, 30 some year-old woman in a blue gingham dress, with a small child clutching each of her legs. The commanding officer returned a casual salute.

"General Bee," said Major Russell, "may I present Mrs. Allison Stoneman, late of Shreveport and newly arrived after a harrowing trek through the Wild Horse Desert."

"How do you do, Mrs. Stoneman? I hope I'm not interrupting."

"Not at all, General Bee." She pegged him as the type of officer who rode a desk chair instead of a war horse.

"Allow me to introduce you to my wife, Mildred, and my two sons who are apparently incapable of walking without the support of my wife's legs."

"Oh, they're just playin' a game, Hamilton," Mildred lovingly rebuked her husband. "It's a great pleasure to meet you, Mrs. Stoneman. I hope you'll come join me for tea sometime, and tell me all about your extraordinary expeditionary adventures."

"I would be most happy to do so."

"Of course, tea time for the English is at four, but I have found many people hereabouts take their siestas at that hour."

"The Mexicans do, I'll warrant," said the General.

"That's only because they are a more taciturn race than the English, Hamilton. I don't believe it reflects on their work ethic, if that's what you are implying."

"I'm not implying any…"

"They are a hardworking people, but now that Texas has been liberated from their failing government, they are understandably afflicted with melancholy, much as you or I would be in similar circumstances. Where will you be living, Mrs. Stoneman?"

"I'm not quite sure, Mrs. Bee, as my husband has recently passed away and my own circumstances somewhat in flux."

"Then you must stay at our *hacienda* in Matamoros. We use it ourselves, time to time, but it's primarily for house guests, of which you are currently the most in need."

"No, I couldn't accept such undeserving hospitality, Mrs. Bee…"

"You'd be doing me a great favor. The house is tended by a charming young Mexican woman, Aurelia, who will do you a world of good learning Spanish, which I have been essaying to conquer with great difficulty for many weeks now. Then after you learn your grammars from her, you may tutor me, and thus repay the generosity you are so admirably reluctant to accept. Isn't that right, Hamilton?"

The three men had been glued to Mildred's every word, so that when she finally stopped, there was a delayed pause before General Bee jumped in with the only response possible.

"Yes, of course. Mrs. Stoneman, you must do us the honor of taking up residence there until you can find yourself better accommodations."

"It's settled, then," smiled Mildred. "At least until you and your husband can find your feet."

"My husband has passed, I'm afraid."

Mildred emitted a small gasp. "Of course he has, you already said that. How rude of me, and now I've reminded you of the tragedy again. There's no more to be said. You are our guest. Major Jessup can escort you to the hacienda, he knows the way."

"*Lieutenant* Jessup, ma'am," Jessup corrected. Over-corrected, really, since nobody cared what his rank was.

"I'm humbled by your kindness," Allie thanked Mildred. "I only hope I can live up to the standards anything as grand as a *hacienda* must require."

Mildred laughed happily. "Grand, is that what you think? Well, I have seen the elephant!" Whereupon she tousled the hair of the boys who still clung to the puffy dress around her knees. They threw their heads around like wet puppies and grinned at her.

"Fine," said General Bee with more than a hint of impatience. "If that's settled, I have some war business to discuss with Major Russell, and you, my dear, must leave us to it." He kissed his wife's hand with a formality she quite enjoyed; then she curtseyed to the group and left awkwardly with her two giggling leg warmers.

General Bee turned to Russell. "Any progress on that jailbreak?"

"No, sir, but I'm pursuing it vigorously. I've put the guard on report—he was relieving himself at the back wall when the Yanks made their getaway."

Bee nodded glumly and turned to Jessup. "Lieutenant. After you take the young lady to Matamoros, I want you to lead a raid on Banco Perdido upriver tonight. Rat's nest of *Cortinistas* camped there, and those escaped Yankees might be with 'em."

"Cortina gonna be there too?" Jessup wanted that prize badly.

"No, he's with his main force, skirmishing with the French. He left some of his *banditos* behind to keep stealing from Texans but I won't stand for it anymore. You sneak up when they're all drunk asleep." He nodded as if he were having a conversation with himself, which he often did. Then he poked Jessup in the chest. "Maybe you can bring some of 'em back alive to hang."

Jessup took Allie, Jersey, Moon and the mule wagon on the ferry to Matamoros. It was a warm day, but nothing compared to the wasteland they'd just come through. Allie was surprised at all the colorful flora after her desert trek—orange bougainvillea, pink hibiscus, yellow primrose, purple frogfruit, peach goldmallow. Not that she knew any of their names yet—but she couldn't wait to start taking pictures of them, certain their colors would make themselves known through the sepia tints of her photography.

She was also taken by the international flavor of the city. Half a dozen languages flew past her, spoken by people in strange clothing, some military, some native, some highbrow, some low down. Strains of unfamiliar music carried across the air, and food smells she couldn't place, and the sounds of construction work, barking dogs, laughing ladies, raised voices. In the near distance a line of black-robed Nuns in grand, white-winged headdress glided by as if on wheels, like disembodied beings.

A fine lady in Oriental silks walked past them holding a leash on a dog the size of a small horse. Allie asked Jessup, "Will there be elephants at the *hacienda*?"

Jessup laughed. "Why would you think that?"

"Mrs. Bee said she had seen the elephant."

"Oh, that's just an expression. Means she'd seen somethin' everyone was crowin' about and it turned out not to be such great shakes after all."

The ferry ride made Moon nervous. He couldn't swim; he hated crossing rivers. Jersey, annoyed with his foolish anxiety, flathanded him in the back. Allie was just annoyed with their bickering. "You two stay close. I don't want anyone stealin' you."

"There's no stealing of slaves down here, Mrs. Stoneman," said Jessup. "Mexicans don't keep slaves."

"Well I'll keep mine, if you please."

At the edge of town they came to an adobe *hacienda* with a still fountain in the front yard and magenta bougainvillea practically engulfing the place. Allie thought it quite lovely. "Well, I have seen the elephant and it looks grand to me," she said.

Jersey and Moon waited outside as Jessup brought Allie in, introducing her to Aurelia, a pregnant 30-year-old woman who spoke only Spanish. Allie wondered to herself if General Bee had sired the woman's baby, as was so common among the landed gentry of the South and their young female slaves.

Aurelia poured them water from an *olla* with floating lemon slices, then showed Allie her room, pointed out *los banos*, mimed pouring the tub full of water, and found Allie a clean dress. It was too big, but to Allie it was divine. Still, she pulled out a wad of the Confederate money she'd gotten from Captain Odeel for her cotton, and gave it to Jersey and Moon, telling them to buy her some proper clothes. Then she went to draw a bath. She might be hot and tired, but there was no law she knew of on either side of the border that said she had to be dirty and sweaty as well.

It rained for about a minute as Jersey and Moon made their way to town, stopping at the first nice clothier's shop they found—Delgado's. It was elegant—worthy of someplace you might find in New Orleans—but the owner, who wore a ruffled shirt and long frock, smelling of far too much cologne, curled his lip as he made them take off their muddy shoes before entering.

"Yessir," said Moon, "that's a good idea, these mud streets ain't like a real city."

The shopkeeper said, "You saying this isn't a real city?"

"Naw, he didn't mean nothin'" Jersey intervened. "We lookin' for clothes for our lady o' the house."

Delgado nodded suspiciously and followed them all over the store as they proceeded to pick out dresses for Allie. But when they tried to pay with the Confederate money Allie'd given them, the owner got cranky. He accused them of attempted thievery, threw them bodily out of the store, and followed them into the muddy street.

"You're probably runaways, too!" the florid dressmaker shouted. "I won't abide a runaway slave in my shop, even if the Mexican government allows it."

"We ain't no runaways, sir," Moon said as he tried to get up.

But the man kicked him back down into a mud patch. "I didn't say you rise. You are not my equal, boy, you stay down where your station at." He turned to a few onlookers. "Lookahere, ain't this something? These picaninnies tried to steal my goods!"

"Naw sir," said Jersey, "Miz Stoneman give us that money to pay with. We didn't know it was bad in your store."

"Did I say you could talk back to me?" He kicked the quaking girl in the belly, but when he pulled his boot back to kick again a strong hand jerked him by the collar. He swung around in a fury; but paused when he saw Isaac, who held a two-foot board.

"Is there a problem here?" asked Isaac.

"I'll say there is. These two tried to foist worthless notes on me and run off with my finest dresses before I saw what they were trying to pull."

"Naw sir, it weren't like that. Miz Stoneman give us that money to pay with. We didn't know it was bad." Moon held out the remaining Confederate bills to show Isaac.

"Looks to me like a simple misunderstanding," Isaac smiled at the shopkeeper. "You just keep your dresses and return their Confederate notes, no harm done. Except for your boot mark on that little girl's ribcage."

Delgado threw a punch. Isaac caught the man's fist in his left hand and popped him in the forehead with the board. Not hard enough to knock him out, but enough to make his legs wobble. Delgado threw his fistful of Confederate money on the ground and lurched back into his shop as Isaac helped the frightened slaves to their feet. "You must be new to town," he said gently.

"Just got in. The mizzus told us buy her some dresses, that's all we's doin'."

"Well, you'd better get back to her now and let her know she needs to turn these graybacks into gold, even if it's just ten cents on the dollar."

"Yes, sir, we'll surely tell her now," said Moon.

But Jersey was staring at the dress shop with a look of barely restrained bravado, like she wanted to storm in and continue the exchange with the shopkeeper.

Isaac said, "You know…there are no slaves in Mexico. You two wanted to walk away from your mistress, I could find jobs for you at Brave River. That's a gambling hall over by the water. You ask anyone, they'll tell you where it is. You ask for Isaac."

"That a bible name," said Moon.

"It is," said Isaac. "Means '*he laughs*' in the old Hebrew language." He growled a throaty chuckle and went on, "That's how a bear laughs. And I'm the old black bear who protects his cubs. You come see me next time you need protection."

Jersey and Moon nodded, wordless—but then that was how a lot of people responded to Isaac's parables. The worried slaves grabbed their shoes out of the mud and walked off, Moon slouching, Jersey shrugging his hand off her arm.

Isaac watched them go, marveling at their endurance. But that's what slaves did, they endured. He remembered when his last owner, Dr. Ellengill, had tired of Isaac's erudition, he turned him out to sport-fighting with slaves from other plantations, for the owners to place bets on. Isaac told Ellengill he thought the fights were good object lessons for the white race—physical representations of the philosophy of human ownership: if somebody won, somebody else had to lose; and sometimes the unexpected opponent came out on top.

Ellengill didn't like that, so he gave Isaac a different object lesson. Made him fight only much bigger men, so he always lost, always got badly beaten. It did teach him how to fight hard, though. He learned a lot of survival tricks that way. And he had endured.

Since escaping that plantation, he hadn't again suffered such abuse. If anyone now treated him the way this merchant had treated these poor, young Negroes, that man would have suffered consequences more severe than a whack on the forehead.

He still had much to learn about the benefits of patience—benefits he preached but didn't always adhere to. In any case for the time being he simply headed back to the casino to paint a polecat coat-of-arms. Isaac figured that was appropriate family heraldry for Clayton—Isaac knew better than most what a skunk old man Wilkes, Clayton's father, was. But knowing Clayton, there was more to this shield than met the eye.

He'd known Clayton Wilkes most of his life—through childhood, and the predations of violent men, and grief, and many a serpentine affair—and the man rarely failed to surprise him.

*　*　*

Sitting at his workbench Clayton fitted two slivers of yellow glass together perfectly, glued the seam and held the joining fixed, in a vise. Then he sat back and closed his eyes. It was the sleepy time of the afternoon and he thought he might give a nod to the fine old Mexican habit of *siesta*. Looking out his window, he saw the long shadow of the building he was in darken the plain to the river, where the rippling water glinted golden red. It was hard to imagine such beauty existing in this ugly old world.

He took a sip of whiskey, feeling its warmth lull him, as his eyes grew heavier, under a flood of voices that pulled him swirling down until he could resist no more and lay his head on the worktable, seeking a measure of peace...

The overseer pulled them out of the flatbed, tumbling them to the dirt, their hands bound behind them as Clayton's father walked up with his left eye twitching.

"They was workin' some kinda game," said the overseer. "Black boy askin' for directions out front while your son robbed the back."

"That true, Clay?" asked his father. Clayton didn't answer. Isaac looked terrified. Clayton's father nodded to the overseer, who left. Clayton's mother ran up, scared.

"It was my fault, Mama. Isaac had naught to do with it. He didn't know I was stealin' from that man…"

His father grabbed him by the shirtfront and yanked him up, slamming him against the wagon. Slapped him. "Shame on you."

The overseer returned, holding a black man and woman by the arms. Isaac's parents.

Clayton's father set his jaw. "Here's what we'll do. I'm goin' to sell these three troublemakers to three different plantations in three different states…"

"No!" screamed Isaac's mother, but the overseer punched her in the mouth and she fell.

"Don't do that, Daddy, it was my fault."

"I know it was, Clay. This is how I'm punishin' you. I expect it won't happen again." He nodded to the overseer, who pushed the black man and woman into the flatbed wagon, then flung the bound Isaac up there, too.

Clayton's mother forced a whisper to her husband. "Can't we think about this for a day?"

"No we cannot!" his father shouted and stormed off, leaving his wife weeping, Clayton standing in the dirt watching the wagon pull away as two lepers wrapped in rags crossed the road into the woods, and Clay met Isaac's soul-dead eyes…

Clayton awoke with a jolt and looked around. This *siesta* wasn't the peace he'd been seeking; only another wrenching memory. He supposed he might as well finish up his war rounds and chalk off another afternoon in hell.

At 3 a.m. Jessup led a patrol across half the river to Banco Perdido, where Cortina's *hombres* were said to be holed up. Jessup spread his men out to surround the clearing where they could see five men sleeping under bedrolls around the embers of a campfire. Then everything went amok.

The bedrolls were decoys and the *Cortinistas* attacked the Rangers from behind. Two of Jessup's men were killed right off, but the gunfire went on for another ten minutes, everyone chasing or hiding in the tall brush while the moans of the wounded got louder.

Once, when Jessup was crouched behind a big log, he saw a man stand up straight out of a thorny patch, just smiling. And by God, if it wasn't Cortina himself. Jessup fired, missing. The bandit chief didn't move, he only gazed at Jessup. Jessup shot again, but his gun was out of ammunition. As he frantically reached to his belt for more bullets, Cortina slowly raised his own gun—first aiming at Jessup, but then raising it higher, finally straight up, discharging his weapon over and over into the sky until it was empty. Then he slid back down into the thorn bushes and disappeared.

Jessup tried to find him briefly. But his bigger obligation was to his wounded men, who he got back to the north side of the river, and then the hospital.

The next day, covered in trail dust, Captain Odeel of the Confederate States of America showed up at the office of Quartermaster Major Charles Russell.

"Captain Odeel, good to see you, though you look somewhat the worse for wear."

"Carting cotton trains across the Wild Horse Desert is never an easy task, Major."

"Last I heard you were chasing Comanche around San Antone."

"That we did. Then as fortune would have it we came upon nearly 5000 bales we impressed for the war effort. I've put all that cotton in your storehouse. So if you'll let me sign the paperwork and write out a voucher for the tariff, I'll be on my way."

"Tell me, Captain, would that be the bales from the Stoneman Plantation?"

"I believe the lady said that was her name, yes sir."

"Well, that presents something of a problem."

Allie stepped into the room, Jessup behind. His cheeks were taut with fatigue from a bad night of chasing *Cortinistas* around Banco Perdido. Three of his men had been killed; Cortina had escaped again. So Jessup was not in a mood to take any guff at the moment. Odeel regarded them with an inkling of what was about to befall him.

Russell took a strongbox from the safe and opened it on his desk—revealing a mound of gold coin. "I have the money all counted, transported from Patricio Milmo's Bank in Matamoros—he'll be taking possession of the goods. But Mrs. Stoneman, here, has already presented me with the bill of sale."

"What bill of sale?" Odeel felt the firmament slipping away.

"Why, this one, sir," said Allie, pulling the paper from her new cloth purse. "The bill showin' I bought the cotton from the man who now owns my plantation outside Shreveport. This documents that I am, in fact, the cotton's rightful owner."

"The Confederate States of America owns that cotton," insisted Odeel. "It was impressed under the authority given me by the Cotton Bureau."

"And yet," said Russell, "you are not in possession of this bill of sale which, under the circumstances, I am compelled to honor. I was informed of the same by the Governor of Tamaulipas Province, who is also Patricio Milmo's father-in-law, and charged with enforcing the laws of the cross-river cotton trade." This was, of course, nonsense. Neither a Mexican governor nor his Irish son-in-law had any say in cotton transactions on this side of the river. But Russell knew the lingo, and how to lace in enough facts to make it sound legit. He pushed the gold across his desk to Allie.

"Now just a damn minute..." Odeel went for the pistol on his belt.

Jessup grabbed the fool's hand and held it there as Allie handed the bill of sale to Russell. Then she gestured at the strongbox of gold coins to a quivering Moon, who was standing in the doorway with a dolly. Allie smiled at Odeel.

"I want to thank you, Captain Odeel, for guidin' my cotton down here. And I thank you, Major Russell. This gold is my stake, and I hope to be an importer of some repute."

"I've no doubt you will overtake us all, Mrs. Stoneman." They regarded each other with recognition of a deal well consummated, hopefully the first of many, as Odeel stormed out in a silent rage. Allie set aside a small pile of coins in front of Russell and turned back to the Ranger.

"Lieutenant Jessup, if you'd be so kind as to escort us to the bank?"

"I can do that, ma'am."

"And after a refreshin' nap, perhaps later you could show me some of the festive night life of Matamoros I've heard so much about."

But last night's gunplay, followed by strong whiskey, little food and almost no sleep, had left the young soldier a bit dizzy. "I'm terrible tired, Mrs. Stoneman."

She took his hand in hers with a rejuvenating warmth. "I won't take no. You've saved my life twice now. I know you have it in you to save my social standing."

Clayton finished his rounds and walked over to *The Daily Ranchero*. As he approached, Jensen, the printer's devil, stalked out, knocking past Clayton without a by-your-leave. Wachtel appeared in the doorway with a contorted face—but when he saw Wilkes he held his tongue and went back into the shop. Clayton followed. "Lose another employee, Simon?"

"The boy will be back. He is just sensitive to criticism—but this is *gut*. Sensitive means he will be a *gut* printer."

They spent a pleasant hour on their chess match. Wachtel surged in his middle game only to realize too late that Clayton had laid a subtle trap. "So now you have me."

"I never make the mistake of claimin' victory before the king has fallen," said Clayton. "I advise you not to claim your downfall until that very same moment."

"There is a measure of honor in bowing to defeat when the end is in sight."

"I don't believe that. Lookit what happened to the Sioux in the Dakota Uprisin'. They were practically annihilated by the Bluecoats *after* they gave up. Which is why the Cherokee Nation joined the Confederacy—Jefferson Davis promised 'em citizenship."

"I hope those Cherokee don't start taking slaves if your beloved South does win."

"Cherokee already keep slaves. And the Cherokee Confederate Mounted Rifle Brigade's mostly what's holdin' the Yankees back, up in Arkansas. Those Yanks better hope the Cherokee don't make *them* slaves."

"If they do, the Union wrath will come down on them like Thor's hammer."

"Just like I'm about to come down on your last bishop." He nodded at the chessboard and Wachtel's face fell. "But you get a reprieve, Simon. I have to go get ready for the evenin's festivities at the opera."

"Go. The Matamoros Opera is a charade of culture." And he went back to studying the board as Clayton exited with a light step, curious to find out what new batch of war rumors would be circulating at intermission tonight.

The Opera House was rumored to have been built at the urging of the Austrian Arch-Duchess Carlota—who, it was said, refused to take the throne of Mexico with her husband Maximilian until culture arrived first. Two tiers high now, it was intended that there be a third story, as well—but construction had been halted, the top floor just storing building materials for completion as soon as multinational hostilities allowed. Tonight, however, hostilities didn't prevent *La Traviata* playing to a full house, the new diva a big draw. Ladies and gentlemen from the upper strata of Matamoros and Brownsville were dressed in their finest. Charles Stillman—who owned most of Brownsville—chatted with General Cobos, the *Imperialista* monarchist-in-exile. Iron Shirt, an Apache chief trying to broker peace with American troops, made small talk with an Austrian Duke. All were here to see and be seen.

Catherine Delacroix flitted from couple to couple, ever the *grande* hostess, handing out compliments as she fluttered her kohl-encrusted eyelashes. In a sneak attack she ushered Clayton to a service doorway, took his hand and placed it on her left breast. "You can feel my heart swell to see you."

"I believe I can," he smiled. A familiar scent caught his awareness, bringing with it a quickening of breath, an excitement; or was it alarm?

He brought his nose to Catherine's neck to see if she was wearing a new perfume. It wasn't coming from her, but she took his move to imply an intimacy he wasn't trying to project. Still, she put her hand behind his head and pulled his lips to the tender spot behind her ear. There was really nothing Clayton could do but kiss her there.

"Come to me tonight," she whispered. Clayton recalled the last time they spent abed together, sweet in the moment, empty in the parting. He was feeling particularly adrift now, though, so he thought he might just take her up on her offer. He slid his hand down toward her backside.

But the moment was interrupted by Confederate Consul Quintero, who approached eagerly. "Wilkes, I am so very glad I found you." Clayton pulled away, Catherine bridling at the *interruptus*—but then she was quickly taken herself by one of the rich patrons who kept the Opera House running six nights a week. "Did you have any success with the water-stained letters?" Quintero asked Clayton quietly under the crowd noise.

"I did. The note said '*Kingston Bar, Bar Sinister.*' That led me to another coded note I'm having translated now—which will, I'm afraid, require extra payment."

Facing the wall, Quintero pulled out a handful of bills, which Clayton expertly palmed and shifted to his pocket. He didn't count the money; but did ascertain they were U.S. Treasury Notes, not Confederate. Quintero smiled. "You are the best purveyor of information, Clayton."

"Well, you pay the best."

"I know, you try to sound cynical. Your loyalty to the Confederacy keeps you on track, though. The money, it is just a way to measure your sympathies."

Clayton did a pretty good job of appearing humble. "We all do what we can." A gentleman of the South like Clayton could always be counted on to honor historical ties, even if his most passionate love had become legal tender.

Legionnaire Scully approached Clayton, looking out of place—though his captain's jacket had been pressed, his hair combed. "Good evening is it, Mr. Wilkes."

"Scully, this is the last place I expected to see a fellow like you. The cockfights, more like. You know *Senor* Quintero, the Confederate *attache* in these parts?"

Scully shook Quintero's hand, and they exchanged pleasantries, though Scully was clearly uncomfortable in this rarified culture. He pulled Clayton aside. "Claire got me a backstage pass. She wanted me to see her perform. What else could I do?"

"Y'all did the right thing, son. I believe after tonight this puts your relationship on solid ground. Long as you're sufficiently admirin' of her voice." Clayton saw General Bee, the Commandant of Fort Brown, approaching with his wife, Mildred, and a Royal Navy officer in full regalia.

On reaching them Bee addressed Quintero. "Consul Quintero, allow me to introduce Captain Smolleigh, Commander of Her Majesty's Ship, *The Sea Queen*."

Formalities were exchanged all around as Mildred Bee, a devilish twinkle in her eye, grabbed a passing gentleman. "And of course you all know Ambassador Pierce."

There was a momentary frosty silence as Quintero and Pierce raised their neck hairs at each other. But, of course, both were diplomats— albeit on opposing sides—who now presented only the warmest of cold smiles.

"My, my, Ambassadors Quintero and Pierce," Mildred went on with flagrant playfulness, "how much you two must have to talk about."

"Why, we talk all the time," smiled Union Ambassador Pierce, "about the extraordinary showcase our Opera House provides at this crossroads to the world."

Confederate Ambassador Quintero turned more serious, but only as a means of extending Mildred's joke. "Madame Bee, I spoke to Ambassador Pierce only recently of my generous plan to relocate the Union army to Canada—but sadly he has declined."

"My counteroffer was to accept Consul Quintero's terms, if we could take all the Confederate slaves with us and give them their own country in Nova Scotia."

"I'd provide the sea transport for that," the British Navy Captain jumped into the good fun. "The Crown needs all the workers it can get in our great Canadian colony."

"The bloody British do love their colonies," said Scully. He spit on the floor. Mrs. Bee gasped, but was clearly loving the show.

Captain Smolleigh scowled. "I'm bloody ready to arrange passage to a special colony in Australia for you, you blighted Irish…"

"Let's not start a new war at the opera, gentlemen," Clayton pled. "There's war enough to go around." And to Scully: "Don't you have somewhere backstage to be?"

Scully exited, jostling Smolleigh on the way out as General Bee pontificated. "I would never let anyone take our darkies. Not even to an English prison colony."

Pierce turned undiplomatically serious. "It is an ungodly, immoral sin for one human being to own another."

General Bee puffed up. "It was God Himself, Leviticus 25:44-46, who said, '*Your slaves are to come from the nations around you; from them you may buy slaves.*' If God said it, I don't believe you can say it's unGodly."

But now Mildred threw in her two cents. "What the bible says is not necessarily God's verbatim instruction manual, Hamilton. Deuteronomy 21:18 states, '*Our son is stubborn and rebellious, a glutton and a drunkard. Let all the men of his city stone him with stones, that he die.*' You think that's what we should do, because the bible says it?"

"It seems to me," said Quintero, "that is exactly what Lincoln's armies are doing. Stoning to death their Southern sons who are only 'stubborn and rebellious.'"

"Let's not forget the gluttons and drunkards amongst them," Mildred said sweetly.

"Really, my dear," the General rebuked her.

"By God," said Clayton, "if we were goin' to stone to death every drunkard and glutton in the country, the slaves would end up bein' the only ones left to run the place."

Everyone laughed at that, tension broken. A bell rang once, signaling everyone to the auditorium. Clayton started to turn, but before he could take a step he smelled that fragrance again, the one he thought

Catherine had been wearing—only stonger now. Strong enough that he couldn't believe he hadn't recognized it before. Lavender. His pulse quickened as a voice spoke up behind him. A familiar voice.

"Clay Wilkes."

He turned. The face he saw utterly stunned him, and the source of the perfume he'd whiffed came into focus like a clear and present danger; like an unsettling nightmare. "Allie," he whispered hoarsely, but could say no more. If he'd felt lost in spirit up to this moment, he now felt at a loss of purpose, of movement, of intention.

They held each other's gaze as Mrs. Bee wasted no time. "Why Mrs. Stoneman, how delightful to see you here, I do hope you're enjoying our humble *hacienda*."

"Yes, Mrs. Bee, it's been a great source of comfort as I sort out my situation. Your kindness has been such a boon."

"Which you may repay with tales of your travels, at tea time tomorrow, as you promised. Now, Hamilton, get me settled in our box so I can watch everyone enter."

And taking her husband by the arm, Mildred aimed them for the box seats, joined by Captain Smolleigh. Ambassador Pierce left as well. Quintero remained in place, transfixed by Allie's face, while Clayton and Allie continued staring at each other. Ranger Jessup, walking up behind Allie, tried small talk.

"She's a firecracker, Mrs. Bee is. She'll take all the words out of a talk-fest before anyone else gets a chance to use any of 'em."

"What are you doing here?" Clayton finally managed to say to Allie, unaware of anyone else in the room.

"I could ask you the same."

Jessup cleared his throat. "So I reckon you two know each other?"

"Mr. Wilkes was a distant neighbor once," she replied in a sham neutral tone.

Clayton tried to regain his composure through social formalities. "Confederate States Special Liaison to Mexico, Jose Quintero, allow me to introduce Mrs. Allison Stoneman. Mrs. Stoneman, the Honorable Mr. Quintero."

"How do you do, Mr. Quintero?"

"Excellently, Mrs. Stoneman. You elevate our poor attempt at culture here in Matamoros with your presence."

Another scratchy pause, during which everyone seemed to forget Jessup was standing there without introduction. He remedied that himself, extending his hand to Quintero. "Lieutenant Jessup, Texas Rangers, now in the CSA. Pleased to meet y'all."

They shook hands, Clayton and Allie peering at each other the whole time.

Jessup went on, "Of course I've bumped into Mr. Wilkes from time to time. Everybody in town knows Brave River." The bell rang twice. "That's five minutes until curtain," said Jessup. "We should go get our seats."

"Yes," said Quintero. "If you'll excuse me. Clayton, perhaps we can continue our conversation later." He tipped his head to Allie. "Madame." And he left.

Regaining some of her composure, Allie said, "Lieutenant Jessup, if you could find our seats, I'll join you momentarily."

"All right, I can do that. Good to officially meet you, Mr. Wilkes." And Jessup left.

Clayton was able to look at Allie more in her entirety now. Over a corseted waist she wore an elegant turquoise silk ball gown, flowing out around the cage of crinoline hoops underneath. Teal buttonhook boots with low heels. "It's good to see you again, Allie. Is your husband here?"

"He's dead, Clay."

Clayton tried to process that information, wondering how, and when. "I'm sorry."

"For whom?"

"Why, for you, of course..."

"Because being sorry for yourself is what I most remember of you."

"You are certainly entitled to your own recollections. My personal memories are of a fonder nature." Both fonder and more bitter; but all sealed away.

"You may romanticize the past all you want. I prefer to be more of a realist in matters of..." She stopped when she realized where her thoughts were taking her.

"The heart?" he finished her sentence.

"Business," she said stonefaced.

"In business—if I recall correctly—realism was not exactly your aim." He sensed a darkness inside her but felt compelled to feed it rather than avoid it.

"'Not exactly my aim,'" she mocked his arch tone. "Self-interested chicanery surely was *your* aim, though. A yellow coward's aim, I might add."

"You always did have a mouth on you, didn't you."

She inched closer, lowering her eyes in a coy come-on they both knew was false. "Is my mouth what you think of, when you think about me?"

"I don't think about you at all."

She slapped him so hard the sound drew startled glances from around the room.

He had a moment of twisted grief but served it back with a gentleman smile. "That's the second time this week I've been slapped. Only this time I didn't feel a thing."

She walked with a regal grace to the balcony seats. He stood there for a long time, missing the first act as his mind drifted, floated, dove deep…

"Hey, Sweet Thang, you gone buy me a drank?" The girl wet the corner of her mouth. She looked no more than 16, though she spoke like an adult who knew her business. Some kind of fancy perfume reached out like wisps of temptation.

"Maybe you ought to buy me a drink. What do you think of that?" said Clay.

The young lady sat beside him. "I think you need a long drank o' me, is what I think."

"Well I have a room above the café. If you'd care to join me, we could play a little game of seein' who buys who what."

She shook her head with a smile from here to there. "How'm I gone pay for my keep ef I give it all to you for free, Sweet Thang?"

They made love all afternoon. They surprised each other with the things they did, wrapped up together in an overheated mist of lavender incense…

Clay jerked awake in the seat he'd taken at the back row of the balcony and exited to the wide *loggia* where tonight's patrons would soon mingle to discuss the first act and gossip. But he crossed the floor quickly, seeking cool air on the veranda, irrationally afraid of the building going up in flames, his world collapsing in ashes. He gripped the filigreed iron balustrade that overlooked the wide boulevard and beyond that low hills at rest beneath the infinite blackness. Clayton closed his eyes. How could she be here? Was this a trap set by his enemies? A sad joke of the gods?

"I couldn't last the whole first act either," said a voice behind him. "That new singer has some work to do."

Clayton didn't have to turn his head to recognize United States Ambassador Pierce's voice. They stood side by side now, looking out at the stars.

"That could be said about all of us, I imagine," Clayton replied. Pierce laughed without making a sound. After a pause Clayton got right to it. "I just heard the Yankee troop buildup around Lafayette's a diversion. The Union invasion of Texas comes by sea, at Galveston. Is that right?"

Pierce weighed whether to confirm this highly classified news; then nodded.

Clayton continued. "Obviously I'll feed Quintero the opposite notion—tell him the Yanks are massing at Lafayette to invade by land. That ought to pull a couple platoons of Rebs out of Galveston. And here, I have somethin' else."

Clayton slipped the coded message he'd found behind the Kingston Bar coat-of-arms into Pierce's side pocket. "It's a cipher, meant for Quintero's eyes only. I'm hopin' you can translate it with the codebook your man took off that Confederate ironclad."

Pierce nodded, but no money was offered for the stolen document, and none requested. Clayton refused to profit from his efforts on behalf of the Union. A man had to take a principled position sometimes, after all. And Clayton's deepest principles were Union blue.

"I'll let you know what I find out," said Pierce. "Meet me Sunday. At church."

"Anybody saw me in a church on Sunday, they'd think it considerable odd, if they know me at all."

"Come in the back door the flagellants and egregious sinners use," Pierce smiled. "That should cover any questions anyone has." He started to leave, then paused. "Good work, soldier," he said into the night, and left.

But the kudos gave Clayton no pleasure. A double agent for the North, he'd just this evening been caught open-hearted by the only Southern belle he'd once have done anything for—except spy for the South.

So what would he do for her now?

CHAPTER 7

"IT'S SO KIND OF you to help me like this, Lieutenant Jessup," said Allie.

"Not at all. I need to spend a few days talkin' to informers in Matamoros anyway, to get a lead on Cortina. I might as well help you find a place in town while I'm about it." Not to mention it was a pure pleasure picking up wafts from her perfume—one of those bright surprises a man who lives on the range rarely got to appreciate. "Place I heard about is just around the next corner, Mrs. Stoneman."

"Please—you've already helped so much—you must start calling me Allie."

"All right…Allie."

"And what shall I call you? Lieutenant Jessup seems a touch overly formal."

"Nobody's called me anything but Jessup since I can remember."

"Well, what's your given name?"

He hesitated. "Ahotay." At her raised eyebrows, he continued. "It's Hopi. Means 'Restless One'. My mother was Hopi, my pa's folks come over from England way back. People mostly just called me Jessup. Never stopped being restless, though."

It was one of the things she liked about him, the way he ranged far and wide—even joined the Rangers to make it official. She'd been quite a roamer herself back in the day, and for the first time had the conscious thought that Jessup might be part of her future. Dependable, resourceful, unafraid to venture out, pretty and strong; what woman couldn't use a man like that? Particularly as a buffer to Clay—who had some nerve showing up in her life again now, as if he were entitled to do so.

They came to a small adobe building with a shack behind it. Once they walked through the madrone door she could see the windows brought lots of yellow sunshine inside. "Good light," she nodded, strolling through the two other rooms. "This suits me to a T. I'll have the front for reception, the middle for studio sittings, and this here will be my darkroom. That little building out back can store my inventory."

"What kind of things are you looking to import?"

"Shoes for our soldiers, I'm told are in high demand. Real coffee, too, and I have a contact in Cuba who can send it in bulk. But I'm also after big mark-up items—jewelry, art, whatever I can overcharge the gentry for my elegant taste. I'll sell my photography, too, if I can, but I'd do that without charge, just to expand my soul."

"My opinion, Mrs.—Allie—your soul's doin' just fine as is."

She regarded him with alert eyes in a neutral face. "I believe I'll call you Jessup in the public domain…and Ahotay in a more private setting, if you please."

He was so taken aback he didn't reply. With a smile to herself, Allie walked around through the bare rooms alone, envisioning where the desks and file cabinets would go; and where Lieutenant Ahotay Jessup would go, as well.

The home of the Commandant of Fort Brown was just outside the walls of the fort itself. One story clapboard, painted light blue, it was spacious and well appointed, with a contented view of the river. The slave quarters were further down by the water, sheltered behind a grove of cedar elm and Texas swamp privet. It would have been an easy swim across the river to freedom, but the slaves were all too afraid of General Bee to try it, since he had a whole fort of soldiers at his command.

Mildred Tarver Bee was a forward thinking woman, enamored of the Enlightenment. She believed in the French principles of *liberte, egalite,* and *fraternite.* She believed in science, universal education, women's suffrage, temperance, and even emancipation—though there were few she would admit that to in the state of Texas. She barely even hinted at it to her husband, who owned close to 70 human beings himself; but whom she nonetheless loved, and hoped to convince of the error of his ways, by utilizing the kind of longterm, nuanced campaign only a wife can.

Allie's knock was answered by an elderly house slave named Sharalee, who led Allie to the parlor, where Mildred was playing Pachelbel's Canon in D on a maple harpsichord. But she jumped up when Allie entered, to give her a warm hug.

"I'm so glad you came! Sharalee, please get us some sassafras tea." Sharalee left as Mildred took Allie to sit at an overstuffed sofa.

"What a delightful house," said Allie. "I just love the cool river breeze."

"Yes, it is nice for garden parties—I do a good deal of entertaining here, as you might imagine. Though I have few friends, sad to say."

"I hardly believe that."

"Oh, it's true. Some avoid me because Hamilton is in charge here, and they fear offending me. Some show up to ingratiate themselves, but they are no friends of mine. Most of the officers' wives find me either too opinionated or too modern, I suspect."

"Well, if you're all that modern, I hope you can direct me to some interestin' men in this town." Jessup was sure enough a good start, but the more names on her dance card, the more she expected Clay Wilkes would fade into the background.

"I believe I still know one or two eligible bachelors."

"I said interestin'. I ain't aimin' to get married again anytime soon."

Mildred laughed. "You and I are going to get along fine. Why, by the time Independence Day arrives—wait, that's it, you can help me organize the Grand Ball for *La Independencia.* It's a perfect excuse for me to introduce you to everyone in town, especially the gentlemen."

"Is it a big party, then?"

"Oh, the biggest. September 16th, at the Opera House, the Plaza, every which where. Fireworks, revelry, the most grand, beyond imagination—but then I have seen the elephant." The thought seemed to sadden her just a bit, and Allie noticed.

"You look so contemplative—would it be forward of me to ask if I could photograph you on that divan? I glorify so many men with their portraits, it would be a treat to capture an intelligent female face on my plate."

"Of course I'll sit for you—not today, I have my horseback lesson this afternoon. Tomorrow, perhaps. I'll have Sharalee…"

But before she could finish, a rattlesnake oozed over the window sill from the sunny side of the house, looking for a cooler spot to rest. It hit the floor with a plop that drew their attention and moved slowly in their direction, darting its tongue in and out until it picked up their scent. Stopped short and gave a rattle with its tail.

Mildred froze in fear. Allie was cool as could be, though. "Never you mind, Mildred, I know how to handle this." She reached into her purse, pulled out a small, lady-sized gun and pointed it at the snake.

"Are you such a markswoman you have that much confidence in hitting it?" Mildred whispered, her eyes wide.

"Not at all. I just know how a blind man can get a snake to kill its own self." She slowly waved the gun back and forth at the snake, which followed the movement of the muzzle with precision. "See?" said Allie, "A blind man." She turned her head away from the snake, closed her eyes and held the gun still. The rattler stopped moving its head as well, intent on the gun—and Allie pulled the trigger. Blew the rattlesnake's head off. "See, the snake aimed the gun for me, I just had to pull the trigger."

Mildred's jaw dropped in amazement. "I never."

"Just an old trick I learned from an old friend. I can't even remember who."

The next morning as Allie directed workmen where to place the furniture in her new offices, Jersey and Moon set up the developing equipment in the back room. Jersey was quiet and Moon could see she was working on something, so he took a small carving of a woman out of his pocket, one he'd made from a piece of mesquite on their desert trek. "I made this to look like you, so's I could keep it near me, case we ever got sold apart. But you keep it. Remember who made it for you." He gave her the carving. "Don't say much, these little folks, but they's good listeners." He tried to smile.

Jersey was silent for a moment. Then she brought the doll up to her face and spoke to it quietly. "I'm thinkin' 'bout goin' to work at that gamblin' hall Isaac told about."

Moon wasn't expecting that. "Whatchu talkin' 'bout, girl?"

"Talkin' 'bout workin' for that Colored man at the dress store, name Isaac."

"I know'd his name!" Moon tried to keep his voice from rising. "You forgettin' you belong to Mizz Stoneman?"

"Ain't no slaves in Mexico. We in Mexico."

He pulled her into the corner and whispered. "Maybe you ain't no slave now but you my wife. And I won't take no more talk like this. You hear me?" She yanked her arm away and pursed her lips. His arm came up as if to strike. "I said you hear me?"

He'd never hit her before so she got scared for a moment; then angry. "You raise your hand to me I'll give you right back, don't think I won't! I ain't your slave neither."

He whispered harshly in her face. "Don't you even think 'bout leavin' here. You make me shamed."

"Shamed is what you oughta be. And if I decide I'll go..." She shouted: "I'll go!"

They faced off like that, neither giving an inch. Everyone knew they bickered all the time; but never a fight like this. They felt hurtful in their hearts toward each other right now. Of the two, Jersey was the most adult, though she was Moon's junior by half a lifetime. And she could see he was terrified. Normally full of jokes and patter, it was clear to her that his world was tipping just too much to take any more. The loss of the plantation he'd lived on most of his life, the desert trek, the Indian attack; the beating at the dress shop. Now the specter of losing Jersey was just more than he could handle.

So she tried to settle him down. "Okay, Moon. You just go on and sing somethin', make you feel better."

Moon lowered his arm, troubled by his own unprecedented threat of violence. "Don't much feel like singin'."

They stared at each other a long moment, then silently went back to work.

Sunday found Clayton circling the massive Cathedral from a distance. Gaily decorated churchgoers congregated around the front steps, entering for services as they mingled in their piety. Here rich and poor, high and low gathered by the hundreds in their glorification of Christ. But not like a dour New England Protestant Sabbath, or a Virginia teetotaling event. In Matamoros God's day of rest was about relaxation and vitality—like a New Orleans Sunday, a day God made for man. Unlike Good Friday, when the effigy of Jesus was put in a gold coffin, and kneeling *senoras* howled like all *los lloronas* wailing for their dead children—that was a day God made for women.

Father Clos, in his purple robes, greeted them all. Clayton saw Catherine, Cortina, Quintero, Tinbury, even Scully, which surprised Clayton, who'd assumed Scully to be as Godless as any he'd ever known. But the young diva, Claire, was on Scully's arm, so for them this was more likely mating ritual than homage to God.

When Clayton reached the back of the cathedral, he entered the small doorway reserved for outcasts. It led down a cool, dark hall, past several closed doors, to a *serape* hanging on the wall. This he pulled aside, revealing a doorway low enough that it forced anyone entering to bow; a kind of compulsory humility that only made Clayton want to act rude. Leonard Pierce sat in a pew facing a gilt Crucifix on the wall, its wood-carved, bloody Christ casting eyes heavenward in agonized confusion.

"I never understood how people can find serenity through meditations on a mortally tortured man," said Clayton.

"Not mortal, if you're a believer. Which I am, most sincerely."

"Then please explain how His eternal suffering can possibly give me peace." Clayton sat down in the pew behind Pierce.

"To understand that, it's necessary to open your heart—which I cannot recommend you do until after the war is over. We need men with hardened souls if we're going to win."

"Glad I can be of service." Clayton's tone was droll, against Pierce's cynicism.

But Pierce was all business now. "I de-encrypted the message you intercepted. It's from a Southern spy, for delivery to Jose Quintero, as you said. Says the Union invasion of Texas is to come by sea, at the Sabine Pass on September 8."

"Up the Sabine River? Why that snaky little stream? Why not go right for Galveston? That's what the omnibus boy at Antoine's heard. That's what makes sense."

"The Sabine's got a fort. Once we take that it's a short march to Galveston's back door." He handed a pamphlet back over his shoulder to Clayton. "This is the Confederate naval codebook I used to decipher the note. Let Isaac have it."

"To forge a document?"

Pierce nodded. "Have him write Quintero a new message, saying the invasion is by land, crossing the Louisiana border in early September. I'll want that codebook back when you're done, it shouldn't really leave my office. But these are extraordinary times."

Clayton felt the weight of great war secrets on his shoulders, not to mention the presence of Allison Stoneman filling all the otherwise unoccupied corners of his mind. Extraordinary times, indeed.

After leaving Pierce, Clayton ran into Father Clos outside the back of the Cathedral. Wilkes usually tried to avoid the man, who generally wanted to corral him into a Mass or a tithe, but he didn't see a way out now.

"Bless you, my son. Are you coming to Mass?"

"No, *Padre*, I have important gamblin' and other sins to conduct this mornin'."

"You try so hard to be *vilain*," smiled Clos, who was French, "but I know one day you will return to the church of your mother."

"What are you doin' at the servants' entrance now, ignorin' your flock?" Clayton hoped if the priest felt poked, he'd retreat inside and leave Clayton to his godless life.

"A humble priest must serve his back door supplicants, as well. *Non?*" He nodded over Clayton's shoulder. Wilkes turned to see four lepers, shrouded in muslin. Father Clos continued, "All God's children deserve the sacrament. Even you."

Clayton cast a glance at the nearest leper—earless, three-fingered, like a wraith in a dream—and he shivered, wondering what piece of himself was missing, at this gathering of outcasts. But he just walked away, unsettled and unsaved.

Without exactly meaning to, Clayton found himself standing outside Allie's new office—he'd learned of its location through his grapevine of informants. But now that he was here, he just stood staring at it, wondering if this was a smart move. His intention, if he had one, was to be an adult about this accidental crossing of paths. They had lives of their own now, and little would be served in holding a grudge, or even a harsh memory. Best way to fill this hole gnawing at him was to face it—face it with Allie—and write it off to old debt. Even laugh about it, in time; even become friendly again, it wasn't out of the question. But in any case, put the past behind and move on. So in he went.

In the front room two Colored workers were snapping at each other like an old married couple. The older one, a gawky man with big ears, carefully lettered a long wooden sign in black paint: STONEMAN TRADEWORKS AND PHOTOGRAPHY. At Clayton's entrance the young girl pulled herself into a haughty posture.

"Moon know his letters and didn't steal 'em neither, he learnt 'em fair and square."

"Then you ought to get him to teach you, too. You look like you could pick it up pretty quick, you ask me."

"I could learn if I wanted to."

Moon glanced at her sternly, then back to Clayton. "Jersey don't mean no offense, sir." He knew Jersey wasn't afraid of insulting a white man, so he often bent over backwards excusing her.

"He can see I don't mean no offense, Moon. He white, not stupid."

That did seem a little offensive to Clayton, but he let it slide. Moon filled the uncomfortable silence. "Miz Stoneman in the back room, if that's who you lookin' for."

As Clayton entered the next room, leaving Jersey and Moon behind in a tense whispering campaign, he found Allie hunched under a black apron, focusing her camera on something outside the window. A moment later she flipped the cloth up over her head, stood, turned, and jumped with a small "Ooh," to find Clayton standing there.

"Sorry, Allie, I didn't mean to scare you."

"You didn't. I was just surprised, is all. How on earth did you know I was here?"

"Some little gopher told me at church this mornin'."

"I don't believe you were at church. But you can help me bless one of God's creatures right here, if you please." And before she could remember how angry she was with him, she pointed out the window at a large white bird with gray wings, sitting in a glasspaper tree, motionless as paint and nearly invisible amidst the white flowers. "Poor thing looks scared to death, which is why it's so still I can get a perfect photograph." She gave him a look of pride mixed with excitement.

"Collared dove in an Anacua tree, what that is. Cousin to *les pigeons de guerre*."

"Like your mama's War Pigeons, I remember when you told me…"

She stopped. Cancelled her smile at the word "remember." She'd lost recollection of this man for many a year. He was hardly a ghost in her mind, certainly not supposed to be mixed up in her Mexican adventure, so full of promise, as he himself had once been. But now he was just as dead in her heart as her husband, her mother, her sister and brothers. "This is my new life, Clay. I don't want you in it."

A hollow opened in the pit of his stomach, like an ache, like an old grief recalled; just a feeling. But feelings were something from another time; he'd forsaken feelings for purpose long ago. And then substituted emptiness into the place purpose held, emptiness surrounded by carapace. And now a crack in that shell, a whiff of something through the crack. Like Allie's lavender perfume that had distracted him in the opera house last night. Like a dream half remembered.

He sensed this all of a piece, in the time it takes to catch breath. Then he nodded to her and left without a word, not trusting himself to speak.

*　*　*

Clay went back to his gambling hall, sat at the bar with a bourbon, feeling sideways about most everything. Milagra could see how out of sorts he was, so she brought him a plate of rice and beans with an eye-weeping hot sauce.

"*Ahora tienes una razon para llorar,*" she told him with a sympathetic scold, and walked away. Now you have a reason to cry.

"*Solo una razon para despedirte.*" Only a reason to fire you.

Barkeep Jim walked up, looking frustrated. "I tried tellin' Rheumy your story about the corpse in the snow, but he wouldn't even let me finish. Said nobody can smell a corpse in a blizzard. I said that's the joke, that's why it's funny. He said didn't sound funny to him. So *you* tell him, you tell it better, then you could finish the end of it, too."

Clayton looked at him blankly and went back to eating. Jim walked off in a huff.

A minute later Teddy sat down beside him, in uniform but apparently off duty. "You appear to be in low spirits," she said. "Anything I can do?"

Clayton looked at her—half woman, half man, probably feeling for him what he was trying to avoid feeling for Allie. Clayton and Teddy, hearts asunder. "You know better than most," he said, "we all pretend to be somethin' we're not. Then you run up against who you are, sometimes, it's a smack in the face."

"You know all about *my* false claims. Tell me one of yours."

He smiled bitterly. "My claim to knowin' what the hell I'm doin'."

"Well ain't we the Liars' League," she grinned in conspiracy.

Clayton's attention was drawn to Isaac breaking up a fight at a pool table. After he threw the brawlers out, he glanced over at Clayton, who signaled him upstairs. Clayton patted Teddy's arm—comrade spies in exile—and went up to join Isaac.

In his study, Isaac gingerly patted a round bruise on his neck. "While I was keeping my eyes on the man with the pool cue, the man asleep behind the table rose up behind me holding the 4 ball. I didn't see him, but I felt my neck hairs rise up like little soldiers. That's when he whacked me. There is a lesson in this."

"I'm sure you'll come up with some historical tale to enlighten us. But right now I'd like you to put away your fables and take up your manly art of calligraphy once more." Clayton handed him Pierce's codebook. "Don't make it look too pretty, though." Clayton explained what was needed—a coded message to Quintero outlining a nonexistent Union land assault, to divert Southern forces away from the Sabine Pass just at the moment they were needed there most by the Confederacy.

"Ugly calligraphy is not really my *metier*," Isaac said.

"Don't use foreign words as a hobble to try resistin' my orders."

Isaac feigned arrogance. "As your superior officer, I need no such hobble."

"You are hardly my superior."

"*Captain* Wilkes—as a Major in the 1st Rhode Island Colored Volunteers, I…"

"An infantry unit not yet recognized officially by the U.S. Army."

"But will be in two months, by order of President Lincoln, now that the 54th Massachusetts Colored has Charleston surrounded."

"Then in two months you may refuse my order. Until then, write the fake damn code letter and hold on to your '*metier*' for your personal projects…Major."

Isaac tossed off a casual salute. "Yes, suh. And you're dismissed, Captain."

Clayton got gone. He'd have to ask Ambassador Pierce to get him promoted in the next two months, so he wouldn't have to take any more guff from Isaac.

Captain Solomon was alone and afoot, having left the crew of the *Bucanneer* in Bagdad with grog money for a few days, while his ship was in dry-dock for repairs. He'd borrowed a 35-foot Jamaica sloop from a friend and sailed it up the Laguna Madre. It drew just six feet of water, a favorite small ship of pirates, with a sleek hull and a topsail that could pull eleven knots in a good wind. Solomon took it now for luck, and for continuity with the long privateering line of his mother's family. He often felt he'd been born a hundred years too late, for the day of the buccaneer was over. Blockade running was the best he could do. That, and this little side show seeking old treasure.

After a couple days easing in and out of inlets, he at last stood on a hillock near the center of Padre Island, gazing over the terrain. Dark clay loam, covered in bluestem grass, it was unremarkable in all respects—except for one gnarled oak, bent over from some long ago injury of wind or wave. But when he saw that oak, his pulse ticked up.

He looked at his tattered map in the red hues of the lowering sun, wondering if this was finally the spot he wanted. The hill, the tree, the position of the sunset on this date. He unstrapped the shovel from his back and approached the crippled tree.

The map had been in his family since the death of the pirate, Jean Lafitte. Descended from a branch of Sephardic Jews expelled from Spain in 1492, Lafitte's ancestors settled in France. He emigrated to New Orleans, fought for the Americans against the British in 1812 and went on to rule a pirate colony. As it happened, Captain Solomon's mother was part of the same clan. Scotland branch. Solomon was orphaned at 14, with a single inheritance. Lafitte's treasure map, bequeathed by his mother—provenance enough for Ryburn. He went to sea, first as a cabin boy, eventually graduating to captain. Now he had his own ship and did damn well what he pleased.

The only problem with the map was, it didn't identify which island the loot was buried on. He'd searched all over Galveston, around New Orleans, the dunes of Point Isabel and the coves of Padre Island. So far, no luck. But as he reached the withered oak, the sun settled and the bats came out, feasting on clouds of dusk mosquitos as they dipped wildly in the air, brushing him with their wings. It felt like a benediction.

Captain Solomon put shovel to sand and dug.

CHAPTER 8

T HE MATAMOROS RACETRACK WAS as famous as its Opera House, but considerably more boisterous. People came to gamble on the ponies, dressing up or down according to the same rules around the world that encouraged lowlifes, high rollers and rich snobs to rub shoulders and bandy money turfside. The stands were 100 yards long, five tiers supported by Greek columns. Box seats clustered at the finish line on the lower levels, while the announcer perched on the top, calling the races through a bullhorn. Behind the bleachers were betting windows, bars, saddle shops and food stalls, while facing the seating was a red dirt track; all of it smelling like dust, horseshit, cigars and beer.

A thousand people milled around awaiting the next race as Clayton made his way past the betting windows and out to the track itself, where the assembled were bantering and laughing. Many leaned against the rail for a good close look when the horses thundered past. Hundreds more sat in the stands, the women holding parasols against the sun, the men holding drinks against their losses.

The horses gathered at the starting line with their jockeys and owners as bets exchanged hands, money like the fluttering wings of colorful birds. A camel wandered across the track. They were stabled here at the end of their cotton caravans down the desert. Then they'd get loaded up with tons of salt mined from the Great Salt Lake 50 miles north, and trek it back up the Wild Horse to Camp Verde. Some fool tried to wrangle this beast off the track, but it bit him in the head with its huge mouth, crushed his skull, and he fell down dead. Someone shot the camel, and both bodies got dragged off the track.

Clayton scanned the box seats for Quintero but didn't see him. As he walked around with eyes on the crowd, however, he came across Ned, the Limey who'd been retaken by ship's law at the Kingston Bar while he danced his drunken jig. He was besotted again.

"Ned!" Clayton shouted above the crowd din.

"I know you," Ned returned the address with a twinkle in his eye. "You run the Brave River, and it's a fair drink you pour."

"That I do. But I also bought you a bottle of gin at the Kingston Bar and you got dragged away by the mate for jumpin' ship. How the hell are you back in port? I thought you'd be keelhauled by now."

Ned closed up beside Clayton, offering a confidence to this half-friend who'd once bought him drink. "I paid the bugger off," he whispered loudly. "Now I'm well and sassy drunk, and goddammed if I'm goin' back to that mealy ship."

"How'd you ever scrounge up enough cash to buy off the First Mate?"

Ned offered a crafty smile as he withdrew a gold coin from his pocket. "It's a dubloon," he said with a whiskey breath. "They go a long way if you stretch 'em out."

"'They?' How many of these do you have?" Clayton examined it as closely as he was allowed. It looked real. "And where did you come by them, if I might ask?"

"There's all manner o' salvage if you…oh, shite."

Clayton looked across the green, where Ned's eyes were aimed— to see a pack of *zocalo* dogs rummaging through the crowd for scraps. "What's the matter, Ned?"

"Those hounds. I don't like 'em in packs, but I specially don't like that big black one. He's lookin' for me." He turned away, then stopped cold again. "Oh, double shite."

From the other direction Clayton saw the same ship's mate who'd cornered Ned in the bar, now forging through the crowd toward them, truncheon in hand.

Ned took off into the stands, far faster than Clayton would have thought possible, the pursuing officer hard on his track. The dogs got chased off by a trainer with a whip, and Clayton went back to searching for Quintero, who he finally saw at a long table of silversmithed work.

Clayton meandered over, and with casual sleight of hand eased Isaac's forged note into Quintero's jacket. "That's the message I got from the Kingston Bar."

"You got it decoded?"

"Sad to say, my man was unable. I'm hopin' you have books to decipher such."

Quintero nodded and left as six horses rumbled past, kicking up dirt clods while the crowd roared. That's when Clayton saw Allie on Jessup's arm, cheering her horse. Clayton winced. The woman was turning up everywhere in his life suddenly, like a recurring dream. Or was he just dreaming it all now, and any minute he'd wake up in a sweat? Or maybe she was following him. Here to seek revenge, to unmask his current deceits in retribution for his past ones. He wondered if he'd have to skip town to escape her reach. But no, by God. He had a life here. If she didn't like it, she could leave.

He watched Jessup tear up his ticket and throw the pieces into the air as Allie laughed joyously. For the moment, it seemed, she was oblivious to Clayton's existence, which felt like the unkindest cut of all. The sight of her, so affectionate with Jessup, so carefree, squeezed Clayton's heart more than he expected; so he headed home alone.

Allie hadn't seen Clayton arrive, but she did see him leaving. The sight put a little cinch in her gut, which annoyed her. Why that man's appearance, at this late date, should even register, more than any of the thousand other strangers here at the track, was an aggravation she didn't intend to feed. So she looped her arm through Jessup's. "Care to go for a stroll along the river to cool down our overheated blood?" she asked.

"I don't mind."

"You've been such an angel in need to me. Gettin' me through the desert, findin' me General Bee's *hacienda*, locatin' my studio—I hate to ask for somethin' more."

"Go ahead, ask. Maybe I'll say no." He gave her a wink.

"I was hopin' maybe you could find me a permanent place to live… Ahotay."

He startled every time he heard his given name come out of her mouth. No one had called him that since childhood. In a public setting like this it was…intimate.

"I'll surely look around for you…Allie."

She squeezed his arm and they walked the rest of the way to the river in a comfortable silence, a sense of buoyant confusion running down Jessup's spine.

But Allie wasn't confused. Just setting a course of action and giving herself to the moment.

In her only flowered dress Jersey slid in the front door of Brave River, staying flat against the wall, trying to blend in to the woodwork. She'd never been to a place like this, she didn't know how to act, and was afraid she'd do something wrong. She just stood there for the longest time, taking it all in with big eyes and a galloping heartbeat.

One old *vaquero* stumbled over, put his hand on her thigh and offered her a peso to go out in the alley with him, but she batted his hand away so wildly he got scared himself and made his way back to the bar. She was just about to bolt after that but Isaac saw her, took her gently to a table and brought her a lemonade.

"Mrs. Stoneman know you're here?" She shook her head. "You looking for honest work?" She nodded. He nodded back, studying her seriously. "What can you do?"

"Everything."

"That's what most of the men here are like to think, you keep wearing pretty dresses like that." She cast her eyes down shyly. He patted her hand. "I'll get you suited up proper, you can sweep out the rooms each morning and clean the tables when they go empty. Payday is every Friday, for work done. That sound all right to start?"

She nodded again. Gave him a tentative smile.

"You look about Little Andy's size, he's the quiet-hours barkeep. I'll get you a change of his clothes and you can start this afternoon."

"I kin start now." There was that defiance he'd seen in her at Delgado's shop.

"I guess you can," he said. He got a broom from the corner and handed it to her. "When you're done with that, you can help Hermano. He's the simple fellow smiling in the corner, pumping water up to the roof. You introduce yourself and give him a hand. Sometimes he just gets lonely, so if you see that, go sit with him. He likes to be talked to. And the cook is Milagra, she may ask you to fetch vegetables from time to time."

With a grin from cheek to cheek, Jersey began to sweep.

As Isaac left her to her work and started out the door, his eyes were drawn to a fascinating sight. Harley, the Opera House janitor, was standing at the far wall peeking behind the bar sinister coat-of-arms Isaac had painted. He was about the last man imaginable to engage in some kind of intrigue. Isaac walked up.

"What are you looking for, Harley?"

"Nothin'." He stuck out a petulant chin. "Thought I saw a critter run up behind this here picture." They stared at each other, Harley sullen, Isaac neutral.

"Let's go talk to Mr. Wilkes." He extended his hand toward the stairs. Harley didn't move. Isaac took his arm, gentle but brooking no debate. "Please, Mr. Harley, sir. I believe Mr. Wilkes wishes a word with you and I wouldn't want to keep him waiting."

Harley shook his shoulders out and walked upstairs, Isaac two steps behind. They stood outside Clayton's office as Isaac knocked twice and opened the door enough to usher Harley inside. Clayton looked surprised.

"You have some interesting war talk from the Opera House for me, Harley?"

Isaac stood between Harley and the door. "The gentleman was looking behind the *Polecatus* bar sinister, Mr. Wilkes."

"If your boy's talkin' 'bout that wood picture downstairs, I weren't hurtin' it none. He's lyin' if he says otherwise."

Clayton could see how scared the meager fellow was. Caught between fear of two men—whoever it was paid him to find what lay behind the coat-of-arms, and the man who stood before him now, his ongoing benefactor, Clayton.

"I don't think you hurt the shield, Harley. I think you do want to tell me who sent you to look at it, though."

Harley shook his head. "Naw sir, he didn't...I mean I don't...I mean I..."

"Let me show you my French doves," said Clayton, standing. He exited his room and walked up to the roof, Isaac encouraging Harley to follow. When they got there Harley was mesmerized, if confused, by the sight of the cage full of cooing pigeons. "Those are my particular eatin' fowl," Clayton went on. "I raise 'em like my French mama taught me, to make a special dish called *coq au vin*. Ever hear o' that fine dish?"

"Naw, sir, I ain't."

"The birds taste better when they grow up at a great height above the earth, like this. Closer to heaven. We're pretty high up now, don't you think?" He walked Harley to the edge of the roof. Nearly sixty feet above the hardpack below; the distant terrain visible for miles: the cacti, the river, the sandy hills, the infinite sky.

Harley tried to back away from the edge, but Clayton held him there. "I know you're lyin', Harley."

"No, I..."

"That's all right, I'm not angry. I know the pressure you're under. This fella mighta paid you good money to snoop around my place. Or maybe he scared you with a weapon. I know how you hate violence." Clayton let the derringer at his belt show.

"Please, Mr. Wilkes..." Harley looked pitiable.

"Just tell me who he was, son. Who put you up to this?" He pulled Harley forward until the man's thin-soled shoes hung over the lip of the roof. "Don't disappoint me now. Remember who takes care of you, even when you have nothin' for me."

Harley's eyes were watery as pools of black tea. "I never met him before, Mr. Wilkes. Don't know his name. Supposed to meet him tomorrow night in Bagdad, with whatever I found behind that wood picture on your wall downstairs."

"What time? Where exactly?"

"Little hut off the back room at Zilley's, Cap'n. Late. He said knock twice, then twice again. What I'm gonna tell him now?" Despair filled his voice.

"Not a thing, Harley." Clayton pulled him back from the edge. "You can keep the money he gave you. I'll let him know it's all right when I see him tomorrow."

"You gonna see him?"

"So you don't have to. I'll take care of it. You just take care of yourself. Go on home, now. And I'll remember you kept yourself honest with me." Clayton nodded at Isaac, who took Harley by the arm and led him back downstairs.

When they got down to the casino Harley yanked his arm away from Isaac and turned cold eyes on him. "Don't you be thinkin' you're better'n me just 'cause you got Cap'n Wilkes payin' you regular." Then he stumbled out the door, still trembling.

Isaac tolerated crackers like Harley, but generally felt more pity than hate. They'd always find someone else to fear or resent for causing their misery, instead of seizing their own destiny; they were their own damned slaves. Something about this interaction put a different feeling in Isaac's heart, though. Something between despair and elation, like a scary new thought he didn't want to look at. But he'd have to chew on it.

* * *

Captain Ryburn Solomon had been on the verge of abandoning the dig when his shovel hit something hard, four feet down. Not rock hard, but teak hard, or mahogany hard. He scraped away a foot of clay to reveal what looked like old, weathered wood. Yet as he drew his palm across the exposed surface, it felt denser than wood; almost soapstone in consistency. By morning he'd excavated away enough dirt to display a four-foot long, one foot wide, flat brown surface. Odd shape for a chest full of Spanish gold, and it didn't sound hollow to his knocking. When he pried it up and out of the deep hole he found it wasn't a box. Nothing like that. It was a huge leg bone.

Long, with rounded cleft ends for bending at the joints. Similar in shape to critter legs Solomon knew. He'd taken a caravan up the Wild Horse Desert once, to escort the arms shipment he'd brought in. He'd seen a thousand bones scattered across that waste. Bones of men, horses, cattle. But this bone was easily four times the size of any of those and hard as rock, to boot. Thigh bone, it looked like, from some enormous, outlandish manner of steer, or bison. But how was that possible?

Bison with a thigh bone this big would have to be ten feet tall, eighteen feet long. A monster with bones of raw granite, or…or a great animal god. Were the Aztec gods real, as some of his *mestizo* friends believed? Could those ancient deities have migrated up here to die when the great Aztec kingdom withered under Spanish rule? It took Solomon's breath away to think of it; to contemplate the massive stony bone lying before him in the sand. This could be the sacred relic of a once powerful people, the evidence of an elemental Spirit. It left him in awe.

When he leaned down to touch it he saw the ragged corner of another artifact sticking out of the hole. He scraped away until it pulled free. It was half a lower jaw bone, almost three feet long, with one big, flat tooth. It made him dizzy just to hold it. This wasn't the treasure he'd been seeking, but riches of another kind. Ryburn Solomon was the keeper of sacred magic now.

He spent hours more digging, exploring the gravesite, unearthing several fragments and one more large piece: a broken horn, six feet long and vicious. The entire span of both horns could have been close to fifteen feet. The horn of an angry god. A God of Wrath, a God of Power. Solomon felt afraid.

But what was he to do now? He couldn't bring the holy relics back to his ship. Couldn't let the crew know, couldn't let the treasures fall into Union hands if he got boarded. Maybe icons such as these had special powers. Maybe the course of the war lay in his hands. He had to give careful thought to how he proceeded from now on.

He put all the big bones but the horn back in their tomb and refilled it, packing the clay hard. The next rain would wash away the traces.

Soon he'd return with a cart and take the magical tokens back to a proper crypt. He didn't know why he was meant to find these remains; he just knew it was a sign.

As sunset came he knew what he'd do. He'd take the horn to his Zuni friend, Shalako, a man on good terms with the spirit world. He'd given Solomon good advice in the past; maybe he could help out now. Until then, Ryburn needed to be careful who he told about his giant stone bones. They were holy relics, easily stolen for profit. And in times of war all men were scavengers. They only varied in the nature of their feast.

Leonard Pierce had a safe house at the edge of one of the *barrios*, a way station for escaped Union POW's, runaway slaves, and Confederate deserters. They all knew from the grapevine they could get a meal and a contact name there—someone who could lead them to deeper cover. But Clayton knew of an outside root cellar door to a private room where true secrets could be left for Pierce; a basement to which only Pierce and a trusted few had access. This is where Clayton stopped now, to get the naval codebook back to him. But it was with some surprise that Clayton found him here now, talking in low tones to the insurrectionist, Juan Cortina.

"I didn't mean to interrupt," said Clayton. "I only came by to leave you somethin'."

"We were just finishing up," said Pierce. Then, to Cortina: "*Adios.*"

Cortina looked insulted to be dismissed so easily, but simply left without introduction, crooning his personal folksong on the way out. "*Cuando los Americanos duermen, Cortina visita sus suenos…*"

"Man sounds crazy," said Clayton.

"Yes," said Pierce. "But a useful ally."

Cortina suddenly jumped back down the steps in a crouch, like a wild animal, shouted at them in Spanish, then strolled back up the stairs singing, and was gone.

Pierce translated. "He said he might be *loco*, but he'll live forever in his song, while you and I will die like dogs without memory."

Clayton shrugged and handed Pierce the codebook, confirming

he'd given Quintero the false dispatch to keep the Rebs unprepared for the 5000 Yanks who were set to land by gunship at Fort Sabine on September 8. Pierce outlined three diversionary plans in motion: drawing Rebel troops away from Galveston by stirring up Comanche trouble around Fort Worth; pretending to invade at Lafayette; and tying up the Rebs here at Fort Brown with an attack across the river, combining Pierce's private army of runaways and escaped POW's with Cortina's nationalist *banditos*.

They toasted a speedy end to the war and Clayton went back to Brave River. Seeing him enter, Isaac got a bottle of rum, two glasses, and sat at an empty table.

Clayton joined him. "I'm goin' to Bagdad tonight to meet Harley's connection."

Isaac nodded as he poured them two fingers of rum. "I've decided not to go back to America after the South loses, which it must—which will open Pandora's Box."

"Why must it lose?" This was the question that interested Clay more than Pandora's box.

"Because the white men who wrestled this country to ground have deluded themselves too dearly. They will never accept the black man as their equal. They will lord their imaginary superiority over us for a thousand years." His mouth twisted bitterly. "Somehow watching Harley tonight lifted a veil from my eyes and I could see what Pandora saw. She was given a box that said 'Do Not Open,' but she opened it anyway, and all the demons flew into our hopeless world. War, Pestilence, Greed, Hate, all filled the land. But at the end, one last little creature flew out of the box, too. That was Hope."

"And what did you learn from that?"

"Hope flew south. After the war I'm going to stay south of the border and start my own colony. That's my last little creature." He downed his rum and left.

As Clayton finished his drink he noticed a young black janitor in work clothes sweeping near the back door. Not a big surprise—he and Isaac frequently took in waifs—but there was something familiar in this orphan's face, or stance, or...he realized it was Allie's young girl house slave, dressed as a man. Same one he'd seen arguing with the sign painter at Allie's studio. So what was she doing here?

He walked over to her. "Jersey is what I think your man called you. Does Mrs. Stoneman know you're here?"

The girl stiffened. "No, sir, and I don't have to tell her neither. Ain't no slaves in Mexico and I a free woman now." She looked defiant, ready for a fight. Clayton saw her fingers grip around the broom handle.

"All right, that's a fact. Isaac hire you?"

She paused, trying to calculate if this was a trap being laid for her—then nodded.

"Isaac's a good man. He runs this place with me. If he took you on, then there must be somethin' about you he regards highly." He put his hand on her back with a warmth that calmed most women he knew. "In which case, so do I."

Her nod was almost imperceptible. "I'll do my best by y'all."

"'Maybe you can even get old curmudgeon Isaac to teach you a little readin'.'"

Her smile grew. Across the room, tuning his cigar box fiddle, Captain Solomon watched them as Clayton said something to her, patted her on the back and headed upstairs. Solomon smiled too. On a captain's ship, even the cabin boy must be treated with respect. It increased his good feeling about Clayton another notch. He plucked out a tune on the cigar box, making up words as he went. *The gambler bowed to the scullery maid, and bid farewell, his anchor weighed...*"

Jersey swept a little harder now, proud that her good work had been recognized by Clayton. But as she swept out the hall for the third time that day she was aware of another fellow staring at her from a corner table. Not the kind of recognition she wanted, not like the owner's gentle appreciation. It made her uncomfortable, so she kept looking away. But whenever she looked back, he was still staring.

She had to get near his table to finish sweeping that corner, and when she did, he motioned her over.

"Cain't stop, I'm workin', sir,"

"You can talk while you sweep, can't you?" said Tinbury.

Jersey didn't want to get in trouble with a customer, but wanted to do her job well too. "I can listen while I sweep," she said. She didn't give much.

And though Tinbury was no great lover of the Negro people, he saw something in her that caught his curiosity. She was hesitant, but unafraid; she wasn't uppity, but she didn't cower, either. And she was hardly bigger than a child. She might be just the person the Honorable Mr. Pierce had asked Tinbury to keep an eye out for.

"I was just admiring the job you were doing here and wondered if you'd like to do more purposeful work for a tidier sum."

"This work got purpose. Purpose to clean the floor."

"How'd you like a job helping to free all the slaves?"

"Mr. Lincoln already done that."

"On paper, yes he did. I'm talking about this world on earth where you and I live. How'd you like to help do for the Southern States what they always done to you?"

She stopped sweeping. "Whatchu talkin' 'bout?"

He showed her his diplomatic badge. "This says I work for Mr. Lincoln. I think you can help us. If you come with me, I'll show you how." He stroked his juvenile mustache; a nervous habit. "I imagine Isaac gave you this job. He'll vouch for me."

She wrestled with mixed emotions for a few moments; then laid up her broom in the corner and stood straight. "If Isaac like you, I guess you okay. Now who I have to kill?"

CHAPTER 9

CLAYTON GOT OFF THE paddleboat in Bagdad after midnight. Scores of bonfires lit the shoreline, one of them consuming a small, beached boat that people were dancing around. He walked past them to the town proper, where torches lit the way through a maze of mud-sticky streets lined by shacks. Unconscious or dead bodies filled the shadows, intermingled with trysting couples or illicit commerce. A fecal smell was sometimes so strong Clayton gagged or mouth-breathed until some beneficent sea breeze diluted the stench. He saw three uniformed police beat a man to death, take all the money from his pockets and roll him into a ditch. Bagdad Sunday night.

He walked along oceanside planking for a short time before turning again into the belly of the beast—where something unexpected caught his eye in a moonlit alley. A familiar figure he couldn't place at first, until the man's posture and beard gave him away. It was Simon Wachtel… doing what? Running down a story? Some piece of corruption in city government? Clayton began walking toward him; but stopped when another man emerged from a doorway, stood before Simon…and Simon kissed him.

Could it be Teddy, looking for male companionship somewhere she wouldn't be recognized? No. It was Jensen, the young printer's devil. Clayton watched as their embrace grew more passionate, Wachtel turning Jensen's back to the wall, then Jensen doing the same, all the time locked in a long kiss. Until they stumbled together through the door Jensen had just come from, and disappeared.

The sight of the tryst glued Clayton to the spot. It put a lot of things into a different perspective—the arguments he'd seen them have at the shop, the praise, the glances—but Clayton wasn't sure how to grasp it, a liaison like this between his kind old friend and the swaggering young deserter. So he put it out of his mind for the time being. He had more important issues to focus on now.

He found the ramshackle structure that was Zilley's—identified by a broken sign with only the *Z* left intact. Inside was an opium den—a warren of rooms packed with sailors, businessmen and languid women lying on pallettes, serviced with pipes by Chinese men. The sweet smell of poppy tar smoked the air. So dark it was hard to see, Clayton made his way more by feel until he got to a closed door in a back room. He opened it and stepped outside, crossing the alley to a tilted shack of driftwood and canvas. He knocked twice. Then twice again, as Harley had instructed.

The door opened at minimal pressure and Clayton entered. At a table across the room, lit by a small candelabra, sat a man pointing a gun at him. Clayton took a step forward into the yellowed light of an oil lamp.

"That's about far enough. Where's Harley?"

"He took ill. Asked me to come."

"I guess you'll do." The man pulled the candles closer to his own face. It was Dupree. The courier Clayton had "killed" at Brave River a few weeks ago with a derringer and a pig's-blood pouch.

"Thought you were supposed to be dead and gone, old son," said Clayton.

"Not quite gone, not yet. Couldn't show my face in Matamoros, though, account everyone thinks I'm dead. So I had to hole up in this stinkpot town. Not sure I wouldn't rather be all the way in the ground."

"So you sent poor simple Harley to check on the classified I put in the paper."

"Harley wouldn't've been my first choice, but my options were limited, as you can imagine. I lay low for your sake, mostly—anybody saw I wasn't dead, they'd knowed you didn't kill me, so you must be a Southern agent."

"Appreciate the consideration."

"What'd you do with the note I gave you for Quintero?"

"It was all smudged, I had to get it figured out. Took me to the Kingston Bar and a hidden message, all coded up."

"Only Quintero was supposed to get that message, no one else. How'd you come to find it?" He was trying to sound curious, but it came off as suspicious.

"You let river water get up your dentures, it smudged the writin' on your note. So Quintero gave it back to me to get it deciphered. That took me to a note at the Kingston Bar, said the Union invasion is comin' by land at Lafayette."

"That ain't what it said."

Dupree was right. That's not what the bastard coat-of-arms coded message said. It said the invasion was by sea. But the only way Dupree could have known that was if he'd been there at its encoding. And since Clayton lied about the contents—and Dupree knew he was lying—Dupree had to know Clayton was a double agent.

"You're a damn Yankee spy, ain't you?"

"Why would you think that?" Clayton tried to sound nonchalant, though by now they were both just trying to figure how this was going to play out.

"I pretty much figured whoever put that ad in the paper was a spy, musta intercepted the code and tryin' to pull whoever wrote it into a trap."

"And you wrote it."

"And you caught me."

Now they both knew what they both knew: for Dupree to give Quintero the true site of the Union invasion—or for Clayton to stop him—one of them had to die.

Clayton leapt at the same moment Dupree's gun went off.

The bullet lodged in Clayton's calf as he wrapped his hands around Dupree's neck, knocking them both to the floor, along with the gun and the candelabra, which fell against the driftwood wall, quickly flaming high. It was a death struggle, nothing less. Clayton gouged Dupree's eye; Dupree stuck his thumb into Clayton's bullet hole.

But just as Dupree got a good grip on his knife, twisting it up toward Clayton's gut, a shape moved behind them, clubbing Dupree solidly in the head. Dupree slumped over, and out. Clayton sat up. The whole back wall was on fire now, illuminating Isaac's face even through Clayton's blurred vision.

"About time you showed up," Clayton said, his voice a bruised rasp.

"I wanted to let you best him on your own, if you could. I believe you might benefit from some self-confidence in the manly arts." He pulled Clayton to his feet. "But we better leave before the whole place burns."

Clayton limped out the back as Isaac dragged Dupree's body almost to the river and beyond sight of the flaming building, which volunteers were starting to douse with water buckets. If the wind picked up, half the town might burn. Some opium smokers were stumbling out to safety while the rest incinerated without ever waking up.

"Find out if he told anybody his suspicions before he came tonight."

Isaac knelt beside the still figure. Put his ear to Dupree's mouth. "Man's dead."

Clayton nodded. "Go on and send him home, then."

For the second time in as many weeks Isaac rolled Dupree into the river.

"I guess he did have two lives to give for his country," Clayton said as Dupree's corpse tumbled slowly in the current, toward the mouth of the river and out to sea.

Isaac examined Clayton's leg wound. "Lost you some blood."

He tore a strip from Clayton's shirt to tie a pressure dressing around the gunshot, which was bleeding freely. Isaac slung him over his shoulder, carried him to the two-horse wagon he'd driven here and flopped him down in back.

A woman Clayton had never seen before was curled up in the wagon—cowering, wide-eyed. Chinese. Her foot-bindings were burned away, the skin blackened by flame. Isaac had never seen feet crushed to that deformed size, though he'd read of the practice. The woman looked at Clayton. "I am Zhi Li," she said. "You take me."

Clayton nodded at Isaac and glanced back at the flaming buildings— three of them now—that crackled like demon fire, making Clayton twitch with an unremembered memory. Or was it a prevision, like the portents his mother told him he had? Isaac climbed on the bench seat, slapping those reins sharply across the animals' backsides. "You two step lively," he advised his horses. And they tore off down the muddy road like beasts in hot pursuit of Clayton's confused images, as he gratefully passed out.

When Clayton awoke, sunlight made the room bright with a lovely blue and red pattern reflected on the wall by the William Morris stained glass. So he was back in his office above the casino, on some kind of bed that had been set up here. And he was alive. He tried to get up, but a mighty pain careered down his leg. Oh, hell.

"I took a bullet from your leg," came Isaac's voice. "It nicked the…" He checked a large, open book he had propped by the bedside. "…popliteal vein. But I tied off the bleeding. Says here 'corruption of the wound' is what we have to guard against now."

Clayton peered down. Thick white bandages were stained by bloody serum. His entire leg throbbed with an excruciating combination of pain and numbness. He waved his hand at the surgical instruments on the table. "How'd this all come about?"

"That Yankee war surgeon we like is gone up to San Juan Potosi, to doctor the Juarez troops. I wouldn't trust a doctor whose politics I don't know treat you in this condition, so I borrowed a book and tools from the Brownsville Hospital, brought you back here and operated. Scully was asleep downstairs, I had him lend a hand."

"You studied up some first, I'm glad to see." Indicating the open medical text.

"You know Dr. Ellengill taught me the basics. I just needed some particulars. Don't know how long the real doc'll be gone to the mountains."

"Well. You're a damn poor healer if you haven't provided for some laudanum."

Isaac held up the bottle. "I borrowed this, too."

Allie was setting up a filing system to invoice her import buyers when Mildred Bee entered all in a rush. "I can only stay a moment, dear one, I'm late to my luncheon, but I just had to tell you—as I predicted, Hamilton is such a peacock, he can't wait to come here in full dress uniform for a sitting."

"How grand of you to coordinate that, Mildred."

"And of course once he does so, Consul Quintero will want to be photographed as well, and that pompous rascal Cortina will, too, he's quite a revolutionary hero to these people. In fact—why didn't I think of this before?—you must set up your camera at the Opera House for Independence Day."

"You think so?"

"Everyone will want a memento! It celebrates the Cry of Dolores, which is the speech the priest Hidalgo made in the town of *Dolores* in 1810 to throw off the yoke of Spanish tyranny. Dolores is such a pretty name, don't you think? It means pain, I believe. Or possibly sadness."

"Then I pity the girl who has to wear the name."

"I pity the whole Mexican people, if it comes to that. I know they feel the pain of America grabbin' up Texas and whatnot, and now France is after the rest of the country. Seems like they are forever destined to enslavement by some foreign power—but then slavery, as you know, is a subject I oughtn't to get into," she added confidentially.

It brought a shadow to Allie's face. "My house girl, Jersey, has disappeared."

"You think she's run off? Some do, here on the border."

"I can't believe she would. I'm more concerned she's dead in the river or stolen by some unsavory types."

"Miz Stoneman?" It was Moon in the doorway, upset.

"Yes, Moon, what is it?"

"Ma'am I wouldn't want you to worry no more'n you need to… but man at the blacksmith tell me Jersey gone to the gamblin' house for a job."

"Gamblin' house? What in the world does she know about that?"

"Don't know. Just a Colored man told us we could work there, and now I hear she went." There was a stunned silence as Allie digested this; then Moon continued. "But don't you worry none, I ain't goin'." He dipped his head and left.

Mildred put her hand over Allie's, a sisterly gesture. "It'll be a better life for her, bein' free. Won't be easier. But better. Better for you, too, not bein' a slave owner."

"How would you know about that? You own dozens of slaves your own self."

"Hamilton owns them, not I. I do what I can for them, and I'll work on Hamilton 'til the day I die, to help him understand the toll this business takes on his immortal soul."

"Sounds to me like your husband's fightin' a second front in his own house."

"Hamilton gives me free rein in matters of spirit, long as I'm no drag on his career. Rest assured I've made my feelin's on the subject of slavery well known to him. To his great credit, he loves me still. He's not a bad man, Allie. He's just of his place and time, as are we all."

Allie in fact had mixed feelings about owning slaves. She felt hurt by Jersey's going. But here was Mildred, her new best friend, making some sense. Though Mildred owned Negroes—well, her husband did—she didn't feel right about it. Yet she did feel comfortable with those contradictions. Allie had lived with many contradictions herself, over the years; so why not this one? It certainly wouldn't be the first time she'd changed who she was. And the notion of becoming a secret abolitionist at the back door of Dixie did have a touch of thrill appeal to her. But then would her businesses suffer?

"I'm sorry, I can see I've made you glum," said Mildred. "Tomorrow I'll introduce you to Catherine at the Opera House, and we'll make grand plans for the Independence Ball on the 16th. But for now I must be going."

"Where are you off to?"

"Oh, it's complicated. I was to meet Hamilton for lunch at the Miller Hotel, but he had to see Major Russell first, who was late comin' back from a visit to cheer up that Wilkes rapscallion, who's laid up from some brouhaha, so Hamilton..."

"Are you..." Allie interrupted with a thin smile, "are you referrin' to Clay Wilkes?"

Isaac finished treating the ragged hole in Clayton's calf with a diluted bleach solution and redressed it with a clean cotton bandage.

Wilkes gritted away the opiate-dulled pain. "Don't you know how to sew it up? I'da thought that was on the very next page o' your medical book."

"Best to leave it open, let the corruption drain."

Clayton stared out the window, hoping maybe the eternity of the Rio Grande's flowing waters would float his pain away, like burning leaves adrift on the surface. "For the love of God, Isaac, give me somethin' to do."

"You could run for congress. Be about as useful as any other politician and never have to leave the bed. Matter of fact in 40 A.D. Gaius Caesar, generally known as Caligula, tried to have his horse elected senator."

"What happened?"

"He was assassinated." Isaac sat down nearby and began reading the medical tome he'd pilfered from a surgeon's office at the hospital, as a knock on the door frame revealed Quintero standing there, with Claire, the flirty replacement diva, on his arm.

"I hear you have suffered an injury," said Quintero. "May I come in?"

"*Buenos Dias*, Agustin," Clayton motioned him forward. Quintero turned first to Claire. "Please remain here, precious one, we have a moment of business to transact." He went to Clayton's bedside, tipping his head at Isaac to indicate he wanted privacy. Isaac walked over to join Claire, who appraised him with a saucy eyebrow.

Quintero spoke in a whisper to Clayton. "I have deciphered the communique you gave me. The invasion comes by land at Lafayette and Shreveport early next month. I have advised General Bee to deploy his troops there. When you are recovered it would be helpful if you were to spread false information downstairs at your gambling hall—so the Yankees who drink there will believe we know nothing of their true plans."

"Manufacturin' belief is my speciality, Agustin. I once staked a claim on an empty cave and called it a gold mine. Then I got some friends to make counter-claims, we filed suits against each other, got court injunctions, had the cave sealed by the law. Then while the legal mess was gettin' sorted out I borrowed half a fortune from the banks, usin' the mine as collateral. Used to love foolin' the banks. Now it's the Yanks."

All at once Allie was elbowing her way into the room past Isaac and Claire. "Clay, my word, I heard you were injured, but this looks halfway serious." She hadn't expected to see him so diminished. When she turned away from his bandages she realized it was Ambassador Quintero beside her. "Mr. Quintero, how nice to see you again."

"It is an honor, Madame Stoneman."

His was an acquaintance she knew she had to deepen if she wanted to advance in Matamoros society; but not now. She turned back to Clay. "Are you in pain?"

He was not, at the moment. The bottles of laudanum and rye whiskey—both nearly empty—had cured him of any such grievances; and released most inhibitions of feeling as well. "Not in pain now that you're here, Allie." He gave her a dose of big moon eyes.

Which caught her up short. She realized that while it was an unanticipated panic of concern that had brought her here, she didn't care to express that to this man she once despised and latterly had succeeded in forgetting. She certainly didn't want to reveal any such notions in front of all these people. So she flipped the concern around to herself. "Jersey has gone missin'," she blurted out, deeply aggrieved. "Missin' for two days, as I'm sure you've heard."

He hadn't heard, exactly; he'd only seen the girl downstairs in the casino. But he didn't want to break the confidence of a runaway slave, even to Allie. "I'm sorry, no, I've been preoccupied."

Glancing at his wounded leg again made her feel foolish for even mentioning her own problems—until Quintero spoke gently, in the most solicitous of tones.

"And who is this Jersey, if I may ask?"

Reflexively Allie fell back on her default, tried and true role, the Plantation maiden in distress. "She is my house girl, sir. Of course, I've been beside myself, this town is so overrun with ruffians—but Moon finally told me she came *here*. For a *job*, of all things. As if taking care of me wasn't job enough." She shared this last as an aside to the room, with a self-deprecatory acknowledgement of her renowned task-driver credentials.

"Isaac will likely know her whereabouts, then," Clayton said, to spare Quintero the obligatory response. "We'll be sure to send her back if she's to be found—though you understand I can't promise she won't run again. That call of freedom, you know."

She cast him a chilly gaze. "I've already spoken with Isaac. He was of little help."

"Perhaps I can be of assistance," said Quintero. "If you gave me a description of the girl, I could make inquiries."

"Why, thank you, sir. It's so refreshing to know there are still gentlemen willing to put themselves out to help a lady."

Clay remembered her theatrics fondly. "Allie, perhaps the laudanum makes me too honest, but I've a mind if you traded in your Witherin' Southern Belle for the savvy businesswoman I know you to be, you could afford to hire replacements for your slaves. Hell, they might even hire on themselves."

She didn't appreciate his dressing-down in front of Quintero. In fact, it all came rushing back to her how annoying, how patronizing, how presumptuous Clayton Wilkes could be. "Have I told you lately, Clay, to go to hell?"

She left in a huff, bumping Isaac and Claire. At Allie's jostling, Claire grabbed Isaac for support, pressing against him just a bit more than absolutely necessary.

Quintero narrowed his eyes at Allie as she disappeared, and leaned in close to Clayton, more confidential than ever. "She has brass, this one. She is yours?"

"Not at all, Agustin. Have at her." He was loving pretty much everyone just now.

"And you, my friend, are welcome to the young lady I came with, Claire. She's grown tiresome, and I lack the patience." He stood erect, squeezing Clayton's arm in the manner of brothers. "Get well quickly. We need you back on the ramparts."

He walked to the door, elbow out for Claire to latch onto. She took it, casting fond glances at Isaac and Clayton; and made her exit with Quintero. Isaac walked to the bed.

"I think I'd better keep visitors at bay for the time being. You speak your mind a bit too loose under the influence of these surgical medications."

"Allie's girl-servant, Jersey—she still workin' for us downstairs?"

"Not any more. Tinbury recruited her. He's always on the lookout for runaway contraband to bring into Pierce's army."

"She's just a child."

"Nobody's just a child anymore."

Jersey stood quietly in Pierce's office where Tinbury had left her, as Pierce continued writing at his desk. Without looking up he said, "Mr. Tinbury tells me you're keen to help the Union defeat the Confederate States of America."

She didn't know if she was supposed to answer to his back. But she guessed a free woman could do what she damn please. "Yes, sir, I surely will do my best. Won't be no slap-and-tickle woman for your soldiers, though."

He turned and looked at her. A girl; the baby fat still on her cheeks. But something of a warrior, too, in her posture. "No, of course not, I wouldn't think so. I think you'd be suited for much more important duties than that."

She lifted her chin an inch, in pride and justification.

"A slight girl like you, you might fit into a very tight space. Are you prepared to put yourself in a portion of danger to shorten this war and ensure your emancipation?"

"Don't know all your words. But I kin do whatever needs doin'."

He smiled with a measure of sadness. "I'd stake your life on it, young lady. Please—sit down and let's discuss the matter."

Moon lifted the heavy jug to pour a measure of photographic fixative into the tray. "Missus, did y'all find anything out about Jersey?"

"No, I surely didn't, but I expect to, you wait and see." It was clear he'd been distraught for days over his young wife's disappearance.

"Moon, I wish you'd get back to your old sweet self. I miss it. Why don't you sing me a song? A happy song!"

"Missus, I don't know that I can."

"Of course you can, it'll cheer us both up. Out with it. I will be made happy."

Moon was torn between duty and his emotions, but he took his responsibilities seriously and would try for her. There was a funny new soldiers' song going around, he'd heard some Graysuits singing it at King Ranch. *"Peas, peas, peas, peas! Eatin' goober peas! Goodness, how delicious…"* But he stopped, throat thick, his eyes watery.

Allie felt bad for pushing him. "There, now, Moon, don't you get in a state. That song always makes me cry too."

"Madame Stoneman?"

Allie turned to find Jose Quintero standing in her anteroom, hat in hand. "Why Mr. Quintero, how nice to see you."

"I just wanted to let you know I have my agents out looking for your servant."

"That's so kind of you. But my, my…" She put her hand to his jaw and turned his head to the light from the window. "What a strong jawline you have."

"And how soft your fingers."

"You flatter me, sir."

"I am schooled in diplomacy, but my upbringing compels me to speak the truth."

"Well, if truth is the game…I want to photograph you. It would be a blessing to show people the state of the art with the most magnificent face in Matamoros."

"But my dear, if I do this for you…what favor may I exact in return?"

They looked at each other a long moment, understanding this was to be a dance. Then she sat him in front of the camera. "If I could just have you turn your head this way and be very still," she cautioned him, tipping his cheek to the light with her soft fingers.

"As still as you decree. I am your slave," he smiled, and thinking his groundwork laid, leaned up to steal a kiss.

She backed off coyly. "*Senor* Quintero, I'm flattered. But you promised to be still. And you are my slave, if I may quote."

In a second story window two houses away Odeel stood with a spyglass watching them. Quintero's visit to the Stoneman woman was an unexpected development, but it pleased him. If he could get some kind of leverage on Quintero, maybe he could get the old ambassador to come down hard on Allie.

CHAPTER 10

RYBURN SOLOMON OPENED HIS eyes and looked straight up at the heavens from the smooth roll of the deck where he lay. This was always his favorite moment, stars fading as the black sky lightened in the holy silence of the cool dawn. It was the death of night, the borning of day, replayed over and over like a recurring dream for the Captain, a certainty that he was meant to live freely on the vast presence of the open sea. He sat up. Stood at the rail.

Across the eastern horizon a line of pink appeared, separating the iron gray water from the lightening sky. Pink, and then orange, bleeding color into the lightest of blues. He grabbed his cigar box fiddle from its water-tight compartment and played a lively tune to meet the day.

His crew began to stir—first, Raoulito the cook, who had this watch, but who always fell asleep in the hour before sunrise. Solomon never faulted the man, though—he had no innate affinity for a sailor's life, but he more than made up for this deficiency with his excellent meals.

Solomon lowered his fiddle, left the port rail and walked starboard to view the coast. The sandy dunes were picking up hues from the sun, which had just crested. The land beyond was still dark, the Gulf waters glinting before…wait. What was that? It looked like a ship, almost too small to see, cruising west, paralleling Solomon's coastal course, off to the north some miles but closer inland. No, this was more than a ship. It was several. And as clarity came with the new morning, the full extent was revealed. It was an armada.

"Raoulito! The spyglass!"

Alarmed at Solomon's tone, the old nightwatchman ran up with the two-foot scope they kept for distant sightings. Solomon put the handheld telescope to his eye and focused. He saw one, two, three… four ironclad steam powered sidewheelers, followed by half a dozen troop ships and more than twenty supply ships, undoubtedly laden with munitions, horses, food, medical goods and the like. It was an invasion force. It was the invasion.

"It's the Yankee Navy, boys."

"Can we outrun 'em?"

"They don't be after this little tub. They're headed for Galveston, same as us."

"Then it's back to Cuba, I say." The crew was all up now.

They'd been headed west to Galveston with a load of arms picked up in Havana. It was a repeat of the run they'd been making when the blockade ship put a ball in their hull and they'd had to set to at Padre Island. This was no simple port blockade, though—they could all see that, taking turns with the scope.

"Our cargo's even more needed by the Rebs now."

"We'd be lucky to make Galveston in eight hours. That fleet'll catch us in four."

They all stood quiet to give the captain time to think. It was a knotty problem. "Sabine Pass is dead ahead," he said. "And the wind is with us. We'll take our load to the fort there and they can haul our guns in wagons the sixty miles to Galveston."

"What if the arms don't get there in time?" The mate was still all for going back to Cuba.

"If the battle's over that fast, it don't matter what we do. So let's do the right thing."

They hoisted sail, tacking leeward. The mouth of the Sabine River was visible without the glass, and they made it there within the hour, Louisiana on the starboard riverbank, Texas on the port. Behind them the Union warships were much closer already, at a steady 12 knots. Two miles upriver the *Bucanneer* docked at the west bank—the Texas side—and Solomon walked up to the earthworks fort amidst cheers from the soldiers. He was greeted with an enthusiastic handshake by a young officer.

"Lieutenant Dick Dowling, at your service."

"Captain Ry Solomon."

"Yes, I know, we met when you ran the blockade at Galveston last year. Whatever you have for us today, it's sorely needed."

"It's nae for you, I'm afraid, laddie. We're just an hour ahead of a war fleet making way for Galveston now. I can try to take my guns down the channel but you might do better with a wagon."

"You're mistaken, sir. The Yank Navy you saw is headed right here, we got word by secret courier two days ago."

"I cannae believe it."

"Can you trust your own eyes?"

Dowling took Solomon to the top of the fort lookout post, commanding a wide view in all directions. When they looked east, sure enough—the entire fleet was fanning out around the mouth of the river, the four ironclads poised at the point, waiting for all the ships to collect.

"I'll be damned," said Solomon.

"Seven thousand infantry and cavalry, I've been apprised. I hope you brought a passel of arms in your hold."

"Guns is one thing. You have enough men here to repel the attack?"

"Forty-six."

"You're joking."

"Forty-six Jefferson Davis Guards. I expect that ought to hold the line."

Solomon still thought the young soldier must be kidding. But when he looked around he now realized there weren't even the 500 regulars who usually manned this fort and environs. In fact he barely saw ten. "You're done, then. I can try to make it to Galveston for reinforcements. If I leave now…"

"You'll find they won't give up a man. We've already asked. They sent whoever they could spare to face off a regiment of Yanks at Lafayette, and our boys here at Sabine have mostly gone to Fort Worth—some kind of Comanche uprising."

"Well…what's your plan, then, man?"

Dowling led him up to the parapets, where six smoothbore cannon were pointed a thousand and more yards downriver, each weapon attended by a nervous Reb slouched behind the wall. They began standing at Dowling's approach.

"At ease, men, hold your positions. Except you, Dunne, I want you to get down to this gentleman's blockade runner with a detail, unload all the arms and distribute them to the men." The Private ran off as Dowling took a knee in his place. Solomon sat against the wall beside him.

"I'm keeping most of us hidden from view, so they can't tell our numbers. We're Texas Irish from Houston, by and large. It's a good artillery unit, and I mean to stop the Yanks from setting foot on the beach." He indicated a wide, clear area on the sandy shores below that they'd obviously cleared to give them a good field of fire. "But if they do make it, I mean to have a turkey shoot as they debark."

"That's all well and good, lad, but you're daft if you think you two score can hold off 7000."

"We don't just have these six cannon. We've got two 24 pounders and four 32 pounders, to boot."

"Och, you got 'em licked, then."

"You jest with me, sir. But if you look out 1200 yards yonder, you can see we placed range stakes at the narrows, stuck into the oyster shell reefs there." Squinting, Solomon could just barely make out two white wooden points stuck into a shallow turn in the river. "My gun crews have been busy as ants, doing target practice at those range markers for two days. They've got it down to a science now—powder's all measured out for each load, for each gun, perfect elevation on the barrels, we even shaved down the balls to be the same weight for that gun, and by Golly these boys have their range down to a grasshopper's ass."

Solomon was impressed, though not necessarily relieved. That's when the lead warship, the *Clifton*, started shelling the fort from two miles out, at the rivermouth.

"Hold your fire, boys, and stay undercover, they're way out of range for us!" Dowling shouted. The *Clifton's* guns, though powerful, had no bead on their position. The cannonballs fell short, or wide.

The shelling went on for hours, but without much effect. Every once in a while a round would breach the top of a wall, or damage some outlying building; but the ships' Union gunnery crews couldn't see the fort well from their position, so it was mostly guesswork.

The Jeff Davis Guards were a game bunch, easing their nerves with card play, reading books, writing letters home, or theorizing about the coming battle. This wasn't armed conflict just yet, though; only a lot of chest-thumping from the Yankee gunners. Solomon sipped at a bottle from his private stash of single malt scotch as he and Dowling passed the time entertaining each other with their own personal war stories, the triumphs and the disasters. Dowling politely declined Solomon's liquor, as he was the commanding officer of this lot, and meant to act in all ways as a ranking leader should. Only eight months ago he'd been a cannoneer at the first Battle of Sabine Pass, where his drunken commander let the Union gunship Dowling had just won sink to the bottom of the Gulf. Talking about having fools for commanding officers was always a great entertainment for the men in the trenches. Which is one reason Solomon had avoided trenches whenever possible.

He was far from drunk now—a seafaring man learns early how to hold his spirits—but he was feeling intimate toward this brave youngster. "It's fortunate for you, laddie, that I stumbled upon you when I did. For I've a secret weapon I expect will get you through this dust-up without a scratch."

"And what might that be?"

Solomon unstrung a leather thong from around his neck. On it dangled an arrowhead-shaped fossil he'd found with the bigger pieces on Padre Island. He'd drilled a hole in it to thread it as a necklace; he was certain it was a potent amulet.

"If that's a grizzly bear claw," said Dowling, "I've been hoping today's fight won't be hand to hand."

"It's a magic stone, is what it is. It's the tip of a great tusk." And here he leaned in confidentially. "A tusk of the Gods."

"And which Gods might those be, then?" The Lieutenant had warmed equally to his new friend, even without the lubricant of liquor—another by-product of being in the trenches together under bombardment.

"Aztec, mayhap. Or Mayan. Or even the ancient forebears of the mighty Kiowa, that I cannot tell you. Neither will I say where I found it. But I do believe relics such as these have great power."

"Relics, plural? You have more of these?"

"I've got the God's skull and shankbone, by thunder, unearthed after centuries and reburied where only I can find 'em. Go on, hold it—it's a powerful thing, you can feel it for yourself. Absorb the power, if you can."

Dowling took the fossil shard, held it in his palm, felt the cool, almost silken induration.

"The power to defeat all your enemies, here in your hand."

Dowling put his lips to the fossil. "Like kissing the Blarney Stone," he smiled, and handed it back to Solomon, who replaced it around his neck. He didn't necessarily believe everything he was saying; but it couldn't hurt to try to imbue this brave young soldier with some self-confidence in these quiet moments before his big storm.

Around four in the afternoon the gunboats advanced single file up the river at a measured pace, shooting as they steamed ahead. When the fort came into sight their aim got better, sending shells into the fort proper. The Jefferson Davis Guards were anxious to return fire, but Dowling ordered them to stay hidden until his say so. As the ironclads approached the 1200-yard marker, he gave the order. And his cannoneers touched firesticks to their guns.

Every round landed on or near the mark. One of them hit what must have been either the boiler or the powder cache of the *Sachem*, the second ship in line, because it exploded violently, leaving Bluejackets aflame and jumping into the water. The ship listed to the far shore, half blocking the path of the following vessels. The third ship in line, the *Arizona*, was unable to pass, so it clumsily backed out of the channel, not wanting to be a sitting duck. The lead gunboat, the *Clifton*, forged ahead, firing its powerful cannon and placing its sharpshooters on the bow as well, to snipe at the fort.

As the artillery men reloaded, one of the Union cannonballs hit a supporting post, sending wood shrapnel across the firing line. The nearest gunner was laid low by a big splinter in his neck. Solomon ran over and picked up the man's fire stick, but it had been snuffed out in the blast. So the old salt pulled the fossil shard off his neck, took a flint from his pocket, and struck the two together, generating sparks that ignited the cannon.

His ball hit the *Clifton's* tiller, running it aground just 300 yards away, on the Texas shore. But as the Union snipers jumped off ship to take up firing positions, another missile from the Rebel fort hit it dead center, creating a blast that sent flames high. Those Yanks who didn't die in the cannonade abandoned ship in a highly disorderly fashion, picked off by the Davis sharpshooters with the brand new Enfield rifles Solomon had brought them; until the rest of the Union sailors on the beach surrendered. The fourth warship, the *Granite City*, unable to advance beyond the two gunboats already sunk in the narrow canal, reversed course out of the river, back into the Gulf.

As the Confederate riflemen flowed over the ramparts to take their prisoners, the two remaining Union ironclads conferred with their troop ships offshore. With no more river access to the fort, and half their firepower dead in the shallows, the 22 vessel fleet, after having attempted the largest amphibious military assault in United States history, turned around and sailed back to New Orleans with their 7000 soldiers, leaving behind 50 some dead, twice that wounded, and 300 captured. Dowling's Jefferson Davis Guard suffered not one casualty but that gunnery corporal with a really bad splinter.

Solomon held up his powerful tusk fragment to Dowling. "Well, lad, I see my work here is done."

"And I thank you well for the rifles, too."

"I'll be off, then. I advise you to guard against relishing too much all the back patting and ribbons bound to come your way for this little skirmish."

They shook hands like battle-shared brothers, eye to eye. "Where to?" said Dowling.

"Matamoros, if I'm able to squeeze past the two iron beasts you've left capsized in the water. I can pick up a load of cotton there and take it to Havana for a good price." He was also returning to Padre Island, better equipped this time, to excavate more totems from the site to which his treasure map had led him.

The sun was setting as he got back to the *Buccaneer*, great puffy grey clouds underlit with the deep peach of day's end. His crew was glad to have survived the battle, and hove to with a quick step. Lightened of its cargo of arms, the speedy craft was going to make good time to Bagdad, and then Matamoros.

The smell of rot crossed Isaac's nose as he redressed Clayton's leg. He cleaned it up with hypochlorite water while Clayton moaned in fitful sleep. Everyone knew leg wounds that festered led to amputation. Isaac had treated many an infection on the doctor's plantation; but he'd never done an amputation and didn't want to start now. So he left to find Ambassador Pierce, who he calculated must know a trustworthy surgeon.

On his way through the casino he nodded at Scully, drinking with Claire at the bar. "You go see what he needs if you hear him shout," said Isaac, and quick-walked out the door.

Scully nodded and turned back to Claire. "I'm half a mind to marry you, darlin'."

"*No, ce n'est pas possible,*" she protested, rubbing her leg against his. She'd acquired some English by now; it wasn't the first time she'd heard the word "marry".

"Well, then, maybe we could just get married for the afternoon."

As she laughed gaily her gaze was averted by a Confederate officer with a dozen medals on his uniform. The officer gestured to an empty seat beside him down the bar. Claire patted Scully's thigh and stood. "I see you later maybe so."

She joined the Rebel Colonel as Scully fell into a brown study. This beauty was the first spark of light in his life since he'd lost his arm. She'd even told him, *in flagrante delicto,* that she loved him. Like the Black Irish fool he was, he'd believed her. And now he had to watch her work her way up the chain of command, like a flitting bird drawn by the shiny objects on men's chests. Scully downed his whiskey, poured another, and eased closer to where they sat.

The Confederate Officer kept his voice low, so Scully only picked up fragments of the confidence he was sharing. But the gist was that Napoleon, now in Mexico City, had promised to occupy Matamoros, to support the Confederacy's defense of Brownsville against Lincoln's Yanks. Claire's eyes widened. The idea of seducing Napoleon, riding triumphant into Matamoros, clearly excited her.

It was too much for Scully. He slammed his wooden arm down on the bar with a loud *crack* that turned heads and startled the old Colonel nearly into falling off his barstool. Claire cast Scully a glance meant to freeze his heart. He stomped upstairs, knocked on Clayton's door, entered, and wrinkled his nose at the foul odor.

"You needn't hide your distaste," Clayton said. "It's the corruption in my leg you smell. If you'd light that bundle of sage, we may both be spared that indignity."

Scully lit the dried herb and set it in a bowl. It smoked away the smell of decay. "I'm sorry to see you feelin' so poorly. I know better than most what it is to lose a limb…"

"I will not lose my leg!"

"Have yourself a funeral for it, man, like you told me Santa Anna did. I'll host the wake meself."

"I'll see you in hell first."

"Be that as it may. I'm here to offer a bit of good tidings."

Despite the pain, Clayton settled his breathing and nodded for Scully to go on.

"It's said by some you're a spy for the South," said Scully, "so I thought you might want to know. I heard from a well-placed source that Napoleon his own self is comin' to Matamoros to stop the Yanks from invadin' Brownsville."

Clayton knew well enough that Bonaparte had promised to recognize the Confederacy's sovereignty in return for their support of his takeover of Mexico. But what was that to Scully? "So you think we're friends now because I'm a Rebel sympathizer and you're a naturalized Frenchie?"

"We ain't friends, boyo. I just want to make a pile o' dough to set myself up out west. I can handle a gun, the iron in my new arm is a wonder at close fightin', and I've worked with explosives. I brought you the news about Napoleon to show you I'm not bad at sneakin' around, either. I hear you pay a fair wage and I've come to curry favor."

Clayton smiled with effort. "You've done well to lay your cards on the table. But I've got a test for you, and I'll pay you smartly for any news you can bring back."

"Tell it, then."

"There's a new lady in town, Allie Stoneman. Livin' at General Bee's *hacienda*. Housekeeper name of Aurelia lives there and I hear she needs a handyman."

"I'm handy enough."

"Tell Aurelia that General Bee said the position was open. Once you settle in, find out all you can about Allie, what she's doin' here, what she's up to. I don't believe she's just in town to set up a business. I want to know if she's here to spy on me."

"I'm thinkin' maybe this is a personal errand, not somethin' to do with the war."

"It's all personal. It's all war." He turned his head to gaze out the window, which Scully took to mean the interview was over. So he left.

Clayton's fever rose. Milagra came up with a bowl of albondigas soup. "*Esto sudara la fiebre de ti,*" she said quietly. This will sweat the fever out of you. But he couldn't drink it so she left it at the bedside. By the time Isaac returned with the doctor in tow, Wilkes was soaked in sweat and half delirious—but smiled when the medic approached. "Am I dreamin' or has a beautiful woman come to soothe my brow?"

"This beautiful woman is Dr. Esther Hill Hawks, a battlefield surgeon of some repute. She took care of the casualties in the 54th Colored, up at Fort Wagner."

Clayton squinted through his fever. "You're a long way from home, ma'am."

"War's a funny road and I'm working here at Ambassador Pierce's behest just now, lucky for you." With that the good doctor put a cotton handkerchief over Clayton's face, opened a bottle of chloroform and sprinkled a few drops onto the cloth.

Clayton bridled but quickly went under. Dr. Hawks flayed his infected wound with a scalpel, irrigated out the purulent discharge and cleaned the cavity with carbolic acid. "Dr. Lister in England recommends this to tamp down contagion," she said, "and I've seen some benefits."

Clay dabbed a paste of yarrow to the gouges on Isaac's back as the young man silently wept in the darkness of the tobacco shed. They had to be quiet—if Isaac was found, he'd be killed for sure. He'd escaped the plantation he'd been sold to and made it back here, where he knew Clay would take care of him.

"This looks bad, Isaac."

"Hard to heal around old scars. You can hide me, at least. You're all I've got, that's how bad my case is." He managed a gritted smile as Clay rubbed the salve into his wounds.

"I'll hide you. That or send you back to the doctor who bought you."

"Be hard to do that. I killed him."

Clay stopped. "You're a bigger fool than I thought."

"He was beating a nine-year-old girl. I pulled him off her. He lay into me with his whip but I wasn't going to abide that anymore, not ever. I stove his head in, put him in bed and told everyone I had to go to town for medicaments he ordered. Everyone knew he was teaching me doctoring, so they believed me. I left and you can't blame me for that."

"I'm not sayin' I blame you. Just sayin' you're a fool."

"I came here for help, did I not?" He offered a smile that leaked tears from his eyes.

"How'd you get talkin' so fancy? Sound like a swanky Yankee gentleman."

"My owner was raised in Delaware before he went to Florida, he taught me proper speech, wanted me to take on Northern airs so I wouldn't sound like an ignorant slave. Said he was blessing me with a white man's education—but he thought of me like his trained monkey."

"Seems the man's monkey changed his mind." He smeared more salve on Isaac's back. "So I suppose it's up to me to change the monkey's bandages..."

"You'll have to change the dressings twice a day," Clayton heard Dr. Hawks tell Isaac through the swamp of pain and anaesthesia.

"Will he lose his leg?" Isaac asked.

"Most likely."

"Well, he never did care to run much."

"I'll bet he was a dancer, though. Even in pain he's an unmitigated flirt. Most of these legs can't be saved, though, and that's a fact."

She left Isaac with a bottle of laudanum. He stood at the bedside window, watching the river roll, unconsciously touching the thick scars meshing his back.

Later Clayton would vaguely recall waking and sleeping during light hours and dark; but he had no real sense of how much time was passing. Hours? Days? Between the pain, the laudanum and the fever, time seemed like a levitation. Sometimes he awoke to find Isaac sitting at his bedside, reading a medical book or practicing calligraphy. Sometimes Dr. Hawks was there, her hand inside his leg. There was pain, but it floated above him like a separate thing, a phantom cloud pierced with lightning. Sometimes he gazed out his window, aware only of the beating wings of birds at dusk.

Concerns would assault him. Was the war over? Had he missed the end? And the ship he'd been awaiting so anxiously from England, the *Defiant*, what had become of it? Its cargo was critical, a positive thing, something he could leave behind besides a web of tricks and bad feelings. Where was it? Where was the ship?

But Isaac would just put a cool cloth on his forehead and reassure him. The ship would dock soon, all was well. If the cloth was cool, then the ship would come in. He just kept telling himself that, and his nerves, if not his infection, settled.

Once, the French Order of Nuns of the Incarnate Word and Blessed Sacrament coasted through the air in a healing circle high above his head, then disappeared in a rain of sparkling, cool water.

Once, he looked out his window to see a French and an Austrian officer dueling with sabers, diva Claire clapping breathlessly nearby. Was it a fever dream? But then he heard Isaac chuckle. "At least she only sleeps with ranking officers now."

Sometimes, when the laudanum was gone, Zhi Li would come— the Chinese lady they'd rescued from the Bagdad fire. Isaac had given her a job in the casino. Now she lit up her opium pipe and melted away

Clayton's pain. But not his delirium. A time came he felt he was floating a foot above his bed, talking to his father, but at a time when his father was a young man. "I'm sorry," Clayton told his young father. "I wish I'd known you when you sailed from Galway and everything was an adventure."

"I forgive you," said the man. "Do you forgive me?"

"Do I have to take on the sins of the father first?" asked Clay.

"You are the sins of the father," said his father. But he wasn't young now. And it wasn't Clayton's father, either. It was Father Clos. He was giving Clayton Last Rites. "In the name of the Father, the Son, and the Holy Spirit…"

"Get away from me!" Clayton shouted, and swung at the priest, knocking the vial of holy water to the floor. Skyrockets exploded behind his eyes.

Time passed.

"Allie Stoneman, may I present Miss Catherine Delacroix, the amazing manager of the grandest Opera House in all of the Americas," Mildred gushed.

They stood in the *loggia*, empty at this time of day except for old Harley sweeping up behind the bar.

"*Bonjour, Madame*, I've heard much of you," Catherine offered a withering smile; she could tell a rival from across the room.

"You have?" Allie raised her brow. "How is that even possible?"

"Matamoros is like an island, Allie," said Mildred. "Everybody knows everybody's business. So I'm sure Catherine has heard how creative you are." And to Catherine: "She'll be invaluable in decorating for *La Grande Fete.*"

"You are offering to hang decorations?" Catherine asked and Allie lifted her hands in a "here I am" gesture. Catherine softened a bit. "*Bien.* Madame Bee can show you how it was done last year."

"I certainly will do that," said Mildred. "We'd also like to set aside a space to photograph guests commemorating the occasion. Where would be a good place?"

"That corner is unused, except for brief trysts. She can set up there." And she swept off to more important concerns.

"She doesn't seem to care for me much."

"She's just preoccupied. Besides which, she's got her bonnet set for Clayton Wilkes, and there are rumors swirling around that you own his heart."

Allie dropped her jaw. "How on earth did that become a rumor?"

"Oh, people see, people hear, people talk. If you just ignore it, it'll go away. Unless, of course, it's true." Mildred laughed gaily, as Harley swept his pile of cigar butts and ticket stubs past them across the floor.

Canvas satchel slung over his shoulder, Scully walked around the back of the *hacienda* where a pretty young Mexican woman, full with child, was hanging wet laundry on a line. He walked over to a ewer of lemonade sitting on a low table, poured a mug full and handed it to the woman. "For you, lovely Miss, on this hot day."

Aurelia eyed him suspiciously, but took the cup. "*Que es esto?*"

"Well if it's Mexican you'll be speakin', we're bound to have a hard time of it. And here General Bee said you might be needin' some help."

Bee's name put a different light on everything. "What kind you mean help?"

"It's a miracle! You've mastered the language just in time to tell me what work requires doin'. Chop wood? Carry water? I do it all, and the finest groundskeeper you shall ever know, at your service." He bowed deeply, with a flourish of the arm.

She couldn't help but smile. "You maybe draw some water for kitchen to wash?"

"I can see my way clear to do that. And where would you like me to put my personal items?" He held up his satchel.

Her brow furrowed. "You no stay."

"That was my understanding with General Bee, darlin', work for a place to sleep."

She sized him up, scanned the property for all the little things that needed to be done, and assumed an air of authority. "You estay out back. Leetle houses."

He looked across the yard at the run-down shacks. "Those appear to be the General's slave quarters."

"*Si, Senora* Stoneman's slaves there now. But room for you, too."

"And just who is this *Senora* Stoneman I'll be bumpin' into? I didn't expect this to be no boarding house."

"She a guest of Heneral Bee. Not your beezness."

"Darlin', *you're* my business. Anything you want, you just shout for Scully." And then he shouted. "Scully!"

She laughed once and stopped herself, placing her hand on her chest. *"Me llaman Aurelia."*

"Aurelia. Sounds like a truce to me, so I'll just go put away my unmentionables and get you your wash water, how's that sound?" He flashed his most charming Irish smile and walked off to the slave quarters with a spring in his step.

She watched him go, took a sip of the lemonade he'd given her and went back to her laundry. But she kept her own smile inside as she worked.

CHAPTER 11

JESSUP TRIED TO SHIELD Allie's eyes from the sight of the middle-aged man and woman hanging by their necks from a cottonwood tree beside a small *pueblo*; but she would not look away. "Dear Lord, how awful! That poor couple, murdered! For their money, do you think?"

Jessup swung the man around to reveal a paper tacked to his chest, reading GO BACK TO THE HILLS. "They're German Unionists—abolitionists from the Hill Country, near San Antone," explained Jessup, unfazed. "Voted against Secession and got run out, a lot of 'em come down here, but Texans don't like 'em much here, either."

Allie shook her head and walked on. Civilian war dead made her angry, but there was little she felt she could do about it. So she let herself be taken in hand by this gentle Ranger, to guide her to some safe haven where she might put these things behind her.

In a *convento* just outside the central district, the little cottage was surrounded by goatweed trees and desert willow, putting the whole place in shade. Jessup opened the front door and ushered Allie inside as Moon tethered their wagon to a front post.

"It's beautiful!" Allie walked around the four spacious rooms, marveling at the elaborate, rococo furniture.

"Rip told me about it just this morning," said Jessup. "Austrian prince put his kept woman here. He got killed in a dust-up with some *Juaristas* near Chihuahua City and she took off with his junior officer down to Veracruz. I believe it would suit you fine."

"But won't someone else want to stay here?"

"The prince leased it for a year and mostly nobody even knows about it. Looks like yours for another nine months at least, if you want it."

"If! My goodness! And look!" She pointed out a rear window toward a weed-overgrown wooden shed. "Moon! Come here and lookit the fine little cabin just for you!"

The young black man entered. "Yes'm." But all he saw out back was a sorry shack that made him wish he'd never left Louisiana. He missed the land there and he missed his wife, who was likely either dead or living on another plantation by now, married off to some new master's house boy. The thought of it made him bitterly sad.

"Now go on and see what it needs." Moon went out back as Allie walked room to room. "I can just move from the *hacienda* in bits and pieces." She twirled 360 degrees, all agrin; then kissed Jessup on the cheek, letting her lips linger there. It tasted salty, and smelled good, a young man smell she let carry her away to a time long ago.

Embarrassed, Jessup gestured through the rear window to where Moon was clearing brush from around the shack out back. "See, now, he's already makin' it home."

From her bag Allie pulled the carved figurine that Moon had given her. "I've been thinkin' about Moon. Everyone keeps tellin' me there are no slaves in Mexico. I'm leaning toward releasin' the boy from his bondage."

"I'm sure he's happy with his situation as it is."

"So I've believed. But I had slaves in Louisiana because folks kept slaves in Louisiana. If there are none in Mexico, well…I kind of fancy the idea of bein' on my own. It's a new life here. A woman needs to be self-sufficient just as much as a man."

"I don't know about that."

She looked into the bedroom again, liking more and more the idea of living without the prying eyes of servants. It was, she had to admit, tied into her growing affections toward Jessup, an emotion she surely hadn't anticipated. It wasn't that many years ago she'd vowed never to love again; even fondness was often a stretch for her.

He rambled on from the kitchen. "…And you'll have all the help you need. From me, of course, and your old friend Clayton Wilkes has a lot of influence around town for favors, though I don't expect he'll be doing much himself once he loses his leg, and I believe Ambassador Quintero is smitten with you, so if you asked him to…"

"What was that?" She appeared quickly in the doorway.

"I was just sayin' *Senor* Quintero is well positioned in town to provide you with…"

"No, that part about Clay losin' his leg."

"Well, I'd say it's likely, given what Isaac told me about…"

"Missus, I got the wagon out front." It was Moon at the back door. "You want, I kin git some o' your things at the *hacienda* and bring 'em here."

She just stared at Moon, feeling scattered. Why was she always the last person to find out about Clay's conditions? Not that she cared—but it was almost as if everyone was keeping things from her. Small town, indeed! But could he really be losing his leg? That surely would put a crimp in his tendencies to run away, which he was always so good at. Damn him anyway. And what was Moon doing, standing there in front of her like a big puppy who hadn't been fed?

"Moon, I'm givin' you your papers."

"Ma'am?"

"I'm settin' you free. You're not my slave anymore. We live in Mexico now, and apparently this country doesn't countenance slavery. So you may go."

"Whatchu mad at me for?" There was a touch of fright to his voice.

"I'm not mad, Moon. I'm givin' you your freedom."

"Missus, where would I go?" Almost beside himself now.

"I'm sure I don't know. I hardly knew where I was going myself today."

The poor man looked stunned and lost. Jessup took pity on him, touching Allie on the shoulder. "Maybe you could hire him. You'll need someone to cart inventory for your import business, that kind of thing."

"That's a perfect idea! Moon, would you care to hire on as my hand?"

Moon nodded, shaken to his core. "Yes, missus."

"Excellent. Then perhaps you'd be so kind as to get my personal belongin's from the *hacienda* and put them in the bedroom yonder."

Moon walked out to the wagon, confused about his new role and uncertain of his fate in life. Torn from his home in Louisiana, then from his wife, and now from his owner. Maybe he ought to just lie down and not get up again.

The *matador* sank his sword into the nape of the bull's neck as the animal turned—so it was a sloppy thrust and only succeeded in angering the beast, which swung its horn around to gore the *matador's* thigh. The crowd went wild, coming to its feet with a thundering chorus of *ole's*. Pierce disliked these events and only came because it was easy to talk without being noticed. In the seat behind him, Isaac spoke.

"I want to buy a Spanish land grant along the Rio Grande, to start a colony."

"The Liberian experiment isn't working out too well. And Lincoln tried to get a Negro colony going on Cow Island, off Haiti, another failure. Why try again?"

"I'm done with white folks telling me what works for me. Even if you mean well. This task is my doing. You people made your own country; that's what I mean to do. But I'm not too proud to ask for help, so I'd like you to set up a meeting for me with Governor Vidaurri."

"Why Tamaulipas State?"

"Land is fertile that section of the river. We'll need a place that can grow crops."

"And who do you propose will populate this colony of yours?"

"Runaways, freedmen."

"You're talking about the men in the army I'm building to attack Fort Brown. Why would I help you thin my ranks?"

"I'll organize them into a fighting force better than you ever could. Then I promise to turn them loose on the Rebs when the time comes— coordinated with the Union invasion. After that I'll take them west and we'll build our own homeland."

The *matador* was dragged out of the arena as the sorry bull got skewered with *estoques*. "Vidaurri won't give you any land. He's pro-French. He won't do anything to hurt the Confederacy."

"Most slave owners would love to see the freedmen move down to Mexico."

"Maybe so. But a better idea for you might be the Sonoita Land Grant, in Sonora State. They're having their own civil war now, and Governor Pesqueira is fighting for his life. He's also loyal to Juarez, so he loves Lincoln and the Union."

"He'd give us land if we fought for Lincoln against the Confederacy?"

"No. But he'd trade you land in return for military service to him. His army's under siege by the French coming up from Mexico City, and from the Texas Rangers who want to annex more territory from the north."

"Where does the grant run?"

"From the Sonoita River west all the way to the Gulf of California." The crowd stood, screaming.

"Get me a meeting with Governor Pesqueira," said Isaac, and left.

✳ ✳ ✳

Clayton swooned in his fever dream, where he stood on the deck of a great schooner in the midst of roiling seas. Waves crashed all around, nearly throwing him into the water, but he held tight to the rail and stood fast. There wasn't another soul on board. Fires raged below decks, sending tongues of flame up the seams of the hatches. The wood beneath his feet was so hot it steamed with every wave that buffeted the boards. The sails were ripped to tatters so the ship was without direction, spinning and tipping in the vast ocean like a dead beetle afloat on its back in a flood-crested river. And Clayton, somehow, was the mind of the beetle, the soul in the charred shell.

In fact he felt like his skin was forged armor, aglow in the heat of the fire beneath the surface. Cooking his insides. Like a tortoise in a pit of hot coals. The whirling ship made him dizzy in the screaming thunder, the crowning waves, his insect carapace red hot, as if covering him in burning shards, agonizing, he could barely stand it, he wanted to tear it all off—when suddenly a tidal wave of seawater lifted the ship high into the night air and thrust it down into the deep, into the cold black brine that snuffed the fires instantly, sizzling Clayton's shell into a cool, brittle little boat that bobbed up to the surface and carried him in the chilly mist on the turning tide toward the dawn, toward...

Clayton opened his eyes. He knew at once his fever had broken. He took a deep breath, chill in the certainty he would not die of this crisis—and a distinct fragrance graced his nostrils; something from *Grasse*, in the south of France. Hands pulled a wet cloth from his forehead and he knew whose hands they were. They were Allie's hands.

"You've been quite a bother to us all," she said, "but it looks as though you may finally give us a well-deserved rest."

"How long have you been here?" he asked hoarsely, voice weak from the ordeal.

"Two days on and off, I count."

"Where's Isaac?"

"That's all you have to say to me? 'Where's Isaac?' After I take leave of my other responsibilities to nurse your crybabyin' back to your usual state of inflated self-importance?"

He felt limp as a kerchief, deeply grateful, at the edge of tears. "Thank you, Allie."

"You're welcome." She placed another moist towel across his bare chest.

"You put me to mind of our early days, tendin' me so."

"I've quite forgotten them."

"As did I for some years, too. I never did marry again."

"We never got married to begin with, in the eyes of the law. It was annulled, if you recall."

"I do recall, though for two months we were as married as any couple I ever heard about. That notwithstanding, you're a widow now, and our daddies lay beyond this mortal coil, at least mine does, so I see no reason to deny the past."

"You may see no reason to. I, on the other hand, am dedicated to moving forward."

"Then why are you here, if I might enquire?"

"This is an act of charity."

"In that case I appreciate your kindness."

"You are welcome, sir."

They looked steadily at each other for the longest time, uncertain of feelings or futures, fortunes or outcomes of war, or of cotton and arms deals, or the fate of ships on the high seas, or Indian raids, or the souls captured on photographic plates; certain of the corruption of neither government officials nor leg wounds, nor tender memories, nor bitter recriminations, nor the invasion of Texas; not the painful recollections of friends or family dead of battle or disease, not the most boisterous memories of love on the run, not the unanticipated, furtive, renewed incursion of one heart upon another; and all of this passed between them in the space of a pulsebeat, of a shimmer on the river outside the window. But then she shook her head, weary as an unwound metronome.

"I'm not havin' any," she said, though it came out a whisper. She rose, and left.

He watched her go as he'd felt his fever go: with exhaustion, a deep sense of gratitude, and a fatalistic anticipation. But anticipation of what? Her return? The return of her absence? A coming close again, to be followed by another annulment? He didn't know what to expect, or what he wanted, or…no, that wasn't right. He knew what he wanted. He just didn't want to know it.

As Allie left the building, she heard the plaintive keening of *la llorona* once more. She'd learned more of the legend in recent days—the Weeping Woman had killed her own children, then drowned herself out of anguish, and now wandered around lakes and rivers looking for new souls to claim, to try to fill the emptiness in her own. To hear her was an omen—but of what, Allie could not be sure. Her suicide sister and mother, come back to beckon her to their depths? The call of her own empty spirit, pulling her to abandon all hope? She could be whoever she needed to be; but who was she?

She put her fingers in her ears to muffle the cries, but they only tore at her all the more. Fine. She could bear it. Wailing women, curse or blessing, were of little concern to her. Any more than the tug Clay

Wilkes gave to her yearnings. She was a fortress, and no siege could make her flee or cave. She was Allie Stoneman; no less. She would survive all challenge, at a time and place of her choosing, alone against all odds.

She rubbed a warm raindrop from her cheek as she made her way home. Though she couldn't credit why a second drop, curling down her lip, tasted so salty.

Clayton put away the opium pipe Zhi Li had left with him. It had become a habit when his leg pain was so great. Now that the pain was simply annoying, the opium had become a habit he couldn't break. He never got so intoxicated that he couldn't function, but he wasn't often able to function at full capacity either. He tried to go without sometimes, but its call was insistent. He'd considered asking Isaac for advice, but then he'd have to sit through one of Isaac's fables—which just made him want more opium.

He grabbed the walking stick Isaac had given him. Filigreed with silver around an ornate ivory handle; functional but beautiful. He set the tip on the floor, pushed himself out of bed and walked across the frayed Persian carpet to the work table, where stained glass fragments lay in the same disarray they had for weeks. Maybe putting them in place now would give him some peace. Order out of chaos. He moved shards around, a green one here, a yellow one that might fit there. Like a jigsaw puzzle. But nothing fell into place. Like the shards of his life.

"I have good news of the war," Quintero broadcast as he entered.

Clayton turned, taking a moment to respond. Good news for Quintero meant bad news for the Union. With a twitch the gears engaged in his brain, all the clockwork machinations fell into place. And Clayton was back in the game. "Tell me," he said.

"The Union incursion into Texas was launched and repelled. At Sabine Pass. 50 brave Confederate troops turned back thousands of Yankee invaders, dozens of warships. It must have been a sight to see. I tell you, revolution is unstoppable."

"So's exaggeration, it sounds like."

"Possibly. Every great conflict needs its legends, though."

"I know for a fact Fort Sabine houses at least five hundred Rebel regulars."

"Yes, but most left to go fight an Indian uprising at Fort Worth."

This gave some credence to the story, since Clayton knew Pierce's plan had been to deplete Fort Sabine with diversions before the Union invasion force arrived. "That's good news, then," he said with quiet enthusiasm, as he poured two glasses of ruby port.

"There is a moment in every revolution when the tide turns. I see that moment at hand now. Momentum is on our side."

"Tell me, Agustin, what are your plans after the Rebellion triumphs? Back to Cuba?" His tone was affectionate. He genuinely liked Quintero—how could he not like a man whose life work was disrupting the *status quo*? He handed Quintero a wineglass.

"No, Cuba is not yet ripe to overthrow the Spanish," Quintero replied. "If the French conquer Mexico I may stay here and offer my services to Juarez. Revolution against Napoleon would be…" He couldn't find a word sufficient to the feeling, though, so he simply drew his fingers together and kissed their tips, exploding his hand.

"By the time that's done, the Confederacy will be a sovereign nation. You can come back and help the slaves set up their own revolt against their tyrannical masters."

"You tease me, I know. But revolution is the lifeblood of humanity, and I will be its most faithful champion wherever it calls me."

"To revolution, Agustin."

"To revolution."

They touched the gilt edges and drank.

Out of sorts, Allie took the glass of lemonade from Aurelia without so much as a thank you. She was annoyed with Clay, and annoyed even more with herself for going to see him at all. He always left her feeling like a mess, and she needed to focus if she was going to keep all these balls in the air. Her import business, her photography business, her love life, the Matamoros gossip mill…and now the issue of her father had risen to the surface again, as it often seemed to in times of stress. Her father, who'd run off when the whole family was dead but her; left her on her own to manage.

Time to go to her darkroom, then; to print a negative. Making something appear out of nothing, like a sorceress, or an alchemist, always gave her the sense of power she needed to feel most at ease. She tossed her lemonade out the window and went to get dressed as Aurelia fumed, picked up a basket of laundry, and walked outside.

"She have no *gracias* in her heart." Aurelia spoke better English than she often let on. She began hanging damp clothes on the line.

Scully was fixing a well-pump nearby. "Ah, but you must pity the empty heart," he replied. Aurelia suddenly winced and grabbed her pregnant belly. Scully ran over. "You all right? Want me to fetch a midwife?"

Aurelia shook her head. The spasm passed. "Is nothing."

Scully trod lightly. "The baby's father off to war, is he?"

"He fights in the hills with Juarez against the French. I hate the French."

He decided not to mention he'd been fighting on the French side until his wounds sidelined him. "Well the Mexicans are a proud people, I'm sure they can hold their own."

She put her hand back on her baby bulge, not from pain, but for comfort. "*Mi esposo* is *no Mexicano*. He is Irish, like you. A *San Patricio*."

St. Patrick's Battalion had fought on the Mexican side against the United States in the Mexican-American War fifteen years before. They were mostly Irish deserters from the U.S. Army, treated so badly for their Catholicism they'd fled to this more welcoming culture. "What's his name?" asked Scully.

"Sean," she said, wiping away a tear. She went into the house.

Feeling bad for causing her grief, Scully went to hanging clothes, but before he'd barely begun Lieutenant Jessup strolled up. "Now there's the work of a married man."

But before Scully could retort Allie came out and her face lit up to see Jessup. *Well there's a man I can trust to help me*, she thought. A man who'd never let her down, someone she could count on. And now more than ever, as the notion of her father crept again to the edge of her thoughts. Here was a problem Jessup could surely help her with—why hadn't she put it together before? "Care to walk me to work, Lieutenant Jessup?" She looped her arm through his and walked Jessup deeper into her life.

✳ ✳ ✳

Feeling housebound, Clayton decided to go to the *Teatro* that night. Not the entire performance, that would have been too much for his recovering leg. But he thought it might be nice to show up at the *Entr'acte* for twenty minutes, mingle, get back in the rumor mill. He dressed in his finest ruffled shirt and cream linen suit, had a short pull on the opium pipe, leaned on his new engraved cane and let Isaac drive him to the Opera House in a buggy, with instructions to return an hour later. On the way they discussed the Union defeat at Sabine pass.

"It was like the Battle of Thermopylae," said Isaac, "when 300 Greeks held off 70,000 Persians for two days at the narrow pass."

"If I recall my schoolin', the Greeks were wiped out on the third day."

"I guess the Yanks at Sabine never learned about flanking maneuvers."

"Maybe you can be a big general some day and stage all your battles like Alexander the Great."

"Maybe I'll do just that."

Isaac left him at the *Teatro* and drove off. Inside, the great hall was empty—everyone was seated at the performance, intermission still ten minutes away. Red, green and white decorations were already up—crepe paper streamers, festive drapes, Mexican flags, all ready for the upcoming Festival of Independence. The Playbill at the foot of the stairs verified what he'd heard—*La Traviata* had closed prematurely, same as its run in Paris. So no opera tonight—but a play, *Macbeth*, which the repertory company knew so well they could bring it out on a moment's notice.

Clayton walked slowly up the grand staircase, using both the bannister and his cane for support. On the second floor *loggia*, bartenders

151

readied their wares for the imminent onslaught. Clayton limped to the French doors and looked beyond the balcony outside. Stars winked in the distance; a delicate fragrance tugged at him from some night-blooming jasmine across the street. It was good to be alive and about.

The theater doors opened, disgorging a crowd of chattering *cognoscenti* into the vast barroom space. But Clayton's gaze went straight to Allie, in full dress—cut low to show off an emerald necklace, among other things—and the world shifted a little. As if the pieces of the stained-glass window had begun to coalesce into an image. Not a clear image yet; but taking shape.

Clayton crossed the room, clacking the tip of his cane to the floor until he stopped before her.

"Why, Clay," said Allie, surprised to see him. "I expected you'd still be abed."

"As you see, your nursing skills have put new life to my limb."

She looked pleased and waved her hand around the large room. "Do you like my decorations for *La Independencia*?"

"You put these up?"

"Yes, with Mildred Bee." She noticed Catherine across the room, watching them. Just to be catty, Allie adjusted Clay's collar with a certain intimacy as she smiled back at Catherine, who glowered in their direction. Then, to twist the knife, Allie brought her lips up to Clay's ear. "And that cow Catherine Delacroix didn't lift a finger to help."

"I'm sure she has enough on her mind, preparin' for the celebration."

"It's amusin' to think a debauchery on the scale this one is reputed to be was started 50 years ago with a Cry of Pain by a country priest."

"Well, Hidalgo wasn't just a priest. He fathered two daughters in his spare time."

She let out a chuckle. "I knew there was somethin' I liked about this country."

He regarded her with great fondness. "You look beautiful tonight, Allie."

Straight from the heart; the compliment actually flustered her. "If you'll excuse me," she said, lowering her eyes. "I see Lieutenant Jessup is waiting." She walked off to where Jessup was talking to Rip Ford, the Ranger Colonel. Clayton was content just to watch her walk until Quintero pulled him aside to talk of the war in murmurs.

Across the room Jessup watched Clayton and Quintero, whose conversation appeared whispered even from afar. "Say, Clayton Wilkes and Jose Quintero are looking kind of chummy, there," he said to Commander Ford.

"Supposed to be some kinda secret," said Rip, "but everyone knows Clayton Wilkes is a Southern agent."

"That a fact? I always took him for no more than a dandy."

"Then I guess it was a secret from you, at least." Rip suddenly realized Allie was about to join them, so he nodded a good evening to her and beat a hasty retreat.

"I must be losin' my charm," Allie opined when she reached Jessup.

"No such thing. Rip's just been out on the *llano* taking Apache scalps. Civilization like this can be a hard business to get used to all at once."

A bell rang twice. Intermission over. Quintero, who'd been telling Clay about Napoleon's promise to occupy Matamoros and recognize the Confederacy, excused himself as the crowd began drifting back in. Clayton moved against the flow, to leave the building. As he neared the bottom of the grand staircase he dropped his cane.

"Let me help you," came a voice behind him. Leonard Pierce.

"I thank you, sir."

Pierce spoke softly as he eased Clayton down, one stair at a time. "Munitions are being offloaded from the *Sea Queen*."

"You want me to have the shipment tracked stateside?"

"I want you to destroy it before it gets there. I've got someone to do the actual demolition but I need you to organize the operation. It's a Trojan horse kind of plan. I'll give you the details in the morning. The thing has to be done tomorrow night."

"That should give me an abundance of time to come up with a dandy raid." They reached the bottom of the staircase. "You are most kind, sir."

Pierce handed him his fallen cane and trotted up the stairs to watch the next act, as Clayton walked out the main entrance. Isaac was waiting for him in a buggy at the front of the building. But beyond the carriage Clayton saw Simon Wachtel and Jensen silhouetted by torchlight, having an argument in pantomime, full of gesticulations and shouts that couldn't be heard at that distance. Jensen stormed off, leaving Simon quivering in place. Clayton felt a twinge of sadness for the old man—and the echo of something similar for himself. A whisper of something that hadn't happened yet, but could easily be lying in wait, in the shadows of the heart, for any who loved too much.

CHAPTER 12

Clayton approached the *hacienda* as Moon was pulling away from Scully in a wagon loaded with trunks of Allie's clothes.

"Isn't that Allie's house boy?" asked Clayton.

"She gave him his papers. He's a free soul now just like the rest of us poor sods."

"Why would she do that?"

"The sorry fellow was wonderin' the very same thing his own self."

"What else have you learned about her for me?"

"Not too bloody much. She's left the *hacienda*, got a place of her own in town."

"You can show me where later. Meanwhile there's a shipment I mean to steal. I'll need a lookout and a few men handy with firearms to make a distraction."

"Distractin' who, if I may ask?"

"Police guards is what I mostly expect. Some Rebs likely too, maybe Rangers, maybe a few British Marines."

"I can distract the hell out of the bloody English for you."

"You're the lookout. Let's see how you handle that job before you get any more responsibility. I want no killin'. Just enough diversion to perform some chicanery."

"You keep payin' me well, I can be a very diverting soul."

"We meet at the Breakers, in Bagdad. Sundown tonight."

Six hours later Clayton had the logistics worked out and his team assembled. It was left only to instruct Pierce's demolition agent what to do. Their handshake code was "Honey" and "Butter", and the meeting was at the *plaza de toros,* empty at this hour. Clayton stood in the *callejon,* a dirt alleyway behind the great bullring. The circular amphitheater itself was covered in sand and crushed shells and the dried blood of men and bulls. He stared at the arena, listening. He'd never enjoyed watching bullfights, but sometimes the echoes of intense battle gave him a sense of things to come.

He put down the sack he'd carried with him and drew a map in the dirt with the tip of his cane as he waited for his secret soldier to arrive. When he looked up he saw a small Colored girl standing in the cool shadow of the overhang. She couldn't have been more than 14. When she moved into the sun he saw it was Allie's runaway, Jersey.

"You go on, now," he said. "This is men's business here."

"I'm your business. You best be tellin' me what you aim for me to do."

"I aim for you to go. Back to Brave River, if what you want's a payin' job."

"Honey," she said.

"This can't be right."

"Mr. Pierce tell me say 'honey', then you say a word. What he called a code so's you know I'm the one."

"You're just a child."

"Say the word." She looked resolute.

"Butter," he came back.

"You awright, then. Mr. Pierce said tell you I'm the only one fits in the dynamite box, is why he picked me." She jutted her chin out. "You just tell me what to do, I'll do."

He gave her one last chance. "You sure you want to get into this war business? You know it mostly leads to dyin'."

She was getting tired of justifying herself to all these white men. "Ima kill as many crackers as took my folks from me. That's twelve since my mammy got whupped dead for pullin' the walkin' boss offa me with his pants down. Let's get started."

He was angry with Pierce for not telling him who the agent was—probably afraid Clayton would turn the whole thing down flat. But what was he going to do now? There was no time for change of plan. And he had to admit, the girl seemed to know her mind.

"Your husband misses you, I've been told."

"Moon be awright. He need a wife who's a better slave girl than me anyhow."

"Just so you flat-out know, and no mistake—you likely won't make it through this mission alive."

"I ain't been alive for some years, now."

He nodded and took her through it. She was to hide in a crate. She'd have a pocketwatch, a lantern, fuses, matches and TNT. If all went as planned, at 3 am her crate would be in a locked warehouse full of munitions, in an unknown location, with guards standing outside the door. When her pocketwatch read 3, she was to go into action. Clayton took a pocketwatch out of his vest and showed her.

She couldn't read time but Clayton pointed out where the hands had to be. That's when she was to get out of the box. She was then to locate any crate labeled BEAN FLOUR—this would be full of gunpowder. Jersey couldn't read letters either, but Clayton showed her how the B in Bean looked like someone's butt—which made her smile for the first time—and how the F in Flour was like a flag. If she saw those two letters, she was to set her dynamite charges behind that crate, with two-minute fuses. He took a stick of dynamite and a fuse out of his sack and showed her how to do it.

She knew this was going to be a lot easier than all these struttin' white men were makin' out. She'd been stealing ways to do tricky things on the plantation for years.

"Once you light those fuses," he told her, "you got two minutes, so you quick open the door and run like hell."

"What if it locked?"

"It's supposed to be you can open it from the inside."

"S'posed." Disbelief was baked into her voice. If she only had a nickel for all the "s'poseds" in her life that hadn't gone the way they s'posed.

"If it doesn't open, just keep bangin' on it, shoutin' for help. When the guard opens the door, you run past him and disappear in the dark before he even knows what's goin' on."

"Kin I kill him first?"

"I don't think you want to be takin' time with that. The whole place is gonna blow in a minute, likely kill a dozen or more."

That seemed to mollify her. "How you gonna get me in there?"

"You'll hear some gunfire and you'll feel your box movin'. Just get out when the watch says 3 and you'll be where you need to be, don't worry."

"I ain't worried." She waited for more instructions, but Clayton was quiet, worrying his own idea. "That it?" Jersey nudged him.

"I was just wonderin'," said Clayton with some difficulty. "You been with Allie quite a long time, as I understand it. How's she been doin'? I mean…is she happy?"

A slow smile of understanding came over Jersey's face. "You the one, ain't you?"

"What one?"

"The one Miz Allie used to dream over. One that got away." She laughed ingenuously, her first open moment. "You white folks ain't got a real problem in the world, so you just make up things to be complainin' on." She laughed again. "You want her, just go get her, she waitin' on you."

"Not any more, I expect."

She shrugged. "Free man do what he want." She held up the dynamite stick. "Free woman, too."

Hamilton Bee stood up, nerves on edge. He was already anxious about pretty much everything in his life—the tides of war, his ability to hold the fort if the Yanks invaded, the kickbacks he was taking from Major Russell—and now he was anxious about how his photographic portrait would look. "You think it will need prettifyin'?"

"Don't you worry none," said Allie. "This photograph is like to go down in history." She ushered him to the door. "Now you let me get to my work while you get to yours."

He exited feeling less than reassured. Allie noticed Lieutenant Jessup way down the road, walking this way, so she closed the door on Bee, to get her mind right. Jessup had to help her, he just had to. She thought of her grief at her father's latest situation.

When Jessup entered a few minutes later he found her weeping.

"What is it, Allie? Did that old goat put hands on you?"

"Nothin' like that." She wiped a tear. "Just got a speck in my eye."

"Allie—please don't mistake me for a fool."

At that she broke down in sobs and let him hold her for a full minute before she confessed. "My daddy's in prison at Fort Brown. He's sentenced to be hung in three weeks—on false charges, I assure you."

"I don't doubt it. What's it about?"

"It's most of the reason I came down here to begin with. I been visitin' him ever since he got transferred to this prison, and payin' Major Russell a toll every time I go."

"That sounds like Russell. But what's your daddy supposed to have done?"

"Before the war he was partners in a gold mine with an Illinois Yankee. Daddy financed the operation and the Yankee did the hard labor. War came and Daddy left home. He wrote a few times—he was workin' the mine, it was packed with gold. But the Yank was hanged for a spy last year, and the Rebs got the idea Daddy was partners with him on that, too. So when he came home to see me..." She shook her head.

"Can't you appeal it?"

"Only way to stop it now is with money to bribe Russell to look the other way and let Daddy escape."

"What about your cotton money?"

"Biggest part of it's already used up in down payments on goods that are still in transit, and payin' off Russell."

"I can loan you some," he said.

She laughed through her tears. "Oh, you sweet man. I won't take your coin. Besides it's way more than you could muster. Ten thousand is the price Russell quoted, to cover his fee, plus the guards, plus a kickback to General Bee. Says he has to factor in funds for his own escape, too, if he gets arrested for dereliction of duty."

"Could you borrow it from the bank?"

"Not if they know what it's for. This has to stay private. That's why I'm tryin' to cultivate friendships amongst the upper crust. Any rich folks who help us free him will get a 20% stake in the gold claim. It's worth millions, if I can just find the right investor."

"I could ask around…"

"No, I trust only myself to find the right man, Daddy's life depends on it. And besides, it's not your money I want." She nestled up to his chest. "It's your strength."

He wrapped his arms around her and didn't say a word. But she thought: *This is the man who can help me. The man who can save my daddy. I could love this man.*

And she held on to him even tighter.

The wind was soft, the night silver with moonlight. Lanterns winked in the bay, where 182 ships lolled on a quiet tide. The last load of crates from the *Sea Queen* sat in a wide pile on the sand near the Bagdad docks as a handful of British seadogs and twice that many Confederate soldiers tied the crates down onto flatbed wagons. In the shadows of a dune removed, Clayton leaned on his cane.

His leg was throbbing from too much activity—he'd avoided the pipe, to stay clear-headed—but this was the moment the deed had to be done, and he was here to do it. Behind him were Scully, Isaac, and a runaway field hand name of Salem, whom Isaac had hired to teach him how to garden. Beside them stood a cutthroat called Pig, who'd done thugwork for Clayton before, and two of Cortina's men who never shared their names. One of them sat on an oblong pine crate with air holes at one end and the words BEAN FLOUR stenciled on top and sides. Clayton spoke softly to the *Cortinistas*.

"When we start shootin' is your signal. Get this crate on any wagon and tie it down. *Comprende?*" The bandits nodded. Clayton turned to Isaac and Pig. "You two split up, Isaac to the pilings at the waterline, Pig to that old scaling shack."

"What about me?" said Scully.

"You set up in the tall grass on that high dune, keep watch. See anybody gettin' flanked, send up three shots and we'll pull back. Isaac, you and Pig make a lot of noise but don't kill anyone. We don't want enough mayhem to get reinforcements called in. Pig, start shootin' a minute after Isaac. And for God's sake don't hit a powder box."

They all slipped into the dark, Salem following Isaac closely—this was a training exercise for him. A moment later a voice eased up behind Clayton. "I can help."

He whirled around, almost tripping on his cane, to find Teddy Beale standing there in roughneck clothes, gun strapped to her belt.

"How in hell did you get here?" he demanded.

"I've been following you, and here's where you ended up."

He was angry at her, and angry at himself for not even being aware of the tail. The damned opium was the problem—he was either too fuzzy from too much, or too preoccupied with his pain from too little. It had to stop.

She saw his pride was nicked. "Don't blame yourself, I'm a pretty fair tracker."

"Well, just go on and track yourself home." He had another thought. "Did Pierce put you up to this? Lookin' over my shoulder?"

"No, sir, I just want to watch you work. That's how I get educated. Watch and then do. Why do you think Ambassador Pierce would've sent me here?"

Clayton realized he might have revealed something he shouldn't have mentioned. Nobody was supposed to know about his relationship with Pierce. Damn opium again. "No reason," he said. "You work for him, maybe he told you to follow me."

"No, I just came to learn. But I can help, too. Looks to me like you're about to stage a raid on some Confederate assets, and that's a good strike against the slave-holders, for my money. Besides that, you could do worse than bringing on a battle-tested war dog like myself with the sorry bunch you got now."

A gunshot rang out. Clayton squinted toward the water. "That'll be Isaac."

"Want me to set off a few rounds down there?"

"No!" He wanted her to disappear, but it was too late in the game to be spending any time on this now. "Just stay here with me."

She smiled. "You bet I will."

Soldiers were returning fire to Isaac and Salem under the docks when Pig began firing from his defilade at the fish shack. Now the Rebs were hunkering down, afraid of crossfire, their backs to the water. The British swabbies huddled behind the lead wagon, trying to stay out of the way: this wasn't their fight. They'd felt lucky to get shore duty because it meant a side trip to the brothels; now they were less happy to be here. And a few moments later even less so. Two of them were shot in rapid succession, one fatally.

Clayton saw what looked like Scully running from a garbage pile to a beached boat, pressing an attack on the English. "The sonuvabitch is fightin' his own damn war," Clay muttered.

Meanwhile the *Cortinistas* were carrying the Bean Flour crate, bumping over the sand toward the middle of the arms convoy. Until it hit a snag. Clayton couldn't tell what from here, some hidden root or tangle of beach grass.

"I can fix that," said Teddy. Before Clayton had time to object, she ran to a mesquite grove where her pony was tethered and galloped to the *Cortinistas*, staying low on her mount's neck to make a poor target. She took her lariat from the saddle, roped the crate, looped the lasso around the horn and rode toward the wagons—pulling the crate right out of the snag. The Mexican bandits ran after her, hoisting the crate onto a wagon when they got there.

Rebel reinforcements showed up, quicker than Clayton had expected; or maybe this was just taking too long. Isaac and Salem got pinned down behind a berm near the water. Clayton unholstered his pistol and shot at the Rebs—too far away to hit, but it might provide enough distraction for Isaac to slip into the tide and swim off. He stopped firing when he saw Scully crawl up behind a Rebel sniper and knock him cold with his wooden arm. Scully picked up the Graycoat's long gun and wounded a British Marine advancing on Isaac's position.

But now Clay saw two Reb infantrymen coming up on Scully

from both flanks, and he was too focused on covering Isaac to realize it. Clayton took off at a lope, pushing off with his cane every other step, headed for the Graycoat closest to Scully. He wasn't making much attempt at stealth; he didn't have time and he couldn't manage it anyway, in his lame state. When he was still ten steps away, the Reb heard his approach, turned and fired. Wilkes shot his own pistol but it misfired, so he just threw his gun and hobbled the last few feet swinging his cane—knocking the gun out of the soldier's hand before the fellow could shoot again.

Meanwhile Scully flipped around at the sound of close-range gunfire in time to see the other Confederate stand up shooting at him. Scully took fire without flinching as he pulled out his own handgun. The two men just blasted away at each other from twenty feet until the Rebel fell, mortally wounded, and Scully ran out of ammunition.

Clayton was now clutching the other Reb from behind, his legs wrapped around the man's legs and pulling his cane hard against the soldier's throat, crushing his air flow as the man kept thrusting his big knife behind him, trying to stab Clayton in the head. But the Reb kept missing, or just slicing a little skin—he was weak and aiming badly, for lack of air, until he finally stopped moving altogether.

Clayton just lay there a moment, panting with his eyes closed. He supposed the Reb was dead, which gave Wilkes no sense of glory or triumph. He hated the times he'd had to kill a man; it only left him feeling depleted, as if he'd failed to find a better solution. He wasn't much of a fighter anyway, and he knew eventually he'd be bound to lose one of these encounters. As Scully made his way over to help, Clayton finally pushed the dead Reb to the side and sat up.

"You all right?" rasped Scully. Clay still only had the wind to nod. "I'll go see how Isaac is makin' out," Scully said, and disappeared into the shadows.

Clayton limped back to his lookout spot in time to see Isaac shoot a man in the buttocks as Salem tore into a Johnny Reb, beating the man senseless. Then Isaac and Salem eased into the dark water.

Pig and Scully vanished on the wind; likewise the *Cortinistas*. Clayton lost track of Teddy. The big wagon train of arms took off for points unknown with a rear guard of Southern troops protecting it and making sure nobody followed to learn where the cache was being stored.

Clayton felt at the knife cuts in his scalp; already clotted, and not too deep. He was wobbly from his exertions, but started the short walk back to Bagdad proper; joined by Teddy along the way, leading her pony on a rein.

"Told you I was pretty fair with a rope," she said.

Clayton took her arm for support. "Don't mistake this for anything but my needin' a shoulder to take the weight off my leg."

"I'll take it for whatever you want." She saw he was in some measure of bad shape from a fight. "Can I give you a hoist up to the saddle?"

"I'm not that lame yet, nor soon expect to be." He took hold of her horse's bridle. "This'll do me fine, thank you very much."

"Any old time, sir." And she just grinned into the dark.

Jersey didn't mind being in the box. It was hot and black and close, but her excitement kept her attentive to the sounds and the changing lights through the air holes above her face; moonlight, or firelight, and later powder flashes. There was jostling first, then sitting for a while, must've been near the ocean because she could smell the salty water through the drill holes.

Then there was gunfire; she was being bumped and dragged. The odor of coal oil filled the space and she realized the lantern beside her must have tipped. She got jerked and pulled against the grainy wood, then plopped down hard. Finally she was moving quick as a horse trot, bounced all over hell, her head hitting the top of the crate over and over, every time one of the wagon wheels whacked a pot hole or a rock.

After what seemed like a long time, the wagon stopped, and a good long time after that she judged her box was being lifted down and carried, it had that swinging feeling, a slow lope and joined by men's voices, until her box set down on something flat and didn't move again. After that the voices disappeared. All was quiet.

She waited in blackness. Time passed slower now, and the box felt hotter. She knew she needed to check the pocketwatch so she found a match in her kit and lit it, sulphur smoke burning her nose. She looked at the watch but couldn't figure out which way to hold it, to get the hands to where they made any sense. Then she realized there was coal oil spilled all over—she'd stopped smelling it—and she was about to light herself on fire. So she snuffed out the match. Time to go. She unhitched a latch and pushed up on the top of the crate. It lifted a few inches.

She sat up, sliding the lid off, onto the hard dirt floor. Felt a little dizzy, so she just sat there a minute, cooling off. The space all around her was almost as black as inside the box, but the air was drier, cleaner, more expansive. Felt like a big space. Slowly she stepped out of the box, onto the dirt. Reached back in, found the lantern, shook it to make sure there was still some fuel left, and lit it.

The place was so big, the dim lantern light didn't come close to hitting the walls. Piled high everywhere were crates big and small, square ones and long ones. They all had writing on them but she knew she just needed to look for the letters B and F. That meant Bean Flour, which really meant gunpowder. These white folks never said what they meant.

She heard voices and crept across the room to a door. Two men were talking outside. She couldn't hear the words, but one laughed, and then one walked away and it was quiet again. She walked around the whole room, holding the little lantern out. It was a big warehouse, wooden crates everywhere, words everywhere, she didn't know how she was going to…and there it was. BEAN FLOUR, the whole damn word was right there, she was sure of it, the B like a butt, the F like a flag. A whole pile of crates full of Butts and Flags.

She ran back to her pine box, grabbed an armful of dynamite sticks and fuses and brought them to the backside of the Bean Flour boxes. The side away from the door. She went back and forth gathering explosives. She took out her 3-inch knife and cut the fuses into 20-foot lengths like she'd been shown, then notched the end of each stick and secured a fuse into it with a blasting cap. As she was fixing the 5th fuse, a rough hand spun her around, knocking her over. It was a big, fat, ugly white man, a Grayjacket sentry with a long, tobacco-stained beard, holding a rifle.

"Thought I heard somethin'. How'd y'all get in here?"

"Don' rightly know, sir. Musta fell asleep in one o' them boxes and when I woke up…"

He slapped her hard. "We gonna hang you for sure. Somethin' else first though." He unlooped the suspenders from his shoulders.

She tried to run but he hit her again. This time it dazed her so she could only lie there, not sure if she remembered how to breathe. He dropped his pants, lowered himself to his knees and yanked her trousers down to her ankles. She felt her mind go numb but she was fighting the feeling too, she couldn't let it end this way. This was like what the walkin' boss was doing just before he killed her mammy. She tried to pull her legs together but the sentry tore her pants off one foot and dragged her legs apart and forced himself into her.

Looking away from his smelly face, she saw her little knife on the ground just a foot away. She slid her hand out. Grabbed it. Brought it back to the side of her body. Pulled it onto her belly and turned it, blade up. So every time his gross body came down on her again, it was punctured by the three-inch blade. Up and down, in and out. He didn't even feel it, he was so taken up with his violation of her, with pushing into her and crushing her with every thrust, he didn't even feel the cuts…until he did.

After a dozen knife punctures he began to register a little pain; and then the sense something was wrong. Terrible wrong. He paused for a moment, still inside her, pushed up on his arms and looked down. There was blood everywhere, streaming from his belly, pooling on hers, flowing down to the floor. And her hand clutching a small knife pointing straight up. He got dizzy and rolled off to the side.

She sat up. Whispered the last words in his ear he would ever hear in this life. Then she put her face in front of his and smiled. It wasn't much longer before he died.

While he was doing that she pulled up her pants, picked up her knife and went back to fixing her fuses. In twenty minutes she had it done. Then she lit them all and walked out the door. There was nobody in the immediate vicinity, but she could see a lot of other guards scattered around a compound of three warehouses and several outbuildings, surrounded everywhere by trees that hid the compound. She ran quietly into the night, avoiding them all until she was well away and heading toward the ocean, by the smell. She had a good nose.

A minute later she heard the explosion, so massive it shook her to the ground, even this far off. Then two more explosions, one bigger, one smaller. She got right back up, kept running all the way to the water and then into it, tearing off her pants again; but this time to get clean.

CHAPTER 13

"**M**OON, YOU ARE BEIN'** just too melancholy. Now what is the matter?"

"It's my fault Jersey gone, Missus. We had a big fight and I said things. Right after that's when she up and left. My fault and now she gone."

"Well it's not right that you take the blame. She was free to do what she wanted."

"No'm, she weren't. That's why she ran." That sank in for a moment. "But she didn't just run from you," he added, feeling even worse. "She felt like I was ownin' on her, too. Girl was feelin' twice a slave."

"All right, we'll both take the blame, then. Now go back to the *hacienda* and thank Aurelia for her kind help and bring the last of my things here, understand?"

"Yes'm." He left, sidestepping Jessup who was just entering.

"How's your father holding up?" he asked her.

Her face turned dark. "I gave Major Russell $1000, which is the biggest remainin' part of my cotton sale. But he says for another five hundred he can bribe a judge he knows to give Daddy a stay of execution for a month."

"The man is bleeding you dry!" Jessup could scarcely contain his anger.

"Yes. But Daddy's goin' to draw a map to his mine for me. With luck I can be there and back with enough gold to buy his escape. It can't be that hard, the way Daddy says it's just waitin' there to get chipped out of the hardrock."

Jessup paused. "Allie…you're sure your father is innocent?"

"How could you even ask such a thing?"

"Well, if I'm going to go all the way to California to dig that ore out of the rock, I don't want to be a turncoat to boot."

She gasped. "You can't do that! What about your Ranger work down here?"

"I got some time off comin'. And Rip owes me a couple favors. Besides, I've done some mining, I'd know what to look for a lot quicker than you would."

She paced the room, thinking. Shaking her head, then nodding. He really was going to help. This Ranger, this sweet man was going to get her daddy out of the hangman's noose. She could barely contain her happiness.

"All right, here's what. You visit Daddy, instead of me. You'll understand his map better anyway. And if you think there's somethin' not right about it, or it's too dangerous, you tell me and I'll just figure out another way. Promise?"

He nodded somberly. "I swear it."

Tears filled her eyes and she kissed him on the mouth with a deep, passionate embrace; then whispered in his ear. "Ahotay. I think I might be falling in love."

Moon walked his mule pulling the wagon piled with the last of Allie's things. He wore the new pants and shirt she'd bought him, and carried his bible, which he used for practicing his reading. He sometimes saw other people reading books with pictures on the cover and wondered what it would be like to read those books.

Just the thought of reading a new book got him a touch excited. What would it be about? Might it be funny? He'd seen people laughing when they read, and he wondered if the books told jokes. It made him smile to think of it—maybe he'd turned some kind of corner, from losing his wife to being a free man, Doo-Dah, Doo-Dah. He laughed at that and started singing aloud. "*Camptown ladies sing dis song, doo-dah, doo-dah…*"

At the first corner of the business district he stopped. Singing so happily he hadn't been watching closely and almost ran over a man in the road. Not just any man, either. Of all the terrible luck in the world—it was Delgado, the dressmaker who'd thrown them out of the clothing store that day. He didn't look any too happy now, either.

"What the hell," he snarled.

"I'm awful sorry, sir…"

"You again. You stealin' this whole wagonload now?"

"Naw, sir, I ain't stealin' it, I'm just takin' it."

"Same thing, takin' as stealin'. I got to beat you to tell me who it belongs to?"

"Belongs to Miz Stoneman." He had a thought and took a carved figurine from his pocket, the one he'd carved for Allie, as proof all these belongings were hers. "This her personal carvin'. You can't beat me for takin' her what's rightful…"

Delgado was so incensed that Moon would tell him what he couldn't do, he raised his walking stick and struck the poor servant in the head. Moon fell to his knees, arms upraised; but didn't fight back.

The dressmaker hit him again. And again. Passersby went on their way, some of them averting their eyes, others staring without hesitation, some even cheering the shopkeeper on. When Moon's hands fell to support himself, the shopkeeper hit him on the head even harder.

Tinbury rounded the corner and stopped. Surely this wasn't the proper place for something like this, even if it was appropriate discipline. "Hear, hear, you needn't get carried away." Ever the diplomat.

But Delgado was breaking a sweat and couldn't stop himself, though Moon was unconscious on the ground, offering no resistance whatever.

Then Jessup showed up on his horse at a walk. "What's goin' on here?" He dismounted and walked over. "That's Moon!" He held the shopkeeper's upraised arm. "Hold on, there, I know this fella, I was just on my way to help him pack."

The dressmaker jerked his arm away and went back to beating Moon. Jessup tore the cane from his hand and whacked him hard three times on the head. When the man moved to get up, Jessup hit him twice more until Delgado sagged, unconscious.

Jessup laid Moon in the wagon, tied his horse to the tailgate and called to Tinbury. "I'm taking him to Mrs. Stoneman's new place—you get a doctor over there in a hurry." He described where the cottage was and drove the rig there, whipping the mule for speed. He wasn't sure if Tinbury could find a doctor who'd take care of Coloreds, but he was pretty sure Allie would want her last slave cared for proper.

Delgado lay unmoving in the street, people stepping over or around him as they passed. He was well known in the neighborhood, and not many tears would be shed for his condition, whatever it turned out to be.

Clayton came through the front door of Brave River and looked around. Teddy played cards at a table occupied mostly by mule skinners and buffalo hunters, comfortable in the company of rough men. Isaac was escorting a belligerent drunk out the back door. Hermano dozed beside the water pump, Milagra threw a bucket of potato peels outside the back door onto the belligerent drunk, said "*Lo siento,*" and walked back inside. Zhi Li paused in her window washing to smoke a cigarette. Claire was tugging on the moustaches of a high-ranking Hungarian diplomat, while Scully drank alone at the bar. Clayton joined him.

Scully raised his glass. "So were we divertin' enough for you, *mi Capitan*? Did you steal what you had to steal?" His words were slurred by a belly full of rye.

Clayton looked peeved. "You were supposed to be the lookout."

"And so I was. I looked out and saw Isaac cornered so I went to help the boyo."

"I said no killin'."

"These things happen when gunplay starts."

"It didn't just happen. Before you helped Isaac you killed those English sailors for no reason but you hate the English."

"The bloody English." He spat on the floor.

"What you do on your own time's your own business. When you work for me, you take my orders. I won't say it again."

"You needn't get so high and mighty…" But as he turned to face Clayton, he bumped into Isaac, who was standing just inches behind him, without a hint he'd snuck up. Scully stood motionless for a moment, then smiled. "Sure and you needn't say it again, boss. Orders is orders. I can keep myself in line."

Isaac took a step back. He'd always been wary of Scully—the New York Irish had no love for blacks, rioting against them in Manhattan just a few weeks ago. It had started as a general protest against the Draft, against the law that allowed rich whites to avoid military service by hiring substitute draftees. But the marches quickly turned into hordes of Irish vigilantes killing hundreds of blacks, burning their churches, lynching and looting. Isaac knew Scully wasn't necessarily of that mind—after all, he wasn't a despised immigrant to America, fighting for leftover crumbs against equally poor northern blacks; he was just an Irish fugitive, running with a French expeditionary force, and now lost in the taverns of Mexico. He'd likely formed his own peculiar opinions about the human condition. But Isaac always kept his eyes, and his options, open.

Clayton took Scully's measure; then put five gold pieces into his pocket. "Be sure you do keep yourself in line. And I thank you for giving Isaac a hand during the fight."

"We're in the same corps, now. Me brothers is who I fight for." He gave Isaac a nod, and Isaac returned the gesture. "Besides, I like the way the weight o' them coins tips me sideways. For that, your honor, I can keep myself in a very straight line indeed." He had another whiskey, to seal the deal with himself.

Down the bar Claire was rebuffed by the Hungarian fop, who laughed in her face and left. She turned as red as a desert rose. Scully excused himself to Clayton and walked over to the lady's side, with a mind to take advantage of the situation.

"Any news of where the munitions went?" Clayton asked Isaac.

"Pretty clear when the warehouse blew. Eight soldiers dead, no women. Nobody on earth can tell black from white after a body's skin is burned off, though."

"Then I hope to God the girl got away. And speakin' of hope, any news of the *Defiant*?"

"No, but I've been preoccupied. Governor Pesqueira was here for a loan from Pierce, to shore up his defenses against the French. I made a separate deal with him."

"You got the land grant?"

Isaac nodded. "Northwest Mexico, from Puerta Penasco on the gulf coast to the Sonoita River. Gives us a Pacific port for trade, farming on the river and mining rights."

"All you have to do is defeat the French."

"I'm gratified you have so much confidence in me."

"Well, you've studied up on all those great historical wars, it's about time you put some of that book learnin' to practical use." But before Clayton could tease him any further, Tinbury entered, buoyant, and ordered a beer.

"What makes you so chipper, Mr. Tinbury? Find a new mustache hair?"

"You can mock me all you want but it's not every day an ordinary citizen gets to save a man's life. Puts a little lift in your step."

"Then I congratulate you, sir, and your beer is on the house. Tell us the news."

Tinbury got confidential. "Well—I don't like to brag—but that nasty clothier Delgado was mercilessly beating on this poor Colored boy in the street, beating him to death by the look of it, and I said stop that, do you hear? But he didn't stop, so I had to restrain him personally, while that Ranger Jessup carried the boy off to his owner."

"Jessup," said Clayton. "He's the one been helpin' out Mrs. Stoneman of late, has he not?"

"Yes, that's right. It was her new house the Colored was going to, Jessup said. I believe that's where he took the boy. He told me to send a doctor there right quick and I put the best medical man I know on the case."

When Clayton asked where the house was, Tinbury told him. But when Tinbury prattled on, Clayton didn't stay for embellishments; he just made for the door.

Moon lay in Allie's gilt, filigreed, four-poster bed in a stupor, eyelids at half mast, staring fixedly to the extreme far right. Allie stood back while a small, ferret-like doctor dressed more like an undertaker finished his exam.

"He'll be dead by morning. Nothing you can do for him. That'll be ten dollars."

Allie noticed Moon's left hand was gripped in a fist. She pried open the fingers, hoping to make him relax, and the small wooden man he'd carved her all those weeks ago fell to the floor. She picked it up with a terrible tugging at her heart. "Can't we make him more comfortable at least?" she asked. "He looks so frightened."

"I can sell you some laudanum. That's two dollars more."

"He don't need laudanum," said a voice at the door. Clayton was standing there, just arrived. "He needs trephination, and a competent doctor who can do it."

"Coloreds don't warrant such amount of effort. Besides, this man is beyond that extreme," said the doctor. "He's dead already, he just don't know it."

"I don't care for your tone," said Allie. "Please leave."

"I'll have my ten dollars first."

Grabbing the doctor by the scruff of the coat collar and the small of his belt, Clayton quick-walked him out the house and tossed him into the dirt. Allie was looking teary-eyed at the little wood figurine Moon had made her when Clay came back in.

Allie felt grateful to Clay for his decisive action but couldn't dispel her sorrow over Moon. "I fear I've taken this poor man for granted for some years."

"I know that feeling," he replied, keeping his gaze fixed on Allie.

"And now he won't be waked up. This loyal companion's the last piece left of my old life. Too much is changing, Clay. I feel quite at sea."

"The war surgeon who fixed my leg is stayin' across the river; she might could help Moon. I fear there's little assistance she can provide for your own self, though, Allie." But when she turned to reprove him she saw he'd said it with a deep affection; and there came upon her a small rush of that old feeling.

"Go on, now, you find you a doctor for this poor soul."

Clayton crossed the river to Brownsville Hospital, where Dr. Hawks was ministering to wounded Union POWs as Ambassador Pierce organized a prisoner exchange in the next room. While Hawks was with a patient Clayton entered Pierce's makeshift office and spoke softly.

"I came for the doctor," said Clayton. "Didn't expect to see you here."

"Nor I, you. But I can tell you now—General Banks is set to attack Brownsville the first of November."

"That's the fallback invasion, then, after the debacle at the Sabine Pass?"

Pierce nodded. "Lincoln wants badly to occupy the Rio Grande—let Napoleon know he'd better not recognize the Confederacy, or we'll push into Mexico after him."

"You'll want someone battle-tested to train your little army to nip at the fort's flank when Banks's troops arrive."

"You volunteering?"

"No. But I know someone who might fit the bill."

The bed was covered with a straw mat and several layers of sheets. Jessup held Moon's head in place while Isaac tied his arms to the bedposts and Clay did his legs. Dr. Hawks, wearing a surgical smock, shaved off Moon's hair on the side of the head his eyes were pointing to; a tray of medical drilling instruments sat on a table beside her. Allie stood nearby, holding a towel and ready to fetch what was needed.

"He won't feel this," said Dr. Hawks, "so you needn't worry on that account. But there will be bleeding. If that's apt to make you faint, you'd do us all a favor by leaving now." She looked gently at Allie.

"I've seen blood," said Allie, and made no move to leave. Clay thought she'd achieved a degree of self-possession he found admirable—though he wondered where she'd seen blood, and what trials she'd been through since last they were together.

Picking up a scalpel, Hawks made a cruciate incision in Moon's scalp, then cauterized bleeders with silver nitrate. She peeled back the four triangles of skin, revealing a two-inch square of white bone. "You see?" she said to the room. "His skull is white as yours. Barely a millimeter of outer skin is any darker. Now you tell me if that's a reason to make another human being a slave." Nobody answered. Allie was the only one here who'd ever owned a slave, and her position on the matter was uncertain.

Hawks took up the trephine—an awl with a circular ring blade at the business end, and a wood-handled T at the gripping end. She put the sharp-edged ring to Moon's skull and twisted the handle while forcefully pushing down—cutting a deeper and deeper ring into the bone. It was hard work and Hawks was soon sweating. "Almost there," she said. Allie watched her work. Clay watched Allie.

Jessup had seen a thing or two Rangering, but never as calculated an intrusion into a man's brainpan as this. Made him queasy, though he'd never admit such a thing. Instead he looked away and thought about a meadow back home, dotted with yellow spring flowers. Whatever else, he was determined not to pass out.

Isaac conversed with Moon in his most soothing voice, to calm whatever was left of the poor man. "Just remember, your name is Moon, and the moon might fall away into darkness but it always rises again, just like you're bound to rise again."

Allie forced herself to watch. She felt she owed Moon that much at least. She knew Clay was watching her but didn't want this to be about them—though she was grateful to him for bringing the doctor, and felt more up to this task knowing Clay had always been able to handle most situations. But she wouldn't think about that now.

Hawks kept turning the circular blade into the skull until there was finally a small lurch. "I'm in," she said, more to herself than the others. Then: "Hand me that elevator, would you?" She pointed to a spatula just out of her reach. Isaac gave it to her.

She insinuated the flat bevel into an arc of the circle she'd cut, leveraging the disc of bone out, placing it gingerly on the table. Exposed now was a circle of glistening, gray-red membrane. Jessup accidentally glanced over. "Is that...is that his brain?"

"No, that's the *dura mater*, it bags the brain. And that's a big blood clot behind it, pressing down on the cerebral cortex. I'm going to cut into the *dura* to release the pressure. A lot of bleeding at first and then I'll bandage it. I'll be needing towels."

Allie stepped up, towel in hand. Clay spoke softly behind her. "May I help?"

"I'm quite capable, thank you."

"I can see you are." Their eyes met only briefly, then Allie nodded to Dr. Hawks to proceed, as she held the towel ready.

Esther Hawks applied the scalpel in a circular motion around the edge of bone, cutting into the *dura mater*. There was a rush of dark red blood mixed with clot, out the skull hole and running down Moon's face. Allie mopped up the gouts of blood as the doctor examined the brain tissue beneath. Suddenly the most extraordinary thing happened. Moon's eyes shifted back to midline and he looked around.

"Is ever'body all right?" he asked.

Jessup fainted. Isaac caught the Ranger mid-crumple, letting him down slowly to the floor. "'*And many that are first shall later be last,*'" Isaac said gently.

"Let him be," said Dr. Hawks, "He'll be fine. And you'll be fine too, Moon. You just had an accident. I'm the doctor."

Moon looked confused. "You the nurse, you mean. I ain't that sick not to know the difference." Allie put the towel to his head to stanch the flow. "Moon," said Allie, "you were very thoughtless to scare us so. I believed somethin' serious was wrong with you."

"No, ma'am. I be back to work for you directly." But he saw a tear curl down Allie's cheek and it made him concerned he was sicker than he thought. He tried to remember what had brought him here but couldn't recall a single event of the day. He remembered going to bed last night—and felt confused again. "Where Jersey got to?"

"She'll be here in a jiffy," said Allie. "We'll make her do all the work for a while."

"Oh, she won't like that. I'll talk to her about it though." Moon grew sleepy. "You want me to sing you a song?"

"Look what I got here, Moon," said Allie, grabbing his figurine out of her apron pocket. "It's the man you made me. Remember? He don't talk, but he's a good listener."

They watched Moon's eyes close slowly, a peaceful smile on his face. The bleeding had slowed to a trickle. "Is he dead?" asked Allie with a thick voice.

"No, but he might be soon, or he might wake up and live a long life. You'll need to change the dressing twice a day." She wrapped Moon's head in cotton batting. "We want it to keep draining. That's why you'll need to change those bandages."

Jessup woke and sat up. "I'm awful sorry."

"We all go where the spirit leads us," said Clay. "Nothin' to apologize for." He glanced at Allie when he said it. She glanced away but didn't know where to look.

The doctor did a bit more doctoring as Isaac helped Allie change the bloody sheets. She was relieved to have something useful to do. Jessup went out for some fresh air, wondering how he could make it up to Allie for his useless behavior.

Allie placed the little wooden carving at Moon's side, within his reach. Then she walked out to join Jessup. Clay wondered what they were talking about.

And Moon lay in bed; whether in a state of grace, punishment, or infinite blackness, none could tell.

CHAPTER 14

CLAYTON WENT ON THE prowl for Scully, to get him involved in the invasion backup plans. The man had disobeyed his order once, killing those British sailors he needn't have; but Clayton didn't think he'd do that again, after their talk; and beyond that there was something about him Clayton connected with. For one thing he'd shown mettle at the firefight on the beach. Saved Isaac, though Isaac had made it out of tougher spots before. And Scully was certainly war-tough enough for the kind of military operation Pierce was envisioning. Clayton thought he'd make a serviceable lieutenant.

But Scully wasn't on his favored barstool at Brave River. Rheumy said he heard the mick had been keeping more time at General Bee's *hacienda* lately, doing chores there. That news puzzled Clayton, since Allie was living elsewhere now—so why would Scully stick around, if he wasn't spying on Allie? Or maybe he knew something Clayton didn't and was working overtime for a promotion. Or maybe he was finding himself a different kind of companionship with General Bee's housekeeper.

On his way out he stopped by Zhi Li. "Things workin' out for you here, Zhi Li?"

She shook her head. "I think you like my pipe too much. No more pipe for you."

"What do you mean?" His stomach flipped just a little.

"Too much pipe no good. Good for my customer, not for my boss. Time make friend with your leg again."

He was irritated. "You made friends with your feet yet? Those burns healed up?"

"Feet never heal. Chinese woman's feet must be small, like Emperor's concubine, so my feet broken, never heal. Not so bad. Don't need opium." She minced away on her foot binding slippers. Annoyed by her stoicism, Clayton just headed for General Bee's *hacienda*.

There he found Scully hanging laundry with Aurelia. They both looked sullen and snappish, making Clayton think it was definitely the housekeeper holding him here. Soon as he arrived they stopped bickering and Aurelia stalked off in a huff.

"Well, ain't you the charmin' lothario," smiled Clayton.

"I don't know what that means but take it back or I'll flatten you."

"Consider it taken. Might I have a word?"

"If you help me with the wash you might. Seems this is the only way I can redeem myself, and I don't even know what it was I said." He gave Clayton a handful of clothes pegs and some wet laundry.

"I'm lookin' for a man to lead a battle."

"If it pays, I'm your man."

"You told me once you were done with war."

"I ain't done with makin' money. When I have enough I aim to buy land out west."

"Well, until I need you to soldier I can pay you to help out with Mrs. Stoneman's injured house man. While you're there you can keep an eye on her comin's and goin's."

"Long as I don't do laundry," said Scully, dropping his wet clothes in the basket.

"I'll take you there now, then. The doctor will likely have some chores for you."

"I got somethin' needs doctorin' meself, so we're both in luck." And the two men went off, Clayton describing the coming invasion in broad strokes.

*   *   *

When they got to Allie's place, Dr. Hawks was packing up her instruments. Allie stood at the bedside adjusting Moon's pillow, Moon unconscious, his head swaddled in bandage. Isaac and Jessup were both gone. Clayton approached Allie.

"Are you all right?"

"Am *I* all right? What about poor Moon?"

"Well, if you tend his wounds as well as you did mine, he'll be around in no time."

She brushed off the compliment and went back to making Moon comfortable. Clayton turned to address Esther Hawks. "Doctor, one of my employees, here, Mr. Scully, apparently has a medical concern. I wonder if I could prevail upon you to see one more patient before you head back."

"Mr. Wilkes, I may as well open up a clinic in your gambling hall, it'd save a lot of travel time. And how's your leg doing, if I may ask?"

"Doin' jim dandy." He pulled up his pants leg. She crouched down, palpated the area around the healing bullet wound, still showing a small hole. "Still leaking some, but it's clear serum, no more corruption. Good thing you've got a strong constitution. She stood up. "I'll check Moon once more, then you can show me your other patient."

As she went to her patient's bedside, Scully pulled Clayton out the door with a grim whisper. "You didn't tell me the doctor was no woman."

"What's it matter? She's a good doctor, I can vouch for that."

"That ain't it."

"Ain't what?"

Scully steeled himself. "I gotta talk to her in private, then."

"What's the problem, man?"

Scully struggled to speak, but finally got it out. "I got sores on me pecker." He plunged ahead. "Got 'em from Claire if I ain't much mistook."

Clayton shrugged. "You best show Doctor Hawks what you got."

"But she's a *female!*"

"Son, I'm damn sure you shown your pecker to a female before. Seems to me that was the whole problem. Just show the doc as much o' your pecker as she needs to help you out. If a red face is the steepest wages o' sin you pay, you're a lucky Irishman."

They went back inside. Clayton stood near Allie as Scully and Hawks walked to the next room. Dr. Hawks paused at the door and looked back at Allie. "I like your grit, young lady," she said; then exited with Scully and closed the door behind them.

"Whatever is goin' on in there?" Allie wanted to know.

"Just a bit of medical consultation. Scully's a good man, and lookin' for work. You think you might have some odd jobs for him around here, now that Moon's indisposed?"

"Indisposed, is that what you call it?" she snapped.

It was plain her pique was a cover for fear, or guilt, or some such; clear to Clayton, at any rate, and it clutched his heart. "It's a hard life on the Rio Grande, Allie. Are you holdin' up?"

The care in his voice broke her down. "I'm holdin', Clay. Up or down is a long walk to figure."

"I been tryin' not to figure for some time, now."

"You seem to be doin' all right. I'm hopin' to be a successful importer myself, and this is the place to get rich doin' it, I'm told."

He nodded. "That it is." He felt like they were having a normal conversation for the first time since she'd come to town; it gave him a tentative thrill, though he tried hard to ignore it. "I'd be happy to make some introductions for you."

It seemed to her as if Clay had changed, had become more mature since the old days. Or was it just an act, like it always had been? She wondered who he really was. She wondered who *she* really was, for all of that; or what she felt. "I'm not sure that's such a good idea, Clay."

"You needn't be beholdin' to me for helpin you out. I've got my own good life here."

But he looked away when he said it, which made her disbelieve him. That, in turn, left her feeling both sad for him and angry at him. And neither of those emotions were the basis of getting on a sound footing with a man.

"Well, that's a fine thing for you, then, Clay. Get you on with your good life, and I'll get on with mine."

While Scully stayed behind at Allie's to help out with chores and Moon duties, Clayton walked Dr. Hawks back to her buggy.

"Your Lieutenant Scully has given me liberty to discuss his case with you, since you'll be collecting his treatment at the chemist." She handed him a slip of paper with medical scribbles on it. "Nitrate of silver, I'll have to cauterize those luetic bubos."

"I expect you will," he said blankly.

"The man has syphilis, and there's no mercury to be had in Texas, so I'll burn the sores on his peter, then he needs to apply black wash every three hours—it's on that paper for the chemist. Tincture of agrimony and green vitriol."

"I suppose there's a lesson in all that."

"He's about to learn it soon enough. Might be prudent to tell the lady he got it from, too. She'll be wanting a visit from me before she catches the next young man's eye, and he catches something else from her."

Clayton thought of all the eyes of all the men he'd seen Claire catch in recent weeks; and thought it might be well to curtail his own amorous activities for a while.

"One more thing," said the doctor. "I need a favor, and Leonard Pierce suggested you might be of assistance."

"I don't really know Mr. Pierce, but whatever I can do for you, I will try my best."

"There's a woman I've been caring for—a survivor of Quantrill's Raid up in Lawrence a few weeks ago. I expect you know about it?"

"Rebel militia burned the place to ashes, is what I heard. Your patient is one of the wounded, I take it?"

"You might say so. She saw some unspeakable acts there, and I believe she now suffers from Da Costa's Syndrome. You may have heard of Soldier's Heart?"

"No, ma'am."

"Well. The things she witnessed have troubled her soul, and her nervous system as well. She fears she will die if she spends one more night on U.S. soil."

"You want me to find a place for her in Matamoros?"

"Temporarily, yes. And I'd like you to give her a job, to boot. She used to nurse but she can cook, clean and tend. I believe getting back to her daily routines might help."

"I've rooms behind the casino, she's welcome there. She can help Milagra cook, make sure those that pass out drunk are comfortable. How long might this go on for?"

"She means to go live with family in England—as far from America as she can get. I don't know how long it will take her to get there, though."

"I expect I can pay her a small wage until she makes enough to book passage."

As they reached Dr. Hawks's buggy, she opened the door and held out her hand. "Mr. Clayton Wilkes, may I introduce you to Mrs. Dinah Singletary?"

Inside the buggy sat a 60-year-old woman, plain of dress and face, with the hollow eyes of a deer who's stumbled unexpectedly into a hunter's camp.

Clayton bowed slightly. "It's an honor to meet you, ma'am."

She neither smiled nor spoke.

"Mrs. Singletary has a taciturn nature," said Esther Hawks, "but I assure you is a hard worker, and eager to get started. Isn't that so, my dear?"

Dinah Singletary looked like she might cry, but extended her hand to shake.

Clayton took her hand gently. "Well, let's get started, then."

Clayton showed Dinah around Brave River. Introduced her to Jim and Rheumy, to Zhi Li, to Hermano. Showed her where the mops were kept, showed her where Milagra was cooking—tortillas, *nopales*, pulled pork—and introduced them.

"Eres bienvenido aqui," Milagra smiled gently, seeing the pain in the woman's heart. You are most welcome here.

Dinah's eyes kept leaking. When Clayton finally showed her to her room—a spare 8 X 6 affair with a thin bed and a tiny table with wash basin—she openly wept. But from start to finish in this orientation to her new life, she never made a sound.

That night while Scully watched over Moon, Allie and Jessup walked through the starlight to the back gate of Fort Brown and waited.

"There ought to be a guard on duty here," whispered Jessup.

"Russell paid the man to take off for a spell," said Allie.

They waited in silence, Jessup still ashamed at having fainted during Moon's procedure, Allie tense at the possibility of getting caught at the illicit gate of the fort. The door opened and Major Russell appeared. He looked suspicious.

"What's he doing here?"

"He's goin' to speak with Daddy. They have to make plans."

Russell looked like he was deciding whether to walk away from the whole thing. "All right. The money's gone up. The judge I found wants a thousand a week to stay the execution, minimum three weeks."

"How much money do you think I have?"

"It costs what it costs."

"Fine, then. Let's you and I go settle the financial arrangements while the lieutenant meets with Daddy."

Russell nodded, ushered them into the fort and shut the door. They walked down a long dark hallway until they came to a row of three barred cells. The first two were empty. In the third a prisoner sat on the dirt floor in the dark.

"You got a visitor," said Russell. Then, to Jessup, "We'll be back in fifteen minutes." Russell and Allie left Jessup standing at the cell door. The man on the floor lit a candle and stood slowly.

In the candlelight he looked gaunt, as if he hadn't eaten much in weeks. Pale, paper-thin skin, with a scraggly beard, sparse hair on his head; and Allie's blue eyes. He opened his mouth to speak, but a soft cough came out with the words: "You must be Allie's young man."

"I'm not sure as I'd say that, sir."

"Be that as it may…I understand you're here to help, and I thank you."

"That's all right. Allie said you had a map to show me?"

He tapped his forefinger to his temple. "It's all up here. I'll have to draw it for you."

He got a pencil and paper from the corner and began drawing a map by the light of the candle. "The mine is five miles beyond Sutter's Mill, where they struck the first lode. You have to raft down the Tuolumne and hike a steep cut. You do any mining?"

"Yes, sir. Silver mines in New Mexico. Never much good, 'cept for a strong back."

"That's all you need. Once you pull the rockslide away from the cave entrance, you'll see quartz veins all through the walls. Gold runs with quartz. Pick-axe those crystals, the gold falls into your hands." He stopped drawing, frowned at his map. "Wait, that's not right." He turned the paper over and started from scratch on the other side.

"Maybe a little more light would help. Want me to dig up another candle?"

"Eyesight's not the problem. Pulling it out of my head, that's the trick." He kept writing. "There's this outcropping shaped like coyote ears on the north bank…no, wait, it's south of the river, I keep getting turned around…" He stopped drawing; stared at the paper; had a coughing fit; then paused, wheezing.

"Want to describe it to me? I'm pretty good with directions."

The old man looked at Jessup with a pleading gaze. "I can't do this, can I?"

"Just talk it out. Writing's a puzzlement to me, too, sometimes."

With great effort the man walked to the bars and spoke softly. "I can find my way there, I have it in my memory—I just can't explain it. I have to go there to know how to get there. Does that make sense?"

"I reckon it has to."

"My mind is failing, I suppose."

"I guess we'll just have to get you out of here first. Then you can ride to the mine on your own."

The old man extended his hands through the bars. Put one softly on Jessup's cheek and took Jessup's hand in the other. "I can see how she favors you. You have a kindness to your manner." Tears came to his sweet eyes.

Jessup felt embarrassed. "I'm just doin' what anyone would."

"You know, my partner's dead, they hung him."

"They won't do you like that. We'll get you out of here."

"That's not what I meant. I meant any son-in-law of mine will get half the gold now. All of it when I die." He took off one shoe, twisted the heel, pulled something out of a secret compartment and gave it to Jessup. It was a gold nugget. "For you," he whispered. "From our mine."

Then he walked back to the corner of the cell and collapsed in exhaustion, leaving the Ranger open-mouthed, but without a thing to say.

As they left the fort, Jessup told Allie her father couldn't draw the map.

"Couldn't draw it!? Why not?"

"He's an old man, he's not well…"

"If he can't locate the mine for us, how'll we get the money to buy his way out of prison?" She sounded devastated.

"We'll come up with somethin'."

"But we won't. I've already given Russell more than I can afford, and now he wants more and I can't credit where to get it."

"There's folks in Matamoros with money. The town's rollin' in it."

"Anyone can see that. Why, I bet those bandits you been chasin' stole more just today than I need altogether."

"That's likely true." He thought of how rich Cortina was reputed to be; rich enough to hire men, to buy guns and horses, to buy his own army. But then Cortina hadn't stolen all of his ill-gotten gains. Everyone knew Leonard Pierce gave money to Cortina to raid across the river into Texas. Cortina and Pierce were thick as thieves, rich with Yankee blood money. Which gave Jessup the inklings of an idea.

Pierce kept all his riches in a strongbox in his house, it was said. If Jessup could discover its location, he might help Allie's father get free. With a move like that he could even vindicate himself after his poor showing at Moon's bedside, as well as strike a blow for the Confederacy, all at the same time. And now that these thoughts were rolling around his skull, hadn't Rip Ford told him that Clayton Wilkes was secretly a Southern spy? It was all coming together.

He took her hand as they walked. "I might just have a plan," he said.

She squeezed his hand a little tighter. This Ranger had her back; a man of word and deed. Her feelings for him grew a little stronger with every connection. And now her father was going to live.

Next day Captain Odeel cornered Major Russell in the Officers' mess hall. "That Allie Stoneman is up to something. I believe she's a spy."

"You see spies under every bush, son."

"She cheated the Confederate States out of their cotton money and she appears to be buttering up the Southern high command, taking their pictures and the like. If she's up to some mischief, I intend to call you in a hurry, and you best come arunnin'."

Russell put some threat into his voice. "You best back away from whatever you think you're getting on about." The last thing he wanted was this idiot stumbling onto the planned jailbreak of Allie's father.

"What do you mean? Is there some intrigue I ought to be privy to?"

"No, sir. Just keep up your good works at the Cotton Bureau and you'll do fine."

* * *

Clayton was feeling shaky. He hadn't smoked the pipe in a day, and Zhi Li said she wouldn't give him another. He imagined he could find an alternate source in Bagdad if he looked hard, but decided enough was enough. So he had another drink instead.

Jessup walked up beside him at the bar. Both were looking forward.

"Afternoon, Mr. Wilkes."

"It is that, Lieutenant. Any luck chasin' down that *mal hombre* Cortina?"

Without preamble Jessup said, "I have it on authority you're a Southern spy."

Clayton broke out laughing. "What authority is that?"

"It's common knowledge in some circles. You needn't deny it. But I'm here on a related matter. I'd like to get the blueprints to Leonard Pierce's house."

"Would you, now."

"I would. And I know this endangers me some to be so open with you, but I want to steal the Federal money from his strongbox—which everyone knows he has."

"Now that's a tall order, Lieutenant."

"I'm thinkin' with his money gone he won't be able to pay Cortina's army to keep harassin' Texas, and as a Southern gentleman you should be in favor of that."

"In favor or not, how would I be likely to get Pierce's blueprints, let alone the location of this strongbox which 'everyone knows he has'?"

"You're a spy. That's the kind of thing spies can find out."

"Well, son, I appreciate your confidence in my snoopin' abilities, but you're just flat out of luck on this one."

Jessup didn't expect to hook him right away. But he had a hole card. "The money's meant to help Allie Stoneman. She's in great need, and I believe you have some affection for her."

As expected, this had an effect on Clayton. But the first reaction wasn't concern, as Jessup had anticipated. It was resentment. "What the hell do you know about my feelin's for Mrs. Stoneman?"

"I'm just sayin' what I heard and what I seen. You want to help her, then you need to help me get a load of money out of Pierce's stash. That way you help her and the Confederacy with the same raid."

Clayton considered all the ramifications. "All right. I'll not say I'm a Southern spy, nor anything else that could send me to Rock Island Prison. But if a man *were* to help you out, he'd need a lot more detail than you given so far."

Jessup smiled. He could feel his hook in Clayton Wilkes; time to give him more line. "All right. It starts with Allie's father bein' in jail at the fort, headed for the hangman in three weeks. But we have a way to buy him a jailbreak, bribin' the right people. Then once he's out he'll lead us to the gold mine he hid before the war."

Clayton nodded, contemplating the plan. "You need money for the bribes, then. For the guards, and the judge, and so forth."

"That and outfitting the gold expedition."

"I'll give it some thought. Just—out of respect for my past relationship with Allie, and for her sense of pride—don't let her know you spoke to me of this."

Jessup gave his most sincere look and extended his hand. "Done."

"You're runnin' the Spanish Prisoner on him!" Clayton was livid with anger, standing in Allie's front room.

Allie looked offended. "No, of course not. How could you think such a thing?"

"Look at who you're talkin' to, girl. Don't even try to finagle me."

She could see he wasn't going to buy any of her denials, so she dropped that charade quick. No use wasting both of their time.

"All right, so what if I am? What's the harm? I'm in need of operatin' capital."

"Who'd you get to play your father? Don't tell me Mose." When she shrugged, he got even more vexed. "Mose died of consumption back in '61."

"That's what he wanted everyone to think. He's fit as a fiddle now and he was pleased to help me out of a jam. Not like some people I know."

Once he cleared the hurdle of knowing he'd been had, Clayton couldn't resist smiling. "By God, Mose was good at the long con. Who'd you get to play the jailer?"

"Major Russell, he already has access to the lockup and he was happy to do it."

"Don't I know it. That man would sell his mother for a kickback."

"He sells the play pretty well, too. Wish we'd known about him back in the day, we could have used him on that English Duke in Virginia. Man has natural talent."

They were falling into the happy banter of their youth, the thrill of the hunt, the sweetness of the con, the skill of the players. And Oh Lord, if Clay wasn't into it now; she could see he was.

"I told Ahotay we're plannin'…"

"Who?"

"Jessup. I told him the prison break is set for the 16th, the big *Independencia* celebration will be a good cover, all the fireworks and gunshots goin' off, half the law drunk as everyone else. And it'll be my daddy's Liberation Day too!" That was always Allie's great gift. Believing her own con.

But Clayton nodded, he was seeing it. "All right, I have an idea, this could work. You'll get some money out of it and so will Russell. But you have to make it look like Mose either runs off or gets killed, so this con is done with, it's got no tail, no comin' back to this well. And then you're on your own with Jessup."

"Fine, then." She looked a little huffy.

He picked up on her attitude. "Wait a minute. You're in love with him, aren't you?"

"What of it?"

But he just smiled, shaking his head. "That's why you're the best player I ever knew. You actually believe in the world you're makin' up. That's why they always fall for it. You believe in it so much they believe right along with you."

"I don't see that that's much of a failin' in our line of work."

"No, not to speak of. It just sometimes gets in the way of our real lives, from one con to the next."

"Well I don't love him for all time," she protested.

"That's a fact, Allie. But then I never did recall what it is you do love for all time."

"Now you're just bein' mean. But tell me, Mr. High and Mighty, what are you gettin' out of hornin' in on my play?"

"I'll get a piece of Pierce's strongbox as well. But it's not just the money. It'll put some other gears in motion for me, that's the main thing."

They paused to stare into each other's eyes for what seemed like an eternity—and only a moment, as well; the two opposite ideas in one. Just like the two of them, opposites and the same, suspicious and attracted, nettled and ardent, chafing, inflamed, exasperated, impassioned…

And they embraced. A long, torrid, overdue embrace. Until he pushed her back at arm's length, gentle but firm.

"And if you cross me," he said sternly, "I'll blow your cover and you'll end up in the women's prison at Blackshear."

She became flushed, and a little breathless. "You know I can't resist you when you take that immoderate tone."

They entwined again. And now their mouths met like hungry animals as their hands pulled away clothes with unsparing desire. Caresses turned urgent, their breaths like one breath, guttural and feral, fingers gripping each other as if they might fall off the edge of the world if they didn't hold tight, didn't howl to the gods of rapture; and the frenzy of spasm. And the collapse.

They lay on the floor, partially clothed, in each other's arms. Breathing quietly.

"I've missed you," she whispered.

"I've been dead without you," he answered.

A soft grunt across the room drew their gazes. Moon was lying in his four-poster bed, 30 feet away, out as out could be.

"You think he heard us?" asked Clay.

"I hope so. The poor man could use to partake of a little pleasure for a change."

Clay thought much the same about himself, until he drifted off into the sweetest slumber he could remember...

They made love all afternoon. He felt as if his whole being were filled with the heady scent of her lavender perfume. They surprised each other with the things they did.

"Lordy, how old are you, girl?" he asked her sometime after dusk had erased the day.

"Old enough, I guess." But her accent was different now, from how she'd spoken down in the café. Allie had lots of different voices.

"Where you from?"

"Why's it matter? You want to write my life story?"

*"I want to **be** your life story."*

She threw on a robe. "They got a fancy inside bathroom here, I been told. Don't go nowhere while I tidy myself." She let the robe fall open as she left, to drive him crazy.

He went through her purse—a man had to make a living, after all. He found a wad of banknotes—the girl did well for herself—but he only took a few big ones.

When she wasn't back in ten minutes he pulled on his pants and walked down the hall, where the bathroom door was closed. He knocked. No answer. When he opened the door, he found it empty.

He hurried back to his room just in time to see her out the window, disappearing around the corner. And did she flash a coquettish smile back at him as she made the turn?

He rushed to his wallet on the dresser. Empty. He couldn't believe this. He went back to her purse, held her paper money to the light. Counterfeit.

She'd taken him for every penny, pure and simple. But he wasn't angry. In fact, he couldn't stop laughing. This girl didn't give away her body for money. She was a pickpocket, thief, counterfeiter, con artist, mimic of dialects and sexual provocateur.

In that moment, he knew he was in love...

Clay woke up actually laughing out of his nap, nuzzling up against her and knowing he was still in love, of all the goddam things. Even better than opium.

CHAPTER 15

T HE STEAMER CAPTAIN HAD off-loaded ten crates of saltpeter and fifty cartons of India tea to the Matamoros dockside. An hour later, when nobody'd come forward to sign for the goods, Allie stepped up and offered the captain thirty cents on the dollar. The captain said he was waiting for someone named Benderbosch, who was to meet him here with the money, fill out the paperwork, and take receipt of the cargo. Allie beamed, said *her* name was Benderbosch, and she was ready to take it all right now. The captain checked his pocketwatch, tapped his foot, looked around, and agreed.

Allie signed the documents *A. S. Benderbosch*, gave the man his discounted cash, whistled to the teamsters driving her wagon and made off to meet them at Fort Brown. Now she was at the fort, taking double her cost from Major Russell—who was still getting the goods for a 30% discount off the transporter's fee. He directed the teamsters to take the crates to his warehouse when a young black man showed up at Allie's side. "Miz Stoneman, I been lookin' all over for you. Miz Bee says please kin you come with me to her house now for somethin' special?"

"Well...all right." She wondered what the mystery was but thanked Major Russell for doing business with her and accompanied the servant in his buggy. They rode the short distance to the Commandant's home outside the fort. "This here's the way," said the young man, and she followed him down to the river.

He led her past the slave quarters—poorly built shacks, mostly empty during the day. A few old mammies cooked over campfires, and a few little ones too young to work ran around by the riverbank. Allie smiled but they turned away, trained not to look a white woman in the eye, on pain of whipping or worse.

Beyond the shacks was a grove of tall cane that opened to a clearing with a large tent at its center. Allie ducked under the flap and went inside. Eight Negro children and two adults sat in the dirt in two ragged rows, holding thin books. Before them was a chalkboard with simple words written on it; and beside the board stood Mildred Bee, who smiled broadly at Allie's entrance. "Why, you're just in time!"

"For what, if I may ask?" Allie was baffled. The slaves on the ground looked nervous, some even scared.

"Well, to help me teach these good folks their letters, of course," said Mildred, as if there couldn't be any other purpose. Then, to the students: "Please excuse us."

Mildred took Allie back outside the tent as Allie shook her head. "What on earth is goin' on?"

"It's a secret school to teach the Coloreds how to read, is all. Hamilton would forbid it if he knew, so you must promise me not to tell. Promise, now."

"All right. I promise." Of course she loved secrets of all kinds, so it was no great sacrifice to keep this one.

"But that's not all. I want you to help me."

"I'm no teacher."

"No more am I. But heavens, they just need to learn letters and a few words to get 'em started, and pretty soon they'll read good as any white man."

"But why me?"

"Because you set your house boy free, so I know your heart is good." She took Allie by the hands. "Will you help?"

Allie had never thought of herself as an abolitionist; or do-gooder of any variety, for that matter. But she did fancy the idea of pulling a little con like this under the nose of that stuffy General Bee, whom Mildred loved for reasons too opaque for Allie to fathom. So if Mildred was happy to sneak around like this, Allie wasn't about to stifle the impulse. "Of course I'll help," she said. "How could I refuse you?"

Mildred squeezed her hands and brought her back inside the tent. "Students, I'd like you to meet your new teacher, Mrs. Stoneman."

All nodded deferentially to Allie. She watched Mildred teach at the board, until she thought she'd got the hang of it; then just stepped up and did it. "Now this is the letter 'M,' y'all. Sounds like 'mmmmmm.' Can everyone say that?"

Before long she was fully inhabiting the identity of a schoolteacher, as if she'd been born to the task, in the organic way only a con woman of Allie's caliber could do. But for now her goal was to be everyone's favorite teacher, and to get these slaves reading better than the man who owned them, that pompous General Bee himself. "All right, who knows this letter?"

"That a O," said a proud 10 year old girl.

"O! O my! O! O! That's right!" smiled Allie, and everyone laughed. "What's your name, smart girl?"

"Shonny," said the girl, more shyly this time.

"Well, Shonny, you're the best reader I ever taught. Course, you're the *only* reader I ever taught, but I hope to make *all* of you the best readers. Will you help me?"

They all nodded. And Allie was immediately everyone's favorite teacher.

Aurelia had a full six-month belly on her now. She was in the kitchen with Scully, showing him how to make tortillas. They'd been soaking the corn kernels in limewater for two days, then letting them dry in the sun and crushing them into *masa harina*, the essential cornmeal. Now she was showing him how to form balls of dough in his fists.

"No, *es* too big," she laughed, pulling the dough from his hands, putting half back in the bowl, then folding his fingers around the smaller lump, her fingers around his—and they both felt it, a little electric tingle. She rolled the ball slowly on his palm with the flat of her own palm. Slight pressure. Their eyes caught. Something was in the air.

"Now we make flat," she said. She put the small ball on the table, rolled it with a clay tube, pressing until it was flat and round. "Now we cook."

"I just have to tend to a little business first."

He walked down a hall into the room he slept in, closed the door and leaned his back against it, collecting himself. He'd felt his pecker getting hard in the kitchen, which made the healing sores shoot pains, which reminded him he'd forgot to apply his last dose of blackwash—Dr. Hawks told him he must paint himself with it every four hours.

He pulled the jar off his closet shelf and uncorked it. The vapors of the green vitriol and agrimony assaulted his nose, making him gag. Best approach was just to do this and get it over with. He let his pants drop to the floor. His pecker was already dark from the mixture, but the doctor said it would fade with time. Scully stuck a rag in the solution, held his pud by the foreskin, pulled it out straight and painted it black.

He had two sores, one almost healed, one still an angry crater—both burning like hell when the blackwash went on. He gritted his teeth, finished the task quickly and put the bottle back in its place. As he pulled up his pants there was a soft knock on the door, and it opened while he was still buttoning up.

Aurelia entered, closing the door behind her. He was so stunned, he couldn't think of a thing to say. She walked quickly up to him and stood close, her breathing shallow quick. "I cannot estop myself," she whispered, and kissed him, and didn't estop.

He grew hard almost instantly, the pain shooting through his diseased part like stabbing knives. He groaned in agony the same moment she groaned in ecstasy, until he pushed her back, shaking his head in a sensual conflict he'd never experienced before. "No," he choked, "we can't do this."

"He is not coming back."

"It's not about your husband. I mean, yes, it is about him. I mean…I can't do this."

She hugged him again, pressing herself close. "You remind me much of my Sean. Not just the red hair, which is like a slow fire. Both so gentle. Both so much warrior. But he is gone now. And you are here."

He pushed her shoulders away again; but maintained hip contact. Certain pressure points seemed to relieve the pain just a little. "No, Aurelia. Please, no."

She looked deeply hurt. "You don't like me?"

"It's not that. I like you very much, I can't stop thinking about you."

Emboldened, she thrust her hand between his legs, rolling his testicles around as tenderly as if they were delicate balls of cornmeal dough.

He closed his eyes; tears filled them. She took this as a sign of deep emotion, rather than the admixture of erogenous agony it actually was, alternating throbs of torment and joy. She kissed him again, pulling his hand to her breast. Again he pushed her away.

Now she was angry. "*Que es?*"

He couldn't tell her his problem. He'd grown to feel close to her. Divulging his true ailment would shame him. So he dissembled. "It's… your baby. You're going to have your husband's baby. What if he came back tonight, what would you tell him?"

After a moment of anger, it was Aurelia's turn to feel ashamed. Scully was right. How could she betray Sean this way, with their child's birth only a few months away? Scully was an honorable man, and courageous to restrain his feelings—his obvious feelings, as her hand still tingled from the grip of his hardness. She was a shameful woman. She wasn't worthy of Scully, no matter what their feelings were. She'd have to confess this episode to the priest on Sunday. She backed away, tears in her own eyes now.

"*Lo siento, mi querido,*" she said, and ran away.

He'd never felt so frustrated, or angry at himself for hurting her. That was the last thing he wanted to do. Hurting her was…ow! Another lancinating pain forced him to the bed, to lie there motionless until full detumescence allowed the daggers to subside.

Captain Ryburn Solomon walked through the tall grass into the Indian camp, arms raised so he wouldn't be shot by some new brave who didn't know him. He was here to see the *shaman*, Shalako, who lived with this Kiowa band, though he was not of them. They'd found him near death in the dirt of a Rio Grande Pueblo village that had been torched to ashes by U.S. soldiers—this was years before the Civil War. He was burned over half his body, including most of his head, but somehow he didn't die. The taut, scarred skin of his face, with the few tufts of hair sprouting out of his scalp made him look like a primitive kachina come alive. A messenger of the gods. They called him Shalako, because they thought he was probably Zuni.

Once they'd taken him in, it was no surprise to anyone that Shalako lived much in his dreams and communicated to the tribe from the spiritworld. He was deeply connected to the weather, the stars, the trees, the animals—especially the animals—and he gave the Kiowa who'd adopted him great guidance in their travels.

He was clearly a holy man. Solomon believed him to be from one of the lost tribes of Israel.

Solomon wasn't a practicing Jew; hadn't been to Temple in 50 years. But the first time he'd met Shalako something had awakened in him. For one thing the name Shalako was a bit like Shiloh, one of the Hebrew names for the Messiah. For another, Solomon had always been told Indians were pagans who worshipped trees and rocks—but Shalako spoke of Creator, the One, with the same reverence Jews referred to Jaweh, the One God. And besides that, Solomon liked the old man's sense of humor.

This band of Kiowa traders was led by Xo Ten, the Kiowa name for Stone Heart. The Kiowa were often middlemen to the warrior Comanche nation, trading guns to the Comanche in return for buffalo skins, cattle and slaves caught in war. Then American government Indian Agents would take Xo Ten's cattle and skins, giving him guns in return, which he then took back to the Comanche for the next trading cycle.

On entering camp Solomon saw a wagon piled with buffalo skins. Captured slaves were bound nearby—two Indians and a young black girl who looked familiar to Solomon, though he wasn't sure why. On the other side of the clearing was a flatbed wagon spread with Union Army Spencer rifles and a few Henry 16-shot repeaters.

Xo Ten and the Indian Agent shook hands and walked to their new possessions. Xo Ten sighted down one of the Henrys as the Agent drove off the wagon of buffalo hides. The slaves were led on a leash to a work area—except the young Negro girl, who was taken to Xo Ten's tent.

Solomon walked over to Xo Ten. "*Ha-cho,* Xo Ten."

"*Ha-cho*, Sol-mon. You have guns for us, mate?" Xo Ten's English was good, but idiosyncratic. He'd learned to speak it from an Aussie sailor he'd kidnapped in a raiding party years before.

"Not today. I've only brought you a gift, and then I would ask to speak with Shalako."

He took a knife from his pocket—a Sheffield springloaded switchblade, Her Majesty's Crown inlaid in brass.

Xo Ten looked pleased. "Strewth, mate! Bloody good knife." He sent Solomon to Shalako.

In a sage-smoked cave Shalako stopped chanting when Solomon entered. "*Ha-cho, Bidau.*" He called Solomon by the Kiowa word for 'foggy,' ever since Solomon had once told him his mother complained his singing voice sounded like bagpipes on a foggy hill. Of course that never stopped him from singing.

"*Ha-cho*, Shalako. You having a conversation with Creator?"

"Yes. Let us sing together your Creator prayer." It was the only Hebrew chant Solomon still remembered from his youth. *Hear, O Israel, the Lord Our God, the Lord is One.* He'd taught it to Shalako, who thought it sounded Zuni. They sang it together now. "*Sh'ma Yisrael, Adonai Elohenu, Adonai ehad.*"

"Creator wishes you sang better, Sol-mon. But I do not mind."

"Nae more do I," said Solomon. "But I have something to show you. I found it in a secret place and I would ask your advice."

Solomon took Shalako a mile from camp to where he'd hid the petrified giant bison horn. Shalako touched the great tusk, moved his hand over its smooth hardness. He closed his eyes, imagining the creature that must have carried this massive weapon on its head. Finally, he opened his eyes. "This is a great creature from the First World. It is one of the First People."

"What does that mean, then?"

"There were many creatures in the First World who didn't look like us. Some were the Great Bison who stood on two legs, like men. They were the Great People and our tribes all came from them. But we forgot the true ways, so the Great People died, and we were made even smaller than their bison little brothers."

"Is that what the Zuni teach?"

"No. This is my own story, that I have learned on the Lake of the Dead. No tribe knows the things I know, or tells my tales the same way. I will have talks with Creator about this great horn you have found. You will return here on the Hunter's Moon."

Solomon nodded. That was the full moon in October, when the White Man's crops had been cleared, so it was easy to hunt game. He pulled two small stone bones from his pocket and gave them to Shalako. "Gifts, for you."

Shalako took the fossil fragments. "These are riches of the Other World, *Bidau*. From the First Men. I thank you."

* * *

Clayton slept badly all night. Shaking, retching; he searched his entire suite for leftover hints of the black ball opiate. But when he could find none, he just nursed the shakes with rum and quinine water. When the sun finally rose he felt spent and tired; but over the crisis. He bathed and dressed in fine clothes, which made him feel better.

As he walked his daily rounds, a jubilant air filled the plaza. Men on ladders decorated trees with streamers, boys ran around trailing strings of popping firecrackers, adobe walls were being whitewashed, a band was playing in the central gazebo. All was being readied for *La Independencia*. The Cry of Dolores. To spit in Napoleon's eye.

Clayton noticed the front page of *The Daily Ranchero* tacked up outside its door, its headline reading EMPEROR MAXIMILIAN ACCEPTS THRONE OF MEXICO! Wilkes thought that was a pretty big event, so he stepped inside to get the details, crossed the floor to Wachtel's inner office, knocked, and opened the door.

As the door swung wide Simon and Jensen quickly pulled apart from a tender kiss. Wachtel looked flustered at Clayton's entrance, Jensen more irked as he swept past Wilkes and out the door. Clayton came all the way in and shut the door behind him.

"Simon, you know…I don't care about this here."

The old man nodded sadly, his hands shaking. "*The heart wants what it wants—or else it does not care.* Emily Dickinson wrote this in a letter, *und* it is true."

"It is that," Clayton said gently.

He wanted to say something more, but Wachtel waved him away, so he exited to the outer office. Jensen, scrubbing down the bed of the press, stood up defiant and said, "He's a brilliant man. You couldn't hold a candle to him no matter what you think."

"You won't get argument from me."

"You gonna talk up what you saw?"

"No reason to. Simon's a good man. I'm not sure what to make of you yet."

"Ain't asking for your opinion."

"You're not givin' me much reason to like you—but I guess I don't need to be friends with both of you. I bid you good day, sir." He exited and went back to his rounds, more curious than ever about the whims of men.

When Clayton entered Allie's offices, he found her in the back room hanging photographs on the wall with Jessup.

She stepped away from the stepladder. "You have arrived at an opportune moment, sir, to help the Ranger with this task so I may get back to even more important business. I've a sitting with Charles Stillman in five minutes."

She and Clay regarded each other only a moment. They'd decided it was in their best confidence game interests not to let anyone know about their liaison; but somehow being in a room together in public while holding that secret felt electrifying. She moved to the door, brushing past Clay, and the physical contact charged them both. Flustered, she took Jessup's hand. "I put you in charge of hanging these properly, sir."

"Yes, ma'am," said Jessup, returning her gaze.

Allie glanced at both men; quite disoriented. Torn between them, it seemed she could only love the one she was looking at, and with both of them in the room she was afraid to move. But wait—she didn't really love Jessup, did she? Wasn't that just the story she'd told herself so well; so well that she felt it to her core? Or was Clay just a story, too? She couldn't separate her feelings when they both pulled at her, Clay with his mastery of the game, his authority of loving, Ahotay with his kind loyalty, his trust, his…She just shook her head and left in a huff, to set up her camera.

"She's got a temper," Jessup smiled as he set the ladder against the wall.

Clayton got right to the point. "I know where Pierce keeps his strongbox."

"I figured you had ways to find out. Is it small enough to carry, or do I have to crack it open right there?"

"I think two men could haul it."

"I know a couple boys I trust."

"Just you and me. I won't let you bring anyone I don't know."

"Think we'll have to kill Pierce to get the money?"

"No, I won't be party to that. I don't want the two guards murdered either, they're only doin' their job and didn't ask us to come do a burglary. I'll arrange for Pierce to be out of the house for an hour when we do the deed—I can set up an Independence Eve pow-wow for him and Jose Quintero to make a joint speech tomorrow, in the spirit of American-Mexican unity, or some such horseshit."

"You mean you want to do it tonight?"

"No reason to wait."

Jessup cast him a steely look. "You best not be settin' me up."

"Why would I do that?"

"Get me outta the way, gives you an open field back to Allie. I could see how you was lookin' at her."

"Lookin' like an old friend, that's all. What tonight's about is buyin' her daddy's freedom while we rob the Federal treasury. You too scared to come with me, I'll damn well do it alone."

Jessup weighed his options. No matter what, he couldn't see any other way to raise as much money as Allie needed. "Let's do it," he said.

"Meet me behind Brave River at nine. I'll set Pierce's meeting with Quintero downtown for ten," said Clayton. "And bring a truncheon."

* * *

Jessup escorted Allie from her office to her house as it turned dark that evening. She'd already made the trip three times between the two buildings and the Opera House as well, getting everything ready for the big day tomorrow—she could talk of nothing but details of the festival, where her camera would be stationed, how much she should charge for a photograph, how supportive Mildred Bee had been, and what a sad woman was Catherine Delacroix, with nothing but that cold Opera House to care for, no love in her life at all. Nothing like Allie, as she held Jessup's hand.

At the house Jessup helped her change Moon's bandage, which had leaked through again; the unlucky man hadn't budged since the day of his surgery. Allie put on the table a fine mutton stew with sweet potatoes and celery, which had simmered for hours; and for dessert, two apples, in season but not all that sweet. After dinner the gentleman insisted on washing the dishes in a bucket of river water tinctured with lye.

Allie could so imagine making a home with this fine, trusty man. But when she took a dish to dry, touching his hand affectionately in the process, he tensed just a little. "You seem preoccupied tonight, Ahotay. Something on your mind I should know about?"

"Not so's I want to talk about. But to put your mind at ease…by tomorrow I expect things gonna work out for your daddy."

"What are you sayin'?"

"Not sayin' nothin'. Just sayin' sometimes things work out."

She hugged him. "Ahotay, I hope you're not puttin' yourself in any danger because of me. I couldn't stand to think I'd got you hurt."

"You didn't get me anything. I just do what I do. And I plan to help you out of your troubles, I hope to say. But now I best be goin'."

He kissed her on the forehead and exited. Allie felt confused. But as these things went, she had a con woman's sense this one was going pretty well.

Jessup walked out of her house, then across the street. He picked up the blackjack where he'd hidden it behind a bush before he'd gone inside with her. Then he turned up the street and headed for Brave River.

Odeel watched him retrieve the bludgeon and walk away. He'd been following Allie all day, going from butcher shop to home, to her office, to the park, to the Opera House, back to her office; sometimes alone, sometimes with Jessup, or with Wilkes; but this business now of Jessup's with the blackjack was interesting. Made Odeel think something rough was going to happen. Made him think it was time to switch his tail, from Allie to Jessup.

He fell into step thirty yards behind the Ranger, staying in the shadows and out of sight.

CHAPTER 16

BONFIRES, FIREWORKS, THE WARM oranges of lamp oil flames, all cradled the town in a festive glow amidst the friendly smells of roasting pig, cedar ovens, floral sprays and the delicate fragrance of perfumed *senoritas*. A cacophony of celebration music wafted from the *Plaza* on a light wind, up to Clayton's office above the gambling hall—trumpets, accordions, violins, guitars and drums competing with each other from different corners of the city—as he studied the map of Pierce's house, deciding on the best access route to the room holding the safe; where the guards were supposed to be at what times, and what tools would be necessary. It didn't look like it was going to pose a lot of problems—but then campaigns never went as planned.

When he was finished, he did a little work on the stained-glass window, an activity that never ceased to calm his internal frictions. It was coming together finally, a picture emerging of an angel in white, hand raised—whether to give a benediction or strike a blow was unclear yet. But the pleasure he extracted from this simple act of creating an image out of colored glass brought him back to a time when colored lights and honkytonk music were part of his world, when he lived in New Orleans in the '50's. He closed his eyes, his mind drifting...

The riverboat was ten minutes from docking when he smelled it again, that curious lavender perfume. He followed the scent until he saw her, the girl who'd stolen his cash and his heart, now dressed in a lady's finery, sitting at a poker game, a sizable pot on the table. The players showed their cards, the young lady won, the riverboat docked, the sun set. Clay followed her into town.

She meandered through the Quarter. Lafayette Square was washed in moonlight as she walked to a British gentleman of high degree sitting on a bench. He stood when she arrived, then they both sat and entered into earnest talk.

Clay eavesdropped from behind a wisteria bush. She was speaking in an educated voice, complimenting the gent on his business acumen—when Clay saw her pick the man's pocket. It was an educated lift, too; Clay was impressed. She stood up, noting the lateness of the hour. The gentleman wondered when he might see her again. Clay decided to have some fun.

He walked around the bush with a troubled face and grabbed her by the upper arms. "Dear God, there you are, I've been lookin' all over."

She was rattled, recalling her last encounter with Clay. "I, I don't know what you are..."

"It's Daddy," he went on. "Some liar accused him of defaultin' on a debt and they threw him in prison and now he's had a stroke!"

She actually began to weep. Clay was impressed. The gentleman of the bench took a tentative step forward. "Perhaps I could be of assistance."

The most fleeting of looks passed between Clay and Allie—sealing their fate, if not their love. She turned to her gentleman and held his arms gently. "No, of course not, I couldn't possibly ask..." And Allie slipped his wallet back into the gent's pocket.

When Clay saw that, it took everything he had not to smile. Instead, he turned his most beleaguered look to Mr. Bench, as Clay had begun to think of the mark. "I beg your indulgence at the interruption, sir, but I must take my sister to see our father now."

"Of course, of course. Can I have my carriage convey you there?"

"Thank you, no. But by way of apology, please allow me to buy you dinner at Antoine's tomorrow evening. My sister will, of course, be there."

"Why...I would be honored, sir." He tipped his top hat. Allie curtsied, took Clay's arm and walked off with him.

"Have you ever heard of the Spanish Prisoner, darlin'?" Clay whispered to her. He got Mose to play their father, locked in an old abandoned Debtors' Workhouse. Allie and Mose hit it off instantly.

"Girl's got natural talent," Mose told Clay after Allie brought Mr. Bench to

meet her destitute father. Destitute, but with a hidden fortune and his daughter's hand in marriage to the man who bought him out of this hellhole. Mose was the only man Clay knew who could keep his lip curled down one side of his face to look like he'd had a stroke.

It took Allie only five days to wrangle $11,250 out of Mr. Bench. "The Lord made everything in six days," she told Clay afterwards. "I made a little less, but I beat His time." And on the seventh day they didn't rest; they hightailed it to Mississippi, where they got a marriage license, a Justice of the Peace, and Mose to witness this holy union before God and man. Then they all got drunk and Mose took off for parts unknown.

They were madly in love, and saw a great future in their partnership, which they took up the coast, living the high life…

Clay opened his eyes, smiling at the recollections like an old man reliving his glory days from a rocking chair on the porch. Nothing wrong with that.

He took dinner downstairs at the bar, where the tattered Brave River anniversary decorations had been replaced with streamers the colors of the Mexican flag, draping the walls and the vigilant giraffe's head. Dinah Singletary served Clay his meal of rice, beans, tortilla. She'd eased into life here without any drama, doing her duties silently and efficiently. She smiled a little more, wasn't quite as jumpy; teardrops didn't streak her cheeks as much. On one occasion she cradled the head of an old farmer who was having the rum fits. People liked her. She just never spoke.

When he was done eating, Clayton ambled over to the bar, where Jim was regaling Rheumy. "So then he says 'I can too smell a dead man in a snowstorm, I been sniffin' dead men in the snow for years!' Then the other fella says, 'Nobody can smell dead meat when it's blowin' this cold…'"

"That's a true fact," Rheumy replied, getting agitated. "What I been sayin'. That's why this story makes no sense!"

Jim threw down his towel. "There's no talkin' to you." He stalked off.

Clayton walked to the back door, where Isaac was instructing a crew of six runaways in how to mulch a garden. "This is the plantation patrol," he grinned at Clay. "They gonna feed our population."

"Well, you won't die of starvation, then. By the by, I'll be doin' a bit of business at the Pierce residence around 10 tonight. I don't want you at my side, but watchin' my back would be a comfort. Perhaps someday I can do somethin' useful for you."

"One can only hope."

✳ ✳ ✳

Clayton and Jessup climbed silently over the high stone wall at the back of the property, dropped to the ground and crouched in a shadow— Clayton grimacing when he landed on his bad leg. He readjusted the canvas sack slung across his shoulder and pulled a bandanna up to cover the lower half of his face. Jessup did the same. Clayton limped to the corner of the two-story house, putting more weight on his cane than usual.

"Seems to me you're already a drag on this raid," whispered Jessup. "Why don't you just tell me where the box is and I'll get it."

"Just watch and learn, son." Clayton jimmied open a window. "Guards mostly stay in the kitchen when Pierce leaves, I'm told. Through this room, down the hall."

They eased over the sill and into a darkened room, where they sat quietly, getting accustomed to the low light. A grandfather clock ticked, a small rodent skittered across a stone floor. Clayton picked up the scents of melting candle wax, cellar mold and gun oil. He inched to the door, listened, and led the way down a long, dark hallway, stopping just outside the kitchen. In the room beyond were voices.

Peeking around the corner of the jamb Clayton saw four men playing a rowdy game of poker and pulled his head back. Jessup gave him a "what's going on?" look. Clayton gestured to another unlit room, which they silently entered.

"There's four at the table."

"Four!" whispered Jessup. "That's not what…"

"Shh. The box is upstairs." He led the way to a long staircase. "Stay close to the wall." They tip-toed up the edge of the steps, to minimize creaking. At the landing Clayton made his way to a bedroom, closed the door behind them and locked it. He lit a match, then a lamp on the bed table, revealing a well-appointed room with a large bed, Oriental carpet, writing desk, American flag on one wall, portrait of President Lincoln on another, and French doors leading to a balcony on a third.

Jessup looked behind the flag but Clayton motioned him over to the end of the bed. "Move it off the rug," he said. They lifted the foot of the bed and swung it several feet toward the wall until it no longer rested on the Oriental. Then Clayton pulled the carpet back. Under it was a seam in the wooden floor. Clayton unslung the canvas sack from his shoulder, pulled out a prybar and inserted it in the seam. Up came a plank at the edge of a trapdoor they lifted out of the way. Inside the space below was a two-foot brass box which they brought out by the handles and set on the floor. It was padlocked. Clayton took a set of lock picks from his pocket and went to work.

"You're a man of some talent," said Jessup.

"I know the things I need to know." He spent a minute manipulating the tools until the lock popped open, then slipped it out of its iron ring and opened the lid. Inside the box were documents and stacks of money; more money than either man had ever seen.

"Holy *Frijole*," said Jessup.

Clayton picked up a packet of $100 bills, wingspread eagle gracing the front. One hundred bills to a packet, $10,000 each. Packets of lesser bills as well; but gold pieces too, from $20 to $100 denominations.

"My Lord," said Clayton.

"There must be, I don't know, a hundred thousand in here."

"More. Much more."

Jessup began loading money into the canvas sack as Clayton looked through the papers on top of the pile. When Jessup was about half done, Clayton touched his arm. "Whoa, girl."

"Come on, let's do this and get out."

"Stop what you're doin'. Read this."

Jessup took the communique from Clayton and read the translation under the coded message. *"General Banks to lead 12,000 infantry from Texarkana November 1. Massing at Ft. Smith. Cortina to march on Laredo same date. Confirm.*" He looked stunned at Clayton. "This is the invasion of Texas."

"It is. And Pierce has been organizing an army with Cortina down here to be part of a flanking attack."

"By God I'm gonna kill that Mexican bandit if it's the last thing I do."

"That's not the point. We have to put this all back."

"What are you talkin' about? This money…"

"Forget the money. Pierce can't know we've been here."

"He'll know when his money's all gone."

"That's what I'm sayin'. He can't know. If he does, they'll change all the invasion plans. If they don't know we have the details of the attack, we can surprise 'em and crush the whole assault. Be the biggest Reb victory of the war."

"I don't see how…"

But Clayton held up his hand. "Let me think on this a second."

Jessup grew increasingly frustrated as Clayton sat there deep in thought, figuring it all out. Finally he nodded. "All right, this ought to work."

"What?"

Clayton pulled a $10,000 packet out of the strongbox. "We take this for Allie's father. We take the same for each of us. That's for our trouble. We put everythin' else back the way it was. I doubt he'll be countin' it closely. Even if he does, with all this cash it'll be chalked up to a miscount."

"But all this cash could be used for the Confederacy."

"Stoppin' the invasion's more important. We're gonna leave all these papers on top, right where they were, move the bed back, leave everything like it's been untouched. They'll never know that we know."

Jessup finally nodded, getting the bigger picture. "Then we tell General Bee, and he tells General Magruder and they get the jump on the Yanks between Ft. Smith and Texarkana."

"And you get to lead your Rangers up to Laredo to take on Cortina, which he don't expect."

"This just keeps gettin' better."

Their heads swiveled to the French doors, where sounds of gunfire and a loud *boom* echoed in the distance.

"That an attack?"

But now came a chorus of trumpets and brass, and a tremendous crowd cheer. Clayton shook his head. "Gettin' an early start on the town party." He pulled a pencil and paper out of his pocket. "I'm goin' to copy the message first so I can show it to Quintero. General Bee has any doubts about the information, Quintero will back us up when he sees this."

Clayton wrote out the code and its translation as Jessup put all the money back in place, except the packet for Allie. Clayton kept one for himself but Jessup declined—he was just here for Allie and for the Cause. They put the padlock back on, returned the box to its hidey-hole, reset the planking, pulled the rug over it and lifted the bed back to its original position. But as Clayton opened the door, they heard footsteps on the stairs.

Jessup pulled a blackjack from his pocket but Clayton stayed his hand and tip-toed to the French doors, motioning Jessup to come along. As they stepped out onto the balcony there was a knock on the bedroom door.

"Mr. Pierce? You home yet? We heard gunshots in town."

They climbed over the railing, lowered themselves to the edge and grabbed it. Jessup hung by his fingers, then let go and hit the ground ten feet below. But before Clayton could drop, a guard walked out onto the balcony to peer around the yard.

Jessup stood flat against the wall, directly beneath the porch. Clayton hung by his hands, swinging slightly, his fingers barely a yard from the guard's feet. A few seconds later the watchman turned and went back inside, closing the French doors behind him. Clayton let loose, falling into Jessup's arms, knocking them both to the ground.

"Appreciate you takin' my fall like that," said Clayton, pushing himself upright.

"Wouldn't've helped anybody if you'd broke a leg." They hurried over to the exterior stone wall, Clayton limping worse than ever. "I'll go first and pull you up," said Jessup, who got some good handholds and made it to the top in a hurry. As he reached down, though, they heard watchmen making their rounds—checking the grounds after the gunfire that had drawn them to the bedroom.

Clayton motioned Jessup to go all the way over the wall to the other side, which he did as Clayton slipped behind a garden bench. He could hear the guards dividing up the search, one this way, one that. And now a third set of footsteps, moving his way. He looked around for better cover. A stunted old *madrone* had a trunk wide enough to hide behind, with good moonshadow as well. He hobbled over to it and stood silent with his back to the wood, listening for movement. Gripping his cane.

Nothing. Then some scraping near the bench he'd just left. Footfalls along the stone wall, first away from him; then toward him. He tensed. Put one hand on the derringer in his belt, though he didn't want to use it unless he had to. The footsteps disappeared. He strained his ears, sensing for direction, waiting for the guards to retreat. Nothing. A whisper of clothing. A hand on his shoulder.

He whirled around, bringing his cane across backhand, at head level, as a voice said, "I can get you..." and his cane hit Teddy Beale's temple with a dull thud. Her eyes went up into her lids and she crumpled at his feet, dressed in her guard's uniform, holding her lariat in one hand.

He crouched beside her in the shadow of the tree, waiting.

On the far side of the high wall Jessup also waited, listening. He pulled his bandanna off his face so he could hear better, but it still sounded quiet. He started climbing back to the top again, to see if the yard was clear to hoist Clayton up—when he heard a revolver cock behind him, and a cold barrel press into the nape of his neck.

"Just what in hell are you up to?" came a familiar voice. Jessup turned his head enough to see. It was Captain Odeel.

"Ain't no business of yours," whispered Jessup, annoyed.

"You and that Stoneman woman set on cheatin' the Confederacy again, I expect. Havin' secret talks with this Union spymaster, Pierce, it looks like."

"You don't know what you're talkin' about."

"Maybe. Maybe General Bee would know." But then he grunted and slumped to the dirt. Isaac stood behind him, holding a gun, which he holstered.

"Mr. Wilkes still inside there?" Isaac asked the stunned Ranger.

"He is. Laying low until the nightwatch passes."

Isaac shinnied up the wall like it was a ladder and peered over the top. Clayton signaled him from the shadows of the *madrone*. Isaac nodded recognition. Clayton took Teddy's lasso, pointed to her unconscious body, pointed to himself, made a tying motion with the rope, and arced his hand overhead in the direction of the wall. Isaac nodded and jumped back down to his own side.

Clayton grabbed Teddy under the arms and dragged her quickly to the wall. He tied the rope around his own torso, threw the other end over the wall, picked Teddy up and wrapped his arms around her, holding her to his chest. In a few moments the rope tightened around him and he was being pulled up the wall from the other side in several smooth heaves, the lasso biting into his skin.

As they neared the top, Teddy's eyes opened, her face just inches from his. She offered a bleary smile. "Glad to be of service," she rasped, bringing her lips to his.

He turned his head to grab the top of the wall and she kissed his ear. Isaac was there in a moment—Jessup anchoring the rope around a stump at the base. Isaac grabbed the girl like a rag doll from Clayton's grasp and pulled her over as Clayton hoisted himself to the top of the wall. By the time he fixed his balance Isaac was back on top. He slung Clayton over his shoulder and climbed down the rockface quick.

Jessup, Clayton and Isaac looked down on the unconscious Odeel and the loopy Teddy. "I told you I'd keep an eye on you," Teddy said to Clayton's knees, and passed out again.

Jessup turned to Isaac. "Obliged to you." Then he pointed at Odeel. "I know this sumbitch." And with a nod at Teddy on the ground: "But what are we gonna do with this Yankee pup?"

"I believe I can make it look like he chased after some ruffians before he got blindsided."

Jessup gestured at Odeel. "I don't believe Captain Odeel saw you, Wilkes, but he thinks there's some kinda shady business goin' on with me and Allie and Pierce."

"Pour a bottle of whiskey on him and put him on the ferry to Brownsville. Tell the ferryman to call the captain of the guard. That'll keep this drunken officer occupied."

"With pleasure."

The three men wrangled the two bodies to Isaac's buggy and dropped Jessup off at the ferry with Odeel before heading back to Brave River, where they put Teddy in Clayton's bed, the very spot she'd most wanted to be for many a week.

Clayton slept on the *chaise* in his office, where his dreamwork churned away...

Her father's detectives caught up with them in Raleigh and brought them back in handcuffs. Her father had the marriage annulled; his father said he'd have Clay thrown in jail if he ever went near that harlot again—the two fathers nearly came to blows themselves. Allie's father took her home. Her two brothers beat Clay almost to death as his father watched, nodding. His mother, beside herself, ran upstairs as Allie's brothers kept beating him, beating him...

Clay rolled off the chaise with a moan, waking himself up. It was the middle of the night, he was panting and his head hurt from the beating he'd just relived in his nightmare. But he had a stiff drink and let the distant music of the street parties lull him back into a fitful reverie...

Clay recovered. His nose fracture healed bent, his shoulder got relocated into its socket by his father's overseer. His father spoke little to him; his mother was caring when his father wasn't around. Clay played the dutiful son, thinking of nothing but getting back to Allie. Until six months later, when a traveling drummer gave him a wicker basket.

"What's this?" Clay asked the man.

"Spanish prisoners, is what I was told to say, and a good day to you." As the drummer walked away Clay looked inside the basket. Two cooing pigeons.

He'd taught Allie all about homing pigeons during their long spree of love and confidence games. How to train them and how to use them. And here they were, undoubtedly imprinted on a home base near Allie.

He stopped the drummer and bade him wait. Then he got one of his mother's carrier pigeons, put it in a canvas sack, handed it to the drummer with $100 in gold coin and instructions to give it to the lady who gave him the basket of birds. The drummer was only too happy to make such good money journeying between the two.

Clay sent one bird flying back to Allie with a message vowing love, swearing he'd come for her soon, and they'd run off together somewhere they'd never be found.

He had hope now. She was waiting for him. Probably watched over like a hawk by her brutish brothers. Now he just had to put together enough money to buy lots of tickets. Tickets for wild goose chases to elude followers and avoid capture.

All would be well now. Love would triumph. And his father—that bitter, slavemongering, abusive tyrant—could go to hell...

Clayton slept late after that, finally dreamless, well into the morning.

Next morning Jessup crossed Matamoros to the ferry on his way to see General Bee at the fort with his urgent business. It was no brisk walk, with thousands of milling celebrants out and about the town. Today was the day, the Day of Independence, and the party was starting early.

There were stirring breakfast speeches at the gazebo by town council members trying to be heard above the shrieks of children running with whistles and noisemakers. He navigated around a parade of bicycles and unicycles, their spokes woven with red and green paper. Drunks accosted him for spare change; even the prostitutes were out in force, a rarity so early in the day. And as a counterpoint to that, the Matamoros Temperance Union was gathered, singing hymns and banging drums.

Jessup finally made it to Fort Brown, where he had to badger General Bee's aide to be admitted to the inner sanctum to tell Bee of his discovery. But Bee was more concerned with getting his dress sash in the proper position for the reviewing stand in Matamoros, scheduled for noon. He was dismissive of Jessup's news.

"I been hearing these rumors about Yankees mustering at Lafayette for months, Lieutenant. You think your so-called intelligence is gonna get me to send my troops up there, you got another think."

"Sir, this is no rumor, and it ain't just Lafayette. Yanks are coming down through Arkansas. I saw the dispatch."

Bee's anxiety raised up a notch. He hated the idea of leaving his fort less than heavily protected, so he generally ignored any rumor that might result in him having to send soldiers to defend someone else's field of battle. An official military dispatch was a little harder to look away from. "What kind of dispatch are we talking about?"

"It came from Leonard Pierce's private safe."

Bee gave Jessup a surly squint. "Then how do you know about it?"

Jessup didn't want to divulge too much more; he didn't want to compromise Allie's operation. "I was shown it by the man who stole it. Then he put it back so the Yanks wouldn't know it was stole."

"Well," Bee wrestled with his options, "I've got a few patrols up near Laredo, they're not doing much to reinforce our situation here anyway, I imagine I could pull some of them off the Rio Grande to head up to the Arkansas line, have a look around."

"No, sir, the message said Cortina was due to attack Laredo on the same day, November first. We gonna need even more men there."

"And what then!" Bee roared, covering his nerves with bluster. "Defend Fort Brown with my wife and her picaninnies? You suggesting I derelict my duty here?"

"No, General Bee, I just think General Magruder would want…"

"And now you know what he wants, too, by God, you're impertinent. How about if I just send you up to Arkansas? You know so much about the Yankee war plans, you can sit yourself in just the right tree to pick 'em off one at a time."

Bee's aide knocked and opened the door. "General Bee…"

"Can't you see I'm about to have a man arrested for insubordination here?"

"He instructed me not to wait," said the trembling aide. "He…"

But Confederate Consul Quintero strode past him into Bee's office, looking grim. "General Bee, we must talk." And to Jessup: "Leave at once, Private."

"Lieutenant, sir," said Jessup, but exited while he could. On his way out he heard Quintero continue with strained excitement to Bee, waving the copy of the coded message Clayton had made. "We've intercepted a military secret. I've just sent word to General Magruder. The Union army will invade at Texarkana on November 1, gathering first at Ft. Smith. You must send all your troops there. I recommended to General Magruder setting a trap in the Ouachita Woods, which the Yankees must pass through on the way to the Texas border. You can surprise them there from a position of cover…"

Jessup breathed a sigh of relief as the door closed him out. Clayton Wilkes had done his job. Now Jessup just had to get the $10,000 to Allie, to set up her daddy's prison break.

* * *

Teddy opened her eyes to find Clayton sitting beside the bed playing a game of chess with himself. "Am I truly in your chambers, or is this just another dream?"

He took her hand in his. "You must forgive me for strikin' you. I was expectin' one of those burlier security men."

"You better show me some stronger apology than that."

He brought his lips gently to hers, kissed her openly and with purpose, generous with his passions. Then he sat back, smiling affectionately. "That's no invitation to more," he cautioned, "but you can hold onto that for the best consolation I can muster."

"You muster pretty good."

He stood. "You can stay here a while. I told Isaac not to bother you. You get gone before I'm back, though. I made a case to Ambassador Pierce that you saw some suspicious behavior and took it on your own initiative to run it to ground before you got codwallopped. Probably get you another medal."

218

"Where you going?"

"To church. I'm bound to wash away the sins of the flesh."

"Don't wash too deep or I'm liable to have to remind you how they go."

He went downstairs, where he saw Claire sashaying off with a wealthy Mexican monarchist—at least he was representing himself as such to Claire. In fact, Clay had paid the *caballero* a tidy sum to whisk Claire off to an estate below Vera Cruz—an estate Clay knew to be currently vacated by the *Imperialista* who actually owned it, and who'd recently relocated to Mexico City, where he was hoping to host Napoleon. Clay had advised his *caballero* friend to refuse sex before marriage—both to protect his own constitution and to lure Claire with visions of marrying fortune; a marriage never to be.

Clay felt only a twinge of remorse about Claire's fate. He'd already asked her to get treated by Dr. Hawks—which she'd refused. He asked her to abstain from carnal delights—which incensed her. He offered her a sizable purse to leave town as a public health measure; but she'd just laughed in his face. He had no doubt she'd land on her feet now— maybe even promoting the Mexican resistance, if she could manage a syphilitic liaison with Napoleon in Mexico City.

He saw Zhi Li trying to teach Hermano mah jongg. Clayton sat beside him for a minute, his arm around the simple man's shoulder. "Good work, Hermano. You'll be beatin' all of us before you know it." Hermano grinned and turned the water pump handle exuberantly. Clayton nodded at Zhi Li and walked out into the town's day-long, night-long celebration.

Near the *Plaza* he skirted a Native Animal parade, the specimens on leashes led by children, escorted by *vaqueros* wearing embroidered *sombreros*, *bolero* jackets and jangling spurs, astride majestic Spanish steeds. Among the animals were two javelinas, a family of goats, a few armadillos, a suspicious raccoon and a skinny Texas longhorn. Most of the game was painted in green, red and white stripes.

There was a brief commotion as the steer got stampeded off-course by a junkyard dog chasing old Limey Ned across the parade grounds. The bull gored Ned in the belly. It was put down fast, and Ned carried by his drinking mates to Brave River, where he wanted to spend his last hours.

Clayton trotted past a band of Irish pipers in the gazebo, mostly deserters from the Army of New York, which they'd fled after mistreatment for being Catholic. He saw Allie photographing them but didn't stop. On general principles it was best if nobody noticed them together today for any reason. Still, he managed to catch her eye. Their gazes felt connected by a magnetic force, neither could look away; as if they were making love just by staying in visual contact, no less than physical caress. Until a party of bell ringers swept him up and carried him down the street in a cacophony of sound.

The next sidestreet was lined with spectators watching the camel races, which were always exciting and nearly out of control. Past that stampede rose the Cathedral, with throngs of penitents, Father Clos in the crowd. He smiled when he saw Clayton walk by and raised his arm in blessing. Clayton ignored him and edged his way past; then around back, into the private chapel, where Leonard Pierce was writing war directives on a makeshift table.

"Did all go as planned?" the Ambassador asked.

"I'd say so. We 'found' the dispatch I gave you to plant in your strongbox. Jessup bought it all, he took the news to Bee, and I left a copy with Quintero, who I never saw so excited."

"They're convinced the invasion is by land, then."

"Absolutely, by way of Texarkana. Of course, to do that I had to sell Jessup on the idea I was there for as much money as I could get without raisin' *your* suspicion that anything was missin'."

Pierce cast him a baleful glance. "So...you took a convincing amount of cash."

"It was a subtle piece of salesmanship," Clayton explained brightly. "But I believe I sold it well."

Allie brought Jessup into her darkroom, lit now only by a single candle. "What is it?" she whispered. "Why are you bein' so secretive?"

He shut the door, causing the flame to flicker and the shadows to jump. "I have something for you nobody can ever know about." He reached into his shirt and pulled out the packet of $100 treasury notes. "There's ten thousand dollars there. That oughta be enough for that scoundrel Russell." He gave her the money.

She held it breathlessly, as if it were a holy icon, some sacred artifact. "Ahotay, how did you get this?"

He hesitated. "I borrowed it from my older brother, who I finally tracked down. He's quite wealthy, you know."

She looked into his eyes, glittering black in the darkness. This was always the sweetest moment for her, making her flush with quiet excitement: the moment the Spanish Prisoner was consummated; the moment the mark handed over the money gladly, joyously, proudly. She felt in awe of Jessup at this moment, that he would do this for her. She'd never been more in love with him than she was at this second.

She embraced him among the jumping shadows, whispering into his chest. "I love you, Ahotay." And she meant it deep down in her soul. Then she stepped back. "But I must get this to Major Russell right away."

"I'll go with you to make sure he doesn't…"

"No, this is for me to do. I'll meet you later and tell you Daddy's escape plan." And before he could protest any further, she was gone, leaving him in the dark.

Allie found Russell examining a stack of bales in his warehouse and gave him the $3000 she'd promised him. He thanked her kindly, deliberately not counting it, in a show of trust. She curtsied, expressed her pleasure working with him and left him to check the money after she was gone. Which he did. Satisfied the count was right, he went back to looking over his cotton bales. He suspected he hadn't demanded enough tariff on this load; he'd have to renegotiate his deal with Milmo, the broker in Matamoros. But now he saw Odeel approaching, and Russell had a pretty good idea why. He put on a fraternal grin, though.

"Captain Odeel, all sobered up, are you?"

"Something's goin' on, Russell, and I don't just say so because I woke up jailed."

"I heard about your misfortunate incarceration, yes. Rough night in Matamoros?"

"Not the way you mean it. I was following the Stoneman woman."

Just what Russell didn't want to hear. "You mentioned that before. Have you learned anything?"

"There was some kind of meeting at Ambassador Pierce's residence last night. I believe they're spies for the North, Stoneman and that Ranger Jessup both. That's why they wouldn't let me impress her cotton for the Confederacy."

"Nobody likes their cotton taken, Odeel."

"Maybe not. But Jessup was meeting with the Stoneman woman all yesterday, then I followed him to Pierce's place—him and that gambler Wilkes."

"Clayton Wilkes?"

"I think so…I'm not sure, I don't remember much after I got there, and then I woke up in jail, stinkin' of whiskey."

"You sure the whiskey ain't the whole story?" Russell oozed condescension.

"It ain't any of the story, and I mean to follow this where it goes."

Russell pulled Odeel close. "I didn't want to say, because this is classified—but I do know something. This can't be official, though, you're not authorized to know."

"What is it?"

"You meet me midnight tonight, you'll get your due. At the back east corner of the fort's an unlocked door. You go down the hall to three cells at the end—that's where the prisoner exchange will be."

Odeel got quietly excited. "What prisoner exchange? What's goin' on?"

"That's all I can tell you. It concerns the people you been talkin' about, though. Jessup, Stoneman, Wilkes, Pierce—this goes to the highest levels, you can't say a word about it, even afterwards. Might even hasten the end of the war."

Odeel was moved. "I appreciate you bringing me in on this."

"As a Confederate Major to a brother who's likely to attain the same rank after tonight…I'm honored to include you." What Russell had in mind would be tricky, but it had to be done. Odeel was just the kind of self-righteous fool who could ruin everything.

A sonorous bell rang far away, across the river—the Matamoros City Hall bell, which clanged only for great events, like fire, flood or royal wedding. It was signaling the official noon start of the Independence Day ceremonies over there; but Odeel took it as a sign of great opportunity for his fortunes.

He was about to join the Big Time.

CHAPTER 17

Most of the town's 40,000 inhabitants filled the streets all afternoon and into the night. Fireworks displays were shot off with skyrockets, Catherine wheels and roman candles colored by potassium, calcium or copper salts. Dancing, drinking, and fighting of every variety swirled in colorful eddies.

There was a *Grande Balle* at the Opera House. The sunken orchestra pit had been raised with its pulleys and gears until the entire floor was flush. Now an 8-piece band was playing the latest reels, polkas, waltzes and fandangos. Ladies and gents from both sides of the river—Confederate officers, Mexican governors, wealthy landowners, Spanish *senoritas* and southern debutantes—had all come to party.

Simon Wachtel was covering the event for *The Daily Ranchero* with Jensen—both dressed in nice suits, Jensen's just bought for the occasion by Wachtel. "I see Patricio Milmo, the cotton king," Simon told him, "*und* Charles Stillman, the richest man in Texas. Anything they say is a story for print." So he took Jensen to interview them.

Clayton worked the room, using his cane to garner sympathy, lubricating relationships with officers on all sides of every war. By the time he made his way over to Allie's photography station, he saw she was busy explaining portraiture to cub reporter Jensen, who'd already abandoned the Stillman interview. Clayton let himself be corralled by Catherine, who looped her arm through his, guiding him to the dance floor.

Jensen soon lost interest in Allie and wandered off to the bar.

Allie—stunning, in a red satin dress—had been hoping for some free publicity, so was doubly miffed by his disinterest. She looked around for redemption, only to see Clay in animated conversation with that theater slattern, Catherine, which annoyed Allie immoderately. So she seized on a young soldier passing by in stiff dress Union Blues with two shiny chest medals in place, making him look both glowing and uncomfortable. Which is exactly how Teddy felt.

"Come over here, soldier," Allie beckoned him. "Have you ever had your photograph taken?"

Teddy inched a little closer, unsure of everything about this fancy ball. "No, ma'am," said Teddy, "I've only worn my dress uniform once before, and I've not been to a dance this elegant, nor rubbed shoulders with so many important folks. Photographs are just one more thing on tonight's list."

"Well come on over, let me put you at ease..." squinting at the bars on his arm—"Corporal...?"

"Teddy, ma'am."

"Well, first off, you mustn't call me 'ma'am,' you must call me Allie."

"All right...Allie."

Allie was taken with the young man's fair skin and purity of feature, almost the embodiment of innocence. "My word," she went on, "you have the face of a cherub—no disrespect meant, Officer."

"None taken. I've never heard of a lady taking photographics before, though."

"Nothin' to stop me, is there?"

"No, I guess ladies can do about anything a man can do." A mischievous smile tweaked the corner of the young corporal's lip.

"Many people take refuge in the *status quo*," said Allie, "but I find the world often refuses to be what it seems, and that's just fine with me."

Teddy smiled even more broadly at that. "You won't find any argument here."

"Then there's nothin' to stop me from recordin' your image on paper, is there?"

The camera was set up pointing at the chair in front of a backdrop of pygmy palm trees. Teddy sat down.

"There you go," beamed Allie. "Now you must let me position you properly, and then you must be very still. Can you do that?"

"I believe I can."

Allie repositioned the young man's shoulders against the back of the chair and turned his head slightly. He had the smoothest cheeks. Allie had a sudden sense memory of her own teenage years, urgent furtive sexual encounters in a family friend's barn—and she turned away from Teddy before he could see the color rising in her cheeks. But in turning she saw Clay had progressed to the dance floor with Catherine. As she watched them do a bold fandango—Clay hanging on to her like a child—Allie did a slow burn.

"I'll tell you what," she said, pulling Teddy out of the chair. "Let's you and I take a turn around the dance floor to relax you for this picture takin'." She led him toward the spinning couples.

Teddy held back, though. "Whoa, whoa, I can't dance."

"Anybody can dance, Teddy. You just hold me and move your feet."

She bustled him onto the dance floor, put her left hand on his right shoulder, and took his left hand in her right. He looked terrified.

"Now you've got it. You just do what I do and I'll pretend to be followin' you."

And before the young corporal could protest again, Allie was moving them into the flow of dancers. She turned her head this way and that until she saw Clay and made sure to move into his line of sight, so he could see he wasn't the only one here tonight who could dance with whomever he pleased.

Clay just smiled when he saw her, though, and tipped his head graciously to her. He could see she was piqued but didn't see any way or reason to stop what he was doing. For one thing this was just a social dance, it didn't have anything to do with his true feelings for Allie. For another, dancing with Catherine was something he'd always done, and he didn't want to raise any suspicions around town that he wasn't the carefree Cassanova he'd always been. That could be bad for his image.

"With my leg so sore, I hope you don't mind my hangin' onto you for support," he confided to her now.

"And here I thought you were trying to tear my clothes off,"

Catherine purred as she nibbled his earlobe. It tickled, which made Clay smile.

But his smile made Allie even madder—so she held Teddy even closer. This gave Teddy a good view of Clay dancing with a beautiful older woman, which caused Teddy a twinge of jealousy, mixed with the confusion of being closely held by this exotic, aggressive lady photographer. And that perfume she wore, heavenly. Teddy breathed it in deep. It made her even more giddy. She could do little but quiver.

"Oh, Lordy, Teddy, you won't pass out on me now, will you?"

Teddy shook her head but felt befuddled and…a bit excited. Allie caught the excitement, which led her to her boldest move yet. "I just hate to think of young men like you goin' off to war and gettin' killed," she said, partly to goad herself into her next flagrant act. Engineering a turn past Clay she gave the young corporal a long, bold kiss.

Teddy felt her heart thumping like a kettle drum in her chest, and wasn't sure whether to flee, faint, or kiss back. So she kissed back.

Allie was thrilled that Clay was getting a good look at this—until she saw how amused he was by the whole thing. But when she noticed the poor boy in her arms had nearly stopped breathing, she pulled away. "Teddy, I hope I wasn't bein' too forward."

"I've got nothing to compare it to, Allie. Don't know what just forward enough is like. But it might be best if I sat down in your photograph chair now. Dancing was likely one thing too many for me tonight."

Allie took the tender soldier back by the hand and sat him down. "You are a dear boy," she told him. "I may just have to take this photo of you free of charge. I'll make two prints, and we can each have one to memorialize the occasion."

"Oh, I don't think I'll forget this night," said Teddy, her head swimming with the sounds and colors of the ball. When Allie was done with her camera work, Teddy got up to leave and bumped into a slightly tipsy General Bee, who was passing with a drink in hand, his entourage behind him. "Excuse me, sir," Teddy said to Bee.

"No, I will not excuse you, you clumsy Yankee fool. If this were a battleground you'd be dead now."

Teddy felt her throat constrict. "You take that back." She took a reflexive step forward and Bee flinched at her approach, spilling his own drink on himself. It was enough to make Teddy stop, and smile at the small moral victory. "Careful not to soil yourself on your retreat," she told him.

Bee stalked off in a huff as Allie walked up to Teddy. "You handled yourself with quite a bit of aplomb, Corporal." Whereupon she kissed Teddy on the cheek and retired to her photography station.

Whereupon the good Union soldier made her own hasty retreat and went home to her quarters, with a lot to think about.

The midnight hour arrived. Odeel, in dress grays with saber, approached Fort Brown under a waning moon, coming to the door at the east corner a few minutes before twelve. When he tugged on the handle it came open easily, as promised. He entered and walked down the long hall, torches set in the walls. When he reached the three cells at the end, all were empty. No one else was in sight. Was he early? Late? Had the prisoner exchange already happened? No, he couldn't think like a pessimist. That's not the kind of thinking that got him here. He waited. After an interminable minute he heard footsteps running down the corridor. A woman was approaching. A hoop-skirted lady.

Mrs. Stoneman threw herself into his arms with unexpected passion. "Thank God!" she wailed. "You've done it!" With her hands behind his back she slid a thin packet of hundred-dollar bills into his waistband. Ten bills, $1000.

He pushed her away. "What in heaven's name are you talking about, Madame?"

"Wait here! I'll go get him," she whispered, running back down the hallway.

"Get who?" Odeel shouted, but Allie was gone. "The prisoner?" A moment later iron bells began clanging. But not distant, not across the river, not celebratory. These were right here in the fort. General alarm bells. What the devil was going on?

More footsteps, lots of them, heavy with boots, clanking with spurs. A patrol came running down the hall toward him. "Arrest that man!"

shouted a voice. Before he knew what was happening he was thrown face to the wall, his hands pulled behind him and shackled.

"Got him some money in his belt, Major," came another voice.

Odeel was whipped around to find himself facing Major Russell, four armed soldiers and a bound prisoner with a burlap sack over his head.

"What's going on here?" Odeel demanded.

"That's what I'd like to know," said Russell, sounding deeply disappointed. "What have you done with the prisoner?"

"What have I done? I've done nothing. The cell was empty when I got here."

Russell held up the stack of Treasury Notes. "What was this doing in your belt?"

"I have no idea!"

Clayton walked up soberly from another direction. "I have some idea. This is the man I saw lurkin' around Leonard Pierce's house last night. No doubt arrangin' this escape." He flicked the bills Russell was holding. "Obviously well paid."

Russell turned to his guards. "You men take the prisoner back to Cell Block Two." Two of the soldiers took the hooded prisoner away. "You two take this traitor's weapons and lock him up. I want two sentries, from two different units, posted outside his door 24 hours a day."

"This is an outrageous mistake!" Odeel shouted as one guard unstrapped his saber and another took his sidearm.

"The mistake was in telling you about this ahead of time," Russell said darkly. "I fear I trusted the wrong man."

"I've done nothing…"

"Do you deny that I saw you lurkin' around Yankee Ambassador Pierce's house last night?" demanded Clay. "I warn you, there were other witnesses."

"Yes, I was there, but…"

Russell nodded to his men. Odeel yelled a continuous string of protests as he was dragged out, alternately whining and indignant. Russell and Clayton lingered in the hall, Clayton slipping Russell another packet of hundreds.

"Always a pleasure doing business with you, Mr. Wilkes."

"Sometimes the pleasure is just a little sweeter, Major Russell."

Outside, the soldiers pulled Odeel past another figure who'd been posted to stand guard in the shadow of some hay bales; a Texas Ranger, by his uniform. Odeel jerked to a stop despite all the hands on him and stared pure hatred at Jessup. "You," Odeel whispered.

"You," Jessup replied in surprise. .

The soldiers yanked Odeel away. But before Jessup could work it out in his head, Allie ran up out of the night. "It's done," she said with a soft excitement.

"But how'd Odeel get caught up in it?"

"Don't matter. Daddy's safe now, that's all I care about. I'll see you in a few days." And with that she disappeared like a ghost woman into the shadows.

Leaving Jessup to find a barracks bunk and mull it over until sleep took him.

The day after *La Independencia* the entire town was either hung over or sleeping in. Trash covered the streets, broken fences lay down like dead soldiers. Mildred Bee was quoted in *The Daily Ranchero*: "*I have seen the elephant, and he has bested me.*" The editorial column of the paper noted that although Mexico's Revolutionary War was won in 1821, Spain didn't recognize Mexico's independence until 1836—the same year that Texas declared its own independence from Mexico. And now that France was trying to subjugate it again, maybe it was time for another *El Grito de Dolores*. Time to champion everyone's right to independence.

Like the American South from the North. Or the black slaves from the South. Which is, of course, where it got complicated. For the Mexicans, too, since some of them wanted Napoleon in power to free them from the tyranny of the peasants. Politics was complicated in 1863.

So though it was a great party on the 16th, the 17th was a freighted letdown. Bittersweet for Clayton, who wanted to reconnect with Allie, but didn't, for reasons of public persona; for Allie, who wanted a vaingloriously free life with Clay, but also wanted the security of steadfast Jessup; for Quintero, who prized revolution above all else, but saw it slipping away in America; for Pierce, who knew his cause was just but hated the lives he had to sacrifice in its service; for Isaac, who kept his eyes on the prize, though the daily struggle was ever a trial.

But the day after was just fine for Russell, who achieved his deepest sense of fulfillment at the conclusion of every deal.

The town remained near comatose for 24 hours. On the 18th it picked itself up, collected its garbage, and resumed its steady roll in the machinery of life.

Ten days later Clayton sat in a wicker chair in front of a *palapa* on the beach south of Bagdad. Whitecaps sparkled across the bay, the sun warm, the breeze cool, puffy wisps of cloud stretching over the infinite sky. He picked up a porcelain cup from the low table beside him and took a sip of coffee, marveling at the magnificence of everything. The sea and sky comprised a far finer cathedral all around him than the dark churches where he'd always refused to confess his sins. Here there was no sin; only joy, only serenity; only glory, however fleeting.

Lying on the table was last week's edition of *The Daily Ranchero*. The headline—PRISONER ESCAPES FT. BROWN—was followed above the fold by a story describing the daring midnight escape of a convicted Northern spy, aided by the most foul skullduggery of one Captain Odeel of the Cotton Bureau. Odeel himself was already in custody and awaiting court martial. In the time since the headline, Odeel had had his trial and been found guilty—though lack of witnesses and the inability of the court to subpoena some classified information relating to the escaped prisoner had allowed him to evade the death penalty. He was now on his way to Camp Ford Prison up near Tyler for further questioning. Anybody with any information, etc., etc.

Information came walking down the beach toward Clayton. A thin, blue-eyed old man, now clean-shaven—Mose—was accompanied by Allie, his recently temporary and beloved daughter. Clayton stood and hugged Mose with great affection.

"You old scamp, I never thought I'd see you again."

"You haven't seen the last of me, sir. I'm certain I have one great piece of theater left in me yet."

"Hell, you ought to be the one sittin' at the beach reflectin' on your salad days."

"And so I shall." Mose coughed uncontrollably for a minute; the others waited until the spell passed. Then he sat down as Clayton and Allie embraced. They'd met a few days before and resolved any outstanding issues. Allie understood Clay had to maintain a certain façade around town—as long as Clay understood she had to do the same. They'd given each other leave to have commerce with whomever; as long as that commerce didn't proceed to emotional or physical entanglement. And they were both pretty good at controlling such things.

"Somethin' for you under that paper," Clayton said to Mose.

Mose pulled an envelope out from under *The Daily Ranchero* and peeked inside at the currency. "Appears to be three thousand," he nodded.

"For your fine work, and to carry you on your travels."

"Goin' to Denver, leavin' tonight. They got a sanitarium for those with consumption, say it's the best one in the country."

"Lot of rich folks take the cure there, I hear."

"You know, I hear the same thing." He coughed once, but it sounded like more for effect than for pulmonary clearance.

"I wish you well, Mose."

"I be well as long as I'm alive. Gonna just set here a spell now and enjoy my great good fortune. You children go on, have yourselves the celebration I know you seek." He waved behind him at the *palapa*.

Clay and Allie looked almost shyly at each other as they walked into the thatched hut, where they lay on a straw mat on the sand.

"I won't even ask how much money you skimmed off the top," she poked him.

"I'd say we all made out like bandits. Except Jessup, he said he was givin' his whole share to you. Did he tell you where he got it?"

"From his brother, he said. That sweet man couldn't lie if his life depended on it."

"Well, he's yours to deal with now. I suppose he thinks you're gonna marry him."

"I suppose you think I'm gonna marry you."

He pulled her face to his and kissed her—a drawn out, perfumed, historical kiss, starting with teen passion, moving into the maturity of their wild years, some angry rough kissing, becoming tender, poignant, grieving slow remembrance; and finally the reconnection, the submission to irrevocable feelings, the vows of the heart, I do, I do...

There was love in Clay's heart; all was set. Train tickets under different names to different cities, ship tickets to Europe. Allie was waiting for him...and then one of the old slaves pulled him aside and took him to the tobacco shed where Isaac lay bleeding.

"I ain't seen you in close to a year, and this is how you visit?" Clay teased him as he examined the gunshot to Isaac's belly. In and out the other side. Hard to say how much damage it had done along the way.

"I didn't know where else to go," Isaac gritted his teeth. "I've been living up north. Did some schooling, met some army folks. They sent me back here on a mission—war's coming, Clay. Georgia Militia's after me." He'd lost his down-home accent; he spoke like an educated Yankee now.

As Clay tended Isaac's wound, he told stories to distract him from the pain. "You'll have to get my Allie to watch your back next time. She's a fine shot, though I don't know where she learned. We ran a confidence game once, she pretended to get drunk at a Selectmen's ball in Virginia. I bet this rich fop Allie could shoot a pigeon at 50 yards. He took that bet and by God we won handily, she's about the best shot with a long gun I ever did see. She couldn't hit her foot with a pistol, but genius is funny that way, a person can be tops bakin' and useless fryin'."

Clay hid his old friend in a lean-to back of the slave quarters—but he was nervous about missing the coach to Allie's place, over a day's ride away.

He sent a pigeon to Allie, explaining why he couldn't come yet, why he had to hide Isaac from the Slave Patrols and nurse him back to the living, why Clay and Allie had to postpone their own getaway a little longer. But she didn't answer.

Isaac got worse. Clay spent his money on an abolitionist doctor. He sent Allie another note. Again, no response. Four months later, Isaac finally on the mend, Clay rode to see her.

But Allie wasn't living with her family anymore. Clay learned from a lady at the General Store that she'd married an old plantation owner named Stoneman, and wasn't her father thrilled she'd finally left behind her wild ways and settled down?

As the lady glowed at the thought, the brightness of her smile seemed to ignite the walls of the General Store until flames surrounded them, threatening to incinerate. But then a fountain erupted in the middle of the floor, showering the conflagration with water, turning into cool rivulets that flowed over their feet like a summer stream...

His eyes still closed, he felt Allie breathing beside him on the mat in the cool shade of the *palapa.* He knew the sound of her respirations so well; her lilac smell, her casual laugh, her skeptical squint, her unbridled ardor. Could he have all that back? Could he take it, would she truly give it? He believed so. He felt it in his heart, their time of trials was over.

When he stuck his head out the door of the shack, Mose was gone, and most of the afternoon with him; October just about here. *What now?* he wondered. But the soft hand on his bare hip told him; and he eased back inside.

Far in the distance came a slow roll of thunder.

Several days later Allie invited Jessup for a walk along the river. The air was muggy, with a light breeze from the ocean, the sky showing haze without a single discernible cloud; but it felt like a storm coming.

She apologized for her absence, but she'd had to parlay with her father's accomplices, logistics had to be worked out, and so on. She spoke excitedly, catching him up on all the news. "His friends took him by sidewheeler up to Laredo, then horseback north. I don't know any details beyond that." She took his hand as they walked. "But he's alive because of you, and I can never repay you sufficient for that."

"Just seein' you happy like this is pay enough."

"Well, here's some extra." She took a sheet of paper from her purse and handed it to him. What he read was as promised—20% interest in all proceeds from the Stoneman Claim, parcel 7618, Tuolumne County, California.

"This ain't why I did what I did."

"I know. But sometimes good deeds are rewarded on earth as will be in heaven."

An egret stood one-legged on the bank, motionless as a statue, peering into the water for a meal. As they paused to watch this particular form of grace, Jessup steeled himself for his graceless question. "Allie, I know I'm undeserving of a high person like yourself, but I'm bound to make myself say the words. Will you marry me?"

She put her hands to her heart with a small gasp. "Ahotay, you mustn't ask."

"I'm not able to stay quiet any more. You're all I think about, and I know nothing will ease the situation but that I marry you. Please say you'll consider it."

"I won't give you false hope, and I…"

"Before you say anything, I want to tell you I asked Rip Ford to promote me, which will improve my circumstances, and I believe he's likely to make me a captain."

"I'm most flattered. And you need no promotion for me to feel for you in the highest regard. You're a dear friend, I know I can depend on. But dear one, no, I can't."

"May I know why? Is there another you're holding out for?" He suspected her old beau, Wilkes, but wouldn't say so to her face.

"No, there's no one else. It's many things, but I simply cannot get past this damnable war goin' on. And with you a soldier…I swear I couldn't live if I lost another husband to this terrible conflict."

He had a momentary confusion. "I thought your husband died of malaria."

"He did, he did. But the doctor was killed by Yankees, and the proper medicines got seized as well." Allie was nothing if not a quick thinker. "The last thing you need is the responsibility of carin' for me when your life depends upon stayin' focused on the field of battle."

"Allie, I can't think of nothing but you, battle or not, married or not."

She grew snappy. "Well you best turn that around, mister, before some Mexican bandit sneaks up on you while your mind wanders."

His case was lost, he knew; but a Ranger never gave up. "I know when I'm licked. But you better believe I'm gonna ask you again when this war is over."

She gave herself up to full affection at that—she wouldn't have to put him off again anytime soon, and he seemed to have completely bought the prison break story. "I hope you do ask again. That'll mean the Rebellion has ended and you're still alive."

With hope came a burst of enthusiasm. "The Rebellion will end victorious, after what we found in Pierce's strongbox."

"All that money pulled out of the Yankee coffers will surely help." Her face turned darker. "Not to mention that weasel Captain Odeel has got his comeuppance."

"They say it was him helped your daddy escape. I saw him go inside there from where Major Russell posted me to stand watch—but I didn't see your daddy get away."

"Daddy left by another door. The whole thing was nearly ruined by Odeel nosin' around. As fate would have it, his appearance made it seem like he was the mastermind of the escape, and Major Russell didn't disabuse them of that notion. You mustn't feel bad, though. Odeel got what he deserved, tryin' to steal my cotton as he did. You just keep your mind fixed on all that Yankee money you found to put in Confederate hands."

"Oh, we found more'n that," he bragged, then immediately had second thoughts. "I shouldn't say, though, it's kind of a secret."

"Surely you can tell *me*." A hint of a pout. "I thought we were closer than that."

"We are, we are. But you can't share this with anyone." Off her reproachful look he continued. "All right, then. We found a Union military dispatch layin' down where and when and how the Yankee invasion of Texas will take place. A great Northern army gonna drive across the Arkansas border from Fort Smith, first of November."

Her jaw dropped. "You don't mean to tell me."

"I do. But we left the dispatch there and copied it, so the Yanks wouldn't know we found it. Now we'll be able to ambush the attack and send 'em packing back into Indian Territory, where I expect the Cherokee Nation will finish them off."

"And you say you and Clay both found this message."

"Well...I'm the one actually found it under Pierce's bed. Wilkes was there mostly to cover me."

She nodded thoughtfully. Knowing Clay as she did, this good fortune on the part of Jessup and the Confederate States of America was not necessarily all that it seemed. In fact, it likely meant the opposite of what it seemed. Which meant this was not good news for the Rebs. Clay hadn't mentioned anything about finding a military dispatch to her, which surely signaled he was keeping it from her. And why would he do that, unless he didn't want her mixing in on any con of his own that he was running? And what kind of con would put supposed Northern military plans in the hands of a naïve young Confederate? Why, that would be a confidence game Clay was running against the Southern States. Which made Clay a Northern spy.

And for all her financial scheming, her flair for high drama, her artistic sense of photography, and her ability to enter whatever state of mind was required to get what she wanted, her heart was with the Rebs; and more intensely, against the damn Yankees who'd ruined her family. Dixie was the land many of her friends had died defending; it was her parents' lifeblood. She was a lady of the South, to the bone, and not at all favorable to watching it undermined by the shenanigans of someone the likes of that cynical rogue, Clay Wilkes. She'd have to consider her next move carefully.

Like lightning the egret ducked its head into the shallows and came back up with a fish in its long beak. A moment later actual lightning flickered inside a distant thunderhead, which had appeared out of nowhere. A warm, fat raindrop hit her cheek.

"Well, you're my hero," she said, kissing Jessup on the lips, and lingering there an extra second. "But we better get back to the house in a hurry, before it comes down so hard I'd be embarrassed for you to see me."

Jessup was embarrassed just thinking about it. But they made it back to the house just as the sky broke loose.

CHAPTER 18

T HE NEXT FEW WEEKS, from the end of September deep into October, were a hum of activity—nationally, internationally, and locally.

The Sioux Uprising that had begun a year earlier was roundly defeated by the U.S. Army at the Battle of Whitestone Hill; in the Civil War the Battle of Chickamauga, Georgia, became just about the bloodiest two days in American history, seeing 20,000 die in a resounding Union defeat; Abraham Lincoln, president of the United States, suspended the Writ of Habeas Corpus and announced a national day of Thanksgiving, to be held at the end of November, though few had much to be thankful for.

In Trieste, Archduke Maximilian of Austria, at the behest of Emperor Napoleon III of France and an official delegation of Mexican *Imperialistas*, took on the solemn responsibility of accepting the throne of Mexico. The United States entered discussions to loan the Mexican resistance government of Benito Juarez 50 million dollars in exchange for Lower California.

General Hamilton Bee, commandant of Fort Brown, Texas, sent Colonel Rip Ford to lead troops up to Shreveport, Louisiana, to meet the anticipated Yankee onslaught coming down from Ft. Smith on November 1. Texas Ranger Jessup—now Captain Jessup, for his instrumental role in catching the traitor Odeel—was given command of a platoon up to Laredo, to ready a counterattack against Cortina's army, which was expected to launch its assault in concert with the Union invasion.

Clayton Wilkes and Allison Stoneman carried on a torrid, secret affair of the heart, soul, and flesh.

And then the rains came.

The Matamoros storm season was torrential. Unlike other subtropics, though, it was river delta surrounded by swaths of wide, open spaces with little foliage to hold back the deluge. So the rains often changed the landscape, altering the course of the river. Some said it was possible to drown walking home if you inhaled too deep; and certainly that was true if you were walking home from a tavern. But sober or not, a man took the storms of the Rio Grande seriously, and stayed indoors until they subsided. So life at Brave River tended to get more chummy.

Limey Ned, who'd been gored by the bull on Independence Day, was unaccountably not only still alive but thriving. Clayton had had him put in a back room to die peacefully; but no such thing happened. Nor did the hole in his belly close. In fact, it knit together with the puncture in his stomach, and the two holes healed up like a tunnel from his innards to just above his navel. Isaac deemed it hadn't gotten infected because of all the alcohol Ned poured in his mouth, which then flowed out the hole in his skin.

This had the unexpected consequence of keeping Ned more sober than he'd been in years, the spirits leaking out this new overflow spout before they got absorbed. Appreciating that Brave River was good luck for him, he decided to stay, and worked out an arrangement with Clayton to do fix-it jobs in return for room and board. On those occasions he did want to experience the effect of his old friend, John Barleycorn, he'd just cork up the hole near his bellybutton and have a few swigs.

His shipmates sailed without him, figuring him for gored and dead. But Dinah Singletary—seeing in Ned a compatriot lost soul of the Brave River—took him under her wing and made it her business to do for him, just as Zhi Li had taken on the caretaking of Hermano. Dinah made sure Ned was well fed; she cleaned his belly hole when the edges of the skin got irritated from stomach juices; she feigned interest in the sailor's knots he tied to entertain her, and which appeared to make him happy. Yet through all of this, Dinah still never spoke word.

Scully was occupied with preparing one of the river islands as a base of attack for Leonard Pierce's ragtag army, naming the place Banco Patricio.

Meanwhile Isaac was doing the same thing with his Colored troops on the Mexican side of the river. He had over 300 refugees under his command now and he was training them into a fighting force—first, to assist the Union invasion, and after that to be an army for his new colony when it was time to occupy their Mexican land grant.

Around the middle of October, the rains paused.

Allie was making a good start of her import business, buying discounted goods left unclaimed at the docks and selling them to the army, thanks to Major Russell. This war was bound to make her rich as long as the Rebs controlled the river that moved goods in and out of the South.

But if she was optimistic about her commercial ventures, she was positively aglow with the success of her photography business. People had been parading through her studio all day buying prints from the Independence Day celebration she had displayed over tables. Photos of the magnificent Cathedral, the robed priest, strolling *mariachis*, the mayor overseeing the parade, mounted *caballeros*, the police force posing with their weapons, prominent personages, sloe-eyed *senoritas*, colonels from five armies, all trying to look stern and important.

In the early afternoon Mildred Bee showed up to get her husband's studio portrait and saw a photograph of Consul Quintero lying nearby. Mildred lowered her voice to Allie, though there was no one else around. "Quintero is a spymaster, you know."

"You don't mean to say."

"I do. In fact, I've heard Clayton Wilkes reports to him directly."

This was of aggravating interest to Allie. In the heat of their affair, she'd more or less put away thinking about the idea that Clay was an active Northern spy. He certainly didn't seem motivated by much but making money and making love. But when the subject of Clay's espionage was just thrown in her face, it was like a burr under her saddle—because it meant Clay was conning her. As if she were no smarter than any other mark. Conning her and everyone else, to help the Union win the war. The notion of it made her furious, not only at him, but at herself. Furious for letting herself be lulled by him, seduced, betrayed yet again. So Mildred's words were goading her now, to get even with Clay's shenanigans. To do to him what he'd done to her.

But it all had to be accomplished with some subtlety, maintaining the illusion of their mutual disaffection—partly since their ongoing flirtations with others generally helped their respective businesses. So she dismissed Mildred's assertion with calculation, assuming the injured tone of an ex-lover. "Clay Wilkes is no spy for the South or anyone else. He is a self-interested cad."

"Well, that's as it may be, but I know for a fact he hates the Yankees for burning down his family's plantation."

Allie knew this to be untrue—she and Clay had quite a history together, after all—but if that's the story he was peddling it gave even more weight to her growing certainty that he was a Northern agent— that he'd contrived to produce information drawing the Confederate armies to a false front in northern Louisiana.

She wondered if Mildred had overheard anything else that might be a clue to Clay's deceit. So she probed. "I hate the Yankees myself, for ruining my own family," she said, "but that hardly makes me a spy." And here she lowered her voice. "Though Captain Jessup did tell me the Union invasion is set for November 1."

"Sugar, you're not supposed to know that," Mildred said, half indignant, half impressed.

"Well, then, I guess maybe I am a spy," Allie smiled.

"What else did that chatterbox Jessup tell you?"

"Texarkana's where he said the big fight is comin'. But I think he mighta been leadin' me astray. Has Hamilton told you otherwise?" She was certain the Arkansas dispatch was a mislead. The question was, where *did* those Yankees plan to invade? She needed to find out, if she was going to thwart their designs on her homeland.

"Hamilton has said nothing to me, I assure you," Mrs. Bee assumed a haughty tone; then broke into a conspiratorial smile. "But I do love our secrets."

"And that Clay Wilkes loves his. Where did you hear he was a spy, though?"

Something in her tone made Mildred ken. "You're still sweet on him, aren't you?"

"I am no such thing." But she flushed a little.

"Yes, you are, I can see it plain as pie. You are all aflutter."

Allie stomped her foot. "I am not, and you must stop sayin' such things. If anything, I despise that man's inconsiderate, self-centered, smug arrogance."

Allie and Clay moaned loudly with the same breath, gripped in each other's arms, their mouths locked, turning them into a single being, flailing amidst strewn clothes, her hands dug into his hips, his fingers in her hair, pulling her head back until an inchoate sound rose from her throat, and he gasped, motionless for an eternity…and they collapsed in a tangle of limbs and sweat and skin on skin, sliding finally to a full stop.

The rains had come again, more gently this time, a continuous patter on the roof of her house that felt calming to them now, a soothing tattoo. She turned into him, brought her lips to his nipple; bit it lightly and snuggled into his arm, laying her head on his chest. "I hate you," she whispered.

"My darlin'." He kissed the top of her head.

"Life surely is a puzzlement."

"Not times like this, it ain't. Nothin' puzzlin' about this. You and I are just suited, in a manner most wouldn't understand."

"I don't understand it."

"There you go."

Clay had once told her the only two minutes in his life he ever thought completely clearly were the two minutes after they made love. Allie had come to believe the same was true for her. And what she was thinking right now, in that window of clarity, was that if the Union attack wasn't actually at Texarkana, there were a limited number of places it might logically come. Galveston was the likeliest since the Yanks had taken that seaport once, only to lose it again. She decided to test Clay's reaction with a small gambit.

"I may need to go to Galveston early November to wrap up some business Mr. Stoneman left unattended."

"Mr. Stoneman, that's what you called your husband?"

"It's customary."

"You gonna stand on protocol while you're layin' between my legs?"

She punched him lightly. "You want to meet me up Galveston way in a week?"

"I'll go up with you right now, if you want."

"No, the man said early November. Besides, I said we should meet there, I don't want us goin' together so everyone here in town sees we're together."

"I'm thinkin' maybe it's time we can be seen sparkin' in public."

"That's a terrible idea. It could hurt my business negotiations with those fellows who give me a good price because they think it'll buy me into their good graces."

"More like they think it'll buy them into your good panties."

She punched him again. "Anyway it would get back to Jessup, and likely hurt his feelin's."

Clay was annoyed. "By God, I may have to sell that man to the Kiowa just to get him off your mind."

This conversation had taken a wrong turn for Allie, but at least she felt confident the invasion wasn't happening at Galveston, if Clay was willing to go there with her. Now she wanted to find a way out of this talk. "I'm just bein' considerate of his feelin's."

"Jessup's a grown-up man, he can tolerate hurt feelin's." When she didn't answer, he suddenly got it. "Wait a minute—*you're* the one's got feelin's for *him*."

"It's not that, exactly," she protested; then steeled herself for his next reaction. "But I may have promised to marry him if he's alive when the war is over."

Clay sat up in a snit. "Well, I'm glad you at least qualified it with him bein' alive. Wouldn't want you to have to marry no dead Texas Ranger."

"Don't be that way, Clay. He'll likely get killed in the next skirmish with Cortina." She watched him get dressed. "You know you're never more attractive to me than when you're jealous."

"I'm not jealous," he said. "I'm just tryin' to remember your name."

She threw a pillow at him as he walked past the bed where Moon still lay unconscious, and continued out the back door.

Allie smiled to herself at Clay's sass. He was the most fun to be with she ever had, and she knew she'd do well not to throw that away again. But that didn't mean she couldn't match his political manipulations with her own, and swell the tides of war to the shore of a more suitable outcome.

She just wished she didn't still love him this bad.

* * *

On his way back to Brave River Clay wondered why Allie was trying to get a rise out of him with talk about Galveston. Did she know something he didn't? He'd have to ask Leonard Pierce if an assault was planned there. More likely Allie was just telling the truth, it was family business, and Clay was overthinking the whole thing. Overthinking because he felt so guilty about lying to her. Pretending his sympathies were with the South, not mentioning his spying for the North, hiding his trickery—it made him feel undeserving of her love, made him feel duplicitous. As if he were betraying her. It filled him with scorn for himself.

So he arrived at the casino conflicted, drenched to the bone and muddy to the knee. The tables were all full, men laughing, making bets, drinking. Zhi Li walked up.

"I put up sign in town," she said. "Free Drink until four o'clock."

"Free!? We're givin' all this liquor away free?"

"Is good trick. Lots come for free drink, then after four they keep drink but not free. They must stay out of rain so they gamble, they lose money. We make big money."

He narrowed his eyes at her, wondering if he should nip this in the bud. Isaac had always assumed management decisions like that. But Zhi Li just smiled, pleased.

244

As Scully made his way out of a light drizzle into the *hacienda* he took off his wet jacket and followed an odd sound to the kitchen, where he found Aurelia weeping on the floor. He sat beside her but didn't speak. She finally stopped crying.

"He is dead. *Mi esposa.* My cousin have tell me. Sean is killed by the French."

"I'm sorry, Aurelia. And…I'm just sorry."

Her face twisted. "I hate the French."

He hated to see her in such pain. They'd been living in the same house, living the domestic routines of a husband and wife, and it had become a comfort to him, even without conjugal privileges; so it hurt him to see her so. He found he wanted something he'd never wanted before. He wanted there to be no lies between them. "I fought with the French. I'm sorry for that, too."

He tried to put his arm around her, to comfort her—but the way they were sitting, it was his wooden arm, and a piece of the tin rigging poked through his sleeve and snagged the back of her blouse. Aggravated, he pulled it back; but this only tore her blouse, scraping skin in the process. She winced but didn't speak.

Scully thought if he shared her pain it might bring them closer; he wanted her to feel that her rawness was also his. So he did something he'd never done before; not sure why it even made sense. He took off his wet shirt and unhooked the harness that held his arm in place. Disengaged the thing and laid it on the floor; a strange tool of oak, iron, leather and tin. Gently he put the side of his exposed stump against her cheek.

She brought the appendage to her lips, tenderly kissed it. Nestled into his embrace. They remained there like that, unmoving, beside the warm coals of the kitchen stove, under the ageless patter of rain on the adobe.

"*Por favor,*" she whispered. "*No mas* kill and die."

It was a promise he couldn't yet make. But he didn't want to lie; so he just kept holding her.

Allie was hanging new portraits on her studio wall when she heard the front door open. A voice said, "I am General Juan Cortina. You will make my photograph." She turned to see a dangerous looking Mexican soldier in an officer's jacket with a bandolier of bullets draping his shoulder; flanked by two scruffy *banditos* carrying rifles.

Allie maintained her composure. "If you think you can just order me about like a slave, I fear you are mistaken, sir."

His first reaction was anger; his second, admiration for her bravery. "*Por favor*, they say you make the picture of great men in Matamoros. I am such a man."

Allie smiled. This would indeed be a fine addition to her collection of local personalities. "Well, since you put it like that, you may have a seat."

"I stand. *El caballero muy fuerte* does not sit."

"That's quite perspicacious of you." She knew to equalize the playing field by using words she was sure he didn't know. "But before we begin, I require a gold piece for my service."

"Those who make my songs do not ask me pay."

"Then perhaps we can both hazard a guess as to what those songs are worth."

Cortina grinned at her cleverness and said something to his bodyguards. One pulled a golden coin from his pocket and laid it on the table.

"Excellent. Now, if I may..." She placed him beside a potted Desert Willow, then took a rifle from one of his lieutenants—who gave it up only after a nod from Cortina—and placed it in Cortina's hands. "Now all will see you're not a man to be trifled with."

"*Bueno*," he nodded with a sense of moment.

She set the camera and got the plates ready as they talked. "I'm surprised to see you here. Everyone thinks you're in Laredo."

"As I wish them to think."

"My fiancé is lookin' for you. He's a Texas Ranger and he'd like to see you dead."

"I will never die. Because my songs no die, *nunca muere*. *Nunca!* And my picture too, *no?* Maybe you better to make your Texas Ranger picture before he meets me." He laughed and his men laughed with him, though none understood what he'd said.

"Why sir, I assumed you wanted this photograph of yourself before *you* met *him*."

He wagged his finger with a smile. "*Que salvaje chica.* Maybe I kiss you."

"Maybe I should tell my fiancé where you really are."

"Then he will die much soon…"

"Shhh! Don't move," she ordered as she stepped under the black cape of her camera. He stood rock still—poised for posterity. She uncapped the lens, exposed the plate, and set off the charge of flash powder that gave the proper lighting.

At the flash, one guard extended his rifle, the other drew his pistol. Angered—and more worldly than his soldiers—Cortina shouted at them even as he tried to hold still. *"No muevas! Idiotas!"*

His men looked confused. Allie came out from under the cape, indignant. "If I have to do this again because they have ruined the sitting, I advise you it will cost another twenty dollars."

Cortina gave his men the evil eye but shrugged to Allie. "For live forever, there is a price, *no*? I will return tomorrow." He motioned his men and they left.

Allie wondered who she might speak to about Cortina's presence in Matamoros. He was known to be in league with Leonard Pierce against the South—so perhaps Quintero would be the best person to pass it on to. Although Russell might well pay for the knowledge and then sell it up the ladder at a higher price.

She took Cortina's exposed plate into her darkroom, washed it in the chemical baths that brought out and fixed the image, placed it on the drying rack and proceeded to print the last of her negatives from the Independence Day party. A boy selling water; an old woman selling *nopales*; a company of soldiers selling bravado.

If she got word to Jessup about Cortina's presence in town, of course, it might bring him back down here from Laredo. Which was good and bad. She loved him truly when she was with him; but she'd become shackled by her lovemaking with Clay. She didn't know how to break that hold and wasn't sure she wanted to. From there it concerned her that she wasn't ever entirely certain who she was or what she wanted. But she couldn't think about that now. For now she needed to remain close to Clay if she was going to find out the real story of the upcoming Northern invasion, so she could warn the men in a position to stop it, like Quintero and General Bee.

She printed the portrait of Cortina; it was a mess. The bandit himself looked fine—a kind of menacing nobility—but he was surrounded by the blurs of his gunmen swiveling around. She was about to toss the print when she noticed something else.

She'd been so rattled at the appearance of the bandits, she'd forgotten the glass plate in the camera had already been used for a previous photograph, then left in place because she'd been too busy with customers to remove it. So there were now two photos on the same negative, a double exposure—Cortina, standing with rifle, surrounded by the blurs of his moving henchmen; and the eerie face of her last portrait—a seated, bearded preacher, who seemed to stare out from behind the leaves of the potted Desert Willow as if he were casting gloomy eyes intently at Cortina.

It gave Allie just the inklings of an idea.

But she put them aside. First she must focus on gathering more intelligence.

Laying her hand on Major Russell's arm outside the Opera House, Allie gushed, "Why Major Russell, you're lookin' quite dashin' tonight."

"I try to clean up when I go to the Opera. Seems only proper."

"It's fortunate I ran into you." By which he understood this to be no accidental meeting. "I've a large shipment of goods arrivin' soon from abroad and I was hopin' you could be my intermediary once more in sales to the army."

"You know I'm happy to do that, ma'am. As you've likely heard, most of the soldiers at Fort Brown are off, or soon will be, to the Arkansas border to fight the Yanks. Any durable goods you might have for that campaign would surely be welcome."

She paused. "Has it ever occurred to you the South is bein' hornswoggled? That our boys are bein' connived to fight where the battle is not bein' waged?"

"Mrs. Stoneman, you and I both know a thing or two about falsification, but in this matter it concerns me not. Wherever the fight is, I hope to profit. Not that I want our men to lose—these grand military strategies are just beyond my ken."

"Well, at least you're an honest thief."

"If it's all that important for you to figure out, you might work your magic on the fellow over there inspecting that shabby buggy. Tinbury."

"What does he know about anything?"

"Likely not much. But he is Pierce's aide, and though I doubt Pierce would confide anything of substance in him, he mighta picked up a snatch of talk here or there. And here's a tip—he's unaccountably prideful of his facial hair."

"In that case, good evenin' to you, sir," she said, and left him for Tinbury, who was circling his one-horse shay, looking for the source of a new rattle. As Allie neared him she stumbled, grabbing the horse's bridle to stop from falling. Tinbury hurried up.

"May I help you, Miss?"

"I may have twisted my ankle. If I could just rest here a moment?"

"Of course. Let me help you into the shay." He helped her up onto the two-seater.

"You are so kind. But now that I'm here—if it's not too forward—I wonder if I could impose on you to take me home. It's ever so close."

"I'd be honored, Miss." He jumped up on the seat beside her. "Where to?"

She looked at him full on and smiled. "My, what a fine moustache you have." In the darkness she felt his heart stutter a beat. "Might I know the name of my savior?"

"Of course, how rude of me, and me a diplomat, to boot. I am Benjamin Tinbury, Aide to Union Ambassador Leonard Pierce, at your service."

"I suppose a Southern Belle like myself should be quakin', sittin' with a Yankee—especially with our boys leavin' Fort Brown to go fight y'all up north."

He knew a bit about the Arkansas divertionary ruse but wasn't about to divulge the few details he had. He didn't want her to fret, though. "You needn't worry on that account, long as you stay south of the border."

She kept fishing for hints. "I don't guess the Union is about to try landin' an army at Galveston again, like they so disastrously did last year."

Tinbury got defensive at that. "Here, now, that wasn't such a bad idea, we got a foothold there in October."

"Until General Magruder tossed you out on New Year's Day!" she laughed gaily. "Once bit, twice shy, I always say."

Her laugh was so sweet, he couldn't be cross. "Well, you may be right at that."

So the invasion isn't coming at Galveston, she thought. *Where, then?* "And I know even you Yanks aren't foolish enough to have another go at the Sabine Pass, after we humiliated you there." She was so tickled by her own words, she actually fell against his arm, then grabbed onto it to steady herself. And then stayed that close.

Tinbury could think of little but the touch of her hand on his arm—though he did try to defend his country's honor. "I wouldn't say we were humiliated. But I will say Sabine might be the worst bottleneck the general staff could have picked to send a navy, and I think they know that now."

"Sounds like you know a thing or two about strategy yourself."

Her admiration emboldened him. "I know there are ten straits wider than Sabine, from Brownsville to New Orleans, and the deepest is right here at Brazos Santiago Pass. So you can bet our military won't make that mistake this time."

Brazos Santiago Pass, she thought. Right here at the mouth of the Rio Grande, off Brazos Island. Brazos was a nearly undefended barrier isle, a good staging area for a landing force. And just 25 miles downriver from Brownsville. In addition, Tinbury had said she'd be safe if she stayed south of the border. As opposed to north of the border—in Brownsville.

She knew it in her heart, now, just as surely as if he'd told her in so many words—which he practically did. The Union invasion was set for Brownsville, just across the river from where they stood.

The Yanks were fixing to barge in the back door of the South, while the Rebel troops were all running up to Shreveport and Texarkana, hundreds of miles away. And Clay must have known that. But she couldn't let him know she knew. She'd have to be especially considerate when he came to her tonight. Though that was in no ways a problem for her.

"I wonder if you could take me home now, Benjamin?"

He flicked his buggy whip, drove the mile to her place and walked her to the door. Then he left, still giddy with the sense-memory of her palm on his bicep; and she went to make her bed ready for Clay.

CHAPTER 19

THE RAINS CAME AGAIN and didn't let up. The streets were mud, and every day one or two drunks were found drowned in some pond or trench. The river was roiling high; some of the smaller islet *bancos* had disappeared altogether. Clayton divided his time between the casino and Allie's place, where he drowned himself in her body, in the flood of their own storm, as the rest of the world washed downstream. He was periodically bothered by having omitted mention of his secret efforts on behalf of the North to invade Brownsville. He convinced himself she wouldn't care, and anyway he didn't want to burden her with military business. Loving her was one universe for him; hating the Confederacy was an entirely different arena.

One afternoon when Clay showed up at the casino, it was pouring so hard the mud got washed off his feet in the step he took before the threshold. Captain Solomon, drinking alone at a far table, raised his glass to Clayton, who nodded back.

Zhi, lighting joss sticks near the stairway, reached behind the backbar for a towel, hobbled over on her deformed feet and began drying him off.

"Here, now, you don't have to do that," he protested mildly.

"You make floor too wet." She stumbled but he caught her, his hand on her shoulder.

From across the room Captain Solomon watched their interaction. It reminded him of something—Clayton's gentle hand on the small woman's back, the way he came down to her eye level as a kindness—Solomon just couldn't place the memory. It didn't have to do with Zhi Li, or puddling rainwater, or tender touches, or—wait, it did have to do with tender touches. And the memory came back all at once. Clayton was turned in the same posture, the same gesture, as he'd taken with that young Negro girl who was briefly a janitor here at Brave River—when was it? A moment later Solomon realized that janitor girl was the same young slave he'd seen in Xo Ten's camp. He motioned Clayton over to his table.

"There was a wee black girl sweeping your floors a few months ago," Ryburn said without preamble. "You might want to know, she's a Kiowa slave now. I saw her in Xo Ten's camp."

Clayton was stunned. After all her heroics blowing up the Yankee munitions depot, only to end up a slave again? "She still there, you think?"

"I'm going back to see Shalako near the end of the month, I can find out."

"I'll go with you. I mean to buy her."

"Xo Ten made her his special new wife. It'd take more than money to get the rascal to part with her now."

"Then I'll have to bring more than money to close the deal." Clayton headed upstairs to include Isaac in his plans.

Ned was at the bar, emptying his pockets of coin for his next round. As Solomon approached to get another drink, he noticed, amongst the copper in Ned's pile, a gold dubloon. The sight quickened the captain's pulse.

"Might I have a look at your shiny penny, there?" And without waiting for leave, he picked up Ned's old Spanish coin. He tasted the coin, bit it, peered at it—but he knew it was real. Likely from the galleon *La Reina*, plundered by Lafitte in 1822.

"It's a beauty," Solomon said with admiration, placing it back down on the bar. "Can I ask where you may have picked it up?" Ned shook his head. "Tell you what," Solomon went on, "it's a 20 dollar peso. I'll give you fifty, hard American for it."

"Not for sale," said Ned. "It's my lucky piece. Last one I got."

"My friend, this coin comes from a Spanish galleon sunk by the pirate Lafitte some 40 years gone. Lafitte is an interest of mine and I'd be grateful if you'd let me buy it from you."

"Not for sale. But if it's Lafitte you be lookin' for, you need search no further than Point Isabel."

"Is that a fact," said Solomon, who'd never found a sou there for all his searches.

"'Tis Indeed. And if you go at the right time, you'll see Lafitte's ghost schooner, *La Dilidente*, sailin' back for the gold they buried in a grotto on the lee side o' the island. Guarded by a black ghost dog with red eyes and yellow fangs, what kills anyone who comes near."

"How is it you're not dead yourself, then?"

"Never got closer than the hound chased me away. I'm leery of dogs ever since. And I won't go near the grotto again."

"I didnae mean to offend you, mate. It's just an old salt's dream to find privateer treasure."

"Privateer, that's what he were," nodded Ned, warming to his subject. "He weren't no pirate, nor evil bastard like some say. Lafitte was a noble gent if ever there was one."

"Here's to Lafitte." They raised their glasses and drank. And Solomon—who'd always kept mum about his quest for pirate gold—found himself opening up. From his forays to Lafitte's reputed haunts, to his family connections to the famous bucanneer.

And the two old salts were soon fast friends.

Clayton went up to the roof, where he released a pigeon into the rain; then came down to Isaac's room, to tell him about Jersey in the Kiowa camp. And Isaac told Clayton the *Defiant* had finally weighed anchor off Bagdad—the ship Wilkes had been awaiting so long. Clayton was thrilled—and anxious to coordinate with Major Russell, to offload the ship and transfer the freight. He hurried to his office to get the requisite cash.

But on entering he found Allie dressed in men's clothing, asleep on his divan. She woke at his footfall. "Where ever have you been?" She sounded half asleep.

"What are you doin' here? I thought you wanted to keep our liaisons a private affair."

"They remain so. I dressed as a man and came upstairs with Isaac, appearin' to conduct business."

"You and Teddy, I swear."

"Teddy who?"

"Never you mind. Why have you come? I'm quite busy just now."

"Most men would forget how busy they were upon findin' me in their bed."

"It's not my bed, it's my *chaise*, and though you are always a fetchin' sight, your garments are hardly what I'd call provocative."

"Then perhaps you should remove the offendin' garments before they quench your ardor any further." She reached up to release his top shirt button. "Or are you hidin' secret war maps under there?"

The question set off a bell in his head. "What are you askin' about war maps for?"

She knew not to push it any further. "Because I'm about to wage a rousin' battle on your person and I don't mean for you to outflank me." She unbuttoned his pants and let them drop.

"I thought flankin' was your favorite approach." He tore open her shirt, pushed her back down on the couch, pulled off her pants and flipped her on her side.

The rain came down harder, muffling the sweet suppressed cries on the divan.

* * *

An hour later the storm broke, leaving a world of steam in its wake. The gamblers at Brave River poured into the street for some outside air, which quickly devolved into a massive mud fight that would be talked about for years. Allie slipped out the back and Clayton made his way unnoticed to Ambassador Pierce's safe house, where he found Pierce waiting expectantly—called to the meet-up by Clayton's carrier pigeon. "What's the emergency?" Pierce asked.

"I'm here for money. We need to buy back a prisoner of war—that girl, Jersey, from Xo Ten. His band took her for a slave."

"Jersey? The Negro girl who blew up the dump?" Pierce sounded annoyed. "That's no emergency. What are you wasting my time on nonsense like this for?"

Clayton's eye twitched in anger. "That girl risked her life performin' a courageous act for the Union, and we owe it to her to get her back. You have enough money to save this child. If that's not what we're fightin' for, then maybe I'm in the wrong war."

Pierce knew not to alienate his best spy over money. "Of course, Wilkes. I didn't realize you felt so strongly. I'll send someone around with whatever you need."

Clayton relaxed a notch. "I'll be off to get her in a few days."

"Make sure you're back before the first. I just got the news. The invasion is on."

Clayton met Russell outside the fort, where some Mexican peasant was being executed against an adobe wall by four soldiers with single-shot rifles. The Quartermaster took him to his personal warehouse near the river, where he unpadlocked the door and they entered. He lit two torches, handed one to Clayton and led the way down aisles of cotton bales, piles of canned goods, bins of copper and lead, wine kegs, brandy bottles, hides, rifles, barrels of gunpowder and a tower of leatherworked saddles. They talked as they walked.

"Let's get right down to it," said Clayton amiably. "How much do you want?"

"First of all, you never told me you were shipping such an advanced weapon of war." They reached a 5X10 foot open crate packed with odd fittings, a large muzzle, gears, wheels and pipes. "Looks to me," Russell went on, "like one of those new Gatling guns I hear they been using on striking workers in New York. Those are 50 caliber, though, and this barrel's a sight bigger."

"Well, you're up to date on your weaponry, I can see that."

"Damn tootin'. War's about to heat up on our side of the Mississippi. Field arms like this could turn the tide. Looks like a highest bidder kind of situation to me."

Clayton had to smile. "I'm afraid you've outfoxed yourself, Major Russell. This is no kind of weapon. It's an ice machine. Showed at the London Exposition last year. Uses ether to make ice."

"It don't."

"Sure as I'm standin' here. Makes tons of it."

"What for?"

"Keeps meat from rottin', and corpses you have to transport. You can cool your animals crossin' the desert. This here model makes 400 pounds of ice an hour. Just let me take the contraption over to my place, I'll give you a demonstration."

Russell looked at the strange invention. Other crates sat beside it, all equally obscure. "All right, say you're tellin' the truth. Item like this could make millions."

"Don't get greedy, old son. We still have a long, prosperous relationship ahead of us, if you don't try to reach further than you can grab."

Russell considered it a moment longer. "You leave this thing here. Have your men set it up and get it running, we'll see what it does. Then we'll talk."

Clayton considered options—including hiring Scully and a team to hijack the thing. But that could end in gunfire, which was bad for commerce and might actually damage the machine. Then he noticed a few more open crates—all full of Henry 16 shot repeating rifles. Best of the best.

"This lot might could be worth more than all the rest of your warehouse combined," Clayton said, picking up one of the long guns and sighting down the barrel. "Most accurate rifle ever made, I hear."

"Loads on Sunday and shoots all week long, they say. Only a few Yankees got 'em now—if they all get 'em, the war's over."

Clay had a thought. "Let's you and me talk turkey, Major."

Clayton enlisted Wachtel to lead the team assembling the ice machine. The old editor refused at first but Clayton enticed him with money, chess, compliments, and the challenge of building a machine even more complicated than the press he'd put together at the newspaper office. In the end Wachtel agreed to spend evenings at Russell's warehouse, supervising one of his *Daily Ranchero* compositors, in addition to Scully and a corporal who'd once been a gunsmith. Dr. Hawks provided the ether necessary for the ice machine's compressor.

On the 23ʳᵈ of October Clayton and Solomon packed up two wagons and set off to Xo Ten's encampment. Two large crates in one wagon, with a large and a smaller one in the other. The smaller was Solomon's—he'd packed it in secret and wouldn't tell Clay what was in it. Clayton trusted him to do what he needed to do, though, so he didn't ask too many questions about its contents.

It was an easy first day over grassland, talking about all the things that they'd seen in their lives; of wars and whales, magic and Oriental gardens and personages of all manner, some kind hearts, some evil devils, some old souls, some bawdy women. By afternoon they'd fallen into an easy silence until Solomon began humming to himself.

"If that's one of your sea shanties, sing it up and make me grin."

Solomon looked perplexed at first, then smiled. "I didnae even know what tune it was, but now I do. As I get nearer to Shalako, the only Hebrew prayer I still know comes over me—he seems to bring it out in me."

"Sing it, then, man."

He sang, as if from far away. "*Shema Yisroel, adonai elohenu, Adonai ehod.*"

"What's it mean?"

"Means I'm on the road to my Maker, most likely."

"We're all on that road, old son."

They made camp at sunset by a stream where the horses could water. As Clay built a small campfire Solomon sat against a wagon wheel and watched the flames dance. After a while an old feeling seemed to fill him, and he closed his eyes. "It's Friday, is it not?"

Clay took a moment to consider, then nodded. "Unless I fell asleep too long."

Solomon tried humming a few notes but shook his head in gentle frustration. "Every Friday at sundown my mother would light a candle and sing the Sabbath prayers—one thanks for bread and another for wine. The fruit of the vine." He shook his head again. "But I can't for the life of me remember how the damn prayers go."

Clay pulled a stick out of the fire and stuck it upright in the sand, its tip aflame. "Well, there's your candle." Then he pulled one of Milagra's tortillas out of his pack, tore it in half and tossed a piece to Solomon. "And there's your bread."

Solomon bit off a chunk, reached into his coat, pulled out a tin flask, uncorked it, had a swig, capped it again and tossed it to Clayton. "And there's the fruit of the vine."

Clayton raised the flask. "To the fruit of the vine." And he took a long pull.

Solomon nodded at his companion in the low firelight as the stars were coming out, just two small souls on a vast plain, and he smiled. "You're a good lad."

It was something Clayton had never heard said to him before.

They rode all the next day and got to Xo Ten's camp on the afternoon of the 25th, the day before the full moon. It was quieter than the last time Solomon had been here. Kiowa women cooked; children played in the dirt, but stopped when the white men entered camp. Xo Ten came out of his tent.

"*Ha-cho,* Xo Ten," called Solomon.

"*Ha-cho, Sol-mon,*" Xo Ten said. "You have guns for me, mate?"

"I have guns," said Clayton, climbing out of his wagon. "*Ha-cho.*"

As Clayton prybarred up the lid of a large crate, Solomon stepped away. "Xo Ten, you and Mr. Wilkes conduct your business, I'm here to see Shalako." He directed two strong braves to pull his smaller crate off the second wagon, and the three of them hefted it through the tall grass to Shalako's cave.

When Clayton got his larger crate open it revealed 20 shiny new Henrys. Xo Ten took one pristine rifle from the crate and hefted it. "Our hides are all gone. Have nothing to trade but slaves. Want a slave, mate?"

"You have a young black girl. She was mine and I'd like her back."

"No. You take Cherokee woman." He shouted a command. One of the braves pulled two women out of a tent and brought them over. They looked scared. "Both good sheilas, you take one."

"That's a good offer, Xo Ten. But the American girl is the only one I want, so I've come prepared to sweeten the pot." He opened the other crate. Twenty more Henrys lay gleaming like treasure. This is how much I want her. Her name is Jersey. If you could find a way to cut her loose, I would owe you a great favor. I have a gift for you, in any case."

He took the crowbar to the crate in the other wagon and motioned Xo Ten over.

It was ice. A solid block, six feet long, two feet deep, covered in ice chips. Clayton dug his hand into the chips, put some in his mouth, and held the rest out. Xo Ten took them in his hand. The two women came forward to experiment with the ice in the crate. Gasps, laughter, shouting. Clayton held up his hand to stop them momentarily. "Wait." He pulled two porcelain cups out of the wagon bed and filled them with ice chips. Then he uncorked a jug of cane syrup and poured it over the ice in one, and poured a dollop of molasses over the other. He tasted them both, smiled, made a satisfied sound and handed one cup to each woman. They tasted the confections and called out. Two children ran up. They nibbled at the sugary frozen treats and ran off to tell their friends.

"My gift to you," said Clayton.

Xo Ten didn't look happy, though. "Buffalo girl is mine, mate."

Whereupon he returned to his tent, giving an order. Clayton was taken by two Braves to a tent of his own. And there he waited.

Clayton awoke at dawn. When he went outside, to his great surprise he found Jersey sitting on the ground, wearing a deer hide dress. She looked proud and fearless.

Solomon walked up. "We're obliged to Shalako for this, and I'm not shy to say you're obliged to me. I gave him a portion of my treasure—bones of the ancient gods. We spent all night thanking their spirits, as Shalako says you must do to all creatures you kill."

Clay was confused. "You killed the ancient gods?"

"We all did, Shalako says. When we got so high and mighty ourselves. In return for my gift—which allowed him to thank our ancestors personally—he had a dream."

"The dream was his gift to you?"

"Nae. Telling it to Xo Ten was the gift—a gift to *you*. In the dream a Dark Queen of the First People brought a great ice storm with her, and the ice froze the sun, and the world went black. Xo Ten kens his dark bride must go, and the ice that followed her gone, to boot."

The wagon with the ice crate had been pulled to the center of the clearing. Tribe members had piled branches all around it and now Xo Ten tossed a flaming branch onto the pile. "Go!" he shouted to Clayton and went back into his tent.

Clayton and Solomon put Jersey into the remaining wagon, where her relief mixed with the conviction that a black skin was always destined for slavery, no matter the color of the slaveowner.

As they began the trip back to Brownsville, Shalako came forward, his fire-scarred face like the mask of a strange demon—and shouted at them, "Behold your future!" They saw the ice wagon engulfed in flame, ice melting into thin rivers over the dusty ground. It was a future Clayton thought for a moment he'd already seen; but couldn't remember where or when.

They returned to Brownsville on the 29th. Jersey got settled at Allie's place, then went to work back at Brave River, where she started getting friendly with Dinah Singletary. Solomon went to Bagdad, to outfit his ship, now fully repaired. He planned to recruit Ned as a mate, to return to the secret location where the Limey's dubloons had come from. And Clayton finalized his war plans. Now that the invasion was only two days off, there was much to do, and much depended on it.

By October 31st he was confident they were ready as they ever could be. He spent the morning with Isaac and Scully. The Union landing was set for Brazos Island tonight. At least 7000 troops would force-march the 25 miles upriver and attack Fort Brown at dawn tomorrow, with the sun in the Confederates' eyes.

"Scully, you lead your *San Patricios* across the river and hit the Rebs from the flank while they're facin' the Union advance. That's how Chamberlain's 20th Maine won Gettysburg at Little Round Top, and I've no doubt you can replicate his success."

"No doubt I'll replicate his casualties, as well." But they all went off to prepare.

When Jersey first got to Allie's she found Moon lying unconscious on a beautiful bed. He looked gaunt; she was afraid to come near at first. But she seized on the courage she'd found for war and sat beside him, forcing herself to hold his hand.

"Moon, whatchu gone and done?" she asked him. Moon didn't respond. "You ain't been eatin' much I kin see. I wish you would, though." He still didn't wake up. "Come on, now, this Jersey here. You gon' tell me you ain't glad to see me?"

His hand twitched in hers, making her jump so much she stood straight up out of her chair. Slowly, she sat down again. Slowly took his hand. "All right, then. I'm here."

And she just sat like that, moist-eyed, for quite some time.

Allie walked into Brave River but Clay wasn't there. With a portfolio under her arm she approached the bar. Rheumy couldn't tell her when Clay was coming back; nor Isaac neither. Teddy Beale took a stool beside her wearing denim pants and a cotton shirt.

"Hey, there, photograph lady."

Allie couldn't place the young man at first; then it came to her with shock and pleasure. "The corporal from the Independence Ball! Lordy, you look like a cowboy! Did they cashier you out of the service?"

"No, ma'am, I'm just enjoying a night off my duties."

"Well, this is opportune. I have your portrait from that night back at my studio, you must come by to pick it up." Allie looked around. "You know where Mr. Wilkes is? I have some photographs for him, he said he might want to put some up here."

"I surely don't. But can I see your pictures?"

Allie pulled some photographs out of the leather folder and laid them out. Teddy held one at arm's length. "That's beautiful," she said, and meant it. It was a shot of the *Plaza's* gazebo at sunset, silhouetting a musician with his tuba. "The way that brass bell catches the light, looks like the fella's holding the sun. I never saw anything like that!"

Allie was as impressed with Teddy as Teddy was with the photograph. "Thank you, yes, that was my intention. You have quite a good eye, young man."

"Nothing like yours, to find a picture that pretty."

Allie got her back up a little. "I didn't exactly just notice him slouchin' around like that. I had the man stand there in that pose in order to create the composition you see."

"Hell, that's even better. Can I look at more?"

The next photo Teddy picked up was a study of Clayton leaning on his cane at a workbench. "You made that photograph right up here in his office. Can I buy it?"

They looked at each other, the photographer and the corporal, both understanding intuitively there was more to them than that. And in a subconscious leap, Allie recalled a conversation with Clay when she'd come up to his office dressed in men's clothing to hide her purpose. And he'd said, "You and Teddy, I swear." And she'd responded, "Teddy who?" And he'd said, "Never mind." And now here was Teddy.

Allie understood now—knew Teddy was a woman, realized they'd held each other close dancing, felt the thrill of that, and then kissing, the thrill of that, oh my Lord! She burst out laughing. The young woman had conned her twice now, and Allie dearly loved a good con, even if she was the mark.

"No, you can't buy it," she told the girl. "You just take it, it's a gift."

"Oh, but I couldn't…"

"Yes, you can. I can see your fondness for the man. It's only right you have a keepsake."

Teddy's heart was nicked by such a generous offer. "Why, I thank you. I can see why he might have fond feelings for you, as well."

Allie put the photos back in the portfolio. "You tell him I stopped by, won't you?"

"I most certainly will."

But Allie paused. "Did you hear that?" she asked. It was the wailing woman she was hearing again—the distant moan filling her ears from all directions. "It's that weepin' woman. *La llorona*. Lookin' for her children. I don't know how it is I hear her."

"Do you have children of your own?" Teddy wondered. Then, "I'm sorry, that was forward of me to ask."

"I did have a child," Allie spoke quietly, almost to herself. "For one day I did."

"That must have been a real hard day," Teddy said with care.

Allie's lip twisted. "There's some things you can't bluff your way out of." Allie fixed Teddy with a complicit gaze—one bluffer to another—then left the photograph of Clay with her and walked out the door.

That night the Opera House was packed. The crowd was festive and made nearly giddy by the keg of ice bits Clayton had given Catherine as a gift, the bartenders putting chips in the cocktails at intermission. In Clayton's mind it was the last party before the war came to Matamoros—though nobody knew that but him and a few others. When he saw Allie talking to Mildred Bee, he walked over to join them.

"Asefetida is a bitter resin of the ferula plant," Mildred was saying. "I have seen some success with it in the treatment of alcohol overindulgence, which is so rampant here on the Rio Grande. These ice chips, I believe, will make that smelly Asafetida easier to go down, and therefore more useful as a remedy."

"Evening, ladies. Yes, I'm hopeful ice on the frontier will have a variety of uses."

"Perhaps you can sleep on it to cool your fevered brow when tempted by the ladies," said Allie with an indelicate glance at Catherine across the room.

"Why would I ever care to unfever my brow in the presence of such lovelies as them who stand before me now?"

The two women fanned themselves reflexively, to ward off the vapors induced by the gentleman's compliment. "Mr. Wilkes, you're shameless," Mildred said gleefully, as the bell rang signaling the crowd to go back into the theater for the final act of the performance. General Bee walked up to retrieve his wife, mumbled good evening and escorted Mildred back into the theater. The rest of the crowd moved in the same direction. Clay and Allie remained where they were.

Clay was careful with his words. "I saw Lt. Jessup was back at the fort today."

"Yes. Are you jealous?"

"A bit. But I mention it because I've a favor to ask. I'd like you to stay away from that side of the river tonight."

"My word, you think I'd go chasin' after him just…"

"I want you to promise you'll stay out of Brownsville the next day or so."

She could see he was dead serious, which gave her pause. "Whatever for?"

"It's just this…feelin' I have. You know my intuitions have saved us a time or two. I hope you'll trust me on this one."

She knew in a heartbeat this was it, and no reason to beat around the bush any more. "The invasion's tomorrow, isn't it. Yanks are comin' up the river to our doorstep."

"I don't know what you're talkin' about, I'm sure." But he knew the more he protested the more she'd be sure she was right. Best to make a tactical retreat. "Just…stay here in town for now."

He left and spent the rest of the night sleepless on his roof with the pigeons and a spyglass and a skyrocket to signal Scully and his ragamuffin army that the Union invasion had begun.

But the night remained quiet. As did the dawn.

November 1st was engulfed in a humid, stultifying haze so thick you couldn't see the sun for the sky. Clayton was cross with everybody at Brave River, and finally just left. He made a stop at Pierce's safe house, but no one was there. He walked past Allie's home to make sure she hadn't crossed the river to Brownsville against his wishes. She wasn't there, but when he passed by her office, he saw her photographing some fop in the front room, so he just walked on. After some searching, he found Scully on *Banco Patricio* with 100 men, his elite force, waiting for the order to attack. "Keep your spine, men," he told them. "This could be a turnin' point in the war." He didn't sense a lot of enthusiasm in the lot. Two men got up and cooled off in the river.

Clayton made his way upriver to Isaac's brigade, where the men looked nervous. Isaac told him they'd do fine, not to worry. They all knew they were fighting for a new country of their own; this was just the first battle. It made Isaac proud of them, but at the same time filled him with self-doubt. Was he up to this? What had he started? Something he could finish? Something that would destroy them all, because he'd promised them something he couldn't deliver? A country of their own? Who did he think he was, Moses and Romulus and Remus and Alexander the Great all rolled into one? Or just baby Isaac, lying on some unknown patriarch's sacrificial altar? But then he saw the abiding bond of trust in Clayton's eye, and his fleeting panic moved on. Nothing to do now but keep steady; and the two men briefly hugged before the startled company.

Clayton crossed the river to Russell's warehouse. The ice machine was in full production mode now, ice blocks stacking up along one entire wall. He had Russell order two privates to drive a wagon full of ice blocks to Brave River, where he showed the bartenders how to chip slivers off and put them in the drinks—a nickel a drink more for the chill. The cold drinks got popular fast. By evening the place was packed, everyone drinking and doing it again. Money was rolling in, both from the extra alcohol sold and the gambling losses of loungers too drunk to calculate odds.

But November 1st came and went. And still no invasion.

November 2nd Clayton woke with a hangover. But he wrapped a handful of ice chips in a silk handkerchief and laid it across his head, to salubrious effect. It reminded him of something Allie had said at the opera, which gave him another thought. So he took Scully to Russell's warehouse, loaded up a wagonful of ice and hauled across town to Brownsville Hospital, where he found Dr. Hawks on the Yellow Fever ward.

"I applied ice to my forehead this morning after too much brandy last night," Clayton told her. "And that remembered me of somethin' Allie said about usin' it to cool my fevered brow when aroused with ardor. She was bein' facetious, but it made me think with all the ice I have now, we could cool down this whole room and lower the fevers on these poor folks."

Dr. Hawks thought it a splendid idea. With Scully's help they suspended canvas bags full of ice from the ceiling rafters, and it wasn't long before the temperature of the ward was palpably lower. They additionally put ice wraps on the foreheads of the febrile patients. Temperatures dropped all around.

"Mr. Wilkes, despite your reputation as a cad and war profiteer, I believe you've eased a great deal of suffering here today. And you, Mr. Scully?" Hawks turned to the Irish Frenchie. "Is your medical problem acting up any more?"

"No, ma'am…Doctor, I mean. I'm just fine," he said. "That is, no more pains."

"Mr. Wilkes, you suppress any more disease on the Rio Grande, I'm going to have to put you up for the Surgeon's Medal of Honor."

"If it's all the same to you, I'll just get back to my war profiteerin' before I'm thrown out of the Scoundrel's Club for good."

Evening of the 2nd, Solomon set out in the *Bucanneer* with a full crew, including Ned, to make a gun run from Havana—to be followed by some treasure hunting. Ned agreed, though with some reluctance. They came up against the edge of a storm, though, and decided to wait it out on the lee side of Padre Island. But as they tacked toward the island, Raoulito called from the top of the mast. "*Mi Capitan*, you better look quick." He tossed the spyglass down to Solomon.

Solomon held the glass to his eye and peered in the direction indicated, into the storm. There in the distance was a ship. No…three ships. No…and as the wind lifted fog from the water, Solomon saw an armada. Flying the Union flag. In disarray from the weather—but more ships than he could count. Headed, undoubtedly, for Fort Brown.

It was, unaccountably, an exact repeat of what he'd seen at the Sabine Pass. Unaccountable but doubtless it was the Captain's fate and lot to be witness to such things. Solomon raced his ship home, rented a horse and galloped to Brownsville, where he tried to warn General Bee the Yanks were coming. He was told Bee was in bed, with strict orders not to be disturbed. Solomon made a stink, but threatened with jailing, hightailed it to the casino, where Clayton, Allie and Scully were having iced cocktails.

"I just saw a Yankee fleet headed this way! Must be close to landfall by now. I've been to the fort but they won't listen. Somebody must make them take up arms."

Allie stood. "I shall," she said, exiting.

Clayton turned to Scully. "You best get gone, too. Join your men on the *banco*." Scully got. And Clayton told Isaac to saddle their two fastest horses.

Allie banged on the front door of the Commandant's house. Banged repeatedly until Mildred came to the door. "My dear, what is it? Are you in trouble?"

"We're all in trouble, Mildred. You must wake the General at once."

CHAPTER 20

Clayton and Isaac crossed their horses to the north bank of the river and rode hard until they reached Clarksville, at the mouth of the Rio Grande on the Texas side, across from Bagdad. They rested on a rise outside town and took telescopes from their bags, scanning the landscape for what was already looking like carnage.

Seven Union steamers lay off the bar in a stormy tide, bombarding the small Rebel force at Clarksville with big-bore guns. In the flashes of cannonfire Clayton counted over twenty warships, some already landing troops into the rough surf and onto the beach at Isla Brazos Santiago. By rough head count of the infantry at the shiprails, Clayton guessed thousands of troops.

Isaac agreed. "Looks like all the armies of Greece come to lay siege to the shores of Troy, and it doesn't appear they need a big horse this time, either. Just a chamber pot." On the beach seasick men were throwing up everywhere.

Clay and Isaac snuck into Clarksville, to the empty telegraph station. Clayton dashed off a message to Fort Brown, stating the Yankees had turned tail and gone back to New Orleans, just like they had at Fort Sabine. Isaac pointed to another ship offloading infantry. "By God, there's a Colored Regiment there, too."

"That won't do you any good with me, Major," said Clayton. "I've been promoted to Lieutenant Colonel, so you're still obliged to take my guff."

"It'd be an honor, Colonel, sir," smiled Isaac. "At your service."

* * *

News of war swirled around Brownsville the next morning like bees on a honey thief. The Yanks were coming, they were here, they were gone, they'd been repelled, they'd taken Bagdad, they'd be at Brownsville by noon, the Texas Rangers had them surrounded. General Bee was trying to weigh Solomon's information that Allie had awakened him with in the middle of the night, against contradictory reassurances telegraphed from some unknown source in Clarksville. He dispatched a company of men to reconnoitre the landing and report back.

But in his heart Bee knew he was now on the fool's errand he'd always feared: having to defend the Confederacy's only remaining open port with the 200 men he had left, after sending the other 2000 under his command to Louisiana and Arkansas to battle an enemy that was even now fixing to crush him right here in his own backyard.

He told his wife not to fret. He told Allie to go back to Matamoros and stay put until further notification.

He told Major Russell to issue rifles to every soldier on the post.

And he began drinking.

Fort Brown was all in a frenzy. Soldiers ran this way and that preparing gun emplacements, civilian workers were racing home, skitterish horses broke rein, camels brayed—and this tone came right from the top, where General Bee could be seen striding the ramparts, shouting orders, rescinding those orders and wringing his hands. Clayton went to Russell's office. Russell sat reviewing inventories.

"All good things must come to an end, I suppose," said Wilkes.

"We'll just retreat upriver. To Fort Ringgold first, until we can set up operations around Laredo."

"What operations?"

"Why, the cotton trade, of course. Just have to reroute the caravans further west, cross the river up there and make a longer trip down the Mexican side to Matamoros. I've already spoken with Milmo. His father-in-law will guarantee safe passage the whole length of the river on the Mexican side."

"Speakin' of safe passage, I'll need to move my ice makin' factory across the river toot sweet. I wouldn't like seein' it in Yankee hands."

"You mean *our* ice makin' factory. I had a mind to take it upriver with me on the retreat."

"The devil you will. It stays with me, and you'll get your percentage same as always. Hand-delivered by courier monthly, if you please."

"Bimonthly."

Clayton nodded as General Bee entered. "Major Russell, you are hereby in charge of organizing the evacuation of Brownsville, commencing now."

"General, I don't know that the citizens of Brownsville particularly want to evacuate. Those businessmen and farmers are just as happy selling their goods to Yanks as Rebs."

"Then I hereby declare martial law. They will evacuate, like it or not." Whereupon he left.

"Well, you have your orders, Major, I won't keep you from them. I'll have some men come across and get the ice maker over to Brave River. Meanwhile, If I don't see you again, you have yourself a safe retreat and a profitable war."

*　*　*

"Is it true?" Allie asked Captain Jessup. "We don't stand a chance against the invaders?" They were seated on a divan in the front room of her home.

"I wouldn't say that. Our scouts say there's a lot of 'em, but we can do some damage. We know every ambush spot from here to El Paso, and those pretenders don't know a thing about Texas."

"You give me hope." She hugged his arm, laying her head on his shoulder. Just this much physical contact always seemed to give her strength; his solidity a balm.

"We'll have to pull out of Brownsville for the time bein'. And General Bee is evacuatin' all the civilians—I know Mrs. Bee would find a safe place to relocate you."

"No, Ahotay. This is my home now. I'm stayin' put."

"As long as you stay here in Mexico while I'm gone—those damn Yankees can't touch you here. If they occupy the Fort, don't you cross the river, though. They have no morals, no respect, no…"

Jersey came to the doorway from Moon's room, where she'd been sponge bathing him. "It true Mr. Lincoln's Army be here soon?"

"In Brownsville, Jersey, not here," said Allie. "They got nothin' over on us in Mexico, this is a free country."

"If Mr. Lincoln's Army get to Brownsville, Texas be a free country too."

"Texans will never let the North enslave us!" said Jessup. But Jersey just looked at him with a curious kind of stink-eye. She let it pass, though, and said, "Moon doin' better, I think. I guess that cracker dressmaker didn't do for him as good as he thought."

Jersey left and Jessup stood up. "I best go. Rip wants me to test their weaknesses tonight."

"You won't do anything foolish, will you?"

"No, ma'am." He pulled her to her feet. "But I hope you will." With that he gave her such a kiss as he'd never given anyone, full on the mouth and pressed bosom to chest. Then he left.

Allie was surprised but not displeased. She didn't know the young Ranger had it in him to be so bold. He just might make it through this war yet.

That night General Bee hosted a grand dinner at the Miller Hotel on Elizabeth Street in Brownsville, a farewell to his friends, political allies, business partners, military peers and social connections. War was near; who knew what tomorrow would bring?

Colonel Rip Ford was here. Charles Stillman was here. Cotton broker Patricio Milmo was here, and Honorary Consul Jose Quintero, and Major Russell, and Clayton Wilkes, and on, and on. It was a night of camaraderie, speeches, glasses filled and refilled; toasts made, adieus bid, oaths sworn, songs sung; and at the last, the guests grew heavy-lidded, aggrieved at what felt like the passing of an age, yet content to be in this proud company on this melancholy night.

"May I ask, sir, what is your plan?" ventured Quintero to General Bee as the hour grew late. "Will you fight? Hold the fort?"

Clayton raised his glass. "There's no shame in retreat from a vastly superior force and come back to fight another day."

"Never!" shouted Bee, more intoxicated than most. "We will hold the fort. We are even now storing goods within the walls to last a powerful long siege."

"Don't be a fool, man," said Stillman. "It's 8000 strong against your 200. Where's the sense in that?"

"I've sent riders," said Bee. "To Lafayette, Shreveport, San Antonio and Fort Worth. Requesting immediate reinforcements. Demanding the 2000 troops I sent out to fight their battles be sent back to me for timely engagement with the enemy."

"What's the soonest any of those boys could be here?"

"Two days' hard ride there. Two back, maybe three. If we can hold out 5 days, by God, we'll show those Federals some Southern hospitality."

"200 strong at the Alamo lasted 13 days against Santa Anna's force of 4000."

"The Union force here is 8000."

"All right, if we can last half of thirteen days, that'll be enough time to get a few thousand Rebs back down here to show them Yankees what's what."

"And if reinforcements don't show up? Like they didn't at the Alamo?"

"Then we'll do what soldiers do," Bee called out with a bravado he didn't really feel. "We'll do what they did at the Sabine Pass, when 47 Confederate patriots repelled 5000 Bluecoats and turned their ships around in half a day's time!"

"We lost that chance when we let these Yanks get off their ships and establish a beachhead. They're comin' for us now, and no mistake."

Bee's face fell at that, the wind knocked out of him.

"The thing you must not do," Quintero said, "is let any of the cotton in the city fall into Yankee hands." He drew close to Bee. "This you must not do."

Bee nodded, as if for a brief moment he'd alerted out of his boozy haze.

Clayton leaned in softly. "Cotton's just cotton, General. It's mother's children in uniform that's in your charge. So many have died, sir. Have a care."

*   *   *

When the party finally broke up, General Bee ordered Major Russell to have every bale of cotton in Brownsville ferried to Mexico, starting right now. And every bale that couldn't be ferried was to be burned. Russell quietly told Milmo to transport as much cotton as he could on his private ferries—Russell would make certain a huge load awaited him on the northern bank, free of charge, in return for favors in the future. Then Russell went back to the fort and passed the orders on to his captain: every bale in town laded onto flatboats, burned, or sunk. Before the sun rose next morning, every ferry was heavy with cotton; and every palette not being crossed was ablaze high into the night sky, all over the city.

There was a frenetic play to the night. Groups of men ran in the firelight shooting guns into the air. Wild parties carried on in bars along the waterfront; laughter mingled with drunken fights. The French Order of Nuns of the Incarnate Word and Blessed Sacrament sailed by twice—once far away, and again later so close Clayton had to jump back to avoid being swept over by them, their starched rustling robes like the fluttering of giant birds, ancient ravens come to scour the city. When Clayton turned away he saw a Mexican cowboy being lynched for some imagined infraction. It was a hard way to go, and Clayton always turned away from such a scene, to give the condemned at least a little privacy during his last moments.

He eased past the deranged crowd as the poor soul swung from the peak of the gazebo in front of Town Hall. It was like the night before the apocalypse. All the rules were off.

Clayton walked the streets under sensory assault: trees afire, people barking, animals screaming, orange shadows on adobe; glass breaking, fists beating flesh, sour smoke, exploded gunpowder, terror sweat. But one vision arrested him more than others, because he had a personal connection to it. In a dark alley Jensen, the printer's devil, was in sexual congress with a burly bartender from the Opera House. But Clayton was soon upended by a tide of noisy partygoers carrying him off to a boulevard in flame.

He stared into the surrounding conflagration, mesmerized by this living hell. A rifle butt hit him in the belly; he went down. Two men beat him, went through his pockets for money as his consciousness swooned amidst the fires, the beating…

His father beat him. "You dare harbor a murderin' escaped slave in my house— my house!—you are no longer any son of mine." He pounded on Clay without restraint.

Clay knew he was about to die. Just too despairing to resist. Across the room Isaac was unconscious, beaten senseless by Clay's father—but not beaten to death; Clay's father wanted to save that for a public gathering. A Celebration Lynching. An example.

His mother appeared at the door and ran to her out-of-control husband. "Stop hurting him!" She tried pulling his father away, but the abusive man backhanded her. She hit her head against a marble bust and fell to the floor, motionless.

Isaac lurched up and lunged, tackling Clay's father. They fell together but Clay's father pummeled him mercilessly, out of control.

Clay couldn't let Isaac die this way. He pushed upright and kicked his father in the head. The old man fell hard, overturning a kerosene lamp, igniting the curtains.

Clay helped Isaac to his feet. He tried to revive his mother—but she was dead.

"Your daddy's dead too," said Isaac, checking the hated patriarch. The entire wall was in flames now. "We gotta get going," said Isaac. "No good come of us staying here." He pulled on Clay's arm. By the time they got outside everything was burning. Slaves were running up, some with buckets of water.

"Leave it!" shouted Clay. "You're all free now! Go on, get out! Let it burn!"

As he and Isaac ran into the woods, Clay looked back. He saw his mother dissolve into smoke, and his father…but he had no father. Just a man who hated music and friendship, who loved whipping and tearing families apart and whose soul was hellfire…

Hellfire surrounded Clay as the town in flames rose before him. He sat up. The men who'd beaten him were gone, his pockets torn and emptied. He stumbled to the ferry. People were jostling, fleeing to Mexico. Clay swam back to Matamoros. Limped to Brave River, took a bottle from the backbar, went up to his room and fell deep asleep.

The next day houses were either burned down or shut down, wagons packed up. Caravans of families took off for points west, north, and south—anywhere but the direction of the advancing Union Army. Scouts from Fort Brown ascertained General Banks had left 2000 men stationed around the landing site at Clarksville and sent 6000 west to Brownsville. They were less than a day away now.

Rumors and fears swirled around like fire in a wind. The Yanks were raping and looting every step of the way. Southern babies were being slaughtered, to prevent them from fighting when they grew up. Thousands of drunken Negro Yankees were the tip of the spear, crazy with revenge and fixed on defiling any white woman they could find. The hysteria was fine with Clayton—just made it easier for him to do what he needed.

He told his shippers where to find Russell's warehouse, describing the necessity of getting the bulky ice machine out of there and across the river back to the casino by end of day. Someone mentioned Allie was likely at General Bee's home, comforting Mrs. Bee; so Clay thought he'd stop by there. He hadn't connected with Allie since the invasion began, and wanted to make sure she was all right.

When he knocked on the Commandant's door it was opened by an old Negro slave woman who didn't even bother asking who he was. She just left the door open and walked away. Clayton called out, "Hello! Mrs. Bee? Are you here? Allie?" When no one answered, he walked across to the drawing room and entered. General Bee sat staring into space with a dark and inward gaze.

"General Bee, I didn't mean to intrude...are you all right?"

"What's a man to do?" he rasped. "I can't work it out."

Clayton sat down before him. "Is there any way I might help, sir?"

Bee looked at him like a man lost. Clayton felt bad for what he was about to do—Bee needed shoring up—but it was war, and Clayton's mission was to get an edge whenever he could. He put his hand on the General's shoulder. "You must leave, sir. A dead man cannot feel honor, and a live one can always fight another day."

Bee didn't say anything; living in his own world now—but finally nodded slowly. "Yes, I can see that." The man seemed mortally paralyzed, and smelled badly of fear.

Clayton patted him on the shoulder. "You'll do the right thing, I know you will."

*　*　*

Late in the afternoon there came a knock at Allie's back door. She opened it to find Mildred Bee with three Negro children behind her. "My word," said Allie, "what is goin' on?"

"We're leavin' directly," said Mildred, "and I'm bound to say goodbye. But I hope you can care for these three, they're too precious to me to waste on this fool's journey."

Allie recognized them now—three of her reading students. Nine-year-old Shonny, twelve-year-old Charles and fourteen-year-old Bootsy, all of whom she'd grown fond of. "I don't know what to say," said Allie.

"Say you'll take 'em, girl, and let me be on my way. We're set to flee and I mean to be at the General's side."

"So the Bluebellies are truly at the gate."

"Once they're in charge I imagine you won't have to be so secretive. But for now I'd feel awful if Hamilton was to learn I'd ferried away three of his prime property. Another five have already run, two were shot and one hung. This is terrible times."

Allie herded everyone into the small shack out back that was to have been Moon's residence. "Y'all can stay in here. I'll buy extra food,

2 7 7

and I'll keep teachin' you to read, but so help me you're goin' to pay for your keep."

"Oh, they're hard workers, you just have to tell 'em what to do."

"First off," she instructed them, "you'll be responsible for takin' care of Moon. He's bedrid, he must be fed, and turned, and cleaned. Is that clear?"

"Yes'm," said Bootsy, the oldest. "We keep your whole house clean, too."

"All right, then. I'm keen to learn what people are talkin' about on the street, so y'all goin' to be my eyes and ears, tell me anything you hear about war plans and such."

"Yes, ma'am, we be your nose too, if you want."

Mildred Took Allie's hands. "Goodbye, good friend."

"Godspeed, and hurrah for Dixieland."

They hugged as if it were the last time, and Mildred ran back to her carriage. Allie turned to her students.

"All right, then. You best clean this place up, and I'll introduce you to Moon."

That evening was chaos. People fled upriver and crossriver, where they competed for space on the ferries with palettes of cotton. Bales had burned all day; they were still flaming along the banks. Soldiers had instructions to drag any partially burned to the river and dump it. When full night fell Bee organized his 172 soldiers along with dozens of prominent families, their possessions piled onto wagons, while a patrol was sent back into the fort to dynamite the munitions dump— containing all the artillery, and all the black powder to boot. Russell took a couple of his own loyal privates with a box of TNT back to his personal warehouse—not that he cared if it fell into Yankee hands particularly; he just didn't want to leave any evidence behind of his bribes, in case it ever came back to haunt him, depending on who won the war.

Bee rode his horse to the front of the wagon train, where his wife, Mildred, insisted on accompanying him. When all was ready he raised his saber high and led his strategic retreat not west, to Fort Ringgold, but north—through the Wild Horse Desert up to King Ranch, which was both fortified and far from the action—with orders to his demolition crew to join them when the destruction of the munitions was done.

*　*　*

As Russell got to his warehouse, Clayton, Isaac, Bartender Jim and two Mexican laborers were already there, dismantling the ice machine under Wachtel's supervision.

"Thought you'd be gone by this time," Russell said to Clayton.

"I thought so too. Ran into a little trouble last night myself." His bruised face told the tale.

"You best hurry it up. I'm burnin' this place to the ground and the munitions dump across the yard is about to get blown to smithereens."

Clayton turned to his crew. "All right, boys, no time to take this thing apart with any delicacy. Just cut it up in chunks you can carry and get it on the wagon."

His team made quick work of the dismantling. Thousands of pounds of ice blocks lined the walls, cooling the whole huge room. Clayton looked at the box of dynamite Russell's soldiers cracked open, distributing sticks of TNT all around the building.

"What munitions are gettin' blown up in the depot?" Clayton asked Russell. Just curious if he could save any of it.

"Artillery mostly. Cannon, muskets, couple thousand rounds of ammunition, few hundred pounds of black powder."

One of his privates walked by just then. "8000 pounds," he said in passing.

Russell stopped him. "You mean 800 pounds, don't you?"

"No, sir, 8000. Most of it just got offloaded from the *Ariadne*, out of Sydney. It was bound for the Red River country, is what I heard. Guess the *Ariadne* got its cotton payment just in time." The private went back to placing dynamite and setting fuses.

"8000 pounds," whispered Russell, taken aback.

"Let's go!" Clayton shouted to his men, with a sickly premonition.

Then came the boom. An explosion so vast, none of them had ever had any experience with the tenth of it, though most had been to war. It knocked them a dozen feet into whatever hard thing they hit first; it blew an entire wall off the warehouse, half the roof came crashing down—and now the building was on fire. Past the gaping maw left by the absent wall, Clayton saw the entire fort in flames; some of it still airborne.

He picked himself up unsteadily, looking around. His ice machine was crushed beyond repair under a tangle of flaming beams. The wall where the ice blocks were stacked was likewise on fire, the ice melting across the floor. And he had a flash of memory, leaving the Kiowa camp, the old medicine man shouting, "Behold your future!" as children danced around the ice wagon engulfed in flame, ice melting in thin rivers over the dry dusty ground. Fire and water, these memories kept recurring, all mixed up into past and future, tantalizing but indecipherable.

Isaac grabbed him, pulling him out of his fugue state. "We have to leave now." He grabbed Wachtel and Jim, too, weaving them around pockets of fire until they were safely outside of the burning building. Russell made it out on his own, as did one of the Mexican laborers. But Clayton didn't see any of the others again.

CHAPTER 21

BROWNSVILLE HAD BECOME A pyre. The fort was half gone, blown to rubble; but what was left of the town itself had been set afire by the flaming debris of the massive powder blast. People ran around like ants in a fireplace, screaming, crying, some of them aflame themselves. One chunk of timber landed on a packed ferry crossing, killing some while others were thrown into the river. Several boats were sunk, people drowned, all their worldly possessions floating downriver or sinking fast. Some fiery shrapnel actually flew all the way across the water, destroying the Matamoros Custom House and igniting other parts of that town, as well. The great bell atop City Hall rang the calamity and rang all night.

Clayton wanted to get back to Matamoros to make sure Allie was safe; but getting across Brownsville to the river was no easy task. Everyone had guns, all shooting at each other. Some were Confederate soldiers who'd deserted; some were shopkeepers, some *Juaristas*, some from Scully's *banco* army, some common criminals; some just stayed drunk for the end of the world, and woe betide any woman caught out in the open. Clayton saw the French Order of Nuns of the Incarnate Word and Blessed Sacrament floating through the smoke like wraiths.

When he and Isaac finally got to the ferry crossings, only two ferries were still functional and people were fighting each other for space on them, pushing others into the water. Flaming bales of cotton floated in the current, mingled with lifeless bodies and floundering horses.

Clayton and Isaac hiked upstream to a relative shallows they knew and waded chest-deep, fighting a belligerent current. On the other side they made it to high ground and rested, to gather themselves and view the scene across the river in Brownsville.

Firestorms, screaming refugees, rape and pillage, gunshots and breaking glass and animal shrieks and the piteous moans of victims dying in pain.

"I won't mind quitting these parts," said Isaac.

Clayton was thinking along the same lines himself. "You stand watch over at Brave River. I've got to make sure Allie's all right."

She wasn't at home, though. Jersey was there, watching over Moon; but she didn't know where Allie was. Three black children cowered in a corner, but Clayton didn't bother with their story just now. Instead he went to Allie's studio. All locked up. He went to General Bee's *hacienda* after that. It was on fire.

Aurelia and Scully were throwing buckets of water on it, keeping the flames at bay—it wasn't a very big blaze. Clayton joined in, pulling up bucket after bucket from the well and handing them off to Scully, while Aurelia shoveled sand onto the hot spots. In ten minutes it was just smoking, with major damage limited to one wall. Scully's wooden arm had taken to flaming, but they put that out quickly, leaving it charred. They sat on the ground, coughing and panting.

Clayton furrowed his brow at Scully. "What happened to your *banco* brigade?"

"They broke ranks and ransacked Brownsville. Rainin' a bit o' wrath down on their old Southern masters, it looked to me like."

Aurelia spat. "Men and their wars." She went back inside to check the damage.

Clayton scoured the town for Allie, without success. He believed she could take care of herself, but riots had a life of their own, and he knew anything could happen. When he finally got back to the casino it was dawn, and the place nearly empty. He stumbled upstairs, tired to the bone; went to his room and pulled off his river-wet, fire-sooty clothes. But as soon as he was naked, a familiar voice rose from a dark corner. "About time you showed up," said Allie. "I was just about to drag the bartender in here."

She crossed the room and kissed him hard. He didn't get to sleep for another couple hours while she lost herself in him, trying to drown out the intemperate wails of *la llorona* and the shrieks of war.

For the rest of that night Rip Ford's Texas Rangers harried the Union troops a few miles outside of Brownsville as they advanced through prime ambush territory. The Rangers picked off a score of Yankees and didn't lose but two men. Still, the odds of 8000 to 60 made standing to fight a suicide mission. So at sunlight they withdrew upriver to Fort Ringgold, to make plans for the coming weeks.

Cortina's army found itself without an enemy to attack, since Bee had run north with the entire Confederate force. What was an army without a battle to do? Cortina rode into Matamoros with his 1600 men and declared himself the head of the new military government. There was some sniping from the local *Juaristas*, who were holding the town in the name of Benito Juarez as a bulwark against the French. But Cortina had the superior force, and the people of Matamoros were mostly merchants, who cared little for which faction would police them. So Cortina simply awaited Lincoln's Army to fully occupy Brownsville. He planned to establish a good working relationship with the new Union commander.

U.S. General Nathaniel Banks rode into Brownsville at the head of his battalion shortly after noon, declaring it Union real estate. By four o'clock all 6000 Yankee soldiers filled the town. Unfortunately Fort Brown itself no longer existed, so the Bluecoats set up tents around the grounds of what used to be the barracks. Banks put Colonel Dye in command of the post. Dye's first order was to locate bricks and timber to rebuild the fort. His second was to round up any Rebel deserters or holdouts and bring them in for interrogation about Confederate troop movements. Dye was an efficient, enthusiastic officer, and planned to make short work of conquering these Texicans.

Clayton walked past the hospital wagon piled high with corpses awaiting transport to the cemetery; and into the hospital to the sounds of moaning, the stench of death and chloroform. Across the ward Dr. Hawks was treating casualties from the two days of rioting. Burn victims, gunshot wounds, beatings, knifings. Some wailing amputees, some unconscious from blood loss or pain. Clayton had just come from Allie's house where two young ex-slaves—Shonny and Charles—told him Allie was at the hospital, helping Dr. Hawks tend the wounded. Wilkes asked them if Jersey were here and if Moon was all right. They told him Jersey left yesterday and didn't come home, but they were taking care of Moon just fine.

He saw Allie wearing a bloodstained apron, giving water to an old man with bandages wrapping his head. Clay loved her dearly in that moment. It made him want to leave all this behind and go off with Allie to a new place. One of the French Order of Nuns of the Incarnate Word and Blessed Sacrament walked over to the other side of the cot and held the patient's head up. Clay approached them.

"Can you use some help?"

His words seemed to frighten the Nun, who put the old man's head back down on the pillow and walked away like she was floating on a cloud.

"The Sisters have taken a vow of silence," Allie explained. "Times they feel tempted to talk, they'll just up and leave." She put down the cup of water.

"How are you doin'?"

"I don't know. The world feels like it's endin'. How'm I supposed to feel?" She looked past the open doors of the ward, out to the river and beyond; unable to grasp the magnitude of what was happening. "Everything is changed now, isn't it, Clay?"

"Some things stay constant," he said quietly and kissed her on the back of the head. "I'll stop by your place later, see how you're doin'."

She shook her head. "Don't come, Clay. I need to spend some time apart from you for a while."

"How's that goin' to help anything?"

"I don't know. I don't know one bit." And she walked off to care for another patient. She'd been feeling a great distance from Clay since the morning after the invasion. A feeling that he was responsible for all this. The burning of the town, the chaos, the death. It was all because of his machinations, his finagling to help the Union Cavalry ride in here like the Four Horsemen, scattering her friends to the wind, turning her world upside down. She would take care of who she could here at the hospital but it wouldn't make up for Clay's betrayal. His betrayal of her, and of the Southern Cause. She had to right that wrong; make the scales balance again. Maybe if she could help the South win Texas again, she could find her way back to the place in her that loved him simple.

Or maybe such things just weren't possible in such terrible times.

Clay watched her go with a hollow in his stomach. Something about her look didn't sit well with him. He'd have to talk to her soon. For now he walked over to Dr. Hawks, who was pulling a sheet over a man's head. "He looked familiar to me," said Clayton. "Do you mind?"

Hawks shrugged. "If you can identify him, so much the better."

Wilkes pulled the sheet down to the corpse's neck, which was slit ear to ear. He tried to recall and then it came to him. "That's Delgado, the haberdasher."

"That might explain this." Dr. Hawks pulled the sheet all the way down. The dead man was clothed in an ill-fitting but beautiful woman's dress. "One of the dresses from his shop?"

"Might could be, I suppose. He's the man beat poor Moon half to death."

"I found this shoved way down his throat, too." She lifted a small wood figurine of a man from the crate beside the cot.

"That's one of Moon's whittlin's." Clay thought he knew, now, where Jersey had disappeared to last night. As he pulled the sheet back up over Delgado's head, his attention was drawn to a man weeping at the end of the row, his torso bandaged. "What happened to him?"

"Tried to shoot himself in the chest and the gun misfired. Burned him all to hell, but he'll be all right. I have to go."

She walked away as Clayton made his way down to the attempted suicide. It was Simon Wachtel, crying quietly, tears running down his cheeks. When he saw Clayton, a moan escaped his lips. "Kill me, I beg you. I have no skill in this."

"Simon, what happened?"

Wachtel sobbed. "He left me. Jensen is gone. I beg you. Put an end to me." The old man reached his arms around Wilkes and hugged him like a baby. Clayton patted Wachtel's back. "That boy was not fit to clean your shoes, Simon. He didn't deserve a companion like you, and some day you'll come to see that."

Wachtel wiped his cheeks. "What will I do?"

Clayton had no words to help, so he just patted Wachtel's back until the old man lay down and fell into a fitful sleep.

* * *

Clayton walked along the waterline, wondering what it all meant. When he had no answer, he went back to Brave River, where he joined Isaac at a corner table and said, "Nothing is the same anymore."

"I surely hope not," said Isaac. "I've got 249 newly freed who look to me for guidance now. We'll head west directly, to claim our land grant. What are *you* going to do, now that the Yanks have found Texas?"

"Pierce has me set up to meet Colonel Dye tomorrow. Wants me to share whatever Confederate secrets I can come up with that might still pertain."

"Pertaining is important."

"Not sure what there is to pertain to anymore."

"You've always got Allie."

Clayton knew that wasn't necessarily true but didn't want to talk about it. Still, war was war, and even with Northern victories from Gettysburg to Brownsville, there might yet be some cleanup operations for which Clayton could be useful. He'd look forward to seeing Colonel Dye about that. He'd look forward to digging up any information he could that might help keep the Union juggernaut rolling. He'd look forward to all the new Yankee soldiers who'd be showing up at Brave River to gamble now.

He had to look forward to something.

Next day found Clayton walking through the debris of Fort Brown. Tents and Union soldiers were strewn as far as the eye could see, busy as termites, digging trenches, making earthwork fortifications, piling stones. He even saw a few Nuns of the Incarnate Word and Blessed Sacrament wafting here and there. Were those women everywhere? Like materialized spirits of the light and dark, they seemed to puff into being at scenes of tortured humanity and tangled feelings.

Passing a long scaffold with a dozen men swinging by the neck, the sign below them reading LOOTERS, he finally found the canvas tent he supposed was the command post, and sure enough Dye was standing there at a long table, looking at a map. Clayton pulled a letter of introduction from Pierce out of his inside jacket pocket.

"Colonel Dye? My name is Clayton Wilkes. I've been workin' with Ambassador Pierce. I hear things, I pick up on things. Anything important I'll pass on direct to you."

"You do that, Dixie, and I'll make sure you get a second helping of grits."

Clayton knew he was being patronized but had no interest in prolonging the talk, so he just left, less than thrilled about having to deal with the arrogant Colonel Dye.

It was sandy earth along the banks, but the dunes were surrounded by a thick overgrowth of vegetation, Calabash trees, Texas Sage and Mexican Fan Palms. Isaac walked among the four groups he'd organized of 30 people each—runaways, pre-emancipation freedmen, liberated contraband slaves newly uprooted since the Union incursion. Each group had a leader, and each leader was teaching his field of expertise—though there were many in each group with skills to contribute.

There were ex-slaves from Hamilton Bee's quarters and from households far and near. Some had already been trained by Isaac as part of Pierce's army. But when that battle failed to join, most stayed on to be the army of Isaac's colony.

He paused at the first group to listen to Salem—General Bee's gardener—talk about what foods were best to plant at what time of year in these riverside soils. Additional ideas came from some who'd worked corn plantations—corn grew well in this part of Texas—and cane growers who'd come from Louisiana. One of Bee's kitchen workers, 10-year-old Bigboy, had a few ideas of his own.

"Long as we at the river we smart to bury dead fish parts with what we plantin'."

"That's a fine idea, Bigboy," said Isaac. "That's Indian wisdom."

Bigboy beamed with pride as Isaac moved on to the next group, which had a few horses at the center of the crowd. A black wrangler named Sal—an escapee from King Ranch—was talking about how to approach a horse, how to gentle a horse, how to sit a horse. How to be kind while still being in control. Isaac thought that was a good lesson to apply in many aspects of life.

In the next group people were learning to read, taught by others who'd been in the secret classes given by Mildred Bee and Allie Stoneman.

And the last group awaited Isaac, who taught self-defense, how to shoot a gun, how to hide. Lying at the center of the crowd were about half as many firearms as there were students, so Isaac partnered everyone up and said he'd teach them in groups of two. But while they were picking their weapons, he noticed a lone figure standing at the edge of the clearing. Shy, maybe. Curious. Or just scared. Isaac walked over with a gentle step. When he got a few yards away he realized it was Jersey, the young hero who'd blown up the Confederate munitions.

"Hey, missy, it's good to see you're all right."

"I'm awright."

"Would you like to join us? I know you're handy in a fight, and we'll be needing all the fight help we can get."

"You goin' make you a new country, is that what you think?"

"No, ma'am, that's what I know. Some place we can do for ourselves and forget about those old overseers, and be proud, and just be."

"Yeah, I heard all about that. I guess I'll stay hereabouts. But I was thinkin'—maybe y'all could teach me how to shoot a rifle."

"I can. But we surely could use a strong woman like you to help us stay the course on our journey."

She looked kind of wistful at that, like she was resigned to a sadder fate. "Guess I'd rather stay here and kill Rebs. Maybe free some more of our people if the Rebs still got 'em in chains. But mostly kill Rebs. Anyway I'd rather kill them than kill some French folks who never done me or mine any harm."

He nodded. "You know, there's an old Cherokee story about a man who dreamed he was fighting two wolves inside him. One was angry, full of hate, the other full of joy and love. You know which wolf won?" She shook her head. "The one he fed."

She pursed her lips, digesting the story. Then nodded. "So that mean you gonna teach me how to shoot, right?"

He put his arm around her shoulder, a little sadly, and walked her over to the group learning firearms—a skill critical to her goals. Isaac had his own goals; he figured she was entitled to have hers. That's what it meant to be free.

CHAPTER 22

NEXT DAY WAS A grand picnic at the Matamoros racetrack, sponsored by all the wealthy Confederates who either lived or had fled here when the Yanks took over Brownsville. They'd invited all the Union bigwigs to powwow—to set up ground rules, establish boundaries, and generally demonstrate how civilized they all were. Cortina showed up with his entourage as well, to proclaim himself Governor, a friend of President Lincoln, and defender against the French, all at once. Clayton was working the crowd, making new friends and lubricating the old, gleaning every tidbit of news he could about troop movements, secret alliances, strategies and suspicions.

Allie took the opportunity to visit Colonel Dye in Brownsville. She'd been told by numerous sources that he was the man to know for news about the Union takeover of the lower Rio Grande. He was billeted in General Bee's residence, which is also where he kept his command center. Allie had to connive to reach the entryway of his office—previously Mildred Bee's sitting room. When Dye saw her there looking so pathetic he waved her in, anxious to address her problem, whatever it was, and move on.

She entered briskly, closing the door behind her. "Commander, thank you ever so much for seein' me without an appointment, I just don't know where else to go."

"Yes, not at all, Miss...?"

"Mrs. Allie Stoneman, but my husband has passed on, I'm afraid."

"I'm sorry to hear..."

"No, that's not why I've come. I have a thrivin' import business, at least it *was* thrivin' until the recent troubles—not that I blame you, you were just doin' your duty—but I put all my goods in Quartermaster Russell's warehouse, and now that's burned to ashes and those cowards left without so much as a down payment on what they owed me, and no I don't expect you to make good on their debt but I am desperate to sell the goods I have left so I might have operatin' capital to keep my business goin', and I'm certain those goods can be as useful to you as they were to the Confederate Army, and yes this is a lot to ask while you are makin' your great plans of war…"

He held up his hand to stop her—already feeling a headache coming on. "Mrs. Stoneman, please. I'm not in a position to…"

But she stepped right up to him and took his hands in hers. Tears glistened on her eyelashes. "No! You must not say no. Tell me anything you want, tell me you'll think about it, tell me you'll make inquiries—but I beg you not to refuse me outright."

He was quite taken aback; but also quite taken. She was a beautiful woman, and he hadn't felt the touch of a woman's hand in over a year. Her story was both tragic and brave—a widow, life torn by war, supporting herself through sheer gumption, only to have it ripped out from under her through no fault of her own. "All right," he said gently. "I will give it some thought. And if your wares are items we can use here at the fort…"

But before he could continue, she kissed him. And not just a peck. This was a passionate, grateful promise.

And that's what Allie felt in her heart. As she got on a roll with her sad tale, she'd begun to feel the burden of her plight, her desperation for a savior, her sense this kind man could help her, her attraction to him—so the kiss was absolutely spontaneous, without guile; for by that time she felt his sympathy for her, and with a gush of relief expressed her deepest emotion in the moment. That was Allie's gift, and no surprise.

The big surprise was that Dye kissed her back. Overwhelmed by her feelings—after having insulated himself from his own during this past year of bloody battle—his deepest yearnings took over and he pulled her close, wanting not to let go.

When she felt that back from him, her emotions took over completely—why, she was practically in love! And while some corner of her mind knew that wasn't possible, she paid no attention to that corner. She just gave of herself, opened herself to him completely. Then, for better or for worse, there was a loud knock at the door.

Dye pulled himself away from her with soldierly fortitude. "Come ahead," he called to the door as Allied turned to the window to gather herself.

"Sir," said the private at the door. "A deserter's been caught. Your presence is requested to address the matter."

"I'll be there directly." As the private exited, Dye turned to Allie. "I hope you'll be here when I get back."

She lowered her eyes modestly. Dye left the room, closing the door behind him. Allie couldn't have asked for a better outcome.

She rifled through the papers on his desk, in his drawers, inside his jacket. And paydirt! An order from General Banks for Dye to send 200 troops to Ringgold Barracks, 100 miles upriver, where the Texas Rangers had their forward encampment. Dye's soldiers were to leave at sunset, travel 50 miles by dawn; then camp unseen in some brushy *banco* the next day; ride another 50 miles the following night; and attack Fort Ringgold at dawn. She had to get this information to Quintero right away.

She left the room, and the building, with intent to depart straightaway. But she paused at the edge of a half-circle of soldiers watching Colonel Dye confront the deserter, who was out of uniform and whose hands were bound behind him.

"There is nothing more noble than battle," Dye was saying to the cowed man, "and nothing more cowardly than desertion. What do you have to say for yourself?"

Allie recognized the deserter. It was Jensen, that news reporter she'd met at the Independence Ball, the one who'd started interviewing her and then just abandoned her in the middle of something interesting she'd been saying. She didn't know he was a deserter, though. She just thought he was rude.

She whispered to a private standing next to her. "What's goin' on?"

"One of our boys recognized this fella in a bar downtown—they were in the Third Ohio Regulars together at Murfreesboro when this fella just up and run."

"What'll become of him?"

"He'll go to the stockade, have a fair trial, then get hanged or shot."

Dye gave an order. "Take this yellow vermin to a cell with high windows, so he can contemplate his God and his treason." Two soldiers took Jensen off to the jail cells.

"Will you do me a favor, Sergeant?" Allie whispered to the soldier beside her.

"I'm just a private, Miss. Private van Dijl."

"That's quite an interestin' name." She opened her eyes wide, to capture his help.

"My people are Dutch, miss."

"Then I may just call you Dutch. Dutch, would you tell Colonel Dye I had to leave on urgent business, but I'll surely come back when I can, to conclude the matter we were discussin'?"

"Yes, miss, I'll tell him."

"Thank you, Dutch." She briefly placed her hand on his arm to cement the deal, then left; and he watched her go, as did a number of the men she passed by. Allie rarely found herself to be a woman alone.

She went directly to the Opera House, to Quintero's private room—which he'd shown her once, with hopes she'd return. She knocked, opened the door and entered.

Quintero and a brand new diva were half undressed on the *chaise*, embraced in a position Allie hadn't imagined Quintero was young enough to hold. All three gasped.

"Madame, please!"

"I'm truly sorry, sir—but I have news that cannot wait for affairs of the heart."

Quintero saw the urgency in Allie's face. Separating from his protégé, he covered her with a shawl. "My dearest," he said to her, "I'm afraid I must ask you to leave for the briefest moment on a matter of state."

She slapped him hard and stormed past Allie with a look of loathing. Quintero put on his frock. "This had better be good."

Allie told him of General Banks's dispatch to Dye, of the raid on the Ranger camp in two days. He nodded his concurrence. This was important. He took her out of the room to an adjacent door and entered. Of all people, there was Quartermaster Russell playing solitaire, wearing civilian pants and no shirt.

"Major Russell," said Allie, "I hardly expected to find you here."

"Nor I, you. I guess we're both living a life of surprise."

Quintero explained, "Major Russell received rear-guard orders from General Bee, and now does special duties for me."

"It's a pure pleasure to see you again, Major Russell." She told him of the impending Union raid upriver and that he must warn the Rangers at Fort Ringgold.

"Anything to help get my old life back. Which reminds me, there's a Turkish Pasha with a load of textile on the Bagdad docks, was meant for me when I was Quartermaster. You might want to claim it and sell it to the Yanks now."

"I thank you for the consideration, Major. I look forward to the day when we can do business together again."

To Quintero, Russell said, "I'll thank you for that letter of introduction to General Bee's *hacienda*." Whereupon Quintero gave him a note.

Russell pulled on a shirt, packed up his guns and left.

* * *

On his way out of town Major Russell swung by the *hacienda* carrying his kit bag. Scully was chopping wood one-handed while Aurelia tended a small patch of corn.

"Afternoon," said Russell. "You must be Aurelia."

She stood up without answering. Scully took a step forward, ax in hand. "Help you?" he said, his tone both neutral and aggressive.

Russell took out a paper. "I'm Major Russell. These are orders from General Bee and Consul Quintero, authorizing me to move in here for the duration of the Yankee occupation, to guard the General's *hacienda* from Union mischief."

"Yankees ain't allowed down in Mexico. Your services are not required, Major."

"Union soldiers on leave don't always follow the rule book. And whether I set a picket here is not your call. This *hacienda* belongs to General Bee and he can situate whoever he likes in his place—which doesn't include you, last I saw the tenant list."

The two men took each other's measure. They didn't much care for what they saw—but Russell thought the ax in Scully's hand had the biggest vote at the moment.

"Tell you what, though," Russell went on. "I'm off on a mission now, and I'm not here to kick anybody out. Just to watch everybody's back. So if you'd show me to a convenient bedroom, I'll stow my bag and scoot for a while."

As Scully examined Russell's document, Russell walked over to Aurelia. "I thank you for your hospitality, ma'am. See any Yanks come across the river, you just holler and I'll be the first one here makes sure they don't treat you with any disrespect."

He dropped his kit at the cabin out back and took off on his horse to warn the Rangers at Fort Ringgold.

Scully glanced at Aurelia. "He looks at you sideways, you let me know."

She went back to her corn. "Men and their wars," she muttered, stalking off.

*   *   *

Allie fell into an on-again off-again romance with Colonel Dye, whom she insisted on calling Colonel, even in their most intimate moments. She could never quite get Clay out of her mind completely, but after all his deceitful Yankee tricks, she was trying. It was near Christmas time, following an episode on Dye's couch that got about as close to an actual act of intercourse as an unmarried lady and gentleman might be expected to get, when Allie found her big military secret.

As Dye went to the kitchen to make her a brown sugar banana *saute* he'd learned from the chef at *Antoine's* in New Orleans, she hurried to a wall safe usually kept locked, but now open a crack—a minor negligence on Dye's part. Atop the papers there was a classified document outlining the *Red River Campaign*—a plan for General Banks to lead 20,000 Union troops up the Red, to take Shreveport, putting all of west Texas in a pincer grip it could not escape. She memorized the broad strokes of the plan quickly and flopped back down on the couch in a disarray of clothing that delighted Dye on returning with the banana desserts.

That night she told Quintero the news—but he disbelieved her. "That's the same ruse they used to get our troops diverted from here so they could invade Brownsville," he countered.

"But I saw the plans. With my own eyes," she protested.

"In the safe, you said. With the door left open. My dear, he intended for you to see it. He knows what you're about, and he's feeding you false information."

She knew he was wrong. She knew Dye loved her and had just been too distracted by her showing up unannounced to bother locking the safe. She knew the Yankees were going to march up the Red River and own all of Texas up to Arkansas. She just had to make Quintero believe it. And she had to do it without alerting Clay to the fact that she was now aware of the North's secret battle plan.

This would take some intricate thinking. But she knew how her mind worked. She simply had to go about her daily routines while the puzzle cooked—until the answer revealed itself, like a fancy dessert coming out of the oven.

So she cleaned her house. She gave Bootsy, Shonny and Charles more reading lessons. She helped them tend Moon, who by now was all skin and bones, sores on his bottom, his cheeks sunken. She reopened her studio—it had been down since the invasion. She buffed her lenses, organized her files, answered the messages people had left wanting photographs of themselves—though some of those folks were now long gone. It was on her third day back that Cortina—now Governor Cortina—entered with two men, asking for the photographic portrait she'd taken of him months ago.

She knew why she hadn't gotten it back to him—it was unusable. His henchmen had been moving, they were blurs around Cortina's standing figure. "I believe I can lay my hands on it," she told him, "but we'll have to do another sitting. My flash frightened your men so, they ruined the picture."

She found the print and showed it to him. He looked disgusted and slammed the back of his hand into his guard's ear. "*Idiotas!*" He stormed out, followed by his men.

But when they were gone, Allie looked more closely at the photo. Blurred, yes; but she saw the double exposure again—registering the photo from the previous glass plate in the camera—so the eerie face from this earlier negative, a bearded cleric, was staring out from behind Cortina's image, seeming to gaze at the *bandito*. Two photos on one plate, making a reality that hadn't actually existed. The notion of it had given her an inkling back then; it was coming into focus now. Like a developing print.

She worked on her idea for days until she had something she liked. And by then it was Christmas.

* * *

Clay closed Brave River to the public on Christmas day, to hold a private dinner for his personal circle. This included Allie, of course—he hoped maybe she could find her way back to him in the company of friends. Allie, for her part, declined at first. But when she learned Colonel Dye would be out reviewing his troops with General Banks over the holidays, she found she didn't want to be alone. So she accepted— though she brought along Quintero as her guest, to buffer any thoughts Clay might be having about inflaming her passions. To add to this buffer she brought Bootsy, Charles and Shonny. Children should not be alone on Christmas, she told Clay. He welcomed her orphans with grace, though—as he did Quintero, who was in a subdued state these days, now that the Yankee takeover of Brownsville was settling into more or less a *fait accompli*.

Tonight's guest list included Catherine and her janitor, Harley; the casino staff—Hermano, Jim and Rheumy—and even Jersey, who was just starting to show a pregnant belly—which, by timing, Clay attributed to Xo Ten. Teddy Beale was here in a fine tailored suit. Simon Wachtel came, still dispirited by love lost. Captain Solomon showed up early in the afternoon play able-whackets with Ned—a sailor's card game in which the winner slapped the loser's palm with rope. Scully was here with Aurelia, her belly looking bigger every day. Zhi Li and Milagra were the *chefs du jour*, assisted by Bootsy and Shonny.

And of course, Isaac, who was more distant than usual tonight.

There were drinks and games and music before dinner. Ned and Solomon sang their favorite shanty, *Fiddler's Green*, accompanied by Solomon on his cigar-box fiddle. Around sunset Solomon dubbed it Friday by fiat and made a speech. "This is the most family I've had since I was a wee bonnie lad. But of a Friday, we used to light a candle and say thanks." He lit one of the candles on the long table and lifted a wine glass—to Clayton in particular, who'd helped him recall the ritual on their trip to Xo Ten's camp. "To the fruit of the vine," he toasted, and drank. And so did they all.

Ned entertained the group with rope tricks—reef knots, clove hitches, ring on a string and a special bowline that came apart with two quick tugs. Allie was particularly fascinated by such dexterous manipulations and returned the favor by showing everyone card tricks— dealing off the bottom, cutting to an ace every time. Clay just smiled in admiration. "Woman's got the best hands with a deck I ever saw."

Dinner itself was a feast of Chinese and Mexican cuisines. From Zhi Li came varnished pig, steamed catfish, glistening noodles, plum wine and candied ginger rice balls for dessert. Milagra provided mole poblano with two wild turkeys, corn tortillas and a hot sauce guaranteed to give a TNT kick. They were joined by Raoulito, Solomon's sea cook, who'd decided he didn't care much for the sea anymore and was more at home in a motionless kitchen. He made an exquisite turtle soup for an appetizer.

Dinah stayed mostly in the kitchen, helping as much as she could, though she'd become so jittery ever since the war had drawn so close, she could barely stand in one spot for longer than a minute, and every time a pot fell or something made a loud noise she jumped and skittered off to a corner. Everyone was gentle with her, though, and nobody expected her to do much.

When all were seated, Clayton made a speech. "I want to thank you for bein' here. I don't have to tell you, it's a time of troubles. If y'all got religion, then God bless you. If not, well, God bless us, we need what help we can get. Uncertainty in life is what we're given. How we take it's somethin' else. I just want to say—you folks here are the branch I hold onto in this angry river. In my life, that's what keeps me afloat." He lifted his cup of plum wine and drank amidst a round of cheers and clinks and drinks.

Solomon dug in on Zhi Li's catfish, noodles and shredded cabbage that tasted oddly sweet and sour. "By God," he announced, "this is exotic fare! You may expect to see me here every December if this is how you celebrate. Chinese food at Christmas, just the thing for a Wandering Jew."

During dinner Clayton bantered sweetly with Bootsy, Charles and Shonny, who had never been invited to a repast such as this before. He was tender with Catherine, to whom he expressed the deeply fond feelings of eternal friendship; to which she responded, "Pfff." Clayton kissed her forehead and moved on to be fraternal with Harley, fatherly to Hermano, ribald with Milagra and courtly with Allie. To Jim and Rheumy—as a special Christmas present to Jim—he told the whole story of the frozen corpse, pretending he could smell it, letting his companions discover it, and reaping a pouch full of gold for his efforts. Rheumy guffawed, which got Jim annoyed.

"What are you laughin' at now, when you always told me it made no sense?"

"You forgot the part about the gold!" Rheumy cackled. "That's what makes it funny!" And they fell to bickering, but in a warm, Christmas-y way. Clayton just smiled and moved on. On this night he felt dear to all.

He made Jersey promise to come to him for help—with the baby, or anything else. He lavished praise on Zhi Li, Milagra and Raoulito, the creators of this magnificent meal, giving them seats at the head of the table. At last he filled his plate and sat beside Isaac, who quickly stood, clinking his glass with a knife.

"Hear, hear. My time in this city is short, like this speech. I leave in the New Year with 262 brave souls to start our colony on the banks of the Sonoita. We'll likely have to fight the French as well as the rattlesnakes. But we'll be fighting for our own land, and that makes all the difference." He sat down.

A cheer went up. Solomon took a thong off his neck—a stone horn tip dangling from it—and hung it around Isaac's. "This is from the horn of a great Aztec Bull-God. It gives protection and great good fortune."

"I thank you, sir. I'll wear it proud. And the French won't stand a chance."

Others came to shake Isaac's hand, or hug him fare-thee-well, or toast his journey, as Clay took Solomon aside, curious. "Ryburn, tell me somethin', if you would. You appear man-to-man with Isaac, but still you run guns to the Rebs, who are fightin' to own slaves. Does that strike you as contrary?"

"Nae, lad. I make every man my equal who treats me the same. Runnin' guns is just a hobby, and great good fun in the bargain. I imagine you could say the same about sellin' information to the rogues you barter with. It's the dance we love, you and I. The rest is all bookkeeping." Whereupon he grabbed his fiddle and struck up a bandy tune he improvised on the spot. *"Was a great man of vision name of Isaac-O, a Stranger in a Strange Land, Like the Wand'rin' Jew when it was time to go, he up and led his Israelite band, They crossed the burnin' sand, aye, they crossed the burnin' sand..."*

As Ryburn took it into a rousing fiddle solo, Clay went to stand at the back door, watching the peaceful river; wondering if it was time for him to leave as well as Isaac. Teddy came up to him. "Allie says you two are on the outs and I can have my way with you if I wish to."

"You get right down to it, don't you?"

"I put in for a transfer to a fighting unit and I hope to have an answer by the first of the year. I could be dead this time next month."

"Well, I hope you're not. And Allie will say a lot of things to stir the pot. But I still feel fondly toward you, and that's a fact. So Happy Christmas." He hugged her warmly. She held on as long as he let her, until it was time to go back in, which they did, just as there came a knocking at the door. Wilkes crossed the room, unlocked the door and opened it, saying, "We're closed for business, tonight, friend, and I..."

But he stopped and stared at the handsome 25-year-old man standing there in long black frock coat, frilly white chemise shirt, curling black hair and droopy moustache. "Hello, Clay," said the man. "I was told I might could find you here."

"Good evenin', John, and Happy Christmas." He hesitated. "Please come in."

The man walked to the table with Clayton, who cleared his throat. "Ladies and gentlemen, I'd like you to meet my cousin—John Wilkes Booth."

"Your bastard step-cousin, in any case." At which Booth bowed to the guests. His accent was a mixture of Southern aristocrat, British uppercrust, and pure theater.

"Not *the* John Wilkes Booth, *bien sur*," said a stunned Catherine, flushing.

Booth raised his left hand apologetically—on the back was a small, blue tattoo, the letters *JWB*. He was the pre-eminent celebrity actor of his day, his name well-known to all, his face at least passingly familiar from playbills and newspaper ads.

"What brings you here, JW?" Clay wondered, suspicious by default.

"I was in the area—touring, of course—and thought what better way to spend this family holiday than with family?"

Catherine made space for him beside her, and his plate was piled high as introductions were exchanged all around.

"Clay Wilkes, you were a rascal never to tell me you were related to such a renowned thespian." Allie kept her coy gaze on Booth the entire time she was speaking to Clay. "Exactly how are you cousins?"

Booth spoke as if it were a stage monologue in a comedy of manners. "Clay's father, Langston Wilkes, is the half-brother of my father, Junius Brutus Booth. My mother—Mary Ann Holmes—was merely my father's mistress. Nonetheless, it made Clay and me relatives by marriage—or at least by adultery. And there you have it. Happy Christmas to us all." He laughed generously. Allie looked smitten. But Catherine wasn't about to let her corner the market on both Clay Wilkes and John Wilkes Booth.

"I am Catherine Delacroix, the proprietress of the Matamoros

Opera House, and I *absolument* insist you shall do a performance while you are here."

"Whatever would I do? I have nothing prepared."

"What is your favorite role? Tell me."

"That, *Mademoiselle*, is easy to answer. That would be the role of Brutus, after whom my father was named. Brutus, the slayer of the tyrant, Julius Caesar."

"Well done!" called out Quintero, the consummate revolutionary, lighting up for the first time all evening. "Rebellion against tyranny must always be championed. In the arts, as in life!"

"In the arts, to *inspire* life," Booth said, raising his cup. "Let us drink to liberty!"

"Liberty for all?" Isaac asked pointedly. He was about as done as done could be with Southern fools and hypocrites who yammered on about freedom from Yankee tyranny while they kept their Negro population in shackles.

Booth didn't try to disguise his distaste for Isaac's outburst. "Are you one of those Coloreds who believes himself to be my equal?"

The room chilled instantly. Isaac stood up but Clay moved between them, facing Booth. "You have no cause to speak that way to my friend, Isaac."

Hermano understood intuitively the hostility that had taken over the room. He ran to his pump handle and began vigorously pumping water up to the roof.

Booth assumed a more conciliatory tone. "I am sorry for makin' such a scene. And a guest in your home, to boot." Then he faced Isaac. "I attended the execution, by hangin', of the traitor John Brown—but I honor him for facin' his death bravely. Perhaps one day you will do the same—and in that spirit I apologize."

Isaac considered his response. He could slap dizzy this arrogant, disrespectful fool, as he'd done to that dress shop owner. Or, having sworn never to lie down for this kind of abuse again, he could easily kill the man where he stood. But Booth was kin to Clayton, and such an act could put his old friend in an uncomfortable spot. So out of respect to Clay, Isaac swallowed his bile and left.

That ended the festivities. Everyone realized how late it was, many thanks, and so on. Allie left with her orphans, her Christmas crush on Booth somewhat tempered by the spat at the end. She wasn't sure what it was about, but old family business between him and Clay. "Good-night, Clay."

"Good-night, Allie." He saw she was carrying a large canvas sack. "Not stealin' the silverware, are you?"

"If I were, you'd never know it. No, this is extra food I promised to deliver to the men at the jail, the guards and the prisoners." And suddenly remembering, "Your young reporter is one of 'em, Mr. Wachtel. Did you know that?"

Simon, who was trying to sneak out without lengthy goodbyes, went pale. "*Vas?*"

"I think he said his name was Jelson, or Johnson? Somethin' along those lines. I'd met him at the Ball, and saw him arrested the other day for desertin' under fire…"

But Simon hurried out the door without another word. Allie, who had no knowledge of Wachtel's relationship to Jensen, merely turned to the new visitor. "A good night to you, Mr. Booth, and welcome." Booth kissed her hand. The other men tipped their heads to her and Quintero escorted her out.

Catherine insisted Booth come by the Opera House the next day and prepare to be impressed. He looked deep into her eyes, saying he was already impressed. She left all aflutter. Jim and Rheumy helped Hermano away from his pump station and to his quarters behind the casino, while Harley swept the floor clean, his particular field of expertise. Ned was passed out drunk in his chair; everyone felt safe leaving him there.

Zhi Li, Milagra, Raoulito, Jersey and Dinah cleared dishes as Scully and Aurelia made their farewells to their host and made their way home—Clayton noticing Scully hadn't been drinking much anymore, since staying at the *hacienda*. Solomon just disappeared in the hubbub. This left only Clayton and Booth alone in the big hall.

"I am sorry, Clay. It's been a long day, I spouted off when I should not have, and now I'm bound to ask you for the favor of a place to stay."

"For how long?"

"Not long. A while."

Clay considered. Partly curious, partly remembering his mother's long ago injunction: *You must always protect your family, they are part of you.* "All right. There's a guest room upstairs, next to my office. You're welcome to stay. For a while."

Clayton showed him to his room, then walked the next flight to the roof. He sat beside his pigeon cage and extracted one of the birds.

"Madeira," he whispered, "you're my favorite, but don't tell the others." He petted her gently, remembering the feel of his mother's hand on his head, the sense of tender protection it gave him, wishing he could go back to that safe place now, as he strained to hear the beating wings of birds at dusk.

*   *   *

The guards at the garrison directed Wachtel to the city jail. At the jail the guards wouldn't let him see Jensen. It was too late, it was Christmas, come back tomorrow. But Simon circled wide around the back and whispered at a series of high, barred windows. "Jensen, is that you? Jensen, are you there? Jensen?"

At the second window came a "Shut up!" but at the fifth there was a familiar voice. "You gotta get me outta here, Simon. They're gonna hang me."

"Shut it, in there!" came a stern shout from inside the building. A jailer.

Simon whispered. "I will be here all night, *und* I come see you in the morning."

Jensen didn't answer. Simon looked around as if there might be someone there to help him; but of course, no one was. He slumped down the wall and curled up on the ground, just six inches of adobe brick separating him from the man he loved.

CHAPTER 23

Early next morning Clayton knocked and entered the guest room where Booth was already awake, writing a letter. Clay handed him a cup of coffee.

"Thank you, Clay. I appreciate the Southern hospitality, so recently vanished from the world."

"Let's not bandy words, JW. I can accommodate you for a few days, but I'm bound to ask what you're doin' here."

Booth nodded. "Earlier this year I was arrested in St. Louis on a tour—some fool heard me say I wished the president would go to hell and the local constables arrested me for 'treasonous remarks'. I was released when I signed an oath of allegiance and paid a substantial fine. No matter—I'm quite wealthy from my stage celebrity."

"Why are you here, then?"

"Last month I was in a play at Ford's Theater in Washington. *The Marble Heart*, by Charles Selby. I was the villain, Raphael, which, to my mind, was a more substantial role than the lead—a sculptor who makes marble statues come to life, based, of course, on the Greek myth of Pygmalion, which I did in New York to a much larger crowd..."

"If you would get to the point, JW?"

"The point is I noticed King Lincoln himself sittin' in his stageside box. Well, sir, I strolled up to him durin' my speech, a speech in which my *character* was makin' threats, and I pointed my finger accusatively at the so-called president—which apparently upset some swooners who interpreted my powerful performance as actually threatening Lincoln."

"Which you would never, of course, do."

"The issue of my St. Louis arrest got raised and it turns out I'd signed that loyalty oath with a false name—purely accidentally—so now between the misperceived threat to Lincoln and the alleged fraudulent oath of allegiance, a bounty was put on my head."

"Well, you can't hide here forever."

"Of course not. In fact, the legal jeopardy is passed. I signed a new document correctly, it was placed in my St. Louis file, and I signed an affidavit with the DC court attestin' to the fact that I was just sayin' my lines, that dialogue was part of the play. Gave 'em a copy of the play to prove it, and I'm damned if the police chief didn't want me to autograph it!"

"So what's the problem?"

"The bounty hunters don't care! Since the initial charge was sedition, the warrant is dead or alive until the bounty is cancelled, which the authorities are draggin' their feet about doin'. Just enjoyin' to watch me squirm, I don't doubt."

"What's your plan, then?"

"I've friends who can smuggle me back to Washington, to straighten it all out—which likely means payin' the bounty myself to some corrupt magistrate. I tell you, Clay, when they know you have money, they try to get it away from you any way they can."

"When are your friends comin' for you?"

"Early January, I was told. I never did hear the exact date."

"All right. You can stay that long. But no longer." He walked to the door. "And don't make me regret my kindness."

"With that he left.

*　*　*

Allie stood in her darkroom jiggling the blank print in the developing solution. She'd come up with a plan to defeat the intended Yankee assault up the Red River, but it depended on a series of untested scenarios.

The first pillar upon which her game rested was the most reliable.

It was the fact that Clay would never step foot into a Catholic church. Certainly he never had, back in the day, and it was such a firmly fixed element of his personality, she felt confident it was still true. His mother had been a devout Catholic, and when her God turned his face from her, leaving her to torment by her own husband, Clay had sworn never to return to a church that worshipped such a God. So that was Allie's first assumption.

Her first uncertainty was based on her ability to reproduce the happy accident she'd discovered in the Cortina photograph—the double exposure that framed two negatives in the same print, to create a seemingly real picture that portrayed a false reality. She was testing that now—developing a photograph she'd taken of Ambassador Pierce sitting in the Cathedral on Independence Day, with the masterful effigy of Christ looking down on him from his gilt crucifix; developing it on top of an unrelated photo she'd taken of Clay, sitting in a chair in a contemplative pose.

Her final uncertainty was Quintero—and how to make him believe that the photo was real. Because Quintero was the key to thwarting the Yankee campaign.

The image emerged on the print. Shadows, lines, shapes. There was Jesus, giving His benediction to the proceedings. And there, Pierce sitting in a pew. And there, another, facing him, serious. Clay. It looked like the two men were in deep conversation, with no one else around. A secret talk. Between Clay and the Yankee Ambassador.

Allie took the print out of the developer, slid it into the fixative, let it dry and took it straight to Quintero's back room at the Opera House. She entered with a breathy excitement that the Confederate Consul misinterpreted. He kissed her hand.

"My dear, how good to see you. My little sparrows around town have informed me you and Wilkes had a falling out. Can I hope you have come to be comforted?"

"No, Agustin that is not why I'm here. I'm here to show you exactly why I've pulled away from Clay." She took the photograph from her purse. He looked at it with some bafflement—still overcoming his dashed hopes.

"What am I looking at?" he wondered.

"I'd hidden my camera in the Cathedral the day of Christmas Eve—Father Clos had asked me not to photograph the Mass, but I saw an opportunity that…no matter, the point is, just as I'd got the camera set, I was stunned to see these two havin' a confidential conversation. Clay and Ambassador Pierce! Can you imagine?"

"What is it you wish me to imagine?"

"Clay is a Union spy!"

"Just because they're talking does not mean…"

"Listen. I will convince you to a certainty that Clay Wilkes is a double agent for the North. Just as I can prove the Yankees intend to invade Shreveport, goin' up the Red River…"

"Please, my dear, please. They tried to fool us once with the ruse that they were going to invade Shreveport, and it diverted all our best armies up there to…"

"I can prove it," she said with aplomb. "Now here is what I propose you do…"

And she outlined the program she had in mind to expose Clay's perfidy. When she was done, she kissed him on the cheek. "That's on account," she said, and exited his office, leaving him with feelings sweet for her, and unsettled concerning the doubts she'd sewn in his mind about his most trusted conspirator, Clayton Wilkes.

As Allie exited Quintero's office, around the front of the balustrade, she saw Booth descending in a Roman toga, and smiled. By way of response he raised his scepter and did an acrobatic leap down five steps, catching himself on the bannister, culminating with an exaggerated performance bow. "At your service, Milady."

"I'm not sure 'Milady' is the proper greetin' from a Roman Emperor. What play are you meant to perform in, may I ask?"

"I'll be doing readin's from Shakespeare's *Julius Caesar*." He plunged his scepter through the space between her arm and torso, shouting, "*Sic semper tyrannis!*"

Allie smiled, having the poise to remain still at his lunge. "Actors are a bit like children, aren't they. Stabbin' make-believe knives into make-believe tyrants."

"There are real tyrants, though—who must be stopped at all costs. Do you not agree?"

"If you refer to that man in the White House, I most certainly do. His destruction of all that was civilized in this country is nothin' less than a mortal sin."

"A sin against God, I could tolerate. We are all of us sinners. But suspendin' *habeas corpus* to jail elected officials so he could station Union troops in Maryland was unconstitutional and tyrannical, and it will not stand!" He'd worked himself up into such a state that he was at first unaware of the applause of Catherine, who'd approached during his brief performance.

"Mon Dieu, que tu es formidable."

"Thank you, *Mademoiselle*, I was lookin' for you. I wonder if you could find me one decent actor to play against who won't try to upstage me."

"Yes, but of course, we have several in our company…"

"And I require a pouch of pig's blood to put under Caesar's tunic, so the spatter will look realistic when I plunge the stake of Freedom into his despotic breast."

"Certainement," said Catherine. "If you meet me backstage in ten minutes, I will show you what I have." She arched an eyebrow and left with a hip sway that invited him to see just what she had.

Booth admired her retreating form, then smiled at Allie. "A Gypsy fortune teller once told me I'd come to a bad end after havin' a grand, short life."

"Well, you better enjoy the grand part while you can."

"I'm tryin'," he said, coming close. "I'm tryin' hard."

And truth to tell, it did set her heart apatter just a little. She lowered her eyes modestly and exited with a decorum that made Booth's nostrils flare.

In the smoky dusk Jersey shinnied up the tall pole to cut the telegraph line. She could see the cookfires of the Rebel encampment throwing soot into the air, mixed with song and laughter. They looked like poor folks from poor families, caught up in the war just like everybody. None of them slaveholders, she imagined. None of them favored getting rid of slavery either, though. They liked having black folks to kick around; someone to look down on. Jersey wouldn't feel bad about killing any of them. But that wasn't what she was here to do. She was here to cut lines and that's what she'd do.

She cut the lines. Then she slid down the telegraph pole quicker than she expected, falling backwards when she hit the ground.

"Here, now," came a voice. "Where the hell you think you're goin'?"

She stood up to face a young Reb soldier with droopy blond moustaches, holding a dim oil lamp. "Goin' home, sir," she said and started to walk off.

He grabbed her by the arm. "You tell me what you's up to or I'll bring you back to camp for a lesson you won't like." As he held the lamp close to her he saw she was practically a child. And a girl in the bargain. "Ima git my captain, he'll know what to…"

But before he could finish she pushed her knife into his chest—between the third and fourth ribs on the left, where Isaac had shown her—and put her foot behind his heel, so as she pushed the blade into his heart he fell onto his back. She pulled the knife out, wiped it on his shirt and stood above him.

Confused, he just stared up at her protruding belly. "You're havin' a baby," he said, and died.

Jersey felt a hint of remorse for a moment. The sentry was barely more than a boy himself. Then she walked off into the darkness, ready for her next assignment.

The Opera House's New Year's Eve performance offered readings from *Julius Caesar* and other works; primarily a one-man show by someone billed as J.B. Wilkens. The audience gasped when Brutus stabbed Caesar, spewing bright red blood all over his chest.

At intermission Cortina—an active patron of the arts since taking over the town—held court on the terrace, making pronouncements on the veracity of the stage murder entertainment. His lieutenants nodded agreement, every one a new theater critic.

Jessup watched the old bandit from afar, incensed that he couldn't just walk up and shoot the man, now that he was Mayor of Matamoros and Governor of the province. Clayton bought Jessup a drink and calmed him with the hope that if Cortina got drunk enough to wander north of the river, Jessup might still bag him.

Quintero pulled Clayton aside and clicked glasses with him. "Happy New Year, my friend."

"To rebellion and whiskey, the two great liberators," said Clayton.

"I was gratified to see you in church this Christmas. God always looks more kindly on the causes of those who venerate him."

"Church? God forbid. I haven't been to church in twenty years."

"Truly? I thought it was you I saw."

"I don't even know what the inside of that Cathedral looks like. Chandeliers drippin' with lies, I don't doubt."

So now Quintero knew Clayton was lying. Lying when he said he hadn't been inside the church—when Quintero had seen Allie's photograph of Clayton and Pierce, sitting close in the pews, huddled in conspiracy. Quintero had seen the evidence with his own eyes. It made him terribly sad to think his trusted friend was a spy for the Union.

"Listen," Quintero went on, "I've been hearing rumors that the North is mounting a campaign up the Red River, to take Shreveport."

"That old story makin' a comeback?" Clay laughed. "Don't believe everything you hear, Agustin."

"No, of course not. Still…put your ear to the ground, would you? Find out about this Red River invasion. Let me know if there is any truth to it."

"I'll get to the bottom of it. And if it's true, you'll be the first to know." What Clayton knew was he had to nip this rumor in the bud. Doing so would take some thought.

Quintero smiled sadly. "It is a relief to know there is still one person in Matamoros I can trust."

Clay cornered Leonard Pierce in a shadow outside the Opera House as throngs were milling out of the building, tonight's performance over.

"Quintero's heard about the Red River campaign," Clay said

quietly. "I'll have Isaac forge a message from Banks to you, tellin' you to spread the *false* rumor that the Yanks are goin' up the Red to take Shreveport. I'll intercept it and get it to Quintero."

Pierce saw it at once. "He'll think Shreveport is another diversion."

"So he'll be certain any more rumors he hears about the Red River campaign are false. Banks will have a free hand to march up there and take it."

Pierce left. Clayton smiled at the thought of effecting the outcome of great battles, even far from home—he extended his arm to touch the far wall with his cane—just like that.

The North owned Matamoros and soon it would own all of Texas. Clayton was back in the game. And Allie's moods be damned.

Soon as tonight's play was over, Allie knocked on Booth's dressing room door to congratulate him. He ushered her in.

"I just came to ask if you'd…"

But he swept her into an embrace with a passionate kiss for punctuation. She was startled at first, then curious; then just a little bit responsive before pulling away.

"Really, sir!"

"Forgive me, my dear, I thought that's why you'd come. It's been much on my mind so I assumed it must have been on yours, as well."

"You must think quite highly of yourself."

"Am I completely mistook to think you were returnin' the feelin' when we kissed?"

"A woman responds to passion; a man mustn't take advantage of the weakness."

"Then I ask your forgiveness." He bowed.

"You may atone for the offense by sitting for a photographic portrait at my studio tomorrow. That is what I came to ask you." She assumed a huffy tone.

His reply was interrupted by Bootsy appearing at the open door, scared and out of breath. "Miz Stoneman, Jersey say please come quick, Moon got a fever!"

Booth was livid. "How'd you get up to my room?"

"I just ran, sir…"

"You were spyin' on us, to boot!" And he slapped her.

Incensed, Allie pulled him away. "Don't you ever lay hands on my houseguests."

"Is that what you call 'em?"

Allie looked into his eyes. It was like getting cold water splashed on her face after she'd been mesmerized. She turned to the quivering child. "You go on home, Bootsy. Tell Jersey I'll be there directly."

The young black girl nodded, afraid to speak now. She closed Booth's door behind her and ran down the hall, past a gathering crowd of well-wishers.

Booth softened his tone. "You must forgive me again—once more consumed by my passions. It makes me a great actor, but a difficult friend."

"Do not think you have achieved the status of friend, difficult or not." She looked deep into his eyes, which her camera had long told her were tunnels to the soul.

Clay went back into the *Teatro* to congratulate Booth on his opening night. As he made his way down the hall through the gaggle of waiting admirers, Booth's door opened. But instead of Booth in the doorway, it was Allie. Booth stood behind her.

She stepped out to Clay as the crowd clamored around Booth. "Hello, Clay," she said quietly. "This is not what you think. We were just arranging a photo session to publicize the play."

"You're right, that's not what I think."

He walked away feeling childish. She called something to him, but he couldn't hear over the din of the giggling theater goers and the first explosions of the New Year's fireworks, celebrating the imminent rebirth of everything and nothing.

CHAPTER 24

B RAVE RIVER WAS PACKED, well known to be the best New Year's
party in town. The gambling was enhanced tonight by a band,
dancing, games, prizes, decorations and unbridled festivity. All the
employees were hired for the full night, two hours on, two off. Raulito
showed Jim and Rheumy how to make Cuban rum drinks. Ned and
Ryburn Solomon, who were fast becoming best friends, alternated telling
fantastical pirate stories and singing shanties, their favorite being *Fiddler's
Green*: "*On Fiddler's Green there's a place I've heard tell, Where old sailor's go if
they don't go to hell…*" Ryburn went on to play a medley of jigs that Clayton
found himself dancing to, and Solomon danced with him as he played.

Clayton later found Isaac in his room, practicing his calligraphic
O's. "I'm glad to see you're celebratin' the new year with joy."

"This is my meditation on January to January, as the year comes full
circle. Like the serpent Ouroboros, who eats its own tail, we endlessly
destroy ourselves and create ourselves anew."

"Myself, I been livin' in the snake's mouth so long his poison tastes
like wine. But I hope you create just what you please for your own self,
I surely do."

"I hope to realize that very thing on the banks of the Sonoita when
I leave here."

Clayton felt a pang at the thought of Isaac's going. "I haven't properly
apologized for the behavior of my cousin Booth. He owes you his own
regrets for how he spoke to you, but I don't expect you'll get any from
him. So you'll have to make do with mine."

"You owe me nothing of the sort. But I'll keep your good feelings in my pocket on my journey and hold on to them during the trials that are bound to come." They shared a long look, drawing on a lifetime of troubles together, now readying to go it alone.

But Clay's melancholy was turned wry by a final gambit. "I do have one last request before you go. I need you to forge a dispatch to Ambassador Pierce, instructin' him to spread the false rumor that the Union is sendin' troops up the Red River."

"By which I take it to mean that is exactly what the Union plans to do?"

They both smiled; but for Clayton it was a sad ending to the year, and to the daily camaraderie with his dearest friend.

He didn't want to go back down to the party, he wanted to wrap himself in his melancholy, to watch the river take the remains of time out to sea. But when he entered his office, he found Allie standing there. Before he could speak she jumped right into what sounded like a prepared speech, spoken to the floor.

"I will admit, in the spirit of honesty, that I did have a little crush on your cousin, and that is why I ended up in his dressin' room. But it was mostly to make you jealous, Clay, since I find I cannot quit myself of feelin's for you." She looked up at him; and her rehearsed speech fell by the wayside. "Clay, I want you back. No man has ever fit me the way you do. Can't we go back to the way it was?"

"Whatever it was, seems like it wasn't enough, one way or another."

"What was missin'? Was it children? Did you want to be a father?"

The question surprised him; then jolted him with a thought. "Wait a minute. You gonna have a baby?"

"No," she smiled. But she saw a touch of disappointment fleet across his face when she said it. Which unexpectedly opened her heart to him even more.

Clay'd felt giddy for a moment; then sad at the letdown. Done in by all his own machinations and the tromp of events beyond his control. He stroked her head gently. "Anyway...I don't know that I'd ever be up to the job, darlin'."

Being held by him like this—so familiar, so loving—she felt

terrible guilty for having revealed his deceitful ways to Quintero; but not guilty enough to mention it now. There was no reason to spoil a moment like this, an island of respite in a sea of turmoil. So she just opened herself to his embrace; then led him by the hand to his adjoining bedroom, where there was a place for resting, and other such activities.

Next day Clayton came downstairs ready to start the New Year with a renewed sense of forward motion. But he was stopped at the bottom of the steps by Zhi Li.

"You order too much different beer," she said.

"What do you mean?"

"People gamble, they no care what beer they drink. You order only one kind from one man, he charge you less, you make more on customer."

"You know a brewer who'll give you a deal if he's all we order from?"

"Know someone, yes."

He nodded assent. She left satisfied, as Clayton surveyed the wreckage of last night's party. Trash and empty bottles littered the floor, interspersed with sleeping bodies and a handful of semi-dozers at the bar. One of the red-eyed slouchers was Wachtel, staring dully into his beer mug. Wilkes walked over and sat beside him.

"Happy New Year, Simon."

Wachtel shrugged, deeply dispirited. "There is more than one witness. The Army has no doubt Jensen deserted in the heat of battle."

"What will you do?"

"Ask the court for mercy. He was only sixteen at the time, he was a frightened boy. With luck, a ten-year sentence."

Tinbury strolled in and made for Wilkes. "Your boy, Isaac, sent me to find you."

"I've told you before, Tinbury, he's not my boy, and if you…"

"He asked me to tell you he's leaving today. And you know I didn't have to go out of my way to…"

But Clayton was already on the move and out the door.

A mild breeze crooned through the long line of covered wagons, cattle, oxen, mules, flatbeds filled with water barrels, ammunition, tools, explosives, dried food, mining equipment, medicines, weapons, bedding, and books—all surrounded by a couple hundred scurrying, milling, excited pilgrims. All of them emancipated—some on their own say-so, some by Lincoln's decree.

Clayton walked up the winding caravan, seeing a number of ex-slaves he knew—General Bee's, or others from around town—until he found Isaac near the front, tying down his calligraphy table to a wagon.

"No, siree," said Clay, "I wouldn't want you to set off for 40 years in the desert without your calligraphin' paraphernalia."

"How else would I keep the ship's log?"

"Appears to me you've got a few holes to plug in the hull before you set pen to paper."

"We'll learn seamanship as we go, I don't doubt." He finished tying off the table and turned to face Clayton. "But I'll miss our conversations."

"You'll find it most hard, I imagine, not having someone to be insubordinate to."

Isaac looked away. "I dislike this convention of saying goodbye. I never got to have it when my parents were taken. Since then it feels false with anyone."

"Fair enough. Leavin's always better if you can look ahead and not back."

"Don't look back, I'll try to remember that. Just like Orpheus told Eurydice, and Lot told his wife."

"I tell you one thing I won't miss is your endless historical and mythological references."

Isaac smiled. "Looking forward, then. Maybe you and I will salt gold mines together on the Barbary Coast one day."

They hugged, long and full.

Then Isaac mounted the big bay mare he'd chosen to lead this procession. He let out a whoop that was echoed on down the line; and set off at a stately walk, followed by a noisy, not yet stately nation.

Clayton took the message to Quintero—the one Isaac had forged. Quintero sat at his desk with his codebook, carefully plotting out the dispatch, letter by letter, as Clayton perambulated the room. It was labeled Top Secret, addressed to Leonard Pierce, and it said the Union's Red River Campaign was a hoax; a hoax that Pierce should spread through his usual channels, purporting to be real intelligence—to divert the Confederacy's forces to that area.

But since this message had been brought to him by Wilkes—who now clearly was a spy for the North—Quintero knew this must be false. Therefore the Red River Campaign was real. The Yankees were going up the Red to conquer Shreveport.

Quintero had to consider his next move carefully. "I think that will be all for now, *mi viejo*. I'll let you know our next move when I have conceived a plan."

Clay left. Quintero rubbed his eyes. It was a terrible thing, war; the price of revolution, but a terrible price. It took lives, ruined bodies, shattered friendships. He felt bitter at the loss of this good friend who'd betrayed him. A man he'd trusted with his secrets and with his heart. So Quintero's additional casualty in this war was he felt ashamed to have trusted this man; and by extension, to have trusted anyone. Revolutions died at the altar of trust; but trust died at the altar of revolution, as well.

When it was tactically appropriate to do so, he'd have to kill Wilkes.

There was a knock on Allie's back door. She was expecting Clay, but when she opened it with a flourish she found Quintero. "Will you join me out here?" he asked.

She glanced behind her to make sure the children weren't around, then stepped out into the moonlight. "Agustin, this is an unusual time for a visit. Is somethin' afoot?"

"You were right, Madame. Wilkes is a spy and the Union is to march up the Red River to Shreveport. Alas, you bore the curse of Cassandra, you could see the future but none would believe what you foretold. At least I did not."

"But you believe me now!"

He nodded. "I have set countermeasures in motion to rectify the situation. General Taylor is, as we speak, preparing a great Southern ambush."

"And Clay knows nothin' of this," she said almost to herself.

"It is critical he be kept in the dark. He must not learn that I know he is a traitor. He must believe I truly think the Red River Campaign is a hoax." He put his hands on her shoulders. "I know you have parted ways. But I beg you to draw close to him once more. Pull him into confidences with your affections, learn his thoughts, seed what illusions you may. But stay close to him—though it may repel you to do so."

"All right. If I must." Truly, the cross purposes of her heart made her dizzy.

"The Yankees must go through with their plan," Quintero pressed. "They must trust that they have fooled us—humiliated us—once again."

"I believe I can help encourage Clay in that line of thinkin'."

"With all due respect, Madame—I am confident in your ability to mislead a man."

Next day Solomon and Ned were playing able-whackets, Ned holding the rope above Solomon's palm. But he didn't strike; he was struggling with something.

"I know I said I'd guide ye to Lafitte's treasure—but I cannot do such to a friend. I wouldn't inflict the curse o' Lafitte's Hell Dog on ye."

Solomon was touched. He put his hand gently over Ned's. "I tell you what, laddie. I've got my own treasure trove. It's a holy site, filled with magic bones of the First Men. I'll share one with you and I guarantee it'll protect you from any Hell Dog curse."

Ned was awed. "You'd give me one o' them bones?"

Solomon pulled a flat, gray stone out of his pocket. "This be a chip off the great beast's horn. Kept one around me neck, but I gave it to Isaac to protect him on his long journey." He put the shard in Ned's hand. "This one's for you, then."

"You're a good friend, Ryburn." Ned waved Clayton over to show him his new treasure, as Booth bounded down the stairs in three great leaps. Making an entrance.

"Clayton Wilkes, good day, sir!" He carried with him a stage sword—an epee with a bulbous button for a tip to prevent actual penetration during a performance. He motioned Clay over to the empty boxing ring and pulled an oilcloth sac of pig's blood from his tunic. "I wonder if you'd give this to Catherine for me. A critical prop for tonight's performance and she was to pick it up, but I must leave and she hasn't yet arrived."

Clayton took the blood pouch. "I can give it to her. Where are you off to?"

Booth spoke quietly. "I've received word the man who's to smuggle me out will be here in a week—I'm off now to get details. All I know is he wears an eagle feather in his hat. So if he shows up here early, tell him to wait in my room."

"With pleasure. We'll both be happier with you gone."

"Don't like me dippin' my fingers in your fruit pie, is that it?" Booth leered. He couldn't help himself from salting old family wounds.

"I'll ask you not to be so vulgar."

"Why, sir, the lady in question told me vulgar is what she likes."

Clayton pushed Booth against the ropes and held him there. "You go too far, cousin." They stood motionless; then Clayton tapped Isaac's Polecat Coat-of-Arms on the wall. "But I reckon this Skunk shield foretold your arrival. You're still the biggest polecat I ever met, JW."

Jersey walked in just then, on her way to the kitchen. Booth glanced at her, telling Clayton, "Leastways I don't smell like that stinkin' blackamoor. How you let her parade around all these white folks…"

Clayton slapped him with the theater prop pouch, which broke, splattering pig's blood all over Booth's jaw. Booth stepped back, whipping his epee across Clay's cheek. Clay pulled a rapier from his cane, where it was sheathed—the cane Isaac had given him. They stood like that a moment—*en tableau*—then jumped off the ropes with three quick steel parries.

Everyone in the casino stopped what they were doing, suddenly aware of this strange, tense battle at the boxing ring. Jim, behind the bar, brought out his shotgun—but Clay motioned him to stand down.

"You're quicker than I recall, Clay. Have you done much stage fencin' since we last engaged?" With a nasty smile Booth pried the button off the tip off his epee.

"You're about to find that out, you sonuvabitch." He lunged at Booth with a *degage*, which John Wilkes parried laterally, coming back with a *coupe* that stung Clayton in the side—as Clay stuck Booth in the arm, drawing blood.

"Well done, sir," said Booth. "I had first blood, but you had first *a pointe*..."

Clayton attacked before Booth could finish his sentence—sick to death of the man's foul behavior, all the more so because he was family. Steel clanged back and forth as they circled each other around the floor—the bar patrons giving them wide berth. Nobody could remember ever having seen Clayton angry like this before. It was a little scary. Both men scored touches, drawing blood from slashes and whippings, and sometimes when the point of Clay's rapier sank an inch into Booth's flesh.

The fight was upsetting Ned, though. Clayton was his savior and benefactor, and it was horrific to see him sliced like this. That's when he remembered the sacred bone Solomon had given him; and he thought it might save Clay. So he leaped between the combatants holding the tusk fragment up like a talisman—just as Booth lunged.

The point of Booth's sword snagged the stone in Ned's hand—first bending the blade, then breaking it in half. The jagged tip of steel that remained impaled Ned's hand. The old sailor yowled and fell to the floor as Clayton and Booth escalated the fury of their fight, Booth's epee now dagger length, with a ragged point.

Clay pressed his attack but Booth was a better swordsman, forcing Clay to stumble until he fell. Booth knelt over him, the jagged point of his broken blade resting under Clay's chin. But a sound made Booth look up, to see everyone in the bar closing in on him grimly, holding knives or guns—their intentions clear enough to Booth.

He stood erect with a broad stage smile. "Here, now. Just havin' some family fun. We used to do this all the time back on the plantation. Like brothers wrasslin."

At that moment Allie entered. Taking in the scene at a glance, she rushed to Clay's side. "Whatever are you on about, sir?" she shouted at Booth.

"Why…I was simply defendin' your honor," Booth said with a bow.

Catherine came in as Allie helped Clay sit up. Catherine saw how bloodied Clay was and assisted Allie. The two women exchanged a savvy glance as each took one of Clay's arms around their shoulders and helped him slowly upstairs to his room.

"Is there no one to aid me with *my* wounds?" Booth asked the room like a sad child. No response. He shrugged philosophically and limped outside.

Zhi Li entered Clay's office with poultice and bandages. The three women cleaned and wrapped his lacerations for the next hour. By the time they were done Catherine and Allie found a new appreciation for each other. Clay asked Zhi Li for a puff on the pipe, but she let loose with a lash of Chinese invective that made itself clear, though nobody else knew the words. Zhi Li left, followed by Catherine, who had to get back to business at the Opera House—including, now, securing a new pig's-blood pouch for tonight's performance.

When they were alone Allie's face grew concerned. "That man might've killed you, Clay. Not to speak of the fact that I don't care for his attitude about my Coloreds."

"I'll get him gone in a hurry and you better believe it."

"Can I help?"

"I don't see how…"

"And I wouldn't mind humiliatin' him just a little along the way," she interrupted with the excitement of the hunt in her voice. "He needs to be brought down a couple pegs after what he did to you. The man is just too in love with himself."

"He *is* an actor."

"I was thinkin' we might run one of our old games on him. I was thinkin' somethin' along the lines of that old story you used to tell about smellin' the corpse in the blizzard."

"Findin' a dead body is never a bad hook," he ruminated, trying to envision it.

"Exactly. A body you couldn't possibly know would be there—but you and Booth findin' it together changes everything!"

His eyes happened to land on the old, motheaten Oriental carpet covering the floor. A plan began to gel. "We'd need a team," he said. "If you can get Scully and Russell up here, we might could work out some travelin' plans for JW."

Allie hadn't felt this sweet on Clay since Virginia. She kissed him deep on the mouth and ran out to gather the troops.

As she exited downstairs through a flood of customers all telling the story of the sword fight the way they'd seen it, Solomon and Ned sat at the bar, Zhi Li applying poultice to Ned's hand wound.

"The bone protected us," he whispered to Ryburn. "Me and Wilkes both, by God."

"It was a brave thing to stand between them like that," said Solomon. "Brave and foolish, mate."

"Wilkes has been my savior, I could do no less. But don't you see? The token you give me can protect me from the Hell Dog curse, too."

"Let's get your hand fixed up proper, then we can talk about that."

"Hand is fix," Zhi Li replied with annoyance and walked away.

Ned held up the tusk fragment and wiped it clean of the blood from his hand—though it had seeped into the grooves and cracks of the stone, creating a kind of etched design in dark red relief, like some ancient scrimshaw.

It made Ned shiver. "Powerful medicine, is what this is. We got protections like these, I can take you to Lafitte's treasure chest, and Hell Dog be damned."

✳ ✳ ✳

Later in the day, shirtless and bandaged, Booth was brushing his teeth with a cinnamon stick when Allie came to the open door, looking concerned.

"I am just about ready for my photograph," he smiled as if nothing had happened.

"I thought you'd want to know, a man came lookin' for you at the casino after you left. Man with an eagle feather in his hat. Said he was an old friend. From Dixie."

Booth was alert. "What did you tell him?"

"Why, not a thing. He heard you lived there and he said he'd be back."

He put on his shirt, excited. "Don't look so glum, missy, that man is my savior."

"There was another man later on," she cautioned. "He was showin' papers on you, sayin' there was a reward. Said he was a bounty hunter from St. Louis."

Booth stopped with a catch of breath. "What'd he look like?"

"Wore an eyepatch. Clay says you want to get away you better meet him quick."

Clay was waiting in one of the small cabins behind Brave River when Allie brought Booth in. Booth was a nervous wreck.

"Clay, please forgive me for the fight I caused. You must help me escape from this one-eyed monster who would shackle me back to Missouri on these trumped up..."

"Settle down, JW, it's all under control. I've parked Mr. Eagle-feather down at the cabin on the end and I sent the eyepatched bounty hunter on a wild duck hunt to Bagdad. You're in the clear for now."

Booth practically wept. "Take me to Mr. Eagle, if you would, and I'll be out of your hair."

"Out of mine, too," Allie said mock-sadly, with a curtsy. "More's the pity."

Booth squeezed her upper arm. "Brave girl." Then nodded to Clay, who led them down the row of cabins to the last one at the rear. Clay opened the door quickly and slipped in, followed immediately by Booth and Allie, who shut the door—as Clay gasped. "Dear God." On the floor was a dead body in a pool of blood, the brim of the eagle feather hat crumpled under the corpse's head. Clayton kneeled next to the body, felt for a pulse and shook his head. He turned the body on its side—the shirtfront was covered in blood, a Bowie knife lying beneath him. Clay let the body drop again.

"Looks like he's holdin' somethin'," said Allie. "What's that in his hand?"

Clayton pried it out of the cadaver's clenched fist. "It's an eyepatch."

"Clay, you have to give me some runnin' money." Booth was in a panic.

"I can help, but not until tonight. You just have yourself ready soon as you're done with the play."

"You can't expect me to go onstage when…"

"Oh, you must!" pled Allie. "If this murderin' lawman knows you're onto him he'll jump you before Clay can organize your escape." She hugged him fearfully. "Please."

"Besides that, you don't show up for your performance, Catherine'll get the local police on your tail, as well. Your best bet's to lay low in the root cellar under cabin four," said Clay. "I'll get you to the theater just before curtain."

Clay ushered Booth to the cellar while Allie waited behind.

Moments later the bloody body stirred and sat up. Wiped his hands on his pants leg and pulled the empty blood pouch off his chest. Allie watched him from the door.

"It's a strange kind of war, all right," said Scully.

"But fun, from time to time," Allie smiled, helping him up. "I'm just tickled to think of John Wilkes Booth lyin' in that filthy root cellar all day."

* * *

The play went badly. Booth's nerves were frazzled. A man with a brand new eyepatch was sitting front row; Booth couldn't stop glancing at him, and then muffing his lines. After intermission the audience was half gone. But the man with the eyepatch was still there, front row aisle. Allie had warned Booth of his presence just before Act I—she said she'd seen him buying a ticket. But she assured Booth she'd distract him when the time came.

Allie sat beside the bounty hunter, flirting ceaselessly, as promised. When the play finally ended to limp applause, Eyepatch stood—but

Allie stood before him, separating him from the stage, her hands on his chest, finishing her story with flagrant innuendo as Booth ran into the wings. From the stage door Clay took him to a grove of trees where a wagon stood, its flatbed filled with rolled carpets. Clay's old Oriental lay spread out on the ground. "Lie down," he said. "No one's goin' to look for you in here. Captain Brancado will meet you in Bagdad and steam you up to Galveston."

Booth hesitated. "Wait. I have no weapon." Clay waved away his concern, but that only made him more anxious. "What if I'm tracked? What if I must fight to the last?" At Clay's reluctance, Booth used his only remaining card. "Your mother told us family above all. Don't let the bloodline fall to thoughtless disregard, man."

Clay didn't like it but he pulled out his .41 caliber Philadelphia Derringer. Booth pocketed it. Clay and the wagon driver—Teddy Beale, dressed like a teamster—rolled Booth up in the rug, making sure the moth holes matched his mouth so he could breathe.

Teddy got up on the wagonseat and slapped reins. The horses took off with a jolt, along the river going east. As the wagon disappeared, Allie and Russell walked out of the Opera House and came over to the grove—Russell removing his eyepatch as he and Allie discussed particulars of the Ottoman cargo still lying unclaimed in Bagdad.

When they reached Clay, he shook Russell's hand. "I thank you, Major Russell."

"It's always a pleasure being flirted at by Mrs. Stoneman. And a joy watching the two of you work. A real schooling in how it's done."

Allie felt that particular inner glow of having consummated a con well-conned. This was the first one she and Clay had run together from start to finish in a long time, too. Just like the old days. It felt good. Which is exactly what Clay was feeling. A sweet moment, like old times, like there was no better place to be, or person to be with. They glanced at each other for only a second, with a smile that shared this core sentiment at a deep place.

But Allie quickly put a pout on her face for Clay's benefit—didn't want him to get too cocky. "Only thing I didn't like about this was helpin' out the Yankees," she said. "Even if it means that vile cousin of yours will get his comeuppance."

"Yankees, Rebs, Frenchies, *Juaristas*—all war is personal, darlin'. None of those big ideas is worth a sow bug. It's about the folks you're connected to. That's all there is."

Whereupon he put his arm around her and walked her back into the *Teatro*.

CHAPTER 25

ISAAC COULDN'T STOP SMILING, settled astride his stoic bay as he watched the procession move west to New America—what they were calling their colony. Hannah—General Bee's cook—and her child helper, Bigboy, waved at him from their wagon perch and Isaac called back, "You keep your eyes open for fish heads, Bigboy, you'll be the king of the garden!" Bigboy jumped down and started looking.

A few cowboys, led by Hannah's son, Jake, and the King Ranch wrangler, Sal, kept the small cattle herd in line. Some folks were singing Gospel tunes; children were running up and down at play. It made Isaac's heart near to bursting just to watch it all.

Salem rode up from far ahead of the caravan. "People comin'."

"Show me."

They rode up the westward moving line, exchanging greetings with all who waved; then kept riding another five minutes. Salem pulled rein, handed Isaac a spyglass and pointed at a range of hills to the south. Isaac brought the glass to his eye.

A dozen armed men rode in their direction at a leisurely pace. Sombreros, rifles, bandoliers of ammunition crossing their chests. Isaac thought: *It begins.*

"Bandits," said Isaac. "You ride back and tell Jake. Do how we talked about it."

"You not comin'?"

"I'll stay here to meet this posse. You go get yourselves set."

Salem rode back to the caravan at a gallop while Isaac sat his horse where he was, waiting for these Mexicans to reach him. The day sparkled with the kind of sunfreshness the air gives off after a rain. Cool breeze made the waiting a pleasant occupation. Isaac used the time to count the critters in this habitat: two prairie dogs, a rattlesnake, some kind of brown lizard, a different kind of brown lizard, a family of armadillos and too many birds to catalogue.

The men on horses grew visible without magnification, and then altered direction slightly to head directly for Isaac. Eleven men. Nine paused thirty yards out and two came ahead until they faced Isaac at thirty feet.

"*Hola, senor!*" shouted the one on the grander horse. He wore a black sombrero with silver coins for a hatband. "*Como esta?*"

"It goes well, *hombre*," Isaac called back, relaxed but alert. "*Juaristas* or *Imperialistas?*"

"No, no, we have no politics. We are only the farmers' *policia.*"

"*Bueno.* We are only farmers."

"On a trip? You must have sold your crops."

"No. We journey now to our first farm. Crops are next year."

"Must be a big plantation! You see? I know this Gringo word!"

"No plantation," said Isaac. "Just families, and farms."

Black Hat shrugged. "You must to pay for passing this way. So we protect you."

"We can protect ourselves."

"Don't matter. You still pay."

Isaac pulled the Henry repeating rifle from its scabbard on his horse's flank and in one smooth move shot the silent man beside Black Hat through the heart. As the dead bandit slumped around his horse's neck, Isaac aimed his rifle at Black Hat before the man could pull his own pistol.

"You're smart not to draw on me," Isaac said. "If you do, you will be *muerto.*"

Black Hat's nine henchmen were already riding up quickly, their guns drawn. Isaac called out again. "Better tell your men to sit quiet too. And look east pretty quick!"

Black Hat looked in the direction of the caravan behind Isaac. Two dozen men and women—Isaac's best shooters—lay spread out prone in the sand, their rifles pointed at the bandit gang. Black Hat raised his arm and shouted at his gathering forces. *"Sin armas! Estate quieto!"* His men lowered their weapons as they pulled up around him.

"Don't come back," said Isaac. "We will make it expensive for you to take from us. *Costoso robar.*" He kept his sights on Black Hat's heart.

Black Hat lowered his arm slowly. Nodded. Two of his men tied the dead bandit to his horse with a *riata*. Black Hat said, "*Vamono*," wheeling his horse around to ride back to the hills, with his men leading the horse of the dead man behind.

When they were too small to see Isaac cantered over to his rifle brigade, who finally stood from their flanking position. After a tense moment—realizing what they'd just done—they all whooped and hugged and jumped around for close to a minute.

"You see them ride off all scared?"

"Damn right they scared. We had 'em!"

"Woulda killed 'em, too, they made a move on Isaac!"

"We the New America Artillery Company!"

They looked jubilant. Isaac smiled down from atop his bay mare. "You did well."

They ran back to the wagon train to tell everyone about their first victory, and with what precision their companions held fire, how the triumph was achieved despite the sun in their eyes, and about Isaac's mastery of the bandit leader, and how well these free black men and women had performed, like free peoples anywhere, what a grand colony was emerging, what a great country they would one day make.

And here, today, was their first piece of history. The beginning of the legend upon which societies were built.

Isaac just sat there, watching his company run back to the rest of the flock. He was indeed a proud father. But he also knew the journey before them wasn't likely to be measured by eleven undisciplined *banditos* in the desert.

Jersey was spooning cornmeal into Moon's mouth. His lips made smacking noises sucking each spoonful but he never woke up any more than that. He was down to about 80 pounds now. He had sores on his butt and his heels, but Jersey and Shonny kept those pretty clean. He had an erection every morning, which made Shonny giggle, but Jersey told her she'd giggle a different tune in a few years.

Mostly Jersey just carried on a rambling talk with Moon every time she fed him. Of course, she was the only one speaking, but it wasn't exactly a monologue, since she often answered responses she expected he'd make if he'd been awake. Usually in the form of bickering, since that had always been their chief method of communication.

"I don't know why you don't show more 'preciation for this fine mush we feedin' you. What? This better corn than we ever had back home, I don't know why you ain't fattenin' up, neither, never mind *sittin'* up. You just lay there like you expect we goin' feed you forever like a baby. You forgot how to do for yourself. You got to fight, you want to get well. Like the frog in the milk pail, he kicked and kicked until he churned it to butter, then he just climbed out. Don't you tell me you can't climb out."

"Will you two do nothin' but argue?" shouted Allie from the next room, where she was giving Shonny, Charles and Bootsy a reading lesson.

"Ain't me arguin'," Jersey called back. "It's Moon. He the disputatious one."

Allie heard a tapping at the back window and looked up to see Clay's moonlit shadow against the shed. "You children read to each other for a while. I'll be back directly." She went out the back door as the kids whispered to each other, gleefully suspicious.

Outside Clay led her behind the shed and kissed without preamble. She gladly absorbed his attentions but when she started pulling away to talk, it just inflamed him. Kisses progressed to fondles. She found herself responding but pushed him back and touched the healing saber wound on his cheek. "That must hurt when you kiss a girl."

"Hurts more when I don't. Kissin's better than laudanum." He leaned in for another but she held him at bay.

"No sir, that's all you're gettin' from me tonight. I've got school lessons to give and receipts to tally and I said I'd help the girls turn Moon over for his bath."

"You could turn me over when you're done."

She felt the time was right to lay out her first piece of bait. Just because she craved this man didn't mean she couldn't use him to help the Confederacy—and hadn't Agustin Quintero given her that very order? She smiled coyly at Clay. "That sounds quite appealin' for some other night." She gave him what was understood to be a consolation kiss. "After gettin' my chores done I must write back to Mildred."

"Mildred Bee? How's that retreat goin' for them?" He put pure idle curiosity in his voice, but Allie knew the timber of his ulterior motives. He was still trying to trick her, so turnaround was purely fair play.

"The poor woman, just when she thinks she has her house settled, her husband gets new orders and all her hopes of domesticatin' him fly out the window."

"What kind of new orders is that?"

"I'm sure I don't know." But she looked away when she said it, reckoning he'd see the tell and figure she did know.

"Well," he put on a pout, "I guess I'll leave you to it, then."

"I guess you will," she smiled back. "And what are you lookin' at?"

He was looking at the changes he saw in her. The wild girl who used to be all about her own playful self had become more thoughtful; more caring of others. If anyone had ever told him Allie would one day be tending a mismatched family of ex-slaves, he'd never have believed it. He kissed her on the cheek.

"Thought I saw a smudge there."

He could also see she was hiding some small thing from him, but he wasn't about to let that come between them again. Besides, whatever it was, he'd figure it out in due time. So he just winked, backed into the shadows, and was gone.

Damn him, she thought. *He just never stops bein' too cute.*

Aurelia screamed, clutching her belly as a growing patch of bright blood spread across the middle of her nightgown. Terrified, Scully lit a lantern.

"What is it? Is the baby comin'?"

"*Si,*" she managed to gasp. "*Consigue a mi hermana.*" Get my sister.

Now Russell ran into the room and saw the blood. "You can't wait on this. Things need to go quick now."

"What do you know about it?" Scully snapped at Russell out of fear.

"I've had truck with such things."

"And how is that, pray tell?"

"I was there when my wife gave birth to both our children."

Scully, taken down a peg, backed off. "Sorry. I didn't know you have a family."

"I don't. They're all dead now." Scully was speechless, but Russell prodded him loudly. "Get moving, for the love of Christ. Find Dr. Hawks. I'll stay and do what I can."

Aurelia let out another loud moan. Scully ran.

Clay waited patiently behind Allie's shed all night. It was where Shonny, Charles and Bootsy slept. In the morning they went off into the world to eavesdrop and whatever other assignments Allie had given them. Jersey left the house soon after, with Allie. Nobody home now but Moon and he wasn't about to give Clayton away.

He entered at the back door and went to Allie's room. It smelled of lavender, her signature scent, though he remained baffled by how she was never without it. It didn't take long, rummaging through her desk, to find a small packet of letters from Mildred Bee, tied together with lace. He scanned the letters and read the most recent.

It was largely a litany of domestic issues—food shortages, the lack of medicinal herbs, the alcohol problem with the locals—but there was one line in the middle of the epistle that grabbed his attention. Mildred was *"so looking forward"* to being alone in charge of her house when General Bee took his 2500 troops *"to guard the new cotton train to Laredo and secure that stronghold as a bastion against Yankee aggression."*

This was critical information for two reasons. All those Rebs headed for the Rio Grande—the Union garrison now occupying Fort Ringgold would have to be advised to send men to Laredo to defend against that attack. More importantly, Bee's army assaulting Laredo left

Shreveport wide open. Which meant the Rebs had bought the story that the Red River campaign was a lie. Which meant now was the time for General Banks' Yanks to move up the Red and storm the place.

Clayton put the letters back in place and headed quickly to the Pierce safe house.

* * *

By the time Scully got back to the *hacienda* with Dr. Hawks in the pale sunrise, a still more pale Aurelia lay half-conscious in bed with a red-haired infant at her breast. Russell sat beside her, leaning his whole weight down pushing a bloody pillow onto her pelvis. "It's about damn time," he rumbled.

"Let me see," said Hawks, lifting Russell off the bed with a strength he hadn't expected. Scully stood motionless as a scared prairie dog while the doctor lifted the blood-crusted nightgown to examine the damage.

"I put the babe at her teat," explained Russell to no one. "They told me once it slows the bleeding."

"That it does," said Dr. Hawks. "But I'll need to get the afterbirth out if we're to stop it altogether. Mr. Scully, boil water, if you please." Scully remained motionless. "Now, please." He ran to the kitchen.

"I didn't know what else to do," Russell apologized to the doctor.

"You did fine, Major. The pressure you applied saved her life. Now sit down there and hold her legs still. She'll want to kick when I get started."

Hearing her wail from the kitchen, Scully was so startled he spilled water on the small fire he'd just started and had to start over with dry leaves on the smoldering coals. He was glad to have this task to focus on, though. By the time he finally got back to the bedroom Russell was putting something in a bucket, Hawks was wiping her hands on a towel, and Aurelia was unconscious, the baby asleep on her breast.

"Will she live?" he whispered.

"I don't know, son. But the baby will, and you've Major Russell to thank for that."

The men glanced at each other a moment, neither having felt so vulnerable before another man. Scully nodded him a silent thanks and Russell nodded acknowledgement. Then they busied themselves with other things.

But when Russell went outside a tear filled his eye, remembering his own fallen family, who he couldn't save at all, leaving him no one to be connected to; except maybe these lost souls now.

It was late afternoon when Isaac's party was attacked from the west by nearly a hundred French soldiers. A dozen of his people fell at the first volley and the exchange of fire was chaotic from then on. The black pilgrims had better cover—their wagons—but they also had the sun in their eyes. And the French outnumbered the émigré shooters three to one. The gunfire quieted after a while. The French used the evening to flank the wagon train. Isaac used it to devise a plan.

"What's a French army want with us?" asked Jake, Isaac's best horseman.

"French don't like Colored folk no more than any other white man do," Salem said and spat on the ground.

"It makes no difference," said Isaac. "We can't fight them much longer."

"They's more of us than they is o' them."

"Not more soldiers, though. Not more guns, or folks to shoot them."

"Maybe we should just rush 'em when it get dark. Beat 'em to death before they kill us all."

Isaac had them circle the wagons while he rode off to scout a better position with Jake and Salem. They came to a rapid river 500 hundred yards to the north, beyond some low hills. Jake tried to ford it but nearly got carried away—it was too deep, wide and fast. Its very power gave Isaac an idea, though.

He left the other two men at the river, showing them each their spot and giving them instructions. Then he rode back to his besieged camp. He picked his thirty strongest men to return with him to the river with supplies—leaving instructions with another twenty riflemen at the wagons to shoot anywhere they saw French movement, a shot or two every few minutes, to keep the Frenchies guessing. He left Hannah, the cook, in charge of everyone else—setting up defenses, hunkering down. Her chief assistant, Bigboy, had endless energy to help everyone do everything.

Back at the river Isaac had his workers dig a wide trench from upriver, in a long arc back around to a spot at the bank thirty yards downriver. Some men piled rocks and boulders along the outer edge of the trench; others set dynamite charges at key points. It took them most of the night to complete, all the while listening to gunfire in the south.

By four in the morning all was silent. Isaac guessed the French were working their way east for a massive attack at sunrise, when the wagon train would be blinded trying to defend itself. For the next two hours Isaac and Salem quietly escorted wagons to the river at a walk, their wheels wrapped in clothing to suppress their sound.

At last everyone was huddled by the riverside. Five wagons had been emptied out and left behind, with just a few marksmen and their ponies stationed there to keep sending off shots into the dark at the invisible French force. Hannah walked up to Isaac.

"You think you Moses now, gonna part the Red Sea for us to git away from Pharaoh's army?"

"No, Hannah, more like Cyrus conquering Babylon at the Euphrates."

"Don't know 'bout the Youfraidies—but this here river too big to cross."

"I don't expect us to cross the river. I expect the river to cross us."

He gave orders to the wagon drivers. He had Jake run to their rear guard at the abandoned wagons; and just before dawn, the rear guard ran back to the river. Isaac didn't want to start their exodus in the dark of night, or half of them would surely drown. As the sun peeked above the long horizon he heard a volley of shots back where the French had had them pinned down, and he knew this was their final attack. He had everybody take cover behind wagons or boulders; everyone with a horse held a tight rein; and he signaled his men to light their fuses all at once.

There was a great blast, carving deeper the channel his laborers had already dug. A channel that cut into the water upriver, curved around and behind their entire caravan, and re-entered the flow again downriver. Roaring water gushed through the channel, overflowing the sides, then merging again with the main riverflow.

And as the daylight grew, Isaac saw his idea working. Enough river had been diverted into the channel around their backs, that the river before them was less raging, and shallow enough to cross.

"Let's move!" he shouted as he heard the French regrouping back at the abandoned wagons; trying to figure out what the explosion beyond the hill was about.

His wagons, horses, cattle and settlers forded the quieter river as the French rode up in force—but were stopped at the edge of the new, turbulent side channel. The French shot at the retreating caravan and wounded a few more. But the French captain didn't want to risk losing any of his own men or animals in the roiling waters. So in the end he just ordered his men to sit their mounts, watch their prey escape and remember this moment of an opponent's brilliant tactical retreat. He actually saluted Isaac.

When he saw that, Isaac turned and saluted in return. This world of wars was surely unfathomable, no matter whose side you were on.

Jersey, Shonny, Charles and Bootsy protested as Allie shut the McGuffey Reader she'd been using to teach them.

"I ain't done readin' yet!" said Jersey.

"You mean 'I'm *not*' done readin' yet. But you did pretty well on the lesson. So here…" She gave them each a nickel. "Now y'all scoot and get yourselves some candy."

"What about Moon?" said Charles. "Don't seem fair he don't get candy just for not readin'."

Allie handed him another nickel. "You buy you some candy for Moon too, then."

They ran out the door whispering as Allie silently thanked the Lord for a little peace to think about her life. She sat beside the dwindling Moon, picked up his bowl of runny mush, dipped a piece of soft bread in it, and slid the soaked bread up against his front teeth. His lips smacked like a sea mollusk devouring its prey, with brainless gusto. Allie repeated the offering as she spoke to her sweet ex-slave.

"My, you are hungry tonight, Moon. These children been feedin' you proper, or you just like the way I do it better? Well, we're just all doin' the best we can. Except I don't know about Clay. I do wish he'd get on the right side of this war. I suppose he's still mad at his daddy and that's why he's takin' it out on our dear Dixie. But one bad daddy shouldn't tar the whole South with the same brush." She dabbed at Moon's mouth with a napkin, almost like he was royalty and she his servant. Then she went on.

"I feel terrible usin' Clay like I am. But forgin' Mildred's letter because I knew he'd find it is simply turnin' his own bad behavior against him. If he hadn't been snoopin' in my room like he shouldn't, he wouldn't have found where I hid it, so he wouldn't have helped out the South in this Red River brouhaha, which is just desserts in my book." She paused, feeling suddenly sad. "I do miss your sweet singin' to ease my mind."

She picked up the McGuffey Reader, still wrestling with herself. "I truly love Clay, Moon. That don't mean I can't help him do the right thing without him knowin' it."

Jensen's court martial, once mounted, was a pretty quick affair. The judge was Colonel Dye. Clayton sat beside Wachtel on a bench in the spectators' section, surrounded by a gallery of noisy fools all certain of the defendant's guilt. Simon held himself together in dread anticipation.

Octavio, the sweet old Mexican lawyer Wachtel had hired, gave a moving closing argument, stressing the possibility of reasonable doubt. It took Dye around 30 seconds to declare Jensen guilty. Wachtel suppressed a small yip in his throat while Jensen stared straight ahead. Octavio asked for mercy in the sentencing phase, citing his client's youthful age at the time of the desertion. Dye told the young man he was sentenced to hang by the neck until dead, with the mercy of the court taking the form of a twenty-foot drop, so death would be quick. Date to be determined.

Two privates marched Jensen unceremoniously back to his cell as

Wachtel burst into tears. Clayton put his arm around the old man's shoulder without knowing what to say; so he said nothing. Wachtel took a deep breath, shrugged Clayton's arm off and walked away. As Clay rounded the building, he saw 500 cavalry troops standing by their mounts, waiting for Colonel Dye, who left the court dais and walked in their direction.

A big dappled roan trotted up to Wilkes. Teddy Beale dismounted. "I'm so glad I found you!" she declared. She wanted to hug him, but this surely wasn't the place for that.

"Well, you found me," smiled Clayton.

"I wanted to thank you for talking to Mr. Pierce. He told me you put in a good word on my behalf and he gave me the transfer. So I'm going." She wanted to say more but wasn't sure what. "Right now."

"Goin' where?"

"I'm not supposed to say—I'm riding with Colonel Dye's company any minute. Assigned to General Banks when we get there."

"That sounds like a front-line kind of postin'."

"I asked for a fighting assignment, so yes, I think that's what they gave me."

"I wish you well, Corporal." He extended his hand—a manly farewell.

She took his hand like a man, to shake—but just held it, unmoving, for the longest time, looking in his eyes. "I wish I could kiss you goodbye."

"These soldiers might not take that in the proper spirit."

"I mean…there's no telling if I'll come back from this war." Her voice choked.

"Teddy, there's no tellin' if any of us will. Time to time it's felt to me like the world was endin'. But we got our memories of each other, and I expect that'll have to do you when them cannonballs come close."

"I expect it will, then." She held his hand in both of hers for just a moment, then dropped it and saluted him. "Begging your leave, sir."

"Gonna miss you, Corporal. Be safe."

She wiped her eye, jumped on her roan and took off at a gallop to join Dye and his 500 men heading north up the Wild Horse Desert.

Clayton turned to walk home, nearly colliding with two Nuns of the Incarnate Word who floated by like an omen.

Clayton entered Wachtel's inner office to find the old man drinking *schnapps*. His eyes were red, his cheeks salty dry.

"I have news, Simon."

"He is dead, *ja?*

"No. I prevailed on Ambassador Pierce to call in a favor with a friend in Washington. Jensen's sentence has been commuted. He's not gonna be hung."

Wachtel stood, propping himself up on his desk. "In prison for life, then? Where?"

"Not prison, no. In return for the commutation he had to agree to go to the front lines—in shackles so he doesn't run again."

Hope rose in Wachtel. "In shackles…until the fighting starts?"

"No, he stays in shackles. He'll be in the first line of attack, though, so best hope is he gets wounded and taken to a hospital. Or maybe left on the field and taken for dead. Either way, it's better odds than a hangin'.'"

Wachtel wept silently. "Thank you, Clayton. For your hand in helping him."

"Wasn't him I did it for." He reached down and moved a piece on the chessboard. "Bishop to King's Bishop six. You'd best go say goodbye now—he'll be leavin' directly."

Wachtel was shown to the jail cell by a private who left Simon alone on one side of the bars, Jensen on the other; Jensen in full uniform, his wrists and ankles manacled.

"You are well? They treat you *gut?*"

"Oh, yeah, very *gut*. So *gut* they gonna send me out first to see if some Reb wants to take a shot at me." His hands shook; he looked at Wachtel with a vulnerability he'd never exhibited before. "I'm scared, Simon. Can't you get me out of here?"

Simon put his hand through the bars, to touch the man he loved. "I will wait for you."

Jensen turned cold, though. "You won't see me again. Find some new entertainment."

"Is *gut* you are harsh. You must protect yourself how you can. Outside and in. I will still wait for you." Stoic now, Wachtel exited.

Jensen was more scared of battle than death itself. He wished they'd just let him hang.

*　*　*

Allie went to visit Colonel Dye, to see what news she might find lying around on his desk, but was told he'd just led his troops north, no telling when he'd be back. She asked if she could leave him a note on his desk but was politely declined. She made a half-hearted attempt to sneak in anyway, and feigned being lost when she was stopped—the *masque* of the flustered Belle.

Well, then, she'd damn well turn this into an import business day. Major Russell had just this morning told her that consignment of Turkish cloth was still lying wanting at the Bagdad docks without a buyer, and he'd be happy to arrange shipment to Matamoros for her, for a reasonable fee. She declined his offer of help, telling him if she did buy it she might just store it in Bagdad until she got Colonel Dye to take it off her hands, whenever he came back from his maneuvers. So she got on a coach to Badgad with her purse full of money and a pistol.

It was evening by the time she got there and located the palettes. Looked like good quality stock, too. When she found the captain and made her pittance offer, he dickered a bit, but soon gave in—they both knew his promised Confederate buyers were long gone. As Allie turned to oversee the loading onto wagons for storage, a bright light exploded in her head; then everything went black.

When she awoke with a headache, two crewmen were holding her up on deck as a Pasha swaggered over. He had a great black beard, a red vest with gold piping, pistols stuck in a colorful sash, and billowing pants. He walked around her, examining, assessing. Once, he pinched her belly, but when she tried to push him away she realized her hands were tied behind her back. He laughed, rubbing the cloth of her dress between his fingers. It reminded her of slave auctions she'd witnessed; only now she was the chattel. She threw up at his feet.

He shouted furiously. The two crewmen dragged her belowdecks to a small storage room full of crates and a single, hanging kerosene lamp. They threw her to the floor, shut the door and locked it.

The back of her head throbbed where they'd hit her, but she refused to pay any attention to that. She knew she was being kidnapped and she knew she had to get away; nothing else mattered. She looked around. No weapons, no tools, no nothing except boxes. She found one with a loose lid and pried it open. Clothing. Useless. But as she studied the cramped space in the dim light she found a glassed-in porthole, not much more than a foot wide, behind a pile of boxes. And just like a con game, her whole plan fell into place.

She pushed the boxes away from the window, stood on the crate remaining just below it and smashed the pane with her elbow; then turned around and cut her binding with a shard of glass still held in place—cutting her wrists as well, though she was so focused she didn't feel the pain. Once free she knocked all the remaining glass from the opening, stuck her head out and looked—a twenty-foot drop to the sea, the bonfires of Bagdad three miles away. She wasn't much of a swimmer, and the distance frightened her, but she didn't mean to give this Turkish clown the satisfaction of seeing her shrink from the challenge.

She pushed a dozen heavy crates in front of the door, blockading it from the inside. Then she grabbed the kerosene lantern, climbed to the window and squirmed out backwards, legs first. Her narrow hips squeezed through pretty easily. When she was up to her armpits through the porthole she twisted and got one shoulder outside, holding on to the edge of the window with that hand; then with her other hand threw the kerosene lamp amongst the wooden boxes, where it shattered and bloomed into flame. She eased her other shoulder out the opening and dropped, a cold plunge into black water. She held her breath, bobbed to the surface, located the shore, and swam.

She knew distraction was the enemy of a well-executed plan, so she kept her mind on nothing but long, slow strokes toward the docks. When her dress dragged her under the swells, she pulled it off and resumed swimming, keeping fear and anger from derailing her. She'd never gone more than a mile in calm waters before, but she knew her life depended on this, and she was determined to stay the course.

But the offshore breeze was blowing in her face and the current pulled her seaward as well. She felt herself tiring, still just barely 50 yards off the ship. Uncertainty gripped her will. She paused to tread water, to regain some strength, but a wave hit her square in the face, making her cough and gag. She thought: *This can't be how I die.* But she went limp with the thought, going under again. Is this what death was like? Black, cold, directionless? No. She couldn't let this happen, she was meant for so much more.

She surged back up to the surface—and immediately heard her name ringing in her ears. It alarmed her. Was she going mad? Was an angel beckoning her to the depths? Or could it be *la llorona*, following her out to a watery grave? There—she heard it again. "Miss Stoneman! Miss Stoneman!" Didn't sound like *la llorona*. Something hit her on the back of the head, like a tap—and when she spun in the water to hit back, she saw a skiff bobbing on the waves, one of its oars extended. "Grab on!" said the voice.

She grabbed the oar, pulling herself along its length until a man's arms lifted her aboard. She flopped onto the flat bottom, grabbing the small mast to steady herself, and focused on her savior, sitting on a bench seat. "Dutch?" she rasped.

"Yes, Miss. It's Private van Dijl."

"Whatever are you doin' here?" Relief swirled with confusion.

Shy, he was trying not to look at her in her wet underclothes. "Well…I was sort of following you."

"My Lord, are you another suitor?"

"No, Miss. But when I saw you get kidnapped like that I just had to help. So I jumped in this boat I saw tied to the dock and here I am. How'd you manage to get away from those slavers?"

She sat up, coughing. "I'm fairly resourceful."

A volley of rifle fire came from the Ottoman ship and two bullets hit the skiff. Allie and Dutch lay low. She saw right away how this could still end real badly.

"You have any weapons with you?" she shouted over the wind.

He pointed to an oilcloth-wrapped bundle lying astern. She unwrapped it and broke into an unlikely grin. "It's a Henry Repeater!" Her confidence soared.

"I brought it along in case of trouble. Mama bought it for me with her savings when I enlisted, said the least she could do was keep me well equipped."

More rounds hit the water nearby. Dutch reset the sail but the offshore gale was getting worse, pushing them back toward the schooner. A lucky shot splintered the tip of the skiff's little mast. Allie took careful aim with the Henry, waiting until they were cresting atop a slow swell—and fired. She saw her bullet go wide, hitting the rail two feet from the man she was shooting at.

"It pulls left," she said. "Or maybe it's just the blow." She adjusted the sights, aimed again and fired. This time the rifleman on deck flew backwards, hit in the chest. She shot four more times in rapid succession—and two more riflemen on the ship fell.

"Damn," said Private van Dijl. "Where'd you learn to shoot like that?"

But now they saw smoke billowing off the great schooner, flames licking up the back end. There were shouts on deck and crew could be seen rushing in that direction. She lowered the rifle with a grim smile. "They can't get in the door to put the fire out, by God, I blocked the way, you slaver bastards."

Dutch was standing up to reposition the sail when another volley erupted from the ship, one round nicking him in the groin. He fell with a cry. Allie returned fire, driving the Turk attackers back from the rail. Then she got down to check on Private van Dijl. The bullet had torn his femoral artery; he was gushing blood all over the boat. "Dear Lord," she said, putting pressure on his wound with a wad of the oilcloth.

He stared up at her with huge empty eyes. "I wisht I didn't die now."

"I'll get us out of here, darlin', you rest easy. Push this cloth down on the bleedin', hear?" She took down the sail, sat on the stern bench, put oars in the water and pulled, edging the prow toward land.

She heard his voice behind her. "I can't meet my Maker with a lie in my heart. I'm bound to tell you I'm here because I saw you through a window, sneaking around Colonel Dye's desk, and then trying to get in his office. I was afraid you were a Reb spy and I wanted to see what you were up to. I'm sorry if that wasn't your intention."

"Sorry, nonsense. You saved my life, showin' up when you did and I'll thank you all of my days, sweet boy." She turned her head to look at him. As their gazes met, his eyes grew darker. Then he died, his life'sblood splashing over the shallow hull. Angry now, Allie strained at the oars with every ounce of her strength, rowing toward shore—focused on the stern of the Turkish ship, engulfed in flame, the entire crew trying to douse it with a bucket brigade of seawater. When she reached the shallows she got out, beached the skiff, sat down hard on the sand and just sobbed.

Scores of onlookers crowded around the nearby docks to watch the fiery show. Allie stopped crying, with an occasional hiccup. This night was almost the end of her. But her luck had held. She'd always been lucky, that's what gave her the edge at a poker table. Alas those around her didn't always share in her fortune. She peered at the dead soldier in the rowboat. He looked even smaller now, depleted of the thing that had made him alive. Griefstruck she tried to remember a prayer to say for the dead, but nothing came. So she just said, "I'm terrible sorry. And you were right, I am a Reb spy."

Far behind her she heard a shout. "Allie? Is that you?"

She turned to see Clay running toward her, which made her start crying all over again. When he reached her he took her in his arms and for the second time that night she just let herself go limp—this time not in the ocean, but in his embrace. "Clay, what are you doin' here?" she finally asked.

"Russell told me he directed you here to buy some goods, but it didn't sit well with me, you bein' alone in Bagdad at night. I came to make sure you were safe." But he could see she wasn't, and it shook him considerably to see her so undone.

She held him tighter, still crying. "This young man came to help me, too, and now I can never repay him."

Clay looked in the boat at the dead Yankee. "Well…we oughtn't to leave him here for the gulls, then. I'll weigh him down with that rifle and put a couple holes in the hull."

She nodded. He put his coat around her shoulders, took off his boots and pants, rowed out and put up the sail. A minute later Allie heard two muffled gunshots—Clay putting pistol balls into the boat bottom. She saw the wind-filled sail pull the sinking dinghy out into the darkness, as Clay swam back the hundred yards to shore and lay her down in his buggy, where she slept the whole way back to Matamoros.

She recovered over the next two days, mostly sleeping, her wrist cuts healing, Clay tending her as the orphans cared for Moon. One evening while they drank wine in her bedroom, talking of nothing in particular, Clay found himself reflecting on his feelings at the prospect of having almost lost her, after so recently having her back in his life. It made him shaky; filled his chest with a terrible ache. He took her hand.

"Allie…will you marry me? Again?"

She was more moved than she expected to be and placed her cheek against his. "Yes, my love, I will." But even as she said it, a little corner of her knew she had to stay set on defeating the Union, which task she'd have a world of trouble hiding from a Yankee husband. She did love him—but it had torn her heart just to see that young Union private die for her; it would shred her soul if anything like that happened to the man she was bound to in matrimony. "But we must wait until the war is over."

"Isn't that what you told Jessup?"

"Yes, but that was to put him off. This is to keep you on." And they kissed.

After that she dismissed them all—Clay and the orphans both— saying she was fine, and surely they had better things to do than treat her like a sick child. Clay said he likely did, and took his leave, telling her he'd be back to check up at a more convenient time. He was pleased, though, that the return of her cantankerous nature meant she was on the mend.

On the third day Clay went to Allie's place to fulfill his promise, to make sure she was doing well after her ordeal. The house was vacant, though, the front door locked. So he went around to the back and climbed in her bedroom window. He was disappointed not to find her, but that being the case the empty house suited him fine. He could take some time to snoop again.

He went through her bureau looking for the packet of letters from Mildred but couldn't find them now. Instead he found Allie's journal in a locked drawer beside her bed. Not a difficult lock. He lay on the bed and started reading the most recent entries. Nothing of note, and by October he was getting sleepy. He relocked the diary and put it back in its drawer. He lay down and closed his eyes, just for a minute, just to rest them. So tired. Might be funny if he dozed off and she discovered him asleep in her bed, just as he'd found her asleep in *his* bed last month. He could pull her down to join him, and she'd scold him fiercely, and he'd say sshhh, sshhh…

"Sshhh," said Clay, creeping through the tall weeds with Isaac. Too late. Rebel bullets sang past them and they took off running. "Must be Home Guard," Clay panted as they ran. Shouts rose behind them, Rebs giving chase. He and Isaac had been on the run for weeks, heading north out of Dixieland. But there were handbills everywhere offering rewards for them, so they ran by night.

Isaac set the tempo and Clay told stories to keep their spirits up. Mostly stories about close scrapes and getting away. And the more stories he told, the softer the shouts behind them grew. They came to a rill and ran upstream a few hundred yards, then out into a meadow, where they finally slowed to a walk.

"You think this is Arkansas yet?" wondered Isaac.

"If it ain't, I'm gonna lie down 'til it is," Clay grinned and flopped onto his back.

Isaac kicked him. "Get up, fool, 'less you want to swing from a Dixie tree. Get up!"

Clay stood. Put a rope around his neck. Pulled it straight up, lifting himself to the top of a gallows, yanking on the end of the rope to make it taut…

Clay opened his eyes, holding his breath against the frightening turn in the dream. He was still in Allie's bed, though, no danger, no ropes. He let out his breath slowly. Unclenched his muscles, breathed easier. So happy to be here, just here. He turned on his side and went back to sleep.

Jersey doused the corn field with coal oil along two sides. The farm was south of the river but owned by a Confederate couple who was a big supplier of corn meal to the Rebel Cause. She'd been told where to find the place by Mr. Pierce, who showed her a map of the area, with the best escape routes. She'd thanked him for giving her meaningful work again, and he'd thanked her for her service.

She held a kerosene lamp turned to its lowest flame. When she'd used up all her coal oil she lit the corn field at the edges in three places and tossed the lamp to the center of the field, where it puffed into flame. And was quickly followed by a bullet whipping past her into the stalks; followed by the gunshot report. Then two more shots—the farmer and his wife barely forty yards away, letting loose on Jersey with all the firepower they had. Then came the dogs. Jersey ran.

She crawled through a hole she'd dug under a briar patch that would slow the dogs, and kept running. As she ran, she took some raw beef slices she had in her pocket, rubbed them in her armpits and threw them in her wake—causing the barking to pause only momentarily as her pursuers gobbled up the meat.

When she ran out of those diversions she ran harder, but the dogs kept getting closer—until she heard them right at her heels. She stopped abruptly, panting, and held out her hands to the four snarling beasts. But as they ran into her, they smelled her hands—hands that had so recently been holding their treats—so they paused even further, to smell her all over. By the time they got to her armpits—the strongest odor on the beef they'd just devoured—they were in love with this woman, and commenced to licking her all over, especially the pocket where she'd been holding the meat chunks.

She sat down and vigorously petted them all, wrestling playfully and pulling their ears as their tails wagged. After a few minutes of that she shooed them away, back to their farmers, and walked off in the other direction, her path lit by the dim orange glow of the now distant corn fire.

She surely loved her work.

As soon as Allie walked in her front door, she saw Moon smacking his lips. "That the only way you can say hello to me?" she teased. But she went directly to feeding him again. She thought he might be putting on a pound or two, which was a good thing; and besides, she found feeding him to be a settling activity when she was confused, or excited, or angry. Right now, just excited.

"I have the finest news," she started, resting the spoonful of cornmeal between his lips. "*Senor* Quintero just told me Colonel Ford is organizin' a force to take Fort Ringgold back from the Yanks. That's just a stone's throw from Brownsville. But the most excitin' development is General Taylor's army's goin' to ambush that Yankee march up the Red. Surround 'em at Mansfield, below Shreveport. And can you believe it, General Bee has been made a field commander. He got so shamed escapin' Brownsville, I guess they're givin' him a second chance. I do hope he's up to the task..."

While she talked, Clay heard it all—awakened by the sound of her voice, and now eavesdropping with his ear to the door. He'd heard enough, though, to make him pale. What Allie was saying made him realize the Rebs knew all about the Union campaign and they were lying in wait.

He had to get this news to the Union General Staff so they could plan a counter strategy before they got surrounded. Pierce could get the news up to General Banks pretty quick. Clay just hoped it wasn't too late.

He quietly climbed out Allie's bedroom window, closed it, and ran.

CHAPTER 26

CLAY MET PIERCE IN the safe house, Pierce already distracted with a dozen other matters. "I haven't much time, I'm off in an hour to parley with Juarez. Lincoln's offered to help defeat Napoleon if Mexico grants all of lower California to the United States."

"Let's keep the United States united first, shall we? You have to telegraph General Banks. Taylor knows all about our assault up the Red River. He's lyin' in wait with thousands of troops. The Union forces will be crushed."

"The telegraph lines are all down again. And are you even sure of this?"

"We have to get word to Banks."

"We might send someone from the fort—but a Union soldier alone through all that Rebel territory, he might get through or he might not."

"All right." It tore him up to contemplate what he was about to suggest. "I'll go."

"I don't know that you should…"

"It was my bad intelligence that led to this. I need to fix what I broke. I can take a lighter up the coast, it'll cut the time gettin' there in half."

Pierce considered the options. Wilkes had a better chance than most—he knew the territory and could pass as a Reb—so Pierce penned a Letter of Passage. "This will get you through any Union lines. And here's a second letter, to be hand delivered to General Banks." He walked Clay to a wall map. "Take your ship here, to the mouth of the

Mermentau. There's a Confederate horse depot there. Steal a fast one and ride him north to Natchitoches. You can make it in a day and a half. Banks should be right there."

Clay studied the map. "That's through 160 miles of dug in Rebel troops."

"If you don't make it maybe the telegraph lines will be back up in time. If not…" Pierce squeezed his shoulder. "Use your charm."

The first person Clayton tried to charm was Quintero, from whom he wanted to get some unwitting documentary assistance, and whom he found in the dressing room of the new diva, giving her advice on which gown to wear. Clay pulled him into the hallway, shutting the door, leaving the diva in a snit.

"Agustin, I have critical news. The Yanks have learned of the Reb ambush up the Red and mean to outflank our boys."

Quintero wasn't sure what to make of this information coming from a Northern agent. "I suppose we must send our troops a message to that effect?"

"Telegraph is down. I'm goin' myself to warn them, but I'll need fresh mounts in Creole. I thought you might authorize that with the Confederate camp there."

"Of course, of course. Come to my office."

In his room Quintero took a leaf of Confederate stationary, wrote a brief letter of authorization and put it in an envelope with his official seal embossed in wax on the front flap. "This orders them to give you two horses. I pray you get there in time."

"Old friend, I thank you. As does our country." He left to finalize details.

"And *my* country thanks *you*," Quintero said softly. "May you burn in hell."

✳ ✳ ✳

Zhi Li took Hermano by the hand. "Come. You help carry food."

He was reluctant to leave his assigned chair by the water pump but

351

Zhi Li's forceful personality convinced him otherwise. She led him to the back door, piled a crate of lettuce into his arms and escorted him to the kitchen, where Milagra took the lettuce from him. "You a good kitchen helper now, Hermano, *bueno!*"

For thank you, Zhi Li gave him a piece of rice candy. He followed her around the rest of the day. When Clayton entered the casino later, she went to him with Hermano at her side, listening attentively to see if any of their conversation involved rice candy.

"I have good idea," Zhi Li said to Clay. "We put opium house behind casino."

"Absolutely not. Poppy users don't spend their money gamblin' or drinkin'."

"We offer free pipe full to anyone who have winning streak."

He had to smile. "I admire your business sense. But no." He left her grumpy, as he noticed Captain Smolleigh toast Captain Solomon and exit Brave River. Looked like a formal goodbye to Wilkes, so he strolled over to Solomon's table and sat down, as Solomon went to tuning his cigar-box fiddle.

"You smile whenever you hear my viole," said Ryburn.

"I do?" Clayton had a flash memory of a broken fiddle, a crying boy. But he put it out of his head. "I could never play such a contraption."

"And I cannae sing, yet I do it all the time, and make up songs to boot. Mayhap I'll make one up about you."

"Any proper song about me would have to be lies and half-lies." He gestured to the doorway Captain Smolleigh had just exited. "What news from the *Sea Queen*?"

"They've off-loaded all their rifles and tin. If they can fill the hold with all the cotton on the Bagdad docks tomorrow, they sail for home at dawn the next day."

Clayton heard a longing in the old sea captain's voice. "Does it make you wish to sail home yourself?" he asked.

"Scotland has naught for me but foggy memories, I've nae home there now," Ryburn answered. He put his fiddle to chin and began playing a sweet highland air.

Clay closed his eyes and let the strain soothe his own troubled waters. He felt a growing kinship with the old would-be buccanneer, a kind of brotherhood of the outlaw heart. It brought him back to the moment at hand. "I want you to sail me up the coast, to the mouth of the Mermentau, near Creole."

"What's there?"

"A horse to carry me up to Natchitoches."

"Ned's all set to take me to Lafitte's gold."

"I have to move right now. But you needn't wait at the river for me. Bring Ned along and after you drop me off you can go get as rich as you please."

As Solomon nodded and took off to ready the ship, Clayton found Zhi Li again, Hermano watching her closely. "I'll be gone for a while," said Wilkes. "A long while, maybe. You're in charge until I get back."

She looked into his eyes. "You go danger now."

He avoided a direct response. "I'll tell Jim and Rheumy and the others to do what you say." He patted Hermano. "Zhi Li is your new boss until I come back, Hermano. Don't give her any trouble."

"I will burn joss for you," said Zhi Li.

"Whatever your religion says. Go ahead on and burn you some joss for me. I'll likely burn in hell for you. That's my religion." But the talk with Solomon about going home gave him another idea. "Now tell me where I can find Dinah."

Zhi Li took him to the laundry room, where Dinah was folding clothes, looking stronger. She jumped at loud noises less often; still not speaking, though.

"Good afternoon, Dinah, are you well?" She nodded warmly. "Good. I've been meanin' to ask—do you still want to go home? Back to England, I mean, to your family."

She looked uncertainly at Zhi Li, lip quivering.

Clayton went on, "I've been advised Captain Smolleigh is taking the *Sea Queen* to England on the tide. I've asked him before if he'd give you passage, and he agreed."

She looked scared; darted a glance at Zhi Li again and ran out of the room.

Clayton looked confused. "What happened?"

"She not want go England. We her family now." She shook her head at Clayton's ignorance, and walked away.

He went back into the casino and sat beside Russell at the bar. "I'm goin' away for a couple weeks. I want you to look after Allie. Make sure she has what she needs. And tell her…" He didn't know how to finish the sentence.

Russell took a closer look at him. "That sounds like more than a couple weeks. Where are you off to?"

He trusted Russell more than most, but it was best if he said no more. Probably shouldn't even have told the two he did he was leaving. But plans had to be made for unforeseeable circumstances. And he was, after all, heading for the front lines, where he'd once promised himself he'd never go.

"Finding parts for a new ice machine. We all know how that ended up last time."

As he started upstairs he had a last thought and signaled Zhi Li to follow him, with Hermano. He took them up to the roof. Walking Hermano to the huge cistern, he said, "I just want you to see how important your work is, old son. All this water is your doin', from that pumpin' you work at down in the casino."

Hermano squinted at the great vat, then walked over to the pigeon coop, where he stared in wonder at the cooing birds. Clay pulled out Madeira and petted her.

"This is Madeira, she's my favorite, but don't tell the others," Clay told Hermano. He passed the quivering pigeon to the gentle man. "Go on, you pet her. But be tender."

Hermano stroked the bird with great care and a sense of joy.

"You let him do this," Clay said to Zhi Li. "Food and water in the cage. They like the petting, too."

He left them there, went down to his room to pack a few things and exited by the back door, so nobody knew he was gone.

It was smooth sailing with Solomon and Ned, hugging the coastline between Padre Island and the mainland. They manned the *Buccaneer* themselves, Clayton helping. It was two days of good wind, tall tales,

Solomon's cigar-box tunes, Ned's descriptions of Lafitte's cave, the Hell Dog, the ghost ship; and everyone's ease in each other's company. Clayton floated in this peaceful bubble, disconnected from the skewed complexities of what was behind him, the fearful uncertainty of what lay ahead, lost in the sad Scottish tunes of Solomon's fiddle, feeling it bring him back to a time of childhood fiddles and banjos, some young year before the reality of the world crushed him. Until the weather turned and the waves began to roll and kick a little…

Isaac kicked him. "Get up, fool, 'less you want to swing from a Dixie tree. Get up…"

He tried to get up but he found himself already standing, not under a Dixie tree, but on a Dixie scaffold. A hooded Hangman was putting the rope around his neck and asking him his last words, but his mouth was too damn dry. "Isaac?" he said, looking around.

"I'm long gone," said Isaac. But there was Allie in the crowd. Everyone he knew in Matamoros was there, drinking, laughing. It was a Celebration Hanging.

"Ain't the war over yet?" he asked the Hangman. "Not for you," came the reply, and he pulled the lever. The trap door opened and Clay felt himself falling, but he yanked off the Hangman's hood as he dropped, the wind rushing past his face…

He jumped awake, top of the third day, the wind buffeting him as he sat up on deck, the ship rolling in the following seas. "Just in time," Solomon called out, and Ned chuckled, shortening sail. "There's the mouth of the Mermentau for your pleasure."

As they weighed anchor Clayton stood, shaky from his dream. Taking it as a warning he decided to break the seal on Quintero's safe passage letter, to see what accords he might be given when he landed. But the letter instructed anyone who read it to seize the man who carried it and imprison him for high treason. Clayton felt a great sadness—for the loss of his friendship with Quintero, who clearly knew Clayton was a spy for the North. First Isaac gone, now Quintero turned against him, he felt fully adrift.

But how did Quintero find out? Tinbury might have known from overhearing Pierce say something—and Tinbury was fool enough to let something slip in the wrong quarters. Jessup, maybe. Or Odeel had put it together from the scuffle at Pierce's, and somehow got his notions back from prison to Quintero. No matter. What was done was done. He just had to move forward on his own now.

So he'd have to go through hostile Rebel territory without papers, using only his guile. All right, he'd made it through worse before. He just hoped he could survive on his wits alone, without resorting to combat. He could generally hold his own in a short fight but it wasn't his strong suit and he avoided it if he could.

"Shall we wait for you?" asked Solomon.

"Better if you left and came back. It's a 30-hour ride to where I'm goin', a day once I'm there, a day and a half back, that's four days. Add another for complications, that's five. If you could drift back here then, I'd be obliged. If I'm not here in seven you'd best be on your way."

They hoisted anchor and sailed out to deeper waters as Clayton swam to shore, to deep waters of his own.

The Rebel camp in Creole was fairly big. Scores of Graycoats lounged around cooking imitation coffee and playing homesick music amidst a patchwork of tents. One small remuda was penned in by ropes strung around a grove of trees 50 yards beyond the main campfires. Clayton sat in the brush that grew a hundred yards inland from the riverside, watching for half an hour, devising a plan. It was mid-morning and there wasn't time to wait until nightfall to steal a horse, so he had to rely on malarkey. Pulling out his thickest Louisiana accent he stumbled from the brush. "He'p me, dear God!"

A picket with a breech loader ran up to help the ailing civilian. He couldn't have been older than 16, and practically shaking with nerves. "Halt! Who goes there?"

"Y'all got eyes, don't you, Johnny? Gimme a hand, here." He fell to his knees. The boy looked back at the camp for assistance, but none was coming so he helped Clayton to his feet. "I got to get to my wife in Lafayette, son. She's havin' a baby."

"Where'd you come from? How come you're all wet?"

"Blockade runner on his way to Galveston dropped me off. Said you boys had horses I might could buy."

"I don't believe the Cap'n'll let you have no horse, but you kin ask him. Come on."

Last thing Clayton wanted to do was talk to a captain. "Lead the way, son," he said. When the boy turned toward the camp, Clayton hit him twice on the head, knocking him out good. "I am sorry, boy."

He dragged the kid into the bushes, took off the boy's gray uniform and dressed in it. About two sizes too small but might make do with luck. He balled his own clothes up in his kit bag, put the picket's rifle over his shoulder and marched into camp bold as you please.

He didn't look anyone in the eyes, just walked straight ahead like he had business to take care of. Nobody paid attention to him. He made it through the core of the encampment, nearing the horses, when he heard the shouts. He cast a glance behind to see the naked sentry waving his arms, bellowing like hell. Men in the camp were walking toward the boy but Clayton just kept on to the makeshift corral.

He picked a powerful sorrel, grabbed a saddle off the ground and cinched it to the animal. He wanted to take a second horse along, for when this one gave out, but a couple men were approaching him now. So he pulled down the ropes of the corral, jumped in the saddle and drove all the ponies ahead of him until they scattered in every direction, while he rode north to diminishing shouts and useless gunshots. He felt bad for that poor young perimeter guard, and whatever his punishment would be.

He rode hard for a few hours, walked his horse for an hour, then picked up the pace again. The terrain was easy, with lots of streams for his mount to drink from and neither civilians nor soldiers to interfere. Pierce had told him due north from the Mermentau, and that's what he did. If his luck held he might even find a farmhouse by nightfall where he could buy, trade or steal a fresh mount.

Plans in the wild were rarely cooperative, though. It was late afternoon when his tired animal stepped in a gopher hole and fell sideways. Clay jumped off before he got hurt, but the horse broke his leg and wouldn't get up. Clay slumped to the ground against the beast, taking a measure of rest as he contemplated what to do.

Just keep walking, is all he could see open to him. He'd passed a few homesteads on the way; he expected he'd run into one again, and somehow promote himself another ride. Meanwhile he was beat and thought a short rest might make his prospects appear rosier. There was the problem of his horse, too. He'd never been able to kill an animal and he didn't think he could do for this one. He didn't want it to suffer, though. So instead of the nap he craved, he hunted for a stick to bind to the creature's leg, that it might be able to limp its way to the smell of other horses.

That plan wasn't destined to work out either, though: in the distant south, Clayton heard hoofbeats. Two horses, it sounded like, heading his way. Likely Reb soldiers from Camp Creole ordered to chase down the horsethief. Wilkes needed a new plan quick.

There was a twisted oak about 50 feet away, newer limbs arching up from an ancient lightning scar. Clayton pulled off the Reb jacket he'd taken from the young guard and wound it tightly around his horse's ankle to give the poor creature's leg some support. He tugged gently on her reins, coaxing her up. But each time she tried to rise, she settled back onto her side, unable to muster the strength to overcome the pain.

In the distance the hoofbeats got louder. Clayton hated doing it, but he had no choice. He yanked the reins hard and shouted at the lame animal. "Get up, damn you! Get up!" he yelled, kicking her flank. The horse lurched upright and stood unsteadily.

"That's a good girl," he whispered now, petting her cheek. "Come on, it's not far."

He walked her, limping every step to the base of the oak tree, and gently pulled her down to the ground again. There was a bad moment when her leg gave and she made a horrible, almost human sound. Clay winced. She finally lay on her side, breathing deeply, exhausted.

He stood on the saddle and hoisted himself up to the lowest branch. From there he climbed two limbs higher and crouched in the thick foliage, waiting. Wasn't a long wait.

Two riders thundered up a hundred yards away; pointed at the horse splayed out at the base of the oak and rode up to it. As they reached the tree Clay looked down on them. One was a tough old goat, a Sergeant likely a veteran of many battles; Clayton didn't think he could win a close-quarters fight with him. The other was the young sentry Clayton had knocked out. The kid was probably being given a chance to redeem himself by catching the thief who'd taken his clothes. Clayton wasn't too scared of him; on the other hand, the boy was probably more inclined to fight to the death than be humiliated a second time. It was the grizzled old Sergeant who dismounted to examine the lame horse. He crouched down, patted the horse's flank, checked the Confederate jacket binding its leg. He looked at the boy, who was still mounted, and said something.

As the Sergeant stood up, Clay jumped. He landed with his feet squarely on the man's shoulders, jamming down with as much force as he could. The Sergeant fell hard, arms akimbo, his forehead planting onto a large flat rock. He lay still; maybe dead.

Clayton immediately jumped up as the young sentry jumped down, drawing his pistol. Clay tackled him and they rolled around punching, wrestling, struggling for the gun. The kid fought like a maniac, desperate for revenge. But even when Clay got stunned by a flailing elbow, he knew not to let go of the gun; and as they rolled into the downed horse, the weapon went off.

The boy yelped. Clayton yanked free and stood up, holding the gun. They both looked at the Reb's side, bleeding freely. "I'm shot bad," he rasped, his voice breaking.

Clay knelt beside him and examined the wound. Through and through the left flank, just above the hip bone. "This is just a bad flesh wound," Clayton tried to sound reassuring. "Not so serious as a center belly shot."

"I'm bleedin' and it won't stop."

Clay wadded up his shirt, pressed it to the entry wound and wrapped it around to the other hole. "You push on this, push hard, it'll clot the blood." He stood up. "I'll send somebody back for you soon as I run into a soul."

"You ain't gonna leave me here?"

"You can't ride, it'll just make the bleedin' go faster, and I can't stay, I'll be hung for a horse thief, and too many lives depend on me gettin' where I'm goin'."

"You leavin' me to die." It wasn't an accusation, it was a realization, and his eyes turned hollow as he saw his fate coming.

Clayton transferred his gear from his own crippled horse's saddlebags to the Sergeant's, donning a new shirt as he did. Then he mounted the officer's horse, with last words to the gunshot sentry. "I'm sorry, son. You're a brave man to've tangled with me again. I hope to God this war gets done with soon."

He took a last look at the wreckage he was leaving—one soldier likely dead, one likely to die, and a horse likely to be killed by the next passing stranger. This is why he fled the army, why he settled in Mexico. This is why he felt so homeless in his heart.

He wheeled the Reb horse around and rode north.

*　*　*

He drove the horse hard into the night until he hit what he thought was the Red River somewhere between Alexandria and Natchitoches. By morning the poor steed was walking, but barely. Clayton began seeing small clusters of Union soldiers walking north up the river. He made sure his horse had no identifying Confederate markings and walked it to the river, shouting at the Federals as he went.

"Hold it right there, pard," came the voice of a guard stepping out of the trees. "Hands up and state your business."

With huge relief Clayton raised his arms and smiled. "I surely am glad to see you, Corporal."

"Don't know why that is, you talk so Dixie."

"Well, this is where I'm from, but I have an urgent message for General Banks from Union Ambassador Pierce in Matamoros. I'm unarmed, so you can tie my hands up without a fight. Just take me to the General so I can give him the dispatch."

"Let me see it first."

3 6 0

"That wasn't my instructions. My instructions was put it in the hands of General Banks and I believe we'd both be better off if you helped me do that."

Something about his tone more or less convinced the sentry, though he wasn't about to take any chances. He turned Clay around, bound his wrists together with a leather thong, searched him for weapons and put him in the back of a supply wagon that was rolling by. "You sit on your hands in there. I'm gonna ride behind so I can keep an eye on you. Take us a couple hours to get there."

They tethered Clay's horse to the tailgate and headed upriver. It was a slow trek but Clayton was so grateful for the rest he dozed most of the trip. Every once in a while he'd stick his head up to look around. Union forces were everywhere now, thousands of them strung out along maybe 20 miles of road, walking casual as a picnic. Every few miles an ironclad chugged upstream.

At last they came to a bivouac of hundreds of men, some organized into units, some just lollygagging around.

"This it?" Clay shouted to the sentry riding behind him.

"No and be quiet. General Banks is still a ways up, this is Colonel Dye's command."

"He knows me! He knows me. You go get him, he'll vouch for me and he'll get us movin' a sight quicker than you are." He saw Dye inspecting some artillery and stood up in the wagon shouting. "Colonel Dye! Colonel Dye, over here!"

"You shut up!" protested the sentry, but Clay yelled louder.

"Colonel Dye, it's Clayton Wilkes, I have important news!"

Dye squinted at Clay. Clay waved. There was finally some recognition and Dye approached. When he got near, he was surprised. "My word, Wilkes, what are you doing up here?"

"I have urgent news for General Banks, direct from Ambassador Pierce, who couldn't telegraph because the lines are cut all over the place."

"Telegraph what?" Dye wanted to know.

Clay hesitated. The information was meant for Banks alone, but he needed some high level allies if he was going to be in time. "Sir, if you could take me a few paces away so we might talk in private?"

Dye helped him down from the wagon, cut his binding and walked him out of earshot.

"You're marchin' into a trap, Colonel. The Rebs know you're comin' and they lie in wait. You need to pull back, regroup and make a new plan."

"Where is this supposed ambush meant to occur?" He sounded unconvinced.

"Sir, if you could take me to General Banks, we could all have a serious talk on that subject."

Dye paused only slightly—excited at the possibility of leading the charge, if this ambush was true. He called for two fresh mounts and rode north with Clayton, escorted by a three-man guard.

They reached Banks's headquarters an hour later at a pretty good clip. It was a large encampment full of tents, corrals, artillery and more men than Clayton could count, all sequestered in an expanse of willow groves. Dye went into the General's tent and motioned Clayton in a few moments later. Clay entered the large canvas enclosure to find Banks poring over a big map laid out on two tables, surrounded by officers; and Teddy Beale standing arears. Their eyes met with a jolt of surprise, until Banks spoke.

"All right, let's see the news from Pierce," he demanded without preamble.

Clayton reached into his shirt to retrieve the letters from Pierce—with the hollow realization it was in the shirt he'd used to stanch the Rebel sentry's gunshot wound. "Sir, I lost the dispatch in a fight with a Reb who was tryin' to stop me. But the long and the short of it is, the Rebs know your plans and they have amassed a secret army in hidin', waitin' to pounce on you."

There was a long silence as Banks mulled over the news. At last he shook his head. "I don't buy it. We have scouts out and about. I'd have heard about any extra Rebel activity in the area."

"Sir, I believe you need to retreat and regroup. Maybe design a flankin' attack."

"I'd be happy to lead such a charge," Dye broke in before anyone else got the assignment.

Banks thought about it. Shook his head again. "I like our plan. Our forces along the river should muster up here by the end of tomorrow. We'll attack at dawn the next morning." He saw the protest rising in Clay's face. "We have overwhelming force, Mr. Wilkes. I'm not concerned about any counterattacks those Dixie boys may try to stage."

"General, if I may," said Colonel Dye. "I've been told by Ambassador Pierce this man's intelligence is impeccable. Dispatch or no, I'm inclined to take him at his word. Seems to me letting me lead a couple battalions to a wide flanking position might cost us a day or two, but it would be good insurance against an unforeseen counterattack."

"I'd hardly call it unforeseen at this point," said Clayton.

Banks looked annoyed at Clayton, but he did give the matter another second of thought before shaking his head. "No, we'll proceed as planned. That's all, Colonel."

Dye shrugged at Clay, as if to say that was the best he could do. Clayton looked around the room for other support, but none was coming. The only thing he saw was Jensen the deserter, still in shackles, seated in a shadowy corner.

"Show this gentleman to the mess tent and give him some grub," Banks ordered one of the Lieutenants. "I'm sure he meant well and it looks like he's had a hard ride."

"I can take him, sir," said Teddy.

Banks gestured in the affirmative and went back to his map. "Dye, come look at this map, I'll show you some strategy that might get you a promotion yet."

Teddy gestured to Clayton. "This way, if you please."

They walked side by side toward the mess tent until Teddy took a detour into a riverside growth of weeping willows. They stood face to face.

"I'm right about this," said Clayton. "We need to get you out of here before the wrath of God comes down on this army."

"It's the wrath of the Reb Army I came here to fight. I don't guess I'm about to give up on that now."

"It's goin' to be a rout, though. It's just…senseless."

"I wanted into the war and I got it. But I admire your concern for my well-being."

"Well…God bless you, then. I never was much good in a fair fight, so I'm bound for gettin' back to Mexico."

They stared, memorizing each other's face like this was a true goodbye; and kissed, not long, but deeply felt. Not long because it was interrupted by gunshots. They jumped apart, unsure where the reports had come from. Pretty soon shouts could be heard downriver, so they ran that way.

What they found was a circle of yammering soldiers. When Clay pushed his way through, he saw Jensen on the ground, dead, his hands still chained.

"Once a deserter always a deserter," said a young captain who was reloading his gun. "I've had my eye on that yellow dog since the day he showed up in camp. I wasn't about to let him betray his country again."

There were general congratulations and retellings of the event as Clayton eased over to the mess tent. Teddy had somehow disappeared but Clay was hungry, thirsty, exhausted and despondent. He got himself a plate of beans, went back to the willow grove where he'd said goodbye to Teddy, ate and curled up under graceful branches that swayed in the cool river breeze like ribbons of green silk.

Isaac's caravan snaked down the Sonoita River until it came to Governor Pesqueira's Mexican Army of Resistance, 400 strong. When Isaac was shown into the *Juarista's* tent, Pesqueira hugged the colonist leader, so glad was he to see reinforcements of any kind, even if they were ragtag Negro runaways.

"You are most welcome, *amigo*, and not one day too soon." His English was good, from the year he'd spent in an American jail at the end of the war for Texas.

"Too soon for what?" asked Isaac.

"We have beaten back the French *puta*, we but they will return in force."

"What's your plan?"

"*Our* plan, *amigo*. *Our* plan is I circle my army around behind the invader while you stay here to beat them back into my fist, to crush them."

"How many will come?"

"Many, I think. But you have time to build a fortification. There are 10,000 rocks here to collect for making walls. And if you build them strong, they will be the first homes on your new land." He stretched his arm out. "This is all yours, now, by Grant. Defend it with your lives, and your honor."

As they exited the tent Pesqueira called out to his Lieutenants. *"Vamanos! Atacamos al sur!"* His men cheered, gathered their gear, mounted up and rode off at speed, splashing through the shallow Sonoita River.

Isaac turned slowly 360 degrees. The river to the immediate south, smooth and wide, flowing west; miles of sandy scrub, covered with rocks, fist-sized to chair-sized; low hills to the north, and beyond that the United States, still disunited. He smiled, deeply content. This land belonged to his people now. After all they'd suffered he'd taken his Israelites through the desert to the Promised Land. And now, by God, he was going to keep the promise. "Salem!" he called out. "Jake!"

His captains came running and he handed out instructions. "French Army is on its way. We'll make a stand here. Want you to organize these boulders into two walls that meet at a corner. The children can collect rocks to pile on—put Bigboy in charge of that. Dig a trench all around, fill it with kerosene."

"Sounds like a fort to me."

"Is a fort. Fort New America. This is our home now."

*　*　*

Solomon walked Ned over the sandy island to the gnarled tree that marked the sacred burial site. The deeper they dug, the more like hardened tar was the matrix; but everywhere throughout, bones beyond counting! The gem-hardened skeletal remains of the First Men, the great Aztec gods. Tokens of power beyond ken: teeth the size of a man's fist, spines like a whale spine; claws and hooves and antlers and tusks, leg bones like trees, finger bones the size of bananas. And skulls! One of a giant cat, with Bowie-knife-sized curving fangs; a towering bear skeleton, all askew but buried more or less upright in the tar, as if it were standing semi-erect, howling at the world's surface above it to be set free. You could almost hear the howl.

"Bless me, Ryburn, it makes me shaky to see and I haven't had a drink in days."

"More valuable far than pirate gold, Ned, and it's yours as much as mine now."

Ned held up a ring of stone, three inches across—once a mastodon's eye socket. "It's like, it's like…the jewelry o' the gods."

"Take that piece, if you fancy it. All of it will protect you, so take what you want."

There were fragments of all sizes, from knuckles to breast bones to brainpans. As the old sailors sorted them, they told stories of imagined interactions between these ancient gods, intermingling them with stories they'd told all their lives about sea monsters and selkies, giant squid and demon whale. When they'd each taken the tokens they wanted and reburied the rest, Ned sat back with a pile of stony riches between his legs and a gaze of awe on his face.

"I'll tell you this, Ryburn Solomon. When we get back it'll be my turn to take you to Lafitte's cave and his chests of plunder. I've been stingy with sharing its whereabouts with you before and I tell you for that I'm sorry—though I truly did want to spare you the curse of the Hell Dog I brought on meself for takin' the bag o' dubloons I did. But you've been a square mate to me and you deserve whatever you can get there."

He stood, helping to support himself with a four-foot, mineralized antelope ulna he appropriated for a walking stick; and sliding the mastodon eye-socket over his wrist like a bracelet, he bowed deep to his dear friend.

And Solomon bowed back.

It was dark the next time Clayton opened his eyes. Small campfires spread across the makeshift barracks, hidden from view by the thick foliage all around the campsite. He washed his face in the river.

What folly this was. So much death, some of it by his own hand. Thousands of men were about to charge bravely into the mouth of Hades. He knew he had to get out. It would be too painful to watch the disaster unfold before his eyes. So he walked around camp until he found the horse he'd come in on, still tied to the supply wagon, but with a feed bag hooked around her nose. He took off the bag, gave her a water bucket, saddled her, climbed up and walked her out of camp.

A few hours later he passed the end of the troop line, still some miles out of the main muster. Most soldiers were bedded down. An hour after that he was getting sleepy himself once more, and since he wanted to ride hard all day he thought it wouldn't be a bad idea to give himself and his pony one last rest stop. He dismounted, walked his horse into a falling-down barn near some poplars and lay down.

The barn reminded him of the structure he and Isaac had bought when they first got to Matamoros. It had been a long journey getting there—to Colorado, then south to Arizona before crossing over into Mexico and heading for the Gulf. By Matamoros they were tired of running, and Mexico meant nobody likely to chase them. So they bought the barn, hired laborers and built Brave River.

He climbed a broken ladder to the loft now and lay down in the hay. A peaceful feeling, smelling of slower times and sheltering barns...

He pulled Allie by the wrist into her father's barn, running and giggling up to the hayloft. "Sshh," she said, "if my brothers hear us they'll kill you."

"I'll die with a smile on my lips," he whispered and kissed her. She kissed him back harder, their hands finding all the sweet spots, urgency growing.

"Hurry," she whispered. "I can't wait one more second."

As they made love, the rhythm was matched by the sound of flapping wings, like doves fluttering at dusk. Clay looked out the loft window, seeing the flock coming right at him, their fluttering feathers made of shadow, Allie's panting getting louder and...

BLAM! He was falling through the trapdoor, the rope around his neck! BLAM! Pulling off the Hangman's hood, the executioner's death-mask face looking down at him, receding as Clay fell BLAM while people in the crowd were shooting guns in the air BLAM...!

Clay jolted awake in the abandoned Louisiana barn, realizing he was hearing cannonfire. Lots of it, from both sides of the river. This was the Rebel ambush, flanking the strung-out Northern troops and attacking while they slept, two days before their own Red River assault was scheduled to commence. In the distance to the north he could see the dim flashes of bombs bursting in a pattern surrounding the main of Banks's army. He was glad he'd gotten to bid Teddy farewell; he was glad he got to Banks in time to warn him, though his warning had been ignored. He could at least feel like he'd done his best. Nobody could blame him for failing. Nobody except himself.

He rode back down to Creole without incident, at a more leisurely pace than he'd come up. He expected to make it back to the rendezvous site within the seven-day window he'd agree upon with Solomon— even giving Camp Creole a wide berth south and then riding back up the beach to the Mermentau. Sure enough, the *Buccaneer* was waiting. Solomon rowed a dinghy to shore and brought Clay back to the ship where Ned was sick with fever. They set a course home. Dr. Hawks would doubtless be a help.

Solomon didn't ask about Clayton's seven days. Clay could only think that God had made everything in that time; and in that time Clay had lost an army.

CHAPTER 27

Rip Ford's 1200 Rangers attacked Fort Ringgold at dusk, from the west, so the setting sun was in the Union force's eyes. It was a tactic Rip favored, since the troops in the fort would be tired as well as blinded. It was a hot firefight but the Rebs knew the good vantage points and the weak spots in the fort's defenses. Ford lost half a dozen men to rifle fire before he realized it was coming from outside the fort, not inside. And from several positions. There were snipers in the hills.

He sent Jessup and five others out into the bush, looking for muzzle flash. Three of them saw the spark in low hills to the north. They circled the spot until another flash erupted 30 yards south of one of the Rangers, who opened fire on the sniper.

"I got one!" he shouted to his comrades. But when they rushed the site, they found only a slight Negro girl, wounded, pregnant, gripping a fine Henry repeater and grimacing in pain. He took the long gun from her. "How many of you are there, girl?"

"Just me," she said. There was a bullet wound in her upper right chest, but it was her belly she gripped with hurting.

"Come on now, you can tell me. We won't hurt 'em, just want to round 'em up."

Jessup came trotting up and stopped in amazement. "That's Jersey."

"You know this girl?"

"I do. Used to be the slave of a fine lady I know."

Jersey moaned loudly once, squeezing her belly. "Ima have my baby now."

The men became uneasy at that. The fight for the fort was still raging and every one of them would rather have been engaged down there. "You boys go on," said Jessup. "I'll tend to this." They all left in a hurry as Jessup sat beside Jersey. "I don't know a thing about deliverin' a baby into the world."

"Just get me back to Miss Allie. She'll know what to do."

Cheers and whoops could be heard down at the fort—the battle was over, the Bluecoats surrendered, the Rangers overrunning the grounds.

"I don't know that I can do that, Jersey. You killed some o' these men."

"I'm dyin' too. Can't matter to y'all where I do it. Just want my baby to be all right."

Jessup didn't think that was such a bad idea. And now with the fighting over he wouldn't have minded an excuse to ride a few hours down to see Allie for a day. "I'll see what I can do," he told her, and went down to the fort to talk to Rip.

"I doubt she'll last the night," he told Ford. "And I could spend a couple days in Matamoros, see if I can pick up any news about Yankee counterattacks."

Ford thought it made sense, now so close to Fort Brown, to get someone snooping around there. "All right. You can put her in a wagon and cross the river right here. One thing, though. This sniper girl don't die, you either bring her back for trial or execute her yourself, you hear? I won't have a mankiller walkin' around on my watch."

"Yes, sir, I'll do that. See you in a few days." And with that he drove a buggy up into the hills, put Jersey in back—she couldn't have weighed 90 pounds, even with the baby—crossed the *Rio* at the shallows below Fort Ringgold and trotted down the Mexican side of the river to Matamoros.

*　*　*

Soon as they landed, Clay helped Solomon get Ned to the Brownsville Hospital, where Dr. Hawks pointed out the rose spots on his chest, declared him to be ill with typhoid fever, and started in to cooling him down with wet compresses. Asked about his chances of survival, all she'd say was, "He's got a chance, same as you and me."

By the time Clay made it back to his room at Brave River it was dead night but he was far from sleepy. Too much churned inside to let him rest. He paced, he drank brandy. He rearranged slivers of stained glass on his fractured William Morris window, which had resisted all his attempts at recreating its original pattern. Until now. Suddenly as he looked at the collection of pieces on his workbench, a picture was emerging.

It had long obviously been a figure, more recently an angel. Now not only an angel, but a warrior angel with wings half-furled. Blue eyes, dark hair—like Allie, he thought—and raising high a sword of milky gray glass. Actually, Confederate grey. The picture coming together in the glass felt like a picture coming together in his life. And all at once he remembered his nightmare, his dream of dropping through the scaffold's trapdoor with the rope around his neck while he pulled off the Hangman's hood…and the Hangman's face was Allie.

He ran out of the room.

Clay knocked loudly on Allie's door until she opened it, wrapped in a dressing gown, holding a kerosene lamp.

"Clay, what on earth…"

He walked past her into the sitting room. "You're a spy for the South, aren't you. And you've been usin' me to help the Confederacy."

"Why, Clay, what utter nonsense…"

"And not just any old spy. You are responsible—and because of my stupidity, blinded by my feelin's for you, I am also responsible—for the rout of the Union Army now underway at Mansfield, on the Red."

"A rout, you say?"

"You misled me so the North wouldn't find out the Rebs were set to ambush them. No, not misled. Those letters from Mildred were likely forged by you, knowin' I'd read them. You conned me!"

"If you were conned, sir, it was because you stole those letters out of my desk, so don't you go gettin' so high-handed with me! You men! Gotta be so right all the time."

"Just need to be not wrong, Allie. You made me so wrong."

The shouting had brought the three children out of their shed to the back door, watching the fight with wide eyes. When Allie glanced at them, Bootsy said, "You yellin' so loud, you gwine wake up Moon."

"Y'all go back to bed. This is none of your concern."

Reluctantly they backed off into the darkness. Clay spoke in a rush.

"I can't believe I didn't put this together before now. I heard you say Quintero told you about the Southern ambush but it never occurred to me you were responsible for it. I mean, you even helped get rid of that traitor cousin of mine, I figured your heart *had* to be on the right side. But my feelin's for you clouded my thinkin' so bad I couldn't see you played me with a simple letter trap…"

She shouted back. "I helped you get rid of John Wilkes Booth because he was a foul human bein' and I am unable to tolerate such a person."

"But I guess you can tolerate General Bee all right, with all his slaves, and I suppose it would be fine with you if he shackled up Isaac!"

"At least I didn't open the back door to let thousands of Yankee marauders in to destroy the entire town of Brownsville!"

"The Rebel command did that when they blew up their own fort and ran away!"

"You're one to talk about runnin' away. You were supposed to come get me after Daddy annulled the marriage so we could run off together, but you never showed, you just run off by yourself."

"Well pardon me but I was savin' Isaac's life and sent you a pigeon tellin' you so. But I guess you couldn't wait a few more months, you rather marry some old rich man."

"What did you expect, when the father of my child abandons me and this kind elder gentleman offers to make sure I'm not an unwed mother and give my baby a name!" She was practically screaming now, as the frightened eyes of the children shown out in the dark, watching. Clay was dumbstruck silent by this last outburst.

"What baby?" he said quietly. "You had our baby?"

Resentment choked her words. "It died, Clay. In childbirth. That was the end of my love for you." But saying it took all the anger out of her heart; nothing left but hollow.

"You never said," he whispered.

"We've both been hidin' things from each other, Clay. We both know that, and we both hate it. Can't we stop?"

But he still couldn't unshoulder all the war-dead on his conscience, let alone this one, new, grievous, personal stillbirth. "Too many people killed on the Red, Allie. That's on both of us. You for trickin' me, me for lettin' myself get tricked. I can't see past that."

They just stood there silently, looking at the floor, when there was a great clamor in front, hooves and clanking wheels; and a haunted wailing that Allie thought was *la llorona* coming to get her. Instead, Jessup kicked open the door, Jersey in his arms.

"She's been shot and she's havin' her baby."

Allie directed him to put the wounded, moaning girl on the *chaise*.

"I just left Dr. Hawks at the hospital," said Clay. "Go bring her on a run, we'll try to take care here."

Jessup ran out as Clay opened the girl's shirt to examine her chest wound and Allie pulled down her pants to see the top of a baby's head peeking out.

"Dear Lord, it's comin' right now." She called out loudly. "Children!"

They showed up back at the door almost before she'd finished saying the word—they hadn't gone far. Allie shouted orders.

"Jersey's havin' her baby. Charles, you stoke you up a fire in the kitchen, boil a pot of water. Shonny, Miss Lacey lives a mile up the road, she's a midwife, you run like hell, bring her right back here. Bootsy, get some sheets over here and help me."

The children ran to their tasks as Clay examined Jersey's wound. "She's lost a lot of blood. Shoulder's shattered, but with luck it didn't hit the lung." He grabbed a pillow from the divan, pressed it hard against the girl's bullet hole. Jersey cried out louder.

By the time Bootsy hurried over with the sheets, the baby's head was fully out.

Clay looked down, stunned. "You ever delivered a baby before?" he asked Allie.

"I have," said Bootsy, putting one hand behind the child's head, easing one shoulder out, then the other. After that the whole baby slid out in a rush.

"I'll be damned," said Clay.

Jersey wailed to break the night. Allie put her hands under the baby's back as she and Bootsy raised it up between Jersey's legs, high enough for the poor girl to see.

"Jersey, looka here, you got a beautiful baby girl!"

Jersey opened her eyes for the first time and looked. Smiled and wept, all in one. Then her eyes closed, her head lolled to the side. No more breath passed her lips.

"She's gone," Clay said quietly. And the baby squawked a long, healthy cry.

Bootsy tied off the umbilical cord with a piece of string and cut it with a knife she always kept on her these days. There was no bleeding from Jersey's end of the cord. The women cleaned the newborn up as Clay swaddled Jersey's body in the sheets.

"Put her there," Allie said, and Clay lay the dead girl in bed beside Moon, pulling the sheet down from her face, nestling her against her husband as natural as he could.

"They look so peaceful there," said Allie. She began quietly crying. For Jersey, for this orphan baby, for the reopened wound of her own dead child, and the death of being with Clay. Bootsy put the blanket-wrapped newborn in Allie's arms, as a comfort.

But comfort was not to be had, and Allie didn't stop weeping. Clay could only stand aside, gazing at the carnage in the small room. There was a time when his life lay before him and everything seemed possible. Now everything only seemed over.

Shonny got back with Miss Lacey an hour later, but there was little for the midwife to do except examine the baby and declare it healthy. Allie thanked her, offered her tea, which she declined, and instructed Shonny to walk her back home.

Two hours after that Jessup showed up with Esther Hawks in tow, but there was naught for her to do, either. She agreed the baby was strong. She gave them a glass syringe without a needle, showing them how to fill it and push the plunger to feed the baby. Jessup took her back to the hospital.

Clay slept on the divan as Allie and Bootsy took turns feeding the baby, letting the other two children hold it between feeds.

Next morning Moon was dead too. When Jessup got back from Brownsville he and Clay dug a single grave for both corpses in the backyard—wasn't much bigger than a grave for one—Moon was so thin and Jersey so small. They dug it deep, though, for lack of coffin. They buried the couple wrapped in each other's arms and put Moon's carvings of his little people in with them. Covered them over while Allie held the baby.

"Ashes to ashes," said Clay. "We'll all be there soon enough. Here was a girl who made some new life on her way out. That's more than most of us can hope to do." He couldn't look at Allie.

"Amen," said Jessup, mostly because he knew Allie felt close to the runaway girl. In his heart he was relieved he didn't have to execute her, like Rip had ordered, so it seemed like a good outcome all around.

Allie quietly sang a few notes of the song Moon liked and Jersey teased him about. "*Camptown ladies sing this song, doo-dah, doo-dah…*" Then she faded out. The others thought that an odd thing to sing at a funeral service, but the world had become an odd place in all sorts of ways.

The children threw flowers on the grave, then made themselves scarce. The baby started crying again; but in the distance beyond that sound, Allie was sure she could hear the blameful moans of *la llorona*. Just to do something, she took the babe in her arms and nursed it with the doctor's syringe. Oddly, when the child stopped crying, so did the Wailing Woman.

Jessup said his awkward goodbyes. "I best do some snoopin' around Brownsville and tell Rip what I can find out. You be all right alone here?"

"I'm not alone. I got Charles and Shonny and Bootsy." She was feeling distant from him—from all men, at the moment—but she could see he wanted to say something as he stared at the baby in her arms.

"Well," he finally nodded, "she sure is black."

He tipped his hat and left. Allie sat down in a rocking chair and kept on nursing as she spoke to the child. "I believe that young man was put off by me bein' white, nursin' a black child. Well, good riddance, I say. We got enough trouble without worryin' about his finger waggin'. How about if I just read you the news of the day?"

She pulled Mildred's latest letter from a pocket in her apron and read to the baby. "*My dear Allie—I hope you are well. I must say I don't miss that Rio Grande. The magnolias of Louisiana are much more to my liking. And how you would love the excitement up here near the bombardments! Our heroes decimated the Union Army and harassed them all the way down the Red River to the Gulf of Mexico. My Hamilton had two horses shot out from under him, but he got right up on a third and back into the fray. I perceive we never truly know ourselves until faced with our deepest fears…*"

Allie put the letter down and talked to the baby, who stared up at her in wonder. "You know, child, I had a baby myself once. That was my greatest fear, and I faced it, though I don't know that I knew myself any better after that, as Mildred suggests. It was Clay's baby, we made it that sweet sweet night sneakin' into my daddy's barn. Once I knew I was in a family way that kind old Mr. Stoneman married me to give the baby his name—though I reckon that wasn't necessary in the end, was it?"

"Who give the baby its name?" asked Shonny, walking up.

"Mr. Stoneman, Shonny. But that was a different baby."

"Well, what *this* baby name? You know it yet?"

Allie considered. "I think her name is Rachel. That was my mama's name, and it's been out of circulation for a while."

"Rachel a pretty name. I'll go tell the others." She ran off.

Allie looked down at Rachel, whose eyes were fluttering into sleep. She wondered what it was like to be a mother and thought it must be nice. She could see herself being a mother to this child. It wasn't her own, like the one she'd lost so long ago; but it had the *feeling* of being hers, a warm, protective feeling. And Allie sure could use a measure of that right about now.

The first stone wall was nearly finished when scouts with telescopes called out the French were coming. Isaac ordered the wagons in two circles near the wall and rounded up all the children inside them. They had two small cannon, which he had placed behind the ends of the wall, and a hundred fused hand bombs to throw. The children were surrounded by men and women with handguns—folks who weren't good with a rifle. And a trench had been dug outside the stone wall, filled with kerosene and coal oil. They were ready as ever they could be. Isaac felt his chest swell with pride.

"This is our land!" shouted Isaac to his followers.

"Amen!" they shouted back, nearly 200 strong.

"Won't nobody take this from us!"

"Let my people go!"

"We been wanderin' in the desert too long!"

"This is our promised land!"

Isaac climbed up on the wagon to take a spyglass from one of the scouts. He raised it to his eye. His breath caught.

The French force was massive. It extended farther back than he could see, and spread wide to flank them. There must have been a thousand. This would be slaughter.

He considered surrendering right away but couldn't bear that. It would crush his people. There was nothing to do but fight. He looked at the scout who'd just seen what he saw. The man's eyes were wide with terror; he wanted Isaac to tell him what to do.

"We make our stand here and now!" Isaac yelled. "Hold your positions!"

When the French were 100 yards away and it was still impossible to see the end of their formation, everyone in the New American colony knew what was coming. But to die free, for their own land, beside friends, seemed something worth dying for.

Isaac gave the signal to the two cannoneers to fire at will—and they set off their charges. The cannon boomed and 5 seconds later explosions erupted in the midst of the French advance. When the French were close enough everyone opened fire. Many advancing troops fell—it was hard to miss them, so many so close. But men and women behind the wall were falling, too. One section of rock exploded with a ball from the advancing army, killing five colonists where they stood. The French were 50 yards away now; now 20. Colonists threw bombs. French soldiers died. Most kept coming.

Bigboy made sure all the children were armed with something—a stick, a rock, a knife if they had one. Hannah did the same with a dozen frail adults—pregnant women, old timers—and led them all in song, a spiritual. Suddenly a miraculous thing happened.

The French troops slowed. Officers shouted orders. The nearest phalanx stopped. There was yelling amongst them, and confusion—and then, dear God, they began to retreat. Faster and faster, running back into their own, it looked like 500 of them bunched up in a stumbling knot, and they were running away!

Isaac was too baffled to be joyous. Could his own people have proven too formidable? Were Pesqueira's troops attacking from behind the Bonapartists with such ferocity the French needed their whole army to turn and engage them? A huge grin filled his face, and he saw others smiling now, as well, standing up atop the wall with arms in the air, defiant.

But then a feeling came over him—the same feeling he'd had in the casino months ago, when that man had risen up behind him holding a billiard ball, to bash his brains in. A feeling of the hairs standing up on the back of his neck. So he kept turning now and saw, behind them, the real reason the French were fleeing.

It was a horde of Comanche coming down from the hills to the north. Three hundred, wild and savage, faces painted like demons, waving rifles, spears and bows, thundering down like they were fused to their horses, like they were mythological creatures come from hell to carry every soul back with them.

They swooped down the hill and the battle was met. Indians and colonists fell to rifle fire, arrows flew. Some Comanches chose to ride up close, to plunge a spear into a foe before being shot by those nearby.

Isaac was struck in the back by an arrow, but it didn't go deep—stopped by the thick cheloid whip scars he'd carried since childhood. The wound made him furious, though, and by the time fighting was hand-to-hand, he'd become a killing machine. Pulling Indians from their horses, stomping their throats with his boot; grabbing a spear from one and sticking it into another; holding a dead body by the neck in front of him as a shield while he took careful aim at three more; and when two jumped him he put out one's eyes with the other's thumb, and stabbed them both without pause.

Yet his own wounds were growing. Hit twice more, another arrow in his back and a spear in his thigh. But he saw Hannah fall. He saw Bigboy and other children captured and taken back to the hills by braves; and this made him even crazier with anger. He lit the trench of kerosene, burning half a dozen horses and men caught unawares. He leapt up on a Comanche pony and rode into the thick of them, slashing with the horn-tip fossil hanging from his neck, gouging flesh and riding on to do more. Vengeance, blind.

An arrow hit him in the back of the head, furrowing under his scalp, creasing the skull, protruding an inch out of his forehead—so it appeared the shaft was going right through his brain and out the other side. Yet he was unfazed, throwing his enemies around with a superhuman strength born of hopelessness.

Dark-skinned warriors of every shade lay dead or dying on the bloody ground. And still Isaac didn't stop. But something else was happening now. The Comanche braves were slowing, just to watch him; like a god on a feeding frenzy. One by one, they dismounted to gaze; stunned, or humbled, or awed, or in thrall. Some dropped to their knees; some danced, or chanted; others bowed silently to this unfathomable warrior.

When Isaac gradually saw what was going on, he stopped. Let the Indian in his grip fall to the dust. Turned in a slow circle, witnessing the killing ground. Over a hundred of his own people were dead. Others had been taken captive. Those that remained were wobbling, bleeding, some on their knees—not like the Comanche, overwhelmed by spirit; but in exhaustion, or blood loss, or grief. Almost as many Indians were dead, or nearly so. Painted to terrify, now they resembled holy dolls, all the colors of the minerals of the earth, dead by Isaac's hands.

Sickened by the sight and the thought of it, he stood, a spear fragment sticking out his leg, two arrows in his back, another in his head, multiple stabs, three bullet wounds.

And now he remembered. It was Shalako, the Kiowa shaman, who'd taught him that when he did have to kill an enemy—like he did that scrofulous doctor who'd owned him—he should always take a moment to thank the body for being an honorable opponent. Same way you thanked the deer you killed for providing you with food. Because in being connected to all, Isaac touched his own mortality with every life he took.

He walked to two dead Comanche and put his hand on their foreheads, and thanked them, and said he was sorry, and made his peace. Then he walked to another, a chieftan's son by the feathers in his hair. The young warrior was moaning and many times wounded, like Isaac. Isaac knelt beside him and tended his wounds. Binding the bloody slashes with torn pieces of his shirt. Pulling a sharpened kitchen knife from an arm. And when he'd done as much as he could with this man, he said, "Thank you," and walked unsteadily to the next; and tended him as well.

And all the hills, and all the sky, and all the people watched.

Clay little wanted this duty but wanted to put it behind him more. As he made his way to *The Daily Ranchero* he felt death swirling around him like a dust devil, making him sometimes the instrument, sometimes the witness. Now here was another friend he'd have to crush with its unbearable weight.

As he approached *The Daily Ranchero,* he saw the front door and surrounding wall scorched black, the smell of burned wood mixed with kerosene smoke. He entered Wachtel's office to find the old printer finishing off a glass of port.

"What happened to your front door?"

The old man shrugged as if he couldn't be bothered to care. He looked much older. "Someone threw an oil lamp. My workers put the fire out quickly, but…" He shrugged again.

"You know who did it?"

"Secessionist Texans who hate me for being a German abolitionist.

Confederate sympathizers who don't like what I write about the war. Bonapartists. *Cortinistas.* Union occupiers angry at my printer's devil for deserting…" He refilled his wineglass.

Clayton hated weighing him down further, but it had to be said. "I have news from the front lines, old friend. More bad news, I fear."

Wachtell closed his eyes. "Is not news. Is only what I knew would be, *ja*?"

"Jensen is dead. I'm sorry."

"*Und* how did he die? Was he beaten for treason? Or for 'bad behavior?'" His lip twisted in a bitter curl at all the ways a man might be cut off at the knees by his fellows.

But Clayton thought, of all the lies he'd been living, at least here was one made to ease pain. "He died a war hero, tryin' to save the Union. You'd have been proud."

This was an outcome Wachtel hadn't expected. He sobered up some. "Truly?"

"I was there."At least that wasn't a lie.

Wachtel pulled himself together. Corked the port and stood. "Then I cannot abandon him. I will rededicate myself to helping the North win, through my publications. I will be a voice for moral truth—so he will not have died in vain."

Clayton left with a new clutch in his gut; but this one felt like a muscle. Wachtel was right. A man made his own meaning, so death was something more than chaos, more than tumbling into the abyss. All this dying, Jensen and Jersey and Moon, all the thousands of soldiers, his own anonymous baby, his great love with Allie—all snuffed out—but it didn't have to be without reason. Clayton would give it reason. He'd turn the Union defeat at Red River into a victory on the Rio Grande. He'd learn the Confederacy's weakness here and funnel it to the Yanks at Fort Brown and redeem his father's sins and honor Isaac's departure and cleanse Allie's betrayal and make peace with everything.

And by God, he'd start right now.

Quintero didn't know Clay was back in town yet, so Clay figured he had some time before it was general knowledge he was a Yankee spy. It took him two hours of bar-hopping in Brownsville to manage to bump into Jessup in a *taberna* frequented by Union privates and corporals.

"There's a friendly face, for a change," Clay said, holding two fingers up at the bartender.

Jessup shook his head. "I'm already working on my third."

"I'm on my fourth. That was quite a night, last night."

"Ain't you a little worried being north of the river with Yanks in charge now?"

"Nobody knows me here. Be weeks more before these daisy recruits know what's what—and I see you've left your Ranger star home too."

"I'm just a local drunk. None of these enlisted men care what a drunk hears."

The bartender delivered their whiskeys, Clayton lay some coin on the bar, the two men clinked shotglasses and drank. "To old drunks on the wrong side of the river."

"Tell me," Clay went on, "how'd you come upon Jersey all shot up like that?"

"In the fight for Fort Ringgold."

"The Yanks took that weeks ago."

"Rangers took it back yesterday. The black girl was sniping at us from the hills."

Clay could hardly believe it. "Last I heard the Rangers were up at Laredo."

"1200 of us night-marched to Ringgold. I'm scouting now to estimate the resistance when we bring the fight here."

Clay was trying to process this new information in a hurry, to formulate some kind of plan. "Better take stock, then. They got at least that many Bluecoats around Brownsville."

"Where'd you hear that? Doesn't look like near that many to me."

"Some in the fort, hundreds billeted in the local *haciendas*. Saw a thousand at Clarksville myself just last week."

"Good to know. Thanks for the tip."

Clay ordered another round. But he'd have to arrange a meeting pretty quick.

The meeting was at the safe house with Clayton, Ambassador Pierce and Captain Avery, who was temporarily in charge of Fort Brown until General Banks and Colonel Dye returned from Red River. The Battle of Fort Brown had been Avery's first engagement and there'd been no fighting to speak of in that contest, if you didn't count confrontations with looters. So Avery was more than happy to take advice from anyone who seemed to know more than he did, which was just about everyone.

"We have credible news of an imminent attack," Pierce advised. "How many men do you have posted at the Fort?"

"Around 200."

"Are they battle seasoned?" asked Clay.

"Compared to what?" Avery wondered.

"Compared to being set upon by 1200 Texas Rangers who've been through the Texas War of Independence and the Mexican-American War." Pierce was annoyed.

"Ain't about numbers," Clay said. "About strategy. Remember the Sabine Pass."

"Better than remembering the Alamo," Pierce muttered.

"That's all right, we can change the odds. I'll make a list of what's needed. Meanwhile have your men do target practice until they know how to hit somethin'."

Avery nodded, relieved to have a task, and went back to give some orders.

Clayton sighed. Maybe the first redemption he could find was saving a fort full of untested, scared soldiers from what might otherwise be pure carnage.

CHAPTER 28

IT WAS A CALCULATED risk but Clayton knocked on Quintero's door at the Opera House and entered without waiting for a reply. Quintero knew he was a spy—now Clay just had to convince him he didn't *know* that Quintero knew. He walked in to find Quintero sitting at his desk writing a letter. When the Consul turned his head to see Wilkes standing there, he dropped his pen in surprise. "Wilkes."

"Good day, Agustin. I trust you're well."

Quintero had heard nothing of the man since he'd sailed off to the Red River; he expected Wilkes would either be a Confederate prisoner of war or hanged by now, after the incriminating letter of transit he'd given him. "Well enough, considering the Tyrant's minions have taken over Fort Brown." Quintero eased a dagger from a compartment on his desk and slipped it into his frock pocket. "Did your ride to Shreveport go well?"

Clay shook his head haplessly. "My canoe overturned and I lost all my documents, so I could get no assistance. Had to just plain steal a horse and run."

"But you made it there and back safely, that's the main thing."

"Didn't make it far enough, I fear. Never did get to report to General Taylor. But I got some critical information for us."

"And what would that be?"

"Layin' low near a Yankee camp I heard those boys sayin' they left Fort Brown practically undefended when they sent everyone up the Red. There's barely 200 men holdin' the fort down here."

"That is not what I've heard."

"Not what they want known. Now the Yanks have lost the Red, they'll send troops back this way. We got to tell Rip Ford to round up every Ranger and attack Fort Brown now, before Banks's army gets here."

Quintero gripped the knife in his pocket; he was in striking distance. But then he thought: If this Northern spy is telling me it's a good time to assault Fort Brown, there must be thousands of Yankees lying in wait. This must be a trap.

"This is important news, Wilkes," he said. "I will get word to Ford's Rangers immediately. Thank you, my friend." He shook Clay's hand and Clay left. Quintero sat down to write a dispatch for Russell to ride to Ford's camp at Fort Ringgold. If the spy Wilkes was saying to attack now, Ford must at all costs hold back, to avoid a catastrophic ambush.

And maybe it would be best to let Wilkes live for the time being. Quintero saw how useful the man could be, despite his own worst intentions. All Quintero had to do was the opposite of whatever Clay told him.

As Clayton exited the building he was guardedly optimistic that his plan had worked—that Quintero, knowing he was a Northern agent, would think Clayton was lying to him about Fort Brown being undefended. He'd think, instead, there must be a battalion of Yankees lying in wait—so he'd tell Rip Ford not to attack.

With luck, this would at least buy Captain Avery time to call for reinforcements before the Confederacy descended on him without mercy.

*　*　*

Isaac carried out his tender mercies all through the day, ministering to the wounded, thanking the fallen and praying for them, gentling the frightened. The Comanche simply watched him. Some chanted healing songs; thank-you songs to Creator, spirit chants. Some did these around Isaac's tending, some did it where braves had fallen or fierce battle done.

As the sun went down Isaac collapsed from blood loss, fatigue, dehydration and the death of his dream. He was placed on a litter and carried north to the Indian Nation, to be cared for and honored as a great warrior and healer.

The five dozen black pilgrims still alive were invited to come too. With nowhere else to go, they accompanied Isaac, throwing their fate in with him no less than they already had.

By the time Clay returned to the casino Ned was there, well on the mend from his bout of typhoid. He'd had the flux bad for a week, but that subsided with his fever. He was here now for a celebratory drink with Solomon before they went off to get Lafitte's hidden treasure. Ned had his stone bracelet and walking stick, Solomon kept a fossil saber tooth sheathed like a knife. But as they stepped outside they sensed all the world coming to a stop: there was a dog, black as burned wood, big as a ram, standing unsteady, white lather frothing its muzzle, swinging foamy strings from side to side when its head turned.

"Mad dog!" someone screamed. "Get away!" People began running.

Ned froze, though. "It's the Hell Dog," he whispered. "It knows where I'm goin'."

Solomon called back into the casino. "Somebody with a gun, get out here quick!"

But the beast locked its eyes on Ned and loped at him. Paralytic with fear, he watched its advance like death itself was set to pounce. But as the creature leapt, Solomon put himself between Ned and his fate—and the dog savaged Solomon, tearing into his right arm and side before a dozen shots rang out, felling the beast.

Russell, Clayton and Scully stood there with guns smoking as Solomon collapsed to the dirt. Ned knelt beside him. "It's my fault," he whispered. "But I'll not let you fall."

They set Solomon up in one of the cabins out back and called for Dr. Hawks, who hurried over to bandage him when she heard the story. "The dog was hydrophobic and Mr. Solomon could succumb to the same. We must be cautious."

"We've got powerful medicine," said Ned, removing his stone bracelet and placing it on Solomon's chest.

Solomon was scared, though. His voice was frail but emotional. "I've heard men kill themselves when they start showing signs."

"Let's not get ahead of ourselves," she said gently. "You may do well."

Clay exited with Hawks as Ned drew a short rope and deck of cards from his pocket to play Solomon's favored game of able-whacketts.

"What should we be watchin' out for?" Clay asked the doctor. He'd seen rabies in a man once before and it wasn't pretty. The good folks of the town had pushed him into a shallow hole, beat him to death and buried him where he lay.

"Early on, fever and headache. After that, agitation, hallucinations. When that happens you'll need to tie him up. He'll want to bite anyone he can. Then they get the sickness. God help us if he gets loose."

"I wish the foul beast had bit me," said Clayton and went upstairs in a dark mood. On entering his office, he found Teddy Beale helping herself to a drink. Still in uniform, she looked torn, dirty and battle worn. Clay hugged her. Awful as she looked, she was a piece of a happier day, and holding her a moment made him want to cry.

"Looks like you got you a story, girl. Let's hear it."

"Was like you warned General Banks. Taylor and the whole damn Confederate army attacked that night, 20,000 strong I'm told, right near Mansfield. We retreated back down the Red. The Rebs diverted the river, too, so low our ironclads grounded."

"What I can tell, war's mostly run by confused fools."

"Corrupt, too. I saw Banks bring cotton speculators on the campaign. Then he used the ironclads that were still floating to load up all the cotton we could confiscate. Confiscate, that means steal when you do it to make money. So a lot of brave soldiers got killed, and some cowards got rich." She finished her glass and poured another.

"Then what happened?"

"We lost another 2000 at the Battle of Pleasant Hill. By then we were running downriver pretty fast."

"How'd you get back here? Reassigned to Pierce?"

She shook her head but didn't speak. A tear filled the corner of her eye but she wiped it off before it went anywhere. "I just kept running. So here I am."

"You deserted?"

"Feels more like they deserted me. We didn't just run. We took our vengeance along the way. Every town we passed through, our troops looted, raped women, beat old men, set fire to buildings…" She shook her head, trying to understand it. "We didn't have to do that. But once the fighting started, even good men went crazy. Crazy mean."

"That's why I live down here now."

"We burned the city of Alexandria to the ground and kept running. I thought we were fighting to end slavery, not end humanity."

Wilkes had no answer. But he did have a tricky question. "People know you here. Pierce knows you. You ran off in the face of the enemy, you're in big trouble, girl."

She took another gulp of liquor. "I've been giving that some thought. I've been thinking nobody knew that Corporal Teddy Beale had a sister, a twin sister."

Clay was surprised. "You've got a sister?"

"Well…I haven't done this in a long time…but I've been thinking I might start wearing dresses again."

Clayton was so tickled by the idea of a con that bold, he poured himself a glass and clinked it to hers. "And what, may I ask, is your sister's name?"

"Ambassador Pierce, may I present you with Miss Edie Beale." The awkward young lady wore a beautiful green chiffon dress.

"It's a pleasure, Miss Beale," said Pierce. It was half an hour before Sunday Mass, the social scene around the cathedral entrance in full swing. Ladies in their finest, landowners and peons, Cortina with medals on his dress uniform, his posse in clean clothes, Scully and Aurelia and their new baby, all mingling, chatting, paying homage to Father Clos on the steps. "But forgive me," the Ambassador went on. "Have we met before?"

She laughed nervously. "Why, no, but people tell me there is a family resemblance to my brother, Teddy. I've come looking for him, but it seems I'm too late."

"Teddy was an excellent Embassy Guard, but he's gone to fight with our troops. I'd be happy to telegraph General Banks, and..."

"No, no, that's not necessary. I'm just in need of some spiritual support."

"To that end, Ambassador, I wonder if you'd escort my new acquaintance into church this morning—since you know my morals prevent me from enterin', myself."

"It would be my honor." Pierce offered Miss Beale his arm, and she took it.

Clay touched her shoulder before taking his leave and pointed to the priest. "That's Father Clos. He's the one keeps that room of clothes for the poor I was mentionin'."

She nodded with a smile and accompanied Pierce into the edifice as Clay watched them go. Life was certainly hard to figure. He wished he could change things up as drastically as Teddy had just done. Take on a new identity, start a new life. But then, after all, what was stopping him?

Clay entered Solomon's cabin with a plate of cornmeal. The old sailor smiled wearily, a thin drool inching out the corner of his mouth. "Call that food, do you?"

"They tell me you've been havin' trouble swallowin'."

Solomon wiped the spittle off his chin. "It sticks in my craw." He swept his arm wide to include the whole world and knocked the tin plate to the ground with a crash that made him jump, jangling his nerves, making him squint. "Cover the window, would you, laddie? The light's like a burr in my eyes."

Clayton hung a blanket over the window, making the room dark. "Can I get you some water?"

But the mention of it made Solomon ill, and he began salivating, the spit collecting in his mouth faster than he could swallow. He spit on the floor and motioned Clayton closer. "When I'm gone you must bury me within a day, it's the Hebrew custom. And ask Shalako to sing a prayer for me, would you, lad? *Shema Yisroel...*" he sang, then fell silent, lost in the memories it produced. "Tell him to light me a candle."

Clay nodded. "You've been a good friend, Ryburn." He picked up the old tar's fiddle, lying near the bed. "I hope you can teach me how to play this thing one day."

"Och, it's not such a conundrum. You put the bow to the strings and scratch. If it's hoping you're about, I only hope I can still lift a pint when this is over."

"I've no doubt of it."

Solomon's eyes got glassy. "I wish I could see the ocean again. It's the only freedom a man can know. Folks fight about land. The sea's what rocks us to heaven."

When he smiled, saliva trickled out the corners of his mouth, overflowing his lower lip. He brought the sheet to his face, to wipe the spit away; and found himself gnawing on the cloth. Goddam but it felt good to bite something.

Late that night Allie and Shonny were playing with the baby, who lay on her back laughing and grabbing at her own feet. Allie loved the way the world was a pleasing place to this infant, and was pleased herself to be providing for the child. She could almost remember her mother being there for her like this, before everything turned so terrible. As if Allie were getting to live this happy part of her childhood all over again. This infant could be the start of a whole new adventure for her.

"Sure is a pretty baby," said Shonny.

"I think so too. But I think a person is pretty because you like him. I think you shouldn't go off with a pretty person 'less you like him first."

"Then I guess we both like this baby if we think she pretty. We goin' off with her?"

"No, I think we'll stay here with her. She has the feelin' of family, which I dearly miss, though I never expected to. All that dyin'...'" She let her mind roam around the old days. Her mother, her sister and brothers, her father. And Clay. "All that's over, though, I suppose. Seems like this baby's just the right thing to make do."

There was a knock on the door. For a brief, elusive moment she thought it might be Clay, come to apologize and forgive, so she sent Shonny off to the bedroom with Rachel—and with an intake of breath she opened the door. Standing before her was a woman in a green dress. A woman she didn't know. She looked a bit drunk.

"I'm sorry to bother you so late but I have nowhere to go and you've been so kind…I mean, I mean I've heard what a kind person you are, taking in strays like myself. So I was wondering if, I mean…" She stumbled, barely catching herself in time from falling. Then she smiled like she was crying.

Drunk for sure, but there was something about her, about her voice, about her posture—Allie had a con artist's sense of the imperative to remember someone you'd seen before. Then it hit her and she put it all together in a second: Teddy Beale was a secret woman who went off to war as a man. Now a woman looking a lot like him was in town. So Allie figured the war had gone badly for Teddy and now Teddy was hiding in plain sight. Allie might have done much the same.

"Well, you can't go back to the Embassy and you can't go back to the fort. But I would love to do another photographic portrait of you in this lovely green uniform."

"I don't know what you're talking about," said Edie, arching her brow.

"I mean you no harm. I imagine the war didn't work out the way you thought."

Edie's eyes watered up. "No, it did not."

"Yes, of course you can stay here. We have become a small orphanage and you but one more lost soul." Allie helped her into the house and took her to the empty bed that once had been Moon's. "I admire your gumption for havin' gone to fight for what you believed in—even if you were fightin' on the wrong side."

"I don't know what side I was fighting on anymore. That's the problem."

"I feel the same way myself, time to time."

Solomon came raging into the casino like one of hell's own fiends. Foamy spit flew from his growling maw. He splintered a chair on the bar. Everyone scattered. Jim jumped over the bartop and Rheumy ducked under it to confront the crazed sea captain—but when Solomon tried to bite them, they backed off, as did everyone in the place.

"He's got the hydrophobia!" someone yelled, and there was a surge for the door.

Solomon paused for a long moment to stare at the giraffe staring back down at him—as if these two wild creatures were communicating in some silent language—then he tore into the crowd, grabbed some poor drunk by the shoulders and threw him to the ground. But when he lunged down to chew, a gunshot slammed into his arm and he fell back. Scully stood nearby, taking aim for a second shot.

"Hold off!" shouted Clayton, stepping up. "Maybe the doctor can do somethin'."

Solomon eyed them like prey—but Clay brought his cane down hard on the sick man's head. Solomon fell like a rock and didn't move. "Call the doc," he said to Scully. He turned Solomon over to look at his face while Scully put away his pistol. Solomon's jaw was slack, his eyes glazed. Fifteen seconds passed while Clay watched him; thirty. No air passed his lips. "Hold off on the doc," he told Scully. "The man's dead."

Ned ran in, dropping to his friend's side, his voice quavering. "I was goin' to show him the pirate gold. It was treasure I promised him. It's my fault he got bit by the Hell Dog. I can never repay him for savin' my life."

"He's beyond carin' now, man," said Scully, and left.

"We drop our dead in the sea," Ned spoke and then sang a somber dirge. "*Thy ship, they say, is in the bay, and thou not of her number; beneath some far and foreign star, they've left our boy to slumber.*"

Clayton told Scully and Jim to carry the body to the undertaker for a quick burial, and he'd pay whatever the cost.

Ned corked up his belly hole and drank until he passed out. While he was down, Dinah conscientiously uncorked him, let the remaining alcohol drain, treated the irritated skin around the hole with one of Zhi Li's poultices, recorked him and put a pillow under his head. She was devoted to his care and feeding.

On waking, Ned staggered to the mortuary that night to say a last goodbye to his friend. The undertaker took him to see the coffin Solomon had been placed in. But the coffin was empty.

Allie and Bootsy were taking the baby out for a stroll, passing her back and forth amidst a torrent of giggles. As they passed the church Allie saw Edie directing two men to load up a wagon with piles of clothes they were moving out the back door. Allie approached with a curious smile.

"Edie Beale, what on earth are you doin'?"

"Clay asked me to round up all these men's clothes and bring them to Fort Brown. Those poor men must be in tatters from previous engagements."

Allie glanced at the wagonload more closely. Trousers, shirts, some military jackets, hats of all sizes. "Wherever did all this attire come from?"

"He bought a wagonload of it in Bagdad. This lot was donated by the church. I'm to meet him at Fort Brown with all of it now. You want me to tell him anything?"

"No, that's all right, I was just curious. You go on with your business, I've got this child to entertain." And with that they went their separate ways.

But Allie gave the baby to Bootsy and ran straight home, where she changed into riding clothes and took off on her horse at a gallop.

By the time Allie got to Fort Ringgold her horse was in a lather. The Corporal of the Guard told her to halt but she said she had urgent news for Colonel Ford—he was to be told Allie Stoneman was here. When the corporal hesitated, she scolded him harshly. The corporal didn't have much experience saying no to a woman, especially one in riding pants, so he asked her to swear she was unarmed and marched her through the gate, keeping three steps behind, rifle poised.

Jessup and Ford were going over an inventory list when Allie's presence was announced. Jessup went out to meet her and spoke the way he thought an officer ought to speak to a visiting civilian. "Good day, Mrs. Stoneman, you look all in. May I..."

"Oh, for heaven's sakes, Ahotay, take me to Colonel Ford, I have critical news."

He took her inside before she decided to get any more personal in front of the troops. "Colonel Ford, may I introduce…."

"The Colonel knows me. This is important, you must take me seriously."

"I know of no other way to take a lady," said Ford.

"All right, then. There are but 200 Yankees defendin' Fort Brown right now. They are vulnerable to attack and you best attack them before they can muster up any help."

"That's not what it looked like when I scouted around there the other night. There was hundreds of tents scattered…"

"Most of 'em empty," Allie insisted.

"How'd you come by this information?" said Ford.

"Clayton Wilkes is distributin' tons of clothes there. Pants, shirts, hats…"

"Which sounds to me like he's outfitting a whole army of…"

"No! It's the same trick he used in Georgia when he was makin' investors think a locked up buildin' was a goin' concern, staffed with hundreds of workers."

"I don't understand what…"

"He had 20 people in there puttin' on different clothes and appearin' in different windows, so it looked like there were lots more than there were. I know his game and this clothes pile is as good as a signed confession." She looked from one to the other.

"That's mighty thin evidence…"

"Colonel, I've never been more certain. You must strike now. If you don't, you lose everything. You lose surprise. You lose superior forces."

Ford looked dubious, Jessup conflicted. "Colonel Ford, Allie Stoneman is the smartest woman I ever met, so her say-so means something. But Allie, I have to tell you, I ran into Clay Wilkes in Brownsville and he said he knew for a fact there was at least 2000 Union troops in the hills and thereabouts."

Allie seethed. "Here's what I know for a fact. Clayton Wilkes is a

Yankee spy, and if you don't believe me you just ask Consul Quintero. He'll set you straight."

Jessup was so stunned he didn't know what to say. He knew Wilkes as an amiable rogue, a lazy war profiteer, a son of the South, a bar owner and sometime rival for Allie's affections. But a spy? Jessup hated spies worse than just about anything. Opposing soldiers, he could abide; they were generally honorable, if mistaken in their sympathies. Even profiteers, just in it for the money, were more or less open about their motivations. But spies were the lowest kind of vermin, who had to be stopped at all costs. He'd not let this information about Wilkes go unremembered.

Ford, terse as ever, reacted to Allie's news without drama. "I'll take it under consideration," was his last comment on the matter. And he left the room.

Allie had done her best. She felt drained and disregarded. Jessup held her arm, but she pulled away; finished with this lot. All she wanted now was to go home and see her baby. So that's what she did.

But the baby was cranky, and wouldn't nurse. "So y'all are turnin' against me too? Seems like Ahotay's about the only livin' soul who holds me in full esteem. He's a man of simple wants, and I'm the main one. Don't I deserve a simple life, at last?"

Somehow the baby responded to her pleading tone and settled down to nurse from the syringe.

Allie smiled at her. "Dear one, now you're tryin' to comfort me. I credit we'll make it through this nasty war yet. And maybe all get the nursin' we need."

CHAPTER 29

Next morning Allie knocked on the door of the *hacienda*, holding baby Rachel. When Aurelia answered holding her own baby, the women smiled and moved into the parlor to swap stories of wiggly feet, cooing smiles, greedy hands and cranky nights.

"Is *bueno* for *mi corazon*," said Aurelia, patting her heart. "You too, *no?*"

"Yes, the experience of motherhood is beyond reckonin'. But I was curious what would be your feelin's about wet-nursin' Rachel sometimes? She's been strugglin' with bottles and syringes and it would be little extra burden on you, would it?" Aurelia looked puzzled, so Allie hurried on, "Of course I would pay you, that goes without sayin'."

"Yes, sure, I could nurse the baby."

Allie hugged Rachel tighter as her confessions leaked out the edges. "I find—beyond just the nursin'—I find it hard to take care of her myself. Of course, the children help, but it seems I'm just not made that way, my own mama was never well enough to show me how it ought to be done, and I fear…" She shook her head. "I don't know what I could have been thinkin' to think I could care for a child."

Aurelia spoke gently. "A baby gives love wanting only love back."

"Yes, but I thought—I wondered—if perhaps you could raise Rachel as your own. With your own. You'd be so good, and I'm so bad, and you have Scully to care for you, stayin' right here. Could you do that?"

Aurelia was even more taken aback. "I could not steal this from you."

"No, no, it would be a blessin' for me and the child both."

Aurelia couldn't fathom it. "You are certain?"

"Yes. Yes, that would be lovely." She tried formality to hold herself together.

"Then of course I will take the child, if you cannot. She will be a good friend for *mi Pablito*. And I will raise her like my own."

"Raise who?" said Russell on entering.

"Rachel," said Allie. "It's Jersey's baby and that poor girl died in childbirth. And Aurelia is bein' so kind as to take this sweet orphan into her home."

"My Scully will help," said Aurelia.

"Hell, I'll help out too," said Russell. "I still remember once when my kids were running through the house..." But then he realized he didn't want to remember that, so he dipped his head to them and left.

Allie put Rachel in Aurelia's arms and left without a word, before she could cry. A person should never cry without getting something for it.

Clayton wrapped himself completely in leper's muslin to avoid detection; he wanted nobody reporting to Quintero that he'd been seen entering Fort Brown—though truth be told, he always found something comforting in leper's garb. It was the cloak of the outcast; but also, the shroud of those witnesses who'd watched Isaac's family torn apart so long ago; and who'd watched Clay do nothing about it. So it was the garb of his own penance. It reminded him he would never do nothing again.

He made his way to Fort Brown now, where he spent all day helping Avery plan a defense against the presumed attack. Where the assault would likely come from, where to place artillery, how to maximize ammunition use, perimeter defenses, fallback positions. There was a large Colored contingent at the fort, which was good—Rebs tended to be intimidated by black soldiers, more likely to retreat.

Around midnight Ned showed up in a sweat to tell him Solomon had been hounded to the drydocks by a posse clamoring for blood.

"He's come back from the dead. Bloody foam at his chin, strong as an ape and snarling like a wolf."

Clayton felt his stomach turn over. Could Solomon still be alive? Could they have been mistaken when they thought him dead? That it wasn't just a body snatcher who'd emptied the old sailor's coffin?

He ran from the fort with Ned, shedding his rags at the river. When they reached the Matamoros drydock, a drunken vigilante mob was all over the place, holding torches into shadows, uprighting overturned dinghys—looking for the monster.

"Evil's reached the city!" someone shouted. "It must be purged!"

There were a dozen ships of different sizes spread out on frameworks for repairs. Nobody wanted to encounter the monster alone so they all went ship by ship together.

"That one looks most like the *Buccaneer*," Ned said quietly, pointing out a sloop at the outskirts. "If Ryburn is here, that's the one he'll have boarded."

They surreptitiously crept to it and climbed a rope ladder off the stern. The floorboards creaked with every step as they walked—Clay with derringer drawn, Ned with his stone-bone walking stick poised defensively. But there was no one on deck. That left the hold. Ned lit up a lantern hanging from the wheel and threw open the hatch.

They went belowdecks, moving carefully, the lantern making every shadow move like it was alive. Suddenly a figure whipped up the stairs and they followed quickly.

When they got topside they saw Solomon at the port rail, readying to jump to the ground—when he was stopped by a voice. "There he is!" And then more voices, and lights swiveling to him, forcing him to shrink back, covering his eyes with his arm.

"Kill the demon! Cut off his head!"

"He were a vampire! I seen one like that in Connecticut!"

The crowd surged against the ship. Solomon turned to run alee but stopped again. Clayton and Ned blocked his way. He screamed at them—a single inchoate wail, at once terrifying and poignant. Crusted blood matted his face, he drooled pitifully.

Ned lowered his fossil cane. "Ryburn, I know this isn't you."

Two men in the crowd below threw torches onto the deck, to burn him out. The flaring light hurt Solomon's eyes and put him into a rage, grinding his teeth.

"I'm sorry, Ryburn," said Clay. "You were a good man, and I'll miss your music."

Solomon paused, understanding in some deep recess of his mind what Clay was saying. He slumped to the deck in bafflement. Clay and Ned crouched before him.

"Ry," said Ned. "I'll hide our spot to the end, you needn't worry on that account."

Solomon choked a sound at them, his eyes pleading. Clay snatched a guttering torch from the netting where it had fallen and stuck it upright in the capstan. "You said you wanted Shalako to light you a candle. Here it is, then."

Solomon squinted at the dim flickering, which pulled a distant chant from deep within his soul. "*Barukh atah adonai…*" he rasped. But that was as much as he could muster. He stared at Clay, baffled and blasted.

"Ryburn Solomon," said Clayton. "You've been a good friend to me. I hope I may be that to you now. Dear man…for this I thank you…"

Clay shot him in the head. He'd killed his first father in hate; this one with love. But he couldn't mull it long. More torches flew onto the deck as the crowd got louder. Clay tipped Solomon's body to the ground, blindside to the mob hysteria; then jumped down and carried it with Ned into the dark. The ship lit up the frenzied docks, as they took Solomon to the cemetery plot designated for unclaimed bodies. They dug the rest of the night and left the grave unmarked, in case any of those fine citizens of the drydocks wanted to go another round of drunken uproar.

Once the ship fire was put out, no body was found, so the next day there was a town meeting at the gazebo. The gent who'd seen a Connecticut vampire informed everyone that if the dead man showed up again the proper disposal method was to cut out his heart. Father Clos shook his head, though, declaring vampire myths to be heathen blasphemies. The issue here was that Solomon was a Jew, and Jews drank Christian blood in their pagan rites. The only way to rectify this transgression was to burn the Jew's body at the stake.

Dr. Hawks declared it was rabies, pure and simple, also called hydrophobia because those with the disease feared water. They also went into a state of deep sleep that could look like death, only to wake up frightful agitated, powerful strong and compelled to bite. If he did show up again, just bury the poor man.

Simon Wachtel wrote it all up in the next day's *Daily Ranchero*, ending with an admonition for all residents to be on the lookout for mad dogs, bats and skunks.

But Ned, nursing a beer in Brave River that night, knew exactly what the problem was. It was Lafitte's Curse, and Ned was the sorry soul to bring it down on his only friend, Ryburn Solomon. And only he could make it right.

Rip Ford sent scouts with long scopes to spy on Fort Brown from the hills. They reported back describing what looked like a thousand soldiers parading the parapets and peering out the windows. But at least one of them was the same man dressed in three different sets of clothes. The scout was sure of this because the man was his cousin, Frank—they'd parted ways when the war began but the scout said he'd know Frank anywhere and he never knew him to have more than one set of clothes.

So Allie's intelligence had been right. Seizing the moment, Ford attacked Fort Brown from three directions at dawn, with 1200 Rangers and 300 Confederate Regulars. The first wave suffered terrible casualties when a trench filled with kerosene a hundred yards beyond the west wall burst into flame, killing or disabling two score advance guard. Explosive mines outlying the other walls took out more. It was a trick Clay had learned from Isaac many a year ago. There were just too many attackers now to make much of a dent in the onslaught, though. Even so, the battle raged most of the day, with losses on both sides.

Cortina rode in with 200 men to support the Yankees. He relished the opportunity to trade fire with Texas Rangers. There was a moment in a gully when Cortina saw Jessup sneaking up on a group of *Cortinistas* preparing a cart full of TNT. Cortina rode full gallop, trampling him, breaking Jessup's leg. Cortina smiled. "I know you," he said. "You tried kill me once on that *banco*. You Rangers are *no* so much."

"Enough to take Texas from you."

Cortina shrugged. "We take back. But I let you live now, maybe the people sing a song of your shame. *La ninita* Ranger cried, *pero el bandito grande* show her mercy, *no?*" He stomped on Jessup's broken leg and the Ranger passed out in pain. Cortina then drove the dynamite cart himself to the wall of the fort, where he lit the fuses. His men gave him firing cover as he ran back to the gully and the cart exploded, collapsing half the wall.

Breaching the wall was the sign Clayton had told Captain Avery his fight was lost. At that point his only options were surrender or retreat. And he hated to surrender. Clay had had him prepare for when a breach happened. As soon as the wall came down, all the remaining Union troops thundered out the riverside door—the one direction Ford had not attacked from. They rode for their lives to the Gulf, 25 miles east.

Ford's men occupied the fort within the hour, sending wounded Yanks and Rebs alike to Brownsville Hospital, where Dr. Hawks finally got to do what battle surgeons do.

Captain Avery holed up his last hundred and ten men on Brazos Santiago, setting up defensive positions. He sent two riders and one mudskimmer north, to sound the alarm for reinforcements or escape vessels.

Jessup, on crutches until his broke leg healed, was relieved of duty until further notice—Rip Ford also asking him to thank Mrs. Stoneman for her crucial advice about the low troop count at Fort Brown. Allie broke down in tears when she saw his leg, feeling the broken bone in her own limb, so closely connected to his pain was she.

Clay, who watched the battle with his spyglass from a good vantage hilltop in Matamoros, was perplexed by the turn of events. Apparently Quintero had taken him at his word that there were only 200 defenders of Fort Brown—so he had presumably instigated Rip Ford's attack. But how was that possible if Quintero knew him to be a Northern spy? It was imponderable.

He returned to the casino. Not much changed here. Men gambled, drank, whored and laughed with the women they loved, or who loved them, or didn't. But the war didn't matter to them. Their lives were smaller than that; and bigger.

Maybe Edie Beale had the right idea. Just walk away. He watched her at the bar, flirting with a handsome *caballero* sporting silver spurs on his tooled boots and a black leather vest festooned with silver dollars, bowing deeply, making her laugh. Clayton didn't think he'd ever seen her laugh before. He wondered if he'd ever laugh again.

Isaac sat in a tent across from the Comanche chief, passing a pipe between them. It had taken weeks for most of his wounds to heal; perhaps some never would. A split over his right shoulder refused to close. His left eye was puffy red and made tears all the time. The leg that had been pierced by the spear remained swollen; he could feel something grinding inside with every step. Yet his chest felt empty as a great hall.

It had taken the tribe time to find an English speaker, finally locating the Kiowa gun trader, Xo Ten. He entered the tent now accompanied by a tall, scarred, limping woman, half bald where she had once been half scalped.

The Kiowa translator said to Isaac, "This is your wife, mate. She's a good sheila, name *Ayasha*, means Little One. A gift, to honor your powers of warrior and healer."

"Tell the chief many thanks, but I wish no wife," said Isaac.

The woman gave Isaac a rawhide bag.

"That's sweet tucker in the tucker-bag, all the dowry she has. Her face is not much, from torn in battle—she is great warrior, for a sheila."

"I bow to her bravery. I have no need of a wife. Besides..." He paused. This memory once caused him pain, but now was just another piece lost in the great cavern of his heart. "I cannot make children. I am torn in that way." His owner, Dr. Ellengill, had forbade Isaac from lying with the slavewoman Isaac had betrothed, because the doctor wanted her for himself. When Dr. Ellengill discovered them violating his order, he castrated Isaac—for "his own good", because he was "too valuable to hang". The doctor then ordered all his men slaves to violate her, to teach her a lesson about obedience. Isaac didn't say all this now; he just said, "I am torn in that way."

Xo Ten told Isaac's infirmity to the chief, who smiled, and replied.

The Kiowa translated, "This is good, mate. Your wife also cannot bear children. So it is fate that put you together, and Creator's wish that you be married."

Isaac had no way to envision what being married might look like. The scarred woman said something in Comanche and the chief nodded. She knelt before Isaac, took his head in her hands and brought her face close to his. He assumed she was going to kiss him. Instead she licked his watering eyeball. He jumped but she held his head tight and licked his eye again. And again. It hurt at first, then not; then it felt better. She stuck her tongue out and pulled a small splinter off of it. She smiled and spoke for a minute.

"She says like you, she is a healer. She says a piece of the spear that stuck you flew into your eye. This is why that eye cries." Xo Ten laughed. "Strewth, maybe a wife like this is not such a bad thing!"

Isaac considered the proposition. His eye felt better. He no longer desired to control his life, or his path. Maybe the chief was right, this was Creator's doing. Maybe Isaac should listen to that. Maybe it was time to turn everything over to a greater guiding power. Greater even than free will.

"Tell the chief thank you. I accept my destiny. I accept my bride, if she cares to accept me. Perhaps we will one day heal each other to have children after all." Then he turned to her and said, *"Ayasha."*

That night was a great wedding party. Thirty-seven of Isaac's colony were still alive. Ordinarily they would have been taken slave, having lost their battle with the Comanche. But out of deference to Isaac they were allowed to become members of the tribe, or at least fellow travelers. One of them was Salem, the gardener.

"What we gonna do now?" asked Salem.

"This is my life. Our dreams are all gone. Maybe I'll find a new one here. What are *you* going to do?"

Salem pondered it. "Stay, I reckon. They seem like peaceful folk when they not killin' you."

The other one of Isaac's immigrants was Bigboy, whom he hadn't seen since the battle—turns out Bigboy wouldn't come out of his tent and the tribe let him stay there. He emerged for the party, though. When he saw Isaac he ran up and hugged him and wouldn't let go. Isaac asked the chief if he could take Bigboy for a wedding present, and the chief agreed. So Bigboy became the son he thought he couldn't have.

Late that night before Isaac went to his bride, he made a trip to his saddlebags, which the Comanche had brought to him from the battlefield, and which he hung on a branch near his tent. He opened the flap and took out a pigeon. When he'd gone through the bag initially, he discovered the bird nearly dead. He gave it great care, though, hand watering and feeding it with a sugary paste one of the Comanche children brought him—until slowly the bird regained its strength. Now it was back to full health.

Isaac wrote a brief note on a small piece of buckskin, telling Clay the colony was lost but he was found. Then he tied it to the pigeon's leg and threw it into the night breeze, where it found its bearings and disappeared into the desert darkness.

Then Isaac went to his bride.

*　*　*

The little red-headed baby, Pablito, squirmed out of Aurelia's arms and crawled backwards—the only way he could get around—over to Russell, in Dress Grays, who scooped him up.

"I haven't seen you in that uniform for some time," said Scully, walking in carrying Jersey's little baby girl, Rachel. "You tryin' to impress someone?"

Russell sweetly bounced Pablito, who kept trying to grab his nose. "I'm afraid it's time for me to leave," he said with a sad note to his smile. "Back to Fort Brown."

"Whatever for? Have you not enjoyed our company?"

"I have a good deal. But as long as the Yankees held the Fort I could say I was here under orders from General Bee to guard his *hacienda*. Now the Confederacy's in charge again I got no excuse. If I stay here all it can mean is I'm a deserter. So I'd best go back to the fort and get back in the war."

"We'll miss havin' you."

"Oh, you'll see me around. I've got to keep my eye on this little guy sometimes, make sure you're turning him into a proper soldier."

"*No!*" Aurelia stamped her foot. "No more soldiers."

Russell put Pablito back in Aurelia's lap, kissed her on the cheek and shook Scully's hand. "You're a good man," said Russell.

"And you," said Scully. "If the Yanks take over again, you know where you're welcome."

"Major Charles Russell, reporting for duty, sir!"

Colonel Ford looked up from his plans with Captain Jessup and a couple lieutenants. He knew he'd seen Russell around, he just couldn't remember the circumstances. "Transferred from where, son?"

"General Bee's *hacienda* in Matamoros, sir. He ordered me to keep it from Yankee seizure, which I have done to the best of my ability. I don't believe that's necessary since your triumphant return, so I'm here to resume my post at Fort Brown."

"What post is that, Major?"

"I monitored the garrison's money, the inflow of cotton and its export for international exchange beneficial to the Southern cause. I was the Quartermaster, sir."

"That's right, now I recall. We can use a Quartermaster who knows the ropes. You may resume your post, Major. I want to get those cotton caravans rolling again."

Ford went back to his maps and Russell went to collar a couple privates into starting reconstruction of his warehouse behind the fort.

Clay was well pleased to hear Russell was back being Quartermaster at Fort Brown. It meant they were back in business.

He went over there to congratulate the scoundrel. With Isaac gone this looked like a chance for a new partnership. He made his way over the rubble from the battle to the southwest corner where he was told Russell's office had been set up. He knocked and entered with a warm grin. "Not as well-appointed as your last quarters, but..."

He stopped when he saw Russell in conversation with Captain Jessup. And on seeing Wilkes, Jessup's expression turned from earnest to dire. He stood nearly at attention, pulled his sidearm and pointed it at Clayton.

"You are under arrest, sir, for treason most foul." Then he shouted. "Guard!"

"What the hell are you doing?" Russell asked almost casually.

"Arresting this man in the name of the Confederate States of America. He's a spy and a traitor, as Consul Quintero will attest, and I expect to see him hung in short order." Two privates ran in and Jessup gave them orders. "Take this man to the stockade and post a guard 24 hours a day. I'll notify Colonel Ford. I expect we'll have the trial tomorrow."

The guards put cuffs on Clayton, who was only able to lock eyes with Russell for a moment before he was taken away. When the prisoner was gone Russell said to Jessup, "Sure hope you know what you're doing, Captain."

"I've had that traitor on my mind for some time. I couldn't touch him south of the river. But this is Reb country again now, and I got him dead to rights."

CHAPTER 30

Russell came to visit Clayton in jail. "This never should have happened."

"Can you do anything for me?"

"The Jessup kid is crazy. Thinks he's upholding some great moral principle."

"He's not in charge here."

"No, but Rip Ford is, and he's a man without imagination."

"We had a good thing goin' with General Bee, and he outranks Ford. Can you get him to stop this?"

"Don't know where he is. New Orleans, maybe. Your trial is tomorrow."

"Do somethin', man."

"I'm trying. You have to understand, I can't stick my neck out too far, though."

"It's *my* neck I'm worried about."

"I'll see what I can do."

"What about Allie? She know about this?"

"Everyone knows about this, brother. You're the latest big news."

* * *

Quintero opened his door to Allie, who was flush with agitation. "Have you heard the news about Clay?" she asked.

"Yes, of course. He's getting his due. The trial was fair. But I am puzzled."

"How so?" she pushed him. Of course, Clay was guilty of spying. But she never wanted him to hang, and she never thought it would come to that. Spying was just another kind of confidence game, it was a game pure and simple, the kind of game she and Clay had played together all their lives. She couldn't let him die for that. Just the thought of it put the depth of her feeling for him in full contrast. They'd hurt each other, surely; but she couldn't imagine a world without Clay in it.

"I was on the verge of killing the man myself," Quintero mused, "so I can hardly fault the authorities for the execution. But…"

"But what?"

"He told me there were only 200 Yankee soldiers in Fort Brown, and Ford should attack at once. I thought he was lying, because I knew him to be a double agent for the North—you proved that to me yourself, with the photograph in the church. But he wasn't lying. There *were* only 200 Yankees defending Fort Brown, and Ford attacked before I could warn him not to. So Wilkes was a Confederate hero."

"Why didn't you bring that up at the trial? Maybe Clay did go astray for a time but has found his Southern soul. You can still tell them that before they hang him. Maybe they'll commute his sentence."

He shook his head. "The Revolution is not sentimental. Innocent or guilty, Wilkes must hang, to avoid needless uncertainties. When he is dead, the simplicity of rebellion will once again be clear."

"What kind of rebellion kills an innocent man just because y'all are confused?"

"A rebellion that must win. We are torn apart. There is no redemption but that we come back together, stronger than before."

His words hit her as if she'd been baptised in cold water. *No redemption but that we come back together, stronger than before.* Her path was clear.

"Perhaps you're right, Agustin. The South is on the rise again. Perhaps we should all celebrate a new day. I thank you for the clarity your insights have provided me."

And she left.

The guard let Clayton play one game of chess through the bars with Simon Wachtel. Clay let Wachtel move his bishop within striking distance.

"I tell you," Simon said quietly, "if I'd known you were a Union agent all along, I'd have let you win more games."

Clay smiled, moving a piece to make his king even more vulnerable. "I liked your editorial today. More forthright in your abolitionism."

"I try to be a *mensch* now. A man of substance must declare his principles to the world. *Und* live by them."

"I'll remember that, Simon." He watched Wachtel studying the board. "But I reckon I might as well give up the ghost right now."

"You told me once, never make the mistake to claim your downfall before the king has fallen."

"And you said, I recall, there's a measure of honor in bowing to inevitable defeat."

Wachtel shrugged. "In that case...checkmate!" he beamed, triumphant.

"Time's up," said the guard.

The joy went out of Wachtel's eyes and he stood. "There will be a reprieve," he said gently. "I have the story already written." He shook Clayton's hand and left.

Clayton looked at the waning moon through his high cell window. How had it come to this? A life of cleverness, come to an unclever end. Done in by a self-righteous Texas Ranger who thought he was doing it for some reason other than to get rid of his romantic rival. What more mundane end could there be to the cavalier journey of Clayton Wilkes?

Pierce had come by to say he was trying to arrange a prisoner exchange. But prospects didn't look good. Spies were afforded no official status; all sides generally turned their backs on them. Nonetheless he assured Clay that President Lincoln would award him a posthumous Medal of Honor. Would he like it sent to anyone in particular?

Friends were already gone forever—Isaac, Solomon, Jersey. Others had visited to wish him hope. Russell, Wachtel, Edie Beale; Catherine, who'd kissed him through the bars as if bars could never separate them; Zhi Li and Milagra, who brought rice candy and albondigas soup for him and the guard; Jim, Rheumy, Ned. Not Dinah, she never ventured beyond the Brave River compound. And not Allie. The only one who mattered was Absent Without Leave. Not that she ever needed his leave to do anything. But Clay was a gambler, and every run of luck ran out eventually.

Announcements were sent out. There was to be a Celebration Hanging the following day. The military court of the CSA was even granting one-day amnesties to anyone who wanted to show up to watch. The guards were particularly happy about the festivities. Clay heard them saying that after the hanging Captain Jessup was getting married to the beautiful widow Stoneman, and everyone in the fort had a six-hour leave to go to the wedding party. Clayton thought that all things considered, he'd rather hang than attend that wedding.

* * *

Two Confederate regular army corporals marched Clay up the thirteen wooden steps to the ten-foot-high scaffold. He looked out at the crowd. Must have been at least 500 people—soldiers from the fort, families from both sides of the river, acquaintances, customers, tourists and shopkeepers. All eating, drinking, gabbing, like it was a picnic in his honor. He still couldn't quite believe it was happening. He tried to say something to the young soldier positioning him on the trap door, but his mouth was too dry and nothing came out. He saw Father Clos start up the steps, presumably for last rites—but he nudged his guard and shook his head No, and the guard motioned Clos back down.

Turning his head slowly from shoulder to shoulder he looked around the lonely hills surrounding town, the scattershot roofs of the adobe homes, the festive assembly, the river—the river would always be here, always changing and always the same—and he wondered if this would be his last vision of this sorry life.

The hangman stood off to the side, wearing a black canvas hood, unmoving. Clay wondered where Allie's wedding was going to be. Maybe they'd have it right here on this scaffold, a two-for-one celebration, and Father Clos could finally come up to perform the ceremony, right around the trapdoor where Clay was hanging. Now that would be a party to remember.

He recognized faces in the audience. Down to the right of the scaffold were Milagra, Zhi Li and Raoulito grilling pork, frying vegetables, handing out treats to children or charging pennies for tortillas, rice and beans. He saw Raoulito look up and cross himself.

Down toward the left he saw the hospital wagon pull up, four bodies already piled in back, room for just one more, his own. Dr. Hawks, holding the reins, needed a little help backing the end of the flatbed up to the side of the scaffold, close to his final hanging place. The gathering of onlookers had to part to let her get through, but a couple of soldiers took the bridles of the wagon horses and helped walk them backwards.

Jim and Rheumy weren't far off, bickering about something, Rheumy holding a canvas sack, Jim a bottle of gin. Ned joined them and Jim shared his bottle, which Ned partook of, letting the spirits flow out the hole in his belly. Clay smiled. He'd miss that little piece of human comedy. Or no. Pretty soon he wasn't about to miss anything anymore. Not Isaac, not the rush of a confidence game done well, not a blow struck against slavery. Not even Allie. But maybe she'd miss him.

Jessup stood not far off, still on crutches, eyes fixed on Clayton. There to witness, to see the deed was done. Clay nodded farewell to him, soldier to soldier. Clay hoped the man had a fine wedding. Jessup looked away as a woman with a parasol approached him—was that Edie?—seemingly asking him a question, as he shook his head in apology.

Wachtel and a few of his black and brown pressmen pulled small wagons full of *Daily Ranchero* broadsides on thin hemp paper, the headline in 48 point Gothic:

Hanging Today!

They handed the large pages out to anyone who'd take one.

Cortina moved slowly to the front of the gallows atop a grand white stallion. Of course, he was considered a wanted desperado now that the Confederacy was in charge again; but Ford had declared amnesty for the day, and that meant amnesty for all. Alongside Cortina were three of his lieutenants, all dressed in their finest military parade clothes. Glittering sombreros with gold coin hatbands, black double-button shirts covered in medals, tooled boots with jangling spurs. The crowd parted to let them through, though some were annoyed that the 18 hands-high steeds would block a good view of the execution. One bold fellow told Cortina to move, but the evil eye the *bandito* cast was enough to silence the man and the rest of the front-row gawkers, as well.

Except for Jessup. He and Cortina locked eyes like cobra and mongoose, Jessup growling in his throat to have a crack at this Mexican revolutionary who'd crippled him. Cortina just slapped his own leg and grinned, though, rubbing salt in the wound. Finally Cortina looked up at Clay with a certain nobility of position, lifted his great hat, and waved in salute. Clay nodded with a half smile—which froze when he saw the hooded hangman approach him from the side.

But as the executioner slipped the noose around Clay's neck, the strangest thing happened. Clay smelled lavender. The subtle scent took him by surprise and he thought this is how it would end—with a rush of powerful memories. Smells and sounds and visions would flood his senses to the last moment. A banjo from childhood, laughing with Isaac when they were boys, the first time he'd made love to Allie, engulfed by her lavender perfume, her perfume…wait. This wasn't a memory. This *was* Allie's perfume.

And then a soft voice, muffled through the hangman's hood as he felt something placed in his shackled hands behind his back. "That's a lockpick," she whispered. "Hope you're as good as you like to brag on yourself about."

His heartrate accelerated with the thrill of what was happening but he forced himself to remain steady and began picking the lock on his cuffs behind him as the hangman tightened the noose around his neck. "This is the knot Ned showed me at the Christmas party," she spoke right into his ear. "Have to yank it hard twice to open it, remember. So if you don't do it once on the way down, your goose is cooked."

Then she stepped away and stood with her hand on the trapdoor lever.

The commanding officer of the detail stepped forward—and it was

Russell. He spoke loudly, for the benefit of the crowd, who instantly quieted down to watch the main attraction. "Clayton Wilkes, you have been sentenced by the Tribunal of the Confederate States of America that you shall be hanged by the neck until dead. Do you have any last words?"

Clay was now frantically trying to work the lockpick at his waist without bystanders seeing what he was doing; but his hands were sweaty and the pick kept missing the mark. He tried to clear his throat but the frog in it kept his voice hoarse. "I regret I have but one life to give for my country." At last! He felt the lock snap open on his cuffs and could not help but smile. "Or two."

Russell took a step back and nodded at the drummer, a private with pimples who applied his drumsticks to the snare in a continuous, stately roll. Russell nodded to the hangman. The hangman raised an arm—almost like a signal—and the next moment a lot of things happened at once.

Raoulito tipped a can of oil onto the cooking fire, which erupted in a plume of flame and black smoke, making everyone on that side of the scaffold back away, waving at the smoke, closing their eyes and coughing.

Rheumy opened his canvas sack, dumping two large beehives to the ground. They broke open, releasing swarms of angry buzzers, scattering the picnic on that side far quicker than Raoulito's smoke bomb.

Wachtel began throwing broadsides into the air, the thin paper flapping in the wind.

Cortina's horses reared up, disquieted by the bees and cookfires and swirling papers. But he and his men held the steeds in place, shuffling back and forth before the gallows, as the surrounding audience backed off to avoid getting trampled underfoot. These were warhorses, though, accustomed to screams and explosions; easily controlled to stay where they were.

Allie pulled the lever. And Clay dropped through the trapdoor.

Time slowed for him, falling through the shaded space under the gallows. His unlocked shackles fell away behind his back as he brought his hands up to the rope around his neck. Like in a dream he watched the soundless chaos all around as he fell—the flaming grill, the great gouts of smoke, the swirling bee swarms, prancing stallions, running people, overturned picnics, Wachtel's fluttering broadsides caught on the wind like rudderless kites, the hangman looking down through the trapdoor, hood raised to reveal Allie's excited face screaming "Yank!" down at him. Was it an accusation? Recrimination for his Northern sympathies? "Yank!" she shouted. No, she was telling him to yank the rope, that was it. And wedging his fingers under the noose, Clayton gave it one, stout, muscular yank. A yank for a Yank, he thought with some amusement…until the rope pulled taut, his neck providing yank number two, exploding a bright white light in his head. And then nothing.

Out of a deep blackness, images floated through his mind. Ned retying the undone noose around another corpse's neck as Clay felt himself being carried to the hospital wagon. Major Russell directing soldiers to put out the fire. Edie swooning at the horror of the event and slumping into Jessup's arms, entangling him as she pulled him down to the ground, his crutches akimbo. Celebratory gunshots going off, the necktie party crowd whooping it up. Jim and Rheumy laying Clay's body atop the other corpses in the hospital wagon. So this was his unsung end, just one more corpse on the pile. But not unsung. Cortina and his men were crooning the bandit's heroic song: *"Cuando los Americanos duermen, Cortina visita sus suenos, y se despierta en Mexico."* When Americans sleep, Cortina visits their dreams, and they awake in Mexico.

Clay wondered if he would awake in Mexico now. But of course, he couldn't. He was dead.

When he first came to, the only thing he was aware of was a burning pain around his throat. He brought his fingers up to touch the spot. It was very tender. Rope burn. He opened his eyes.

He had to squint, though he could tell it was dim inside the tent. No, not a tent. A *palapa*.

"About time you woke up, mister." It was Allie's voice.

He looked around. He was in the *palapa* on the beach south of

Bagdad, the place where they'd paid Mose and spent the rest of the day making love. But now it was half collapsed after the winter storms. Half collapsed is just about how he felt. On the blanket beside him was Allie.

"I appreciate it," he whispered, unable to move much air through his windpipe. "I must say, that wasn't the most original con. The rope trick was a nice touch, though."

"Russell's the one made it all possible, givin' me the hangman job. I've brought you here now to make a truce, or a peace, call it what you will."

"What brought that on?"

"It came to me that my ride to Fort Ringgold urgin' Colonel Ford to attack…"

"That was you the cause of that?"

"It most certainly was. I saw your plan a mile away. All them clothes for those Yankee soldiers to change into, my Lord, and you thinkin' yourself so clever."

"So that's why Quintero didn't take my bait. I must tell you, it's gratifyin' to know I didn't fail to fool *him*—I just failed to fool *you*."

"That's not the point. Point is, me gettin' the Rangers to take Fort Brown is what saved your life. Wasn't for that victory, Quintero might've killed you himself—though that was never my intention. My intention was just to get Fort Brown back in Confederate hands. I figured you'd wiggle out of the consequences one way or another, like you always do."

"I must say, this is all too bafflin' for me to interpret in my postmortem condition," he said.

"It's fate pure and simple, is what it is. We have come full circle, back to where we were at the start. The South is in charge again, the North is wishful thinkin', and they will all carry on their great conflict just fine without any help from you or I. Clay, we are too clever by half for our own good, and yet here we are in a shack on the beach, drinkin' wine amidst these great surges of history—and to what end?" She sipped from a wine glass.

"Tell me, darlin'."

"To realize our destiny. Not fight it. To have done with these wars on the land and in our hearts. It's time to make amends, Clay, and go off together."

"Didn't I hear tell you were marryin' that Ranger?"

"The weddin' is set for the church at sunset. But I always intended to call it off."

"I expect your young captain will have somethin' to say about that."

"I'll just leave him a note that I got a message from my daddy and urgently had to go west. Jessup is a fine young man, and he'll get over it. The point is, you must leave these parts forever, now that everyone thinks you're dead. And you need me to go with you. We are fit for no one but each other." She kissed him, as proof. "But we do need a stake to start over, and I have an idea how to raise it. Ready? Well. You must be aware how big spiritualism is gettin' to be."

"Spiritualism."

"Seances. Talkin' to folks' dearly departed relatives. Lookit this." She took a photograph out of her bag. A double exposure. Two men at a table and a third man, just a hazy face, seeming to float behind them in the background. "I did this by printin' two different negatives at once. Don't it look like that fella in the background is a ghost?"

Clay looked at the print with an artist's eye. "You did this?"

She preened a little. "All we need do is check the obituaries for the wife of some dead Duke or Earl. We hold a séance, I take a photograph of everyone at the table, then I get an old portrait of the dead fella, I photograph that, and I can compose his ghost hoverin' over the séance."

"I'm impressed with your talents, as ever, Allie. But hangin' does somethin' to a man, and I must tell you, I am through with con games. All my efforts here have only got the South in charge of Fort Brown again, except now the estimable Rip Ford is in charge instead of that idiot Hamilton Bee."

"That's what I been sayin', this war ain't no business of ours, we just got caught up in it like everyone else. But you and I need to get gone together and realize what's truly important. If cons are not to your likin' anymore, why I'm sure we can find somethin' useful to do."

"Well, you're right about one thing. I need to disappear." He sat up slowly. "Your young man would kill me for a traitor if he ever saw me again. Or I'd kill him, which I don't fancy. But the main thing is, he trusts you and loves you, while I love you but don't know that I could ever follow the straight and narrow with you."

Emotion filled her face like an invisible color, though she laughed to cover it. "My word, but you've got the vapors now. If I recall, the first time I conned you out of your wallet in that New Orleans bedroom is what made you fall in love with me to begin with."

Remembering that moment now made him smile. And he loved her still. But if he truly wanted what was best for the woman he loved, he knew he had to give her up to the man who adored her without reservation, and would support her to the day he died. Allie needed that stability in her life to overcome the chaos of her past. And Clay just wasn't sure if he could ever provide such. He wasn't certain exactly what his future held. "I fear I must go alone, dear heart. And you must stay with the Ranger who worships you."

"Please don't say that, Clay. After all we been through."

"After all that I can't bear the thought I might let you down again. Let me do this for you, Allie. Let me give you the gift of a man who will always be there for you, even if the man ain't me. Allow me to do this for you, I beg you." He hugged her a long minute, letting her feel the love of his sacrifice.

She resisted at first; this wasn't the end she'd foreseen. But his love felt so deep, his impulse so genuine, she finally let it in; and returned the embrace, reciprocating the emotion, and the finality.

But as she pulled away, she turned chilly, to keep her face from falling apart. "All right, then, I suppose I might as well have that weddin' with Ahotay. I'd thought for a moment, after savin' your life and all, you might have stronger feelin's for me than that. But I surely am in no need of rescue."

He brought his hand to her cheek and she closed her eyes and he whispered. "No, you never were. There's no one I'll ever love like you."

She kissed his palm. "Where will you go?" A tear brimmed her eye.

"I hear the Barbary Coast is wide open to those with a strong will. Mayhap I'll go into politics. Make sure California never has slaves, even if your South wins the war."

"Our South, once."

He kissed her cheek, stood unsteadily and left.

As she watched him go, the ancient cry of *la Llorona* seemed to rise over the hills. Allie collapsed in sobs. But when she finally cried herself out, the Weeping Woman's moans were gone, replaced by a clean offshore wind.

Clay went in the back way of the casino to avoid being seen, walked up to the rooftop and opened the pigeon coop to bid farewell to Madeira. But he saw a bedraggled, featherbent bird in the cage, as well. The one he knew Isaac had taken with him. He grabbed it to get the message. But there was no message; just an empty, broken foot.

So there was the end of Isaac, if not the whole colony. If he'd been alive to send the bird, he'd have included at least some brief words. *All well.* Or maybe *Help.* Nothing but a ruined bird, though. So Isaac was defeated, like Fort Brown, like Clayton himself. The end of so many things. He looked at the river. Like leaves on the water, the people in his life were drifting away in the current. Time for him to drift, too, it seemed. It was a feeling of emptiness, but there was a kind of raw purity to it.

He pet Madeira one last time, reminding her she was his favorite. When he closed his eyes he could still hear the beating wings of birds at dusk, and knew all was well, but all things ended.

Allie stood beside Jessup in the cathedral, near the apse, waiting for Father Clos to arrive. Jessup was on crutches, in his best captain's shirt; she was in a pretty blue dress, not too fancy, as befitted her husband-to-be's rank.

"This is the happiest day of my life," he told her. "I never thought it'd come."

"You are my truest friend ever, Ahotay. I trust this is the beginning of a new chapter for both of us." She noticed him shift his weight to the other foot. "Maybe you ought to sit down and rest your leg until Father Clos gets here."

"The leg'll heal up. It's my pride that hurts. Cortina's left me gawkin' twice now."

"Well, if he's left you alive, there must be meanin' in that." She saw a flock of the French Order of Nuns of the Incarnate Word and Blessed Sacrament float by. "If anything ever happened to you I believe I'd join a nunnery."

"Well, don't make any promises you can't keep."

Father Clos walked up with a beatific smile. "Are we ready?" They both nodded, a little nervous; though Allie, having been in this situation twice before, was less so. Father Clos turned earnest. "Dearly Beloved…"

She glanced at Jessup. He *was* dearly beloved. She knew she could always count on him, and she knew she had it in her to *know* she loved him. Even if it was a little bit of a con at first, she was still her own best mark—she believed the reality so deeply. And Jessup was a reality she could already imagine surrounding herself with.

If only she could get that little pang out of her heart, she was well on her way to imagining Ahotay being a comfort for the rest of her life. "I do," she said.

Ahotay and Father Clos looked a little surprised. "We've not reached that part of the service, Allie," Jessup smiled. "But I know I'm just as anxious to get there as you."

As the afternoon sun edged lower in the muggy heat Clay packed two big bags. He meant to dress in leper's rags to keep away prying eyes, and take a wagon to Bagdad—there to board the *Saro Jane*, a clipper ship bound to set sail south, through the Drake Passage around Cape Horn, where the Atlantic met the Pacific; and then up to San Francisco.

Fitting that he should be garbed as outcast on this last night casting himself out. Before him lay adventure and a new life. A life alone. He wished Allie could see him now, she'd laugh so. He loved her laugh. And when he thought of that it led down a winding road of thinking about all the things he loved about her, from the sparkle in her smile to the brilliance of her intuitions about human nature, to her sensual caresses, her wild abandon, her gentle caring, her wry jokes, her sass, her voice, her strength. Her love of him. Her love.

He stayed in his room until full dark, then called Zhi Li upstairs and told her he was giving her the casino. She thought that was a good idea. She understood why he had to leave, since he was supposed to be dead. He told her the pigeons on the roof belonged to Hermano from now on. He told her to make sure there was always a bee hive out back for Rheumy. He signed the deed over to her. She promised she'd never sell opium here, and she gave him the photograph from the backbar mirror: Opening Day at Brave River, workers posed with serious faces, Clay and Isaac toasting each other—but they were blurs, they'd moved at the moment the picture was taken. In his lepers' rags he felt like a blur now.

He went down the back stairs and peeked in the kitchen, where Raoulito was asleep in the corner, Milagra bent over a pot of something cooking for tomorrow; garlic, cilantro, cayenne. He took a moment to witness her; to remember her like that.

He paused to look at the giraffe over the bar. He thought it nodded at him. Somehow the silly dead animal seemed like just one more member of his big misfit family on the river, and it gentled his heart. So much sweeter than the family he'd left behind on the plantation—and now he was running away from it. Just like he'd run from the first one. But he was *glad* to leave back then; not now. His only solace was that the folks here would go on without him just fine. Just fine.

He went to the cabin out back where Solomon had spent his last days. Only the cigar-box fiddle was left now. Clay took it—who knows, he might learn to play it in his new life. Maybe even write a song about himself, now that Solomon wasn't around to make one up.

At last he went to his wagon. He meant to make Bagdad before sunrise. He didn't know what lay in store for him. All he knew was, there'd been a time when he envied pride; maybe now he'd try to earn it.

As he slapped the reins, the French Order of Nuns of the Incarnate Word and Blessed Sacrament wafted down the river, sounding like nothing so much as the beating wings of birds at dusk.

His intention was to make San Francisco by Christmas; but come what may.

ONE YEAR LATER

April 14, 1865
Washington, D.C.

WELL-DRESSED LADIES AND GENTLEMEN milled, chatted and took their seats as Clay edged his way past those already ensconced, amidst apologies and not-at-alls. When he got to an open section, he remained standing, looking slowly around the theater, feeling a sense of deep content with himself and the world. The war was just about over. A touch of gray in his hair for his part in that ending seemed a small price to pay.

It was only a moment after he sniffed the lavender that he spun around and there she was, pretty as a picture in a scrapbook from a different life. "Hello, Allie," he said.

"Hello yourself. I didn't expect to run into you here after all this time."

"Nor I you. Is Captain Jessup with you? No, must be Colonel Jessup by now."

"I'm afraid he had a run-in with that bandit Cortina shortly after you left, and sustained a belly wound that proved to be the end of him."

"I'm terrible sorry to hear that."

"Yes, I'm twice-widowed and once-anulled now. I count that bad luck, for a gamblin' woman." She paused, then asked, "Are you here with a friend?" Meaning a woman friend, of course.

"No, my duties keep me pretty busy. I'm a Pinkerton man these days, on the presidential detail—so no more hidin' my sympathies. Tonight's my night off, though, and I was told this is an excellent entertainment. My deepest condolences about your Ranger, though—he was a good man. May I ask what brings you here?"

She took a moment to frame it. "When Ahotay died, I followed you to San Francisco. It's where you said you were headed. You weren't there, but I stayed. Made a pretty penny on my séance photographs. But the odd thing is…I sometimes saw my own ghosts. Spirits that I didn't photograph—that weren't part of my con."

He didn't think he was understanding her right. "Whatever do you mean?"

"I saw my mother, my brothers, Ahotay—you'll think me mad, but I even saw my dear sister in a photograph, and it wasn't a picture of my invention, she was just there starin' at me. I came to believe the spirit world is real, and I am connected to it. It has informed my life ever since. Isn't that the strangest thing?"

He took a long look at her and saw the change. Something of substance inside now, something she'd claimed as her own, something to be true to. At one time he'd have thought she was just believing her own con; that had been her great gift. But that wasn't the case here. "I perceive you were brought to that conviction by a dedication to your photography," he said. "Though it took you in a direction you hardly expected."

She appreciated his insight. "We all of us must hold deep to a serious thing, I believe, if we are to survive these terrible times."

She looked a grown woman now. "Why are you here, Allie?" he asked.

"I've stayed in touch with Dr. Hawks. She lives in Boston at present but suggested I meet her here, where she can introduce me to friends who conduct a well-regarded spiritualism salon—as well as friends who might support my efforts establishing a photography studio. It's become quite the art form, you know, since Matthew Brady's battle images have seized the public's imagination."

He was unable to suppress a broad smile, just to look at her. "Allie, it's so good to see you again."

She poured herself into his gaze. And by God if her heart didn't flip-flop just a little. "You know, seein' all those spirits who've passed to the other side—I never once did see you."

"No, I am very much alive," he said with a small sparkle in his smile. Then, more quietly: "I wonder if you would do me the honor of havin' dinner with me after the play."

Her eyes almost watered. "Yes, that would be lovely. I look forward to it."

A man in formal attire emerged from between the curtains at center stage and addressed the audience. "Ladies and gentlemen, kindly take your seats. Ford Theater's presentation of *Our American Cousin* will begin in five minutes."

Clay and Allie found two empty seats together and sat, barely touching but savoring the anticipation of what might come next.

POST-SCRIPT

Teddy Beale went back to her father's farm, where she bred horses, married a bronc buster, had four children and died an old woman on the eve of World War I, determined never to witness another war.

In August 1864 Ned dug up Solomon's body and reburied it with the fossils on Padre Island, along with his last dubloon, to appease Lafitte's ghost. A month later came a wild storm, breaking a limb off the oak, gouging a chunk of earth out of the far side of the tree—revealing a chest full of gold coin, jewels and such like. But the hole got storm-filled with clay, no one the wiser to this second treasure bracketing the same ancient tree.

In January, 1865, French forces made their move on Matamoros, toppling Cortina and expelling US Ambassador Pierce.

On April 9, 1865, Lee surrendered to Grant, effectively ending the Civil War.

On April 14, 1865 President Lincoln was assassinated at Ford's Theater by John Wilkes Booth, using a .41 caliber Philadelphia Derringer—Clay's departing gift.

On May 13, 1865, Rip Ford's troops, still stationed at Fort Brown, beat advancing Yankees at the Battle of Palmito Ranch, outside Brownsville, in what was considered the last battle of the War Between the States—a month after Lee surrendered to Grant, and a week after what was commonly accepted as the end of hostilities. It was believed Rip Ford knew that, but he just wanted to whup the Yankees one last time.

Scully stayed in Matamoros with Aurelia, raising both her child and Jersey's—as well as Shonny, Bootsy and Charles—as his own. He was never cured of syphilis, but it lay dormant in him and he never passed it on it to Aurelia, as far as anyone knew.

After the War, Dr. Esther Hill Hawks and her husband began a Florida orange plantation with freed slaves, in their own land-granted colony—until a blight killed the crop and the colony disbanded. The Hawkses retired to New England, living a long, happy life.

The years 1865-67 were a heyday for Bagdad, with a huge French presence and a construction boom. Unfortunately, the hurricane of 1867 wiped the port town off the sand, and with the end of all the wars, it never came back.

That same storm washed away forever Lafitte's treasure, the invaluable cache of prehistoric fossils, and the bones of Ryburn Solomon from Padre Island—flooding him out to sea, which is what he would have wanted.

In January, 1866, with the United States Army stationed at the border and threatening to enter the fray on the side of Juarez, Napoleon began withdrawing French troops from Mexico.

On June 19, 1867, the Emperor Maximilian was executed by the forces of Benito Juarez, ending Napoleon's expeditionary adventure to the Americas.

With the French, the Confederates, the Yankees, and all other interested parties gone, Matamoros returned to being the sleepy town it once was—from a population of 40,000 at the height of the Conflicts, to the few hundred who had always resided there.

At the end of the US War of Secession, Charles Stillman was recorded as being the richest man in the world. He invested a small amount of his wealth in his son's New York bank—now called Citibank.

Colonel Dye, who loved the warrior life, joined the Egyptian Army, got wounded in the foot at the Battle of Gura, and was later court martialed for striking an Egyptian officer over a reputed insult about men who limped.

General Santa Anna's prosthetic leg is still in US custody, currently under glass at the Illinois State Military Museum.

ACKNOWLEDGEMENTS

There are many people who made this work possible. First and foremost, my wife, artist Jill Littlewood, who patiently supported me and abided my obsessive plunge into the research and writing process. But the book would not have happened at all without the family lore my old friend, Gene Ringgold, told us about his Great-great-grandfather, Bvt. Major Samuel Ringgold, the inventor of "flying artillery," and the first U.S. Officer killed in the Mexican-American War, in 1846—for whom the fort upriver from Brownsville was named.

I'd like to thank my editor, Patrick J. Lobrutto, for helping me pare the manuscript down from 750 pages to its current, abbreviated form. Also, thanks to Charles Pratt, Jr., for being a trusted soundingboard, and suggesting the epilogue. And further gratitude to Milagro Hernandez of the Special Collections section of the University of Texas Rio Grande Valley; Ayla Jaramillo, the Collections Manager at the Brownsville Historical Association; and Eugene Fernandez, Commissioner of the BHA and Chairman of the Texas State Historical Marker Program. Mr. Fernandez gave me invaluable insight into the bandit Cortina, among other colorful characters.

Finally I'd like to give thanks to the actual historical figures who led exciting enough lives in tumultuous times to provide fodder for a tale such as this: Confederate States of America Commander of Fort Brown, General Hamilton Bee and his wife, Mildred Tarver Bee; Texas Ranger

Col. John Salmon "Rip" Ford; CSA Quartermaster of Fort Brown, Major Charles Russell; CSA Lt. Dick Dowling of the Jefferson Davis Guards, and hero of the Second Battle of Sabine Pass; Confederate Consul to Mexico and Cuban revolutionary, Jose Agustin Quintero; U.S. Ambassador to Mexico Leonard Pierce; Union Surgeon, Dr. Esther Hill Hawks; the infamous actor, John Wilkes Booth; Our Lady of Refuge Cathedral priest, Father Clos; Union General Nathaniel Banks; the notorious bandit Juan Cortina, Red Robber of the Rio Grande; Sonora State Governor Pesqueira, Mexican Army of Resistance; and Union Col. William McEntyre Dye, who soldiered around the world after the Civil War, ending his career as military advisor to the King of Korea.